W9-AEI-734

THE KING'S MEN

Nora Sakavic

Tredyffrin Public Library
582 Upper Gulph Road
Strafford, PA 19087
(610) 688-7092 9/16

ALL FOR THE GAME
The Foxhole Court
The Raven King
The King's Men

Copyright 2013-2014 Nora Sakavic

CHAPTER ONE

Even after a semester at Palmetto State University and a couple weeks practicing on the largest Exy stadium in the United States, Neil was still struck breathless by the Foxhole Court. He lay flat on his back on the half-court line and soaked it in. He counted rows of alternating orange and white seats until they blurred into an indistinct mess near the rafters, then studied the spring championship banners hanging in numerical order around the stadium. There was one for each of the Foxes, including the late Seth Gordon. They hadn't been there before the Foxes split up for Christmas and Neil wondered what Allison would say when she saw them.

"You forget how to stand up, Josten?"

Neil lolled his head to one side to look at his coach. He'd left the court door open behind him, and now David Wymack stood in the doorway. Neil didn't think they'd been here long enough for Wymack to finish his paperwork. Either Wymack didn't trust Neil to keep his promise not to practice until he was fully healed or Neil had lost track of time again. Neil hoped it was the former, but the knot in his stomach predicted otherwise.

He'd agreed to spend Christmas break at Edgar Allan, but the Ravens operated on sixteen-hour days during their holidays. What should have been two weeks passed like three, and Neil's internal clock was going haywire even after two days back in South Carolina. Classes were supposed to start Thursday though, and the spring season kicked off the following week. Wymack was sure having a normal routine again would help. Neil could only hope he was right.

"It's time to go," Wymack said.

That was enough to make Neil get up, though his battered

body protested. He ignored the pain with the ease of long familiarity and resisted the urge to work at the ache in his shoulder as he crossed the court to Wymack. He didn't miss the critical once-over Wymack gave him but chose not to acknowledge it.

"They landed?" Neil asked when he was close enough.

"You'd know if you were answering your phone."

Neil pulled his phone out of his pocket and flipped it open. He pressed a couple buttons, then tilted the dark screen toward Wymack. "I must have forgotten to charge it."

"Must have," Wymack said, not at all fooled.

He was right to be suspicious; Neil had let his phone die on purpose. Before going to bed on New Year's he'd shut his phone off and left it unplugged. He still hadn't read the messages his teammates sent him over the break. He couldn't avoid them forever, but Neil hadn't figured out how to explain his actions. The ugly injuries he sported were an expected consequence of facing Riko. The tattoo on his cheek would take a little more work to justify, but it was doable. What Neil couldn't get around was what Riko had done to his appearance.

After nine years of colored contacts and hair dye Neil finally had his natural coloring back. With auburn hair and bright blue eyes he was a spitting image of the murderous father he'd spent half his life outrunning. He hadn't looked in a mirror in two days. Denial wouldn't change his appearance back but he'd throw up if he saw his reflection again. If he could at least dye his hair a couple shades darker he might breathe a little easier, but Riko made it clear what he'd do to the Foxes if Neil changed his looks.

"They're at baggage claim," Wymack said. "We need to talk."

Neil bolted the court door behind him and followed Wymack up to the locker room. Wymack cut the stadium lights behind them and Neil looked back as the Foxhole Court was swallowed by darkness. The sudden absence of light sent a chill

[2]

down his spine. For a moment he was back at Evermore being smothered by the Ravens' malevolence and the court's forbidding color scheme. He'd never been claustrophobic but the weight of so much hatred had almost crushed every bone in his body.

The jangle of keys brought him back from that dangerous edge and Neil turned, startled. Wymack had gone into the locker room ahead of him and was unlocking his office door. Although they were the only two here—except for the security guard making obligatory rounds somewhere—Wymack had locked the office in his short absence.

Neil had been in there enough times to know Wymack didn't keep anything particularly valuable on his shelves. The only thing of any import was Neil's duffel, which he'd tucked into the office corner before heading to the court. On Neil's first day in South Carolina he had asked Wymack to protect his things, and seven months later Wymack was still keeping that promise. It was almost enough to make Neil forget all about Riko.

Wymack stepped aside and gestured for Neil to help himself. In the short time it took Neil to pick up his bag and sling the strap over his shoulder, Wymack disappeared. Neil found him in the lounge, sitting on the entertainment center to one side of the TV. Neil held onto his bag's strap for courage and went to stand in front of him.

"Kevin called me yesterday morning when he couldn't get a hold of you," Wymack said. "He wanted to make sure you were okay. Apparently he knew all along where you were."

There was no point in lying, so Neil said, "Yes."

"I made him tell the others," Wymack said, and Neil's heart stopped. He opened his mouth to protest, but Wymack held his hand up and kept going. "They needed to know what they're coming back to—for your sake. Think for a moment how they'd react if they came back to this with no warning. You flounder when they call you 'friend'; you'd probably have a psychotic break when they freaked out over you."

Neil wanted to argue with that. The best he managed was an unconvincing, "I was figuring something out."

"You were stalling," Wymack accused him, "so I did it for you. I told them you look like you've gone six rounds with a Sasquatch and said you probably wouldn't want to talk about it. They promised not to smother you, but I don't know if they'll keep that promise when they see you up close. This, though, I didn't tell them about." He gestured vaguely at his own face.

Neil touched the bandage on his cheekbone that hid his new tattoo. "This?"

"All of that," Wymack said, and nodded when Neil moved his hand to his hair. "I don't know why Riko did it but I'll wait for my answers. What you tell them is on you."

It was almost enough to thaw the ice in his chest. Neil didn't know what to say, so he nodded and looked at the clock. He didn't have to pick the others up from the airport because Matt had paid to leave his truck in long-term parking. Neil was supposed to meet them at Fox Tower, but if they were just now getting their bags it'd take them another twenty minutes or so to get to campus from Upstate Regional.

"Should I come with you to referee?" Wymack asked.

"To the dorm?" Neil asked.

Wymack spared Neil a brief, pitying glance. "I meant to Columbia."

Andrew was being released today. As soon as the others dropped their things off at the dormitory they'd be on their way to Easthaven Hospital. It'd been seven weeks since the Foxes last saw him and nearly three years since Andrew was clean. Two of them knew what Andrew was like when stone-cold sober; the others knew only unpleasant rumors and speculation. It was highly unlikely Andrew would care that Neil was half-carved to pieces, but Neil had broken his promise to stay by Kevin's side in Andrew's absence. Neil doubted Andrew would take that well.

Despite that, Neil wasn't concerned. "We'll be fine."

[4]

"If not, at least Abby will be back in town tomorrow to patch you up." Wymack checked his watch and slid off his perch. "Let's get going, then."

It was a short drive to the athletes' dormitory. The parking lot behind Fox Tower was mostly deserted, but a couple of the Foxes' cars were still parked there. Supposedly security guards made rounds to ensure the cars didn't get broken into during their owners' absence, but Neil still had Wymack pull up next to Andrew's car. He tried the door handles first, then checked the windows for cracks or vandalism. He kicked the tires and decided them satisfactory for the trip. Wymack waited with his engine idling until Neil was done.

"Do I need to stay?" Wymack asked.

"I'll be fine," Neil said. "I'll have Kevin call you when we've got Andrew."

"Charge your phone and call me yourself," Wymack said. "Good luck."

He pulled away, and Neil went into the dorm. The hallways smelled faintly of air freshener and cleaners; someone had been by during the break to tidy the place up. His room was on the third floor, the furthest of the Foxes' three rooms from the stairs. He let himself in, locked the door behind him, and made a slow lap of the suite. Finding nothing out of place, he plugged his phone in to charge and unpacked his duffel. The last thing he pulled out was a pack of cigarettes. He carried them to the bedroom window and lit up.

He was on his second cigarette when the front door opened. The quiet told him Matt had come alone; Nicky couldn't be sneaky to save his life. Neil heard the thump of a suitcase being set down and the click of the door catching in its frame. Neil took one last deep breath of smoke and stubbed his cigarette out on the windowsill. He forced the tension from his shoulders, prayed his neutral expression held, and yanked the window closed. When he turned around Matt was standing in the bedroom doorway with his hands deep in his coat pockets.

[5]

Matt's mouth moved soundlessly for a few moments before he finally managed a choked, "Jesus Christ, Neil."

"It's not as bad as it looks," Neil said.

"Don't. Just—don't, okay?" Matt said. He carded his fingers through his hair, mussing his gelled spikes, and turned away. "Wait here."

Neil went to the bedroom doorway as Matt left the suite. Almost as soon as the door closed, there was the heavy sound of a body hitting the wall. Neil heard Matt's furious tone as he lashed out at someone, but the walls were just thick enough to hide his words. Neil shifted from one foot to the other and made the mistake of looking to his right. The bathroom door was open, giving him a good view of his reflection. The technicolor bruises splattered across his face were awful, but the blue eyes staring back at him were a thousand times more frightening. Neil swallowed hard against a rush of nausea and tore his gaze away.

He went back to get his phone and tugged it off the charger. It wasn't anywhere near done, but hopefully there was enough power in it to last until Columbia. Neil turned it off until he needed it and slipped it in his pocket. The temptation to crawl into bed was almost overwhelming. He was exhausted already and he still had seven teammates left to deal with after Matt was done with him. There was no way he'd survive if the girls were coming back today; luckily the three were flying in tomorrow morning. He'd have the night to retreat and recharge.

He made himself go into the main room to wait. Matt rejoined him a minute later and closed the door firmly behind himself. He made a visible effort to calm down, but there was still an edge in his voice when he spoke. "Did Coach already yell at you?"

"Loudly and at length," Neil said. "It didn't do any good. I'm not sorry, and I'd do it again if I had to. No," Neil cut in before Matt could argue. "The Foxes are all I have, Matt. Don't tell me I was wrong for making the only call I could."

Matt stared at him for an endless minute, then said, "I want to break his face in six places. If he ever comes within a thousand yards of you again—"

"He has to," Neil said. "We're going to play the Ravens in finals."

Matt shook his head and grabbed his suitcase. Neil stepped off to one side so Matt could pass, but Matt cast one last look at Neil's face on his way by. Surprise took the edge off his outrage. Neil didn't return the look but started for the door. He almost made it; he had his hand on the knob when Matt spoke up.

"Coach said not to ask about your eyes," Matt said. "I'd assumed Riko blackened them."

It wasn't really a question, so Neil didn't answer it. "We'll be back in a few hours."

He left before Matt could argue. Kevin, Nicky, and Aaron were waiting two doors down in front of their bedroom. Nicky was holding two gift bags but dropped them at Neil's approach. Neil was halfway to them before he saw the bruise on Kevin's face. The red stain across half his cheek said a second bruise wouldn't be long in forming. It wasn't the first time Matt hit Kevin and it definitely wouldn't be the last, but Neil made a note to talk to him later. None of this was Kevin's fault.

With that, he pushed Matt from mind and focused on the three men in front of him. Unsurprisingly, Aaron was the safest one to look at. The frown tugging at the corner of his mouth was curiosity, not sympathy, and his gaze lingered longer on Neil's hair than it did on the bruises staining Neil's face. Neil gave him a moment to see if he'd ask, but all Aaron did was shrug.

Nicky, on the other hand, looked absolutely crushed as he took in Neil's wrecked appearance. He reached out as soon as Neil was close enough and wrapped his hand around the back of Neil's neck. He carefully pulled Neil up against him and propped his chin on Neil's head. Nicky was tense as stone but the long breath he let out was shaky.

"Oh, Neil," he said in a choked voice. "You look awful."

"It'll fade," Neil said. "Most of it, anyway. Don't worry

[7]

about it."

Nicky's fingers tightened a fraction. "Don't you dare tell me you're fine. I can't hear that from you today, okay?"

Neil obediently went quiet. Nicky held on a minute longer, then finally let him go. Neil turned to Kevin last and felt his stomach drop. Kevin was staring at Neil like he'd seen a ghost. The others might find Neil's abrupt change in appearance startling—the cousins less so because they'd seen Neil's blue eyes on their trips to Columbia—but Kevin knew who Neil really was and he'd met Neil's father. He knew exactly what this meant. Neil shook his head in a silent plea to keep quiet. He wasn't entirely surprised that Kevin ignored that, but at least Kevin had the decency to speak in French.

"Tell me the master did not approve this."

"I don't know," Neil said. The last several days in Riko's care were a painful, meaningless blur he was still trying to make sense of. He only dimly remembered Jean's hands working dye through his hair. He thought it was one of the last things they'd done to him, but he couldn't remember if Riko's uncle Tetsuji had been present for it. "Riko said he'd hurt us if I change it back. All I can do is duck my head and hope for the best."

"Duck your head," Kevin echoed. He gestured incredulously at his own face. "Riko called me on Christmas to say he inked you. How long do you think he'll let you hide before he forces you to show it off? The press will be all over this, and they won't stop their questions at your tattoo. He's trying to get you found."

Fear was ice in Neil's stomach, eating its way up his throat. Keeping it from bleeding into his voice took everything Neil had. "I'll take it as a compliment. He's trying to take me out of the game before semifinals. He wouldn't waste his time unless he thinks we really are going to be a problem for his team. That means something, doesn't it?"

"Neil."

"I'll worry about this, Kevin. I'll worry about me. You do

[8]

what you do best and focus on Exy. Take us where he doesn't want us to go."

Kevin's mouth thinned to a hard line, but he didn't argue. Maybe he knew it was pointless; maybe he knew it was too late. Nicky looked between them as if making sure they were done then scooped his bags up again and held one out to Neil.

"Belated Christmas present," he said, a little sadly. "No one knew your address in Millport so I figured I'd just give it to you in person. Erik helped me pick it out." At Neil's confused look, Nicky said, "He flew to New York for a couple days as a Christmas surprise. Kevin's got something for you in there, too. He wouldn't let me wrap it, so it's in an ugly plastic bag. I'm sorry."

Nicky jiggled the other gift bag as Neil took the one offered him. "I've got Andrew's with me, too. Actually I got you two the same thing because you are like the most impossible people in the world to buy for."

"I'm sorry," Neil said. "I didn't get anyone anything. I'm not used to celebrating Christmas."

"You mean you were too busy getting pulverized to shop," Aaron said. Nicky looked like he choked on his cousin's rudeness, but Aaron continued like he hadn't said anything wrong. "Kevin said you went because of Andrew. Is that true?"

Neil flicked Kevin a warning look. "Yes."

"Why?" Aaron asked. "He won't be grateful."

"He won't be grateful to you for killing Drake," Neil said. "It doesn't matter. We did what we had to do. I don't care what Andrew thinks."

Aaron studied him in silence. He was looking for answers, but Neil didn't know what the question was. All he could do was gaze back until Aaron finally shook his head and looked away. Neil wanted to push for an explanation, but he needed to save his energy for Andrew. He distracted himself by opening the present Nicky gave him. Wrapped in orange tissue paper was a black coat. It looked small but was heavy in his hands; it would

[9]

keep out the bitter chill that had settled in South Carolina. Neil let Nicky take the bag from him.

"Thank you," he said.

"You still don't have any proper winter clothes," Nicky said. "We should just take you out and expand your wardrobe again, but I figured we'd start with this. You can't keep wearing team hoodies and not expect to catch a cold. Does it fit?"

Neil unzipped it and started to shrug into it. He only got one arm through before his entire chest and side lanced white-hot with pain. He froze and blinked away the fuzz eating through his vision. "I'm sorry," he said, and regretted it immediately. He could hear pain in his voice, thick enough to slur his words. Nicky looked stricken with guilt. "I can't yet."

"I'm sorry," Nicky said. "I didn't—I wasn't thinking. Here, here. Let me. I've got it." Nicky eased the coat off Neil's arm and folded it. "I'll hold onto it until you're better, okay?"

"Okay."

Neil gave himself another moment to breathe before digging Kevin's gift from the bag. He knew what it was as soon as he felt the weight of it. He'd worried over this notebook too long not to recognize how it felt in his hand. At a first glance the binder was an obsessive fan's shrine to Kevin and Riko. A little more digging would unearth everything Neil needed for a life on the run. Money, underworld contacts, and his uncle's phone number were hidden between the countless Exy articles.

"You're not going to look?" Nicky asked.

"I know what it is." Neil clutched the bag close and looked to Kevin. "Thank you."

"I didn't open it."

Neil didn't want to deal with Matt again, so he figured he could take the binder with them to Columbia and lock it up later. "Are we ready?"

"If you're sure you're okay with a drive," Nicky said.

Neil started for the stairs without answering. The three fell in behind him and followed him to the car. Kevin took his usual

[10]

spot in the passenger seat and Nicky followed Aaron into the backseat. Neil hid his binder under the driver's seat and ignored the way his body ached as he got in. As soon as everyone was settled Neil got them on the road. He'd looked up directions to Easthaven on Wymack's computer yesterday. It was an easy drive from here, almost the exact same path they took to Eden's Twilight when they went drinking in Columbia. The only real difference was in the last fifteen minutes, when they looped around the capital and headed northeast.

Neil didn't realize he'd expected Easthaven Hospital to look like a prison until it finally came into view and the lack of barbed wire on the fence startled him. The gate was unmanned and the parking lot relatively empty. Neil killed the engine and got out. Kevin wasn't far behind him, but Nicky and Aaron were slower to move. The look Nicky flicked the front door was nervous. He hid his unease behind a smile when he realized Neil was watching him.

"Are you honestly afraid of him?" Neil asked.

"Nah," Nicky said unconvincingly.

Kevin was close on Neil's heels as they headed indoors and Neil didn't miss the way Aaron and Nicky both hung back a bit. He thought their last-minute reservations should make him a little more apprehensive of what was waiting for them here, but he felt nothing.

He cased the lobby on his way to the front desk. Floral paintings added a bit of color and a fireplace facade was built into the far wall. The place was trying for homey and came off like a catalogue showroom. At least it didn't smell like antiseptic and sickness.

"Gracious," the clerk said when she looked up from her computer and saw Neil's battered face. "Are you all right?"

"We're here to pick up Andrew Minyard," Neil said.

"That's not what I meant," she said, but Neil only gazed at her in silence. At length she motioned to the clipboard on the desk in front of her. "If you'll sign in, I'll ring Dr. Slosky and let

[11]

him know you're here."

They crowded the desk and took turns scrawling their names on the top sheet. Neil was the only one who hesitated when his pen touched the paper. Riko hadn't let him be "Neil" at Evermore. Every time Neil answered to it on the court, Riko beat him for it. Neil hadn't had much choice, since the Ravens hadn't known what else to call him, but Riko wanted him to know how much trouble he'd caused the Moriyamas with all of his alibis.

The clerk was waiting with her hand out, so finally Neil gritted his teeth and jotted his name under the others'. He passed her the clipboard and tried to force the new tension out of his shoulders.

They didn't have to wait long before a middle-aged man joined them. He smiled and shook hands down the line. His eyebrows went up when he saw Neil but he didn't ask. "My name is Alan Slosky. I've been Andrew's primary therapist during his stay here. Thank you for coming today."

"Primary," Nicky echoed. "How many did you assign him?"

"Four," Slosky said. At the look on Nicky's face, he explained, "It is not unusual for our patients to see multiple doctors. For example, a patient might see me for group counseling, a colleague of mine for intensive one-on-one, and one of our rehabilitation specialists for medication management. I handpicked Andrew's team and I assure you they were some of my finest."

"I'm sure it made a world of difference," Aaron said.

Slosky didn't miss the sarcasm in Aaron's voice, judging by the look he slid Aaron, but he didn't take the bait. Neil wondered if it was prudence or an unintended confession of failure. "Can I trust that he will have your support in the days ahead? If you have any questions or need advice on how to proceed please feel free to call me. I can give you my card."

"Thanks, but we've got Betsy," Nicky said, and at the questioning look Slosky sent him, said, "Dr. Dobson?"

[12]

"Ah, yes." Slosky gave an approving nod. He looked over his shoulder at the empty hallway, thought for a moment, then gestured to the adjoining waiting room. "Please, make yourselves comfortable. He should be down in a moment; he just needs to sign out of his room."

They arranged themselves around the room, Nicky and Aaron on separate chairs and Kevin sharing a couch with Neil. Neil gazed at the fireplace without seeing it. His mind was half a world away, drifting between Lebanon and Greece. The room was just warm enough to make him sleepy. He had three—two?—weeks' worth of sleep to catch up on. The Ravens' nights were short, and pain and violence had broken up most of Neil's. He didn't realize how close he was to drifting off until Kevin's subdued French startled him awake.

"I know what he's like," Kevin said. Neil looked at him, but Kevin was studying his hands. "Riko. If you want to talk."

It was the most awkward and uncomfortable thing Kevin had ever said to him. Kevin was known for his talent, not his sensitivity. Consideration and tact were as foreign to him as the German the cousins spoke. That he tried at all was so unexpected Neil felt it like a balm to every bruised inch of his skin.

"Thank you."

"I know what he's like, but I can't—" Kevin made a helpless gesture. "Riko was cruel but he needed me to succeed. We were the heirs of Exy; he hurt me but there were lines he would not cross until the end. It was different for Jean. It was worse. His father owed the Moriyamas a great deal. The master paid those debts in exchange for Jean's presence on our court. He was property, nothing more. You are the same in their eyes."

"I am not property," Neil said in a low voice.

"I know how he sees you," Kevin said. "I know it means he did not hold back."

"It doesn't matter." It sounded like a lie even to him, but Kevin didn't call him on it. "It's over now and I'm back where I

[13]

belong. The only thing that matters now is what comes next."

"It's not that easy."

"I'll tell you what's not easy: finding out from Jean that Coach is your father," Neil said, and Kevin gave a violent flinch. "Were you ever going to tell him?"

"I was going to when he signed me," Kevin said. "I couldn't."

"Were you protecting him or yourself?"

"Both, perhaps," Kevin said. "The master is not like his brother, nor is he like Riko. His kingdom is his court and that is the only sphere he chooses to exert control over. He has never raised a hand or voice against Coach before because Coach has never been a real threat to him. I didn't know if a confession would change things. I couldn't risk it. Maybe when all this is over."

"Is it ever going to be—" Neil started, but movement in the doorway made him forget his words.

Andrew stood in the doorway with Slosky at his back. He was wearing the same black turtleneck and jeans he'd been committed in. A bag hung off his shoulder, but Neil didn't remember him packing before Betsy led him out of the house. Neil might have asked what Easthaven was sending him home with, except his gaze finally caught on Andrew's face and he forgot his words. Andrew's expression was blank and his stare empty enough to put a knot in Neil's gut. Andrew lingered just long enough to see who'd come for him and turned away.

Aaron was the first to react. He'd been ignored by his brother for years; being looked at like he was no more interesting than a rock was old hat by now. Aaron motioned to Nicky and started after his brother. Neil and Kevin exchanged looks, calling a temporary and silent truce, and stood. Slosky said something to them as they filed out of the lounge, but Neil didn't waste time deciphering his words. Slosky had served his purpose by getting Andrew off his medication. Neil didn't need or want anything else from him.

[14]

By the time Neil reached the door Andrew was halfway down the building already. Aaron didn't follow but cut across the yard toward the parking lot. Nicky went with him, but Neil and Kevin stopped to watch Andrew. Two dumpsters sat against the corner of the building. Andrew upended his bag into one of them and Neil saw clothes fall out. He doubted Easthaven had supplied them; it was more likely Betsy Dobson and Andrew had picked a couple outfits up on the way to getting Andrew admitted. Andrew found his family in a sweeping glance and used their path to locate his car. When he set off for it, Neil and Kevin started after him.

Nicky had his keys on him, and he got the car unlocked so he and Aaron could pile into the backseat. Andrew opened the driver's door but didn't get in. He stood with his back to the car, one arm propped on the hood and the other draped along the top of his door, and watched the strikers approach. Kevin stopped right in front of him to inspect his returned teammate. Neil hesitated by the open back door so he could watch their reunion.

If Neil hadn't known Andrew spent the last year and a half fiercely protective and territorial of Kevin, he'd think they were strangers. Andrew treated Kevin to a bored inspection, then flicked his fingers in dismissal. Not even the bruises were interesting enough to get a comment, it seemed. Kevin nodded and went around the front of the car to the passenger seat. Neil didn't wait to see if Andrew's gaze swung his way again but got in the car.

Andrew slid into the driver's seat when everyone was settled and held a hand up between the seats. Neil dropped his key ring into Andrew's palm. Nicky caught Neil's wrist as he lowered his hand and gave a short, fierce squeeze. Nicky likely meant it as an apology for his cousin's cold shoulder, but fire sizzled up Neil's forearm and down to his fingertips. He'd rubbed his wrists raw fighting Riko's handcuffs, and his bandages weren't thick enough to protect him from Nicky's tight grip. Neil flinched before he could stop himself.

[15]

Nicky let go like he'd been burned. "Sorry, I'm sorry, I didn't—"

Neil's hand was throbbing, but he said, "It's fine."

"It isn't," Nicky insisted, and looked to his cousin. "I mean, Jesus, Andrew, aren't you even going to ask—"

Andrew cut the radio on loud enough to drown out anything else they had to say. Nicky's mouth twisted, but Neil shook his head and waved it off. It didn't ease the sick look in Nicky's eyes, but Nicky let it drop for now.

Kevin reached for the volume controls only once. Andrew popped his hand out of the way and pointed a warning finger at him without taking his eyes off the road. Kevin crossed his arms in a silent declaration of displeasure that Andrew ignored. Neil's head started pounding before they even reached the halfway point to the upstate. He was glad to see Fox Tower, gladder when Andrew parked and the car went mercifully silent.

Neil was the first out and he caught Andrew's door before Andrew could close it. Andrew didn't move, but there was just enough room for Neil to lean in and get his binder. He straightened and turned to find Andrew had shifted closer. There was nowhere for Neil to stand except up against Andrew, but somehow Neil didn't mind. They'd been apart for seven weeks but Neil keenly remembered why he'd stayed. He remembered this unyielding, unquestioning weight that could hold him and all of his problems up without breaking a sweat. For the first time in months he could finally breathe again. It was such a relief it was frightening; Neil hadn't meant to lean on Andrew so much.

At length Andrew took a step back and slid his gaze to Nicky. "You stay. The rest go."

Neil looked to Nicky to see if he was okay being alone with Andrew. At Nicky's slight nod, Neil went around the car to join Aaron and Kevin. Kevin stared hard at Andrew over the roof of the car as if he could see through Andrew's blank mask. Neil had to forcibly turn him toward the dorm.

[16]

They took the stairs up to the third floor. Aaron got the suite door unlocked, but Neil shook his head at Kevin's gesture to join them. He waited until they closed the door behind them before going to the end of the hall and powering up his phone. When the flashing logo finally gave way to his home screen, he dialed Wymack.

"I was starting to think he'd killed you and left you to rot on the side of the road," Wymack said in lieu of hello.

"Not yet," Neil said. "We're back now."

"If anyone needs anything, I have my phone on me. Attempt to keep yours on."

"Yes, Coach," Neil said, and turned his phone off again as soon as he'd hung up.

He'd given his keys to Andrew, so he had to knock to get into his room. He carried his binder into the other room and dug his safe out of the closet. The safe held only a well-worn letter now, but he tucked that into his binder and locked it away for safekeeping. He went back to the living room to see Matt waiting for him on the arm of the couch. Neil returned Matt's searching look with a guarded expression of his own. He waited for the inevitable questions and accusations, but when Matt finally spoke, it was only to say,

"You okay?"

"I'm fine," Neil said.

"For the record, I don't believe you," Matt said.

Neil lifted one shoulder in a tired shrug. "You probably shouldn't believe anything I say."

Matt huffed, too strained and quiet to be a real laugh. "I get the feeling that's the most honest thing you've said to me all year. But Neil? We're here when you want to talk about it."

"I know."

It surprised him that it was the truth. He knew just from looking at Matt that Matt would accept any truth Neil gave him right now, no matter how cruel or unbelievable. He'd done the right thing by going to Evermore; he was making the right

[17]

choice in standing his ground here with the Foxes. It didn't matter how much his reflection freaked him out. If this was the only way to keep his teammates safe from Riko's cruelty it was an easy price to pay.

Neil said, "I've never been to New York."

It wasn't what he needed to say or what Matt wanted to hear, but Matt didn't push it. He regaled Neil with stories of their holiday, from the cousins' awkward first meeting with his mother to Nicky's crazed shopping sprees. Matt took Neil into the kitchen to show him the whole beans he'd brought back from a local coffee shop. It was late in the day to have coffee, but Matt was tired from traveling and Neil was still out of sorts. Neil dug filters out of the cabinet while Matt ground enough beans for a pot.

Neil was filling the pot with water when there was a knock at the door. Matt was closer, so he went to answer it. Neil couldn't see their guest from this angle, but when Matt stepped back in silent invitation Nicky stepped into the doorway. He looked unharmed but nervous, and there was no hiding the guilt in his expression as he faced Matt.

"I'd uh, lie low for a while if I was you," Nicky said. "Andrew just found out who put the bruises on Kevin's face. I tried defending you because Kevin deserved it and you paid Aaron's bail, but I don't know how much good it's gonna do. Logic and Andrew aren't exactly on speaking terms."

"Thanks for the heads-up," Matt said.

Nicky looked to Neil. "He sent me to get you."

"How much did you tell him?" Neil asked.

"Nothing about you." Nicky stuffed his hands in his pockets and gave an uncomfortable shrug. "He wanted an update on everything else, Aaron's trial and Kevin's face and the Ravens. I told him we made it to championships and told him about the fight at Christmas banquet. I didn't tell him you weren't with us in New York."

Neil nodded and went back to his bedroom. He grabbed his

pack of cigarettes first and tucked it in his back pocket. Andrew's armbands were under his pillow where Neil hid them last November. Nicky grimaced at the sight of them.

"Maybe not a good idea to arm him right now," Nicky said.

"It'll be fine," Neil said, and headed down the hall for the stairs.

Andrew was waiting in the stairwell, arms folded loosely over his chest and back propped against the railing. His gaze dropped immediately to the dark cloth in Neil's outstretched hand and he took them without a word. Neil had already seen Andrew's scars in passing, but Andrew turned away to tug the bands on. When his sleeves were hiding the bands, Andrew headed upstairs instead of down.

The stairwell dead-ended at a door marked "Roof Access – Maintenance Staff Only". Neil assumed it would be locked, but Andrew only needed to give the handle a couple hard jiggles to get it open. Judging by the neat cuts on the door and frame, Andrew had sabotaged the lock long ago. Neil didn't ask but followed Andrew out into the chilly afternoon. The wind felt stronger this high off the ground and Neil wished he'd been able to wear his new coat.

Andrew went to the edge of the roof and surveyed the campus. Neil stepped up beside him and looked cautiously over the side. Heights didn't make him squeamish, but the lack of a safety rail was unnerving when it was a four-storey drop. Neil pulled his cigarettes out, shook two free, and lit them. Andrew propped his between his lips. Neil cupped his in his hands to shield it from the breeze.

Andrew turned to face him. "I'll take an explanation now."

"You couldn't ask for answers inside where it's warm?" Neil asked.

"If you are worried about dying of exposure you're a little late." Andrew raised a hand to Neil's face but stopped with his fingers just a breath from Neil's skin. Andrew wasn't looking at his injuries; he was staring at Neil's unguarded eyes. "Did I

[19]

break my promise or were you keeping yours?"

"Neither," Neil said.

"I know you have had ample time in my absence to come up with your precious lies, but remember I gave you a truth on credit in November. It is your turn in our game and you will not lie to me."

"Neither," Neil said again. "I spent Christmas in Evermore."

He shouldn't have been surprised that the first thing Andrew went for was the bandage on his cheek. Aaron and Nicky had looked past it, not even noticing it amongst the rest of the gauze and tape. Andrew had spent too much time watching Kevin's back to not put the pieces together. He scratched up a corner of the tape and ripped the bandage off like he wanted to take Neil's face with it. Neil braced himself for violence, but Andrew's blank expression didn't change at the sight of Neil's new tattoo.

"This is a new low for even you," Andrew said.

"I'm not wearing it by choice."

"You chose to go to Evermore."

"I came back."

"Riko let you go," Andrew corrected him. "We are doing too well this year and your feud is too public. No one would have believed you willingly transferred to Edgar Allan mid-season." Andrew smashed the bandage against Neil's face again and pressed the tape flat with hard fingers. "You weren't supposed to leave Kevin's side. Did you forget?"

"I promised to keep him safe," Neil said. "I didn't say I'd hound him every step of the way like you do. I kept my end of the deal."

"But not like this," Andrew said. "You already said this had nothing to do with Kevin. Why did you go?"

Neil didn't know if he could say it. Thinking about it was almost too much. Andrew was waiting, though, so Neil choked back his nausea. "Riko said if I didn't, Dr. Proust would—"

Andrew clapped a hand over his mouth, smothering the rest of his words, and Neil knew he'd failed.

[20]

Riko said Easthaven's Dr. Proust used "therapeutic reenactments" to help his patients. It was a thin line between psychological cruelty and real physical abuse, and Riko made it clear Proust was willing to cross that line if Neil disobeyed. He should have known better than to trust Riko's word. Hatred thawed a little of the new ice in his veins, but the bored look on Andrew's face was hard to stomach. A couple months ago Andrew was so drugged he laughed at his own pain and trauma. Today he didn't care enough to do even that. Neil didn't know which extreme was worse.

Andrew lowered his hand when Neil went quiet. "Do not make the mistake of thinking I need your protection."

"I had to try. If I had the chance to stop it but did nothing, how could I face you again? How could I live with myself?"

"Your crumbling psyche is your problem, not mine," Andrew said. "I said I would keep you alive this year. You make it infinitely more difficult for me when you actively try to get yourself killed."

"You spend all this time watching our backs," Neil said. "Who's watching yours? Don't say you are, because you and I both know you take shit care of yourself."

"You have a hearing problem," Andrew deduced. "Too many balls to the helmet, perhaps. Can you read lips?" Andrew pointed at his mouth as he spoke. "The next time someone comes for you, stand down and let me deal with it. Do you understand?"

"If it means losing you, then no," Neil said.

"I hate you," Andrew said casually. He took a last long drag from his cigarette and flicked it off the roof. "You were supposed to be a side effect of the drugs."

"I'm not a hallucination," Neil said, nonplussed.

"You are a pipe dream," Andrew said. "Go inside and leave me alone."

"You still have my keys," Neil reminded him.

Andrew dug Neil's keys out of his pocket and pried his car

[21]

key off it. Instead of handing the rest back, he tossed them after his cigarette. Neil leaned out to see if they'd land on anyone, but the sidewalk below was empty. His keys clattered harmlessly against the ground. Neil straightened and looked at Andrew.

Andrew didn't return his stare but said, "Not anymore."

Neil opened his mouth, changed his mind at the last second, and turned silently away. He took the stairs down to the ground floor and pushed open the front glass doors. His keys had landed further out than he expected, but sunlight glinting off the metal made them easy to find. Neil scooped them up and spotted Andrew's cigarette a couple feet away. The ash had broken off on impact, but the end still gave off a thin tendril of smoke.

Andrew was watching him, still perched on the edge like he had a death wish. Neil wasn't sure why he did it, but he plucked Andrew's cigarette off the sidewalk and stuck it between his lips. He tipped his head back to meet Andrew's unwavering gaze and tapped two fingers to his temple in Andrew's mocking salute. Andrew turned away and disappeared from sight. It felt like a win, though Neil wasn't sure why. He ground the cigarette out beneath his shoe on his way back indoors.

Matt was on the couch when Neil made it back to his room. The coffee pot was done brewing and a hot mug felt good to Neil's chilled hands. Matt checked him on his way to the couch, likely looking for new injuries. Neil sat down as carefully as he could on the far cushion and breathed in the steam from his drink.

"Where were we?" Neil asked.

Matt sighed but picked up where he'd left off. He told Neil about snow in Central Park and a New Year's countdown spent in Times Square. Neil closed his eyes as he listened, trying to picture it, imagining for a moment he'd been there too. He didn't mean to fall asleep, but a careful tug at his coffee mug had him jolting awake. Matt narrowly avoided getting hit and held up his hands to ward Neil off.

"Hey," he said. "It's just me."

[22]

The mug was cold in his hands and the light in the room seemed wrong. Neil looked to the window, needing to see the sky, but the blinds were drawn. He let Matt take his coffee away and lurched to his feet when Matt stepped back. He crossed the room as quickly as his battered body could move and yanked the cords to pull the blinds up. The sun was down, but there was still some light in the sky. It was twilight or dawn; Neil didn't know which.

Neil pressed his hands flat against the window. "What day is it?"

It felt like forever before Matt answered, and his words came slowly. "It's Tuesday."

Twilight, then. He'd only lost a couple hours.

"Neil?" Matt asked. "You all right?"

"I'm more tired than I thought," Neil said. "I'm going to bed early."

The unhappy frown on Matt's face said he didn't believe Neil for a second, but Matt didn't try to stop him. Neil closed the bedroom door firmly behind himself and began the painstaking process of getting changed. He was breathing through clenched teeth by the time he finally got his sweats on. He clenched his hands to stop them from trembling, but the climb into his loft just sent the quakes to his stomach. It was too early and he was too sore to fall sleep again yet, but he pulled his blankets over his head and willed himself to stop thinking.

CHAPTER TWO

Getting out of bed Wednesday morning took a herculean effort, one Neil managed only because he was as keen on self-preservation as he was on maintaining his lies. He needed his teammates to think he was okay. That meant going about the day as if Christmas had never happened. He bought himself time to lock his thoughts down by going for the world's slowest run down Perimeter Road. Every step sent pain jolting up his legs and Neil was numb from knees to toes by the time he made it back to Fox Tower.

Matt, who'd disappeared to the gym before Neil got up, was waiting for him in the living room with an incredulous look on his face. "You're crazy, you know that? Tell me you didn't really go out like that."

"What time does Dan land?" Neil asked.

For a moment Neil thought Matt wasn't going to play along and let him change the subject. Matt's mouth thinned to a disapproving line. Instead of launching into a lecture, though, Matt said, "I'm going to get them at eleven and bring them straight to the court. You catching a ride with Andrew?"

"Yeah," Neil said. "Coach wants me to check in with Abby before the meeting."

Neil locked himself in the bathroom for a quick shower. Drying off afterward was almost more painful than his run had been despite his best efforts to be careful. He dressed at a snail's pace, grimacing the entire way, and took a minute to catch his breath afterward. It bought him time to put a fresh bandage over his tattoo, but his heart was still pounding in his temples when he left the muggy heat of the bathroom.

Matt was sprawled on the couch with the TV on when Neil

left the bedroom fully dressed. He said nothing when Neil left, maybe assuming Neil was going two doors down to bother the cousins. Instead Neil left the dorm and took the winding path down to Perimeter Road. He cut a slow path across campus to the library.

He saw only a couple other students on his way up the stairs to the computer lab. Despite the relative privacy Neil went to a computer on the very last row. He'd stopped obsessively keeping up with the news in September but today he wasn't looking for dredges of his past. He looked first for anything about his stint in Evermore, found nothing, and moved on to researching the other teams who qualified for spring championships. It was an easy way to stop thinking and waste a couple hours.

He didn't remember putting his head down and definitely didn't remember falling asleep. Fingers digging into the back of his skull startled him awake. He grabbed for a gun, for a knife, for anything close enough to buy him room to flee, and sent the computer mouse skidding across the table. Neil stared blankly at it, then at the screen in front of him. Fingers clenched into a fist in his hair and Neil didn't resist as Andrew forcibly tilted his head back.

"Is your learning curve a horizontal line?" Andrew asked. "I told you yesterday to stop making my life difficult."

"And I told you I wouldn't promise anything."

Andrew let go of him and watched pitilessly as Neil rubbed at his head. Neil sat up straight and started shutting his browsers down. He went through three tabs before he saw what time it was. It was after eleven, which meant Matt was greeting Dan and the girls at Arrivals and Neil was supposed to already be at the stadium with Abby. Neil didn't know what was worse, that he'd lost two hours like that or that he'd fallen asleep in the open. He silently counted to ten in French and Spanish. It did little to take the edge off his frustrated anger.

Andrew started for the stairs, rightfully assuming Neil

would follow. The car was at the curb, hazards flashing. The other three of their group squished into the backseat. Neil didn't know who'd talked Kevin to giving up the passenger seat or why, but it wasn't worth asking about. He got in and buckled up.

"I didn't tell anyone I was going to the library," he said when Andrew got them on the road.

"You only have a couple hiding spots," Nicky said. "Coach said you weren't at the stadium. You didn't answer your phone when we called."

Neil patted his pockets and dug his phone out. When he flipped it open the screen stayed dark. He'd charged it yesterday, but not for long. He flipped it shut and dropped it in the cup holder between the front seats. Andrew reached across the car and popped open the glove compartment. A charger was tucked inside. For a moment Neil thought Andrew had gone through his things, but the red sticker on the cord wasn't familiar. This had to be Andrew's, then; they had the same model phone. Neil pulled the charger out and snapped the glove compartment closed again.

A key was fastened to the adapter head with a rubber band. Neil had used Andrew's car key often enough in the past couple months to recognize the shape of it. Neil looked from it to the key in the ignition. Either Andrew had confiscated Nicky's copy or he'd gone out and gotten Neil one of his own. Neither option made much sense to Neil. He'd only used Andrew's car because Andrew needed a second driver in his absence.

It was a short drive to the Foxhole Court and Andrew didn't follow them inside. Neil keyed in the code to let them in and preceded the others into the locker room. Wymack and Abby were waiting for him in the lounge. Abby looked immeasurably sad as she took in Neil's sorry state, but she didn't chastise him for what he'd done or ask him why. Maybe she'd gotten satisfactory answers from Wymack already, or maybe Wymack was here to make sure she didn't pry. Neil was grateful either way.

"I can't believe you trusted David to patch you up," Abby said. "The man can barely wash a dish, much less clean stitches."

"Shush, woman," Wymack said. "I was careful with him."

Abby beckoned with both hands for Neil to follow. "Come on, let's take a look at you."

She led the way into her office and closed the door as soon as he was inside. Climbing onto the bed wasn't quite as painful as climbing the ladder to his loft was, and Neil perched on the edge of the thin mattress. Abby collected gauze and antiseptic while Neil tried to get his sweater over his head. He gritted his teeth at the heat that knifed down his shoulders into his back and tried to take shallow breaths through the pain.

Abby helped him with the sleeves and carefully set his sweater aside. Neil picked a spot on the far wall to look at and sat silent while she worked. She started at the top, gently rubbing her fingers through his hair for hidden bumps, and worked her way down. Wymack had just checked Neil yesterday morning, but Abby peeled off all of Neil's bandages save the one on his cheekbone.

"He told you about my tattoo," Neil said.

"And these." Abby slid her thumbs along the tender skin under his eyes.

"You won't ask?" Neil said.

"I've seen your scars, Neil. I'm not as surprised as I should be to find out they're not the only things you hide. I want to ask, but you told me once already not to pry."

She went back to work, but it was a long time before she finished. When she was done with his upper half she still had to take care of his legs. The striped bruises across his thighs, left there by heavy racquets, had her pursing her lips in outrage. There were layers of them, fresher purple ones over fading green and yellow. Neil's knees weren't better off, consequence of falling to them so many times.

"Coach won't let me on the court until you clear me," Neil

said. "How soon can you?"

Abby looked at him like he was speaking a foreign language. "You can gear up when you don't look like you were trampled in the derby."

"I'm getting better," Neil said. "Besides, I played in worse shape at Evermore."

"This isn't Evermore. I know the season is important to you, but I won't let you risk your safety and health any further. You need to take it easy for a while. For a week," she said, raising her voice when Neil started to protest. "Next Tuesday I'll decide whether or not I want to let you play. If you do anything strenuous between now and then I will bench you for another week. Understand? Use this week to rest. And when you can, leave the bandages off. These need to air."

"A week," Neil echoed. "That isn't fair."

"No," Abby said, and cupped his face in her hands. "This isn't fair. None of this is."

The pain in her voice killed Neil's argument in his throat. Abby looked him over, tracing his vicious scars and new wounds with a desolate gaze.

"Sometimes I think this job is going to kill me," Abby said. "Seeing what people have done, what people continue to do, to my Foxes. I wish I could protect you, but I'm always too late. All I can do is patch you up afterward and hope for the best. I'm sorry, Neil. We should have been there for you."

"I wouldn't have let you be," Neil said.

Abby folded her arms around him and pulled him into a hug. She tried to be careful, but it hurt regardless. It wasn't pain that made Neil go still, but uncertainty. The only people who'd ever hugged Neil were his teammates, and those were quick squeezes throughout a good game. His mother had pulled him close before, but usually it was when they were sidestepping curious eyes and she wanted to shield him with her body. She'd never held him like he was something to be sheltered. She'd always been hard. She'd been fierce and unbreakable until the

[28]

end.

Neil thought about her clawing at the air and choking for one last breath. He remembered the tear of her body where her blood had glued her skin to the vinyl. Neil's fingers twitched with the need for a cigarette, for the smell of smoke that was as awful as it was reassuring. Fire was all he had left of her. There wasn't even a hint of her in his reflection; he was every inch his father.

She was gone. Even if she was here, she wouldn't have comforted him for this. She wouldn't have held him like he was a hard breath away from shaking apart. She'd have cleaned his wounds because they couldn't risk being slowed by infection, but she'd hit him for choosing the Foxes over his own safety. Neil could almost hear her harping at his ear. He wouldn't survive long enough to forget the sound of her voice. It was at once reassuring and depressing, and a sudden swell of grief threatened to swallow him whole.

"I need to go," Neil said. "Are we done?"

Abby slowly let go of him and helped him get dressed again. He could have tied his shoes, but Abby did it for him. Neil let her and focused on smoothing down his sweater. Abby moved so he could get down from the bed and didn't follow him out.

Instead of heading down the hall to the lounge, Neil went out the back door into the court. He couldn't breathe until he was in the inner ring with his hands crushed against the wall, and then the first real breath he managed almost tore him apart. Neil could feel every wall he'd put up to survive at Evermore crumbling around him. He clung to control with his fingertips, knowing he'd drown if he let himself go. His heart felt like molten stone, but every breath soothed the heat a little. Neil willed his shaking fingers to go still and headed back to the locker room.

Wymack and Andrew were missing, but Matt and the girls had shown up in Neil's absence. He didn't want to look at them yet, so he stalled by looking for an open outlet. He found a spot on the surge protector behind the entertainment center and plugged his phone in to charge. When the light on his phone turned red, he headed for the couch. His casual act worked only until he had to sit down. Nothing he did could disguise how carefully he needed to maneuver onto the cushion.

That was where Dan's temper finally snapped. "That motherfuck—"

She cut off so abruptly Neil had to look at her. Renee had a hand on Dan's shoulder. Renee smiled when Neil looked her way and said, "We were just debating what to order for lunch. Abby said she'll call it in and pick it up for us so we don't have to wait on delivery. Any suggestions?"

"I'm fine with anything," Neil said.

Allison raked him with a skeptical look. "Can you even chew?"

"Yes," Neil said. "Where is Andrew?"

"Saw him on our way in," Matt said. "He and Coach are talking at the far end of the parking lot. Getting to know each other all over again, I guess. Here's hoping it goes better than their last first meeting."

"I'm still talking to you," Allison said.

Neil rewarded her persistence with another dodge. "Have you seen Seth's banner yet?"

It took a moment for the words to sink in, and then Allison was out of her chair and striding toward the court in six-inch rainbow heels. Dan looked for a moment like she'd go after her, but she changed her mind with a short shake of her head.

"Sandwiches or Chinese?" she asked Neil.

"Either one is fine."

"I'm with Allison on the chewing thing." Nicky gestured at his own face, indicating the bruises staining Neil's cheeks and jaw. "Noodles and rice are softer than subs. Let's go with Chinese."

Matt got up and went to relay the decision to Abby. He was

on his way back when the outer door thumped closed. Across the room Dan sat up a little straighter and shot Renee a meaningful look. Renee dropped her hand and laced her fingers together in her lap. It wasn't the eager response Dan was looking for, judging by Dan's disappointed frown, but Dan didn't have time to push it before Andrew stepped through the lounge door alone.

Matt made the mistake of stopping to look. Andrew didn't even hesitate but punched Matt hard enough to knock him off his feet. It should have been impossible to topple him; Matt had more than a foot on Andrew and could out-press any of them at the gym. Andrew had the advantage of surprise, though, and didn't stop when Matt fell. He smashed his fist into Matt's face as soon as Matt hit the ground.

Dan was on her feet in a heartbeat, but somehow Neil made it to Andrew first. He didn't even remember deciding to move. He used his body and momentum to shove Andrew back. He expected Andrew to hold his ground, but Andrew let himself get pushed and flicked Neil an unconcerned look. Neil put his hands up between them in case Andrew tried to go around him.

"Enough," he said. "Matt didn't do anything wrong."

Andrew flicked his fingers in dismissal. "He knew what would happen if he laid a hand on Kevin, yet he was stupid enough to do it twice. If he does it again I will not be as friendly."

"You're not seriously threatening him," Dan said, incredulous. "Who do you think paid Aaron's bail? If it weren't for Matt, Aaron would still be in prison waiting for his trial."

"Doesn't matter," Aaron said from his chair.

Yesterday Nicky looked guilty when he warned Matt to lie low. Today he closed ranks with his cousins and shrugged expansively at Dan. "Matt helped Aaron by doing that, not Andrew. You can't count a favor for one as a favor to both just because they're twins, you know. That's cheating."

"Nice to see you too, monster," Matt said, a little sourly. Neil looked back as Matt got to his feet again. Matt dragged a

[31]

hand through the blood sliding from his nose, gave a thick sniff, and grimaced a bit at the taste. "Good to see you're still fuck-all crazy."

"Don't look surprised," Aaron said. "It wasn't the drugs that made him crazy."

"Hello, Andrew," Renee said.

Andrew said nothing but slid an impassive look her way. A pleased smile curved Renee's lips and she gave a slight nod, acknowledging and accepting whatever she saw in Andrew's heavy stare. That two-second exchange was the entirety of their reunion; Andrew turned his attention back to Neil as soon as Renee had looked her fill.

Abby walked in a moment later and hesitated with her purse half-slung over her shoulder. She looked from the Dan's obvious anger to Matt's tight expression and bloody nose. It didn't take long for her to put the pieces together, and she turned a guarded look on Andrew.

"Andrew," she said. "Welcome back. It hasn't been the same without you." Andrew gazed at her in silence. Abby waited, then figured out she wasn't going to get a response. She glanced awkwardly around at the rest of the gathered Foxes. "The food should be ready by the time I get there. I'll be right back, okay? Try to behave while I'm gone."

"Thanks," Dan said.

Abby flicked one last look at Andrew and left. The door had barely banged closed behind her before Wymack strode in. Neil wondered if he'd been smoking or just wasting time, letting his team acclimate to Andrew's abrupt reentry and Neil's injuries the same way he'd abandoned them to Allison's grief in September. Wymack quirked a brow at Matt, then looked to Neil and Andrew.

"Didn't we have a talk about not killing your teammates?" Wymack asked. Andrew feigned not to hear, so Wymack looked around. It took him a split-second glance to realize they were down a Fox. "Allison was just here. Where did she go?"

"She went to see the championship banners," Neil said.

"She'll come back when she's done crying," Nicky added.

"She's not crying," Neil said.

Nicky grinned. "Five bucks says she is."

Neil should have brushed it off. Maybe a month ago he would have. He knew his teammates were obsessive gamblers; they would bet on everything from final scores to Andrew and Renee's nonexistent relationship to who'd take the first swing in an argument. Putting money on someone's psychological trauma wasn't new or unexpected, but Neil wasn't in the mood to put up with it today. His meeting with Abby had rubbed his nerves raw and he was barely holding it together for his team. The acrid scent of cigarettes that clung to Andrew's coat was the final straw.

Neil kept the edge out of his voice, but barely. "Don't you dare bet on someone's grief."

"Oh, hey, hey." Nicky put his hands up in self-defense. "No harm intended, right? No offense. I was trying to lighten the mood."

"Lighten your chair and go check on her," Wymack said. "We've got a lot to go over today and I can't start until she's back. She'll be angrier at us if we start without her than she will be if you interrupt her. And yes, I mean you, Hemmick. I don't want Neil moving more than he has to."

"I can walk," Neil said.

"Proud of you," Wymack said. "Didn't ask."

Nicky hoisted himself out of his chair and left.

Andrew dug a fingernail into the hollow of Neil's throat until he had Neil's undivided attention. "Sit down and be still."

Neil batted Andrew's hand away and turned back to the couch. Andrew claimed the middle cushion, so Neil eased into the open spot at his side. His body regretted interfering with that fight, but Matt gave a slight nod in thanks when Neil caught his eye across the room. Neil looked to Andrew, trying to gauge his mood, and followed his hooded stare down. Andrew had brought

[33]

a small knife out and was turning it over and over between his fingers. It wasn't one of the ones he kept in his arm bands, but Neil wasn't surprised he didn't recognize it. He almost never saw the same knife twice.

"It is not that fascinating," Andrew said.

"No," Neil agreed.

He didn't know how to explain the complicated emotions a sharp blade stirred up. His father was called the Butcher for a reason. His favorite weapon was a cleaver sharp and hefty enough to take limbs off in a single hack. Before the cleaver Nathan Wesninski used an axe. He still kept that axe around for when he really wanted someone to suffer. The blade was dull enough now it required a bit of extra weight and effort to cut through bone. Neil only saw him use it once, the day he met Riko and Kevin at Evermore Stadium.

"It's just..." Neil grasped for words, too-aware that the conversation across the room had quieted down a little. The upperclassmen were trying to listen in without being obvious. Neil settled for the vaguest explanation he could and hoped his teammates would mistake the pronoun for Riko. "I've never understood why he likes knives."

Such simple words should not have gotten the reaction they did. Andrew went still and looked up, but he didn't look at Neil. He looked at Renee, so Neil did, too. She'd stopped mid-sentence to stare at Neil, but the Renee studying him wasn't the Foxes' redeemed optimist. Her sweet smile was gone and the too-blank look on her face reminded Neil of Andrew. Neil instinctively tensed for flight-or-fight. Before his body figured out what to do Renee shifted her inscrutable gaze to Andrew.

They stared each other down, soundless and still, oblivious to the bewildered looks their teammates sent between them. Andrew didn't say anything, but Renee lifted her chin. Andrew hummed in response and put the knife away.

"He will lose his taste when he has one in his gut," he said.

Neil looked at Renee again in time to see Other-Renee

disappear. A calm mask melted away the death on her face and Renee picked up right where she'd left off. She didn't acknowledge what had just happened or the obvious questions on Dan's face but gently bullied her friends into rejoining the conversation.

Allison and Nicky returned together. Allison's cheeks were dry and her eyes fierce with determination as she took her seat. Renee's smile was encouraging and Dan grinned in approval. Allison drummed impatient fingernails on the arms of her chair and fixed Wymack with an expectant look.

"Who are we eliminating first?"

"Round one: southeast versus southwest." Wymack picked up his clipboard and skimmed the top page. "Odd-ranked teams play on Thursdays this year, so we've got Fridays. January 12th we're away against University of Texas. Good news is that Austin's just outside the thousand-mile range, which means the board's going to let us fly there.

"The 19th we're home for a rematch against Belmonte. January 26th we're away against Arkansas. It's two out of three to proceed to death matches. Belmonte is fourth-ranked, but you remember what they were like last fall. SUA is also fourth-ranked. UT is second-ranked, and they have been second in their region for the past five years.

"All three of these teams have been in spring championships before with varying results. They know what they're doing. They know what it takes to qualify. We are the weak link. That doesn't mean we're going to break. It just means we have to work twice as hard to keep up. If you're willing to do that, we have a fighting chance."

He unhooked a stack of papers and waggled them at Matt. Matt got up and passed them out. Wymack had put together round-one packets for them. The first page was UT's fall schedule, complete with results. Notes at the bottom detailed UT's last seven attempts at spring championships. For three years they'd made it as far as the third round before getting

[35]

knocked out. Neil flipped the page and skimmed the team roster. The next four pages followed the same pattern for Belmonte and SUA.

"Monday we'll break down their playing style in depth and pin down strategies," Wymack said. "By then I'll also have copies of all of their fall games burned onto discs. Watch them in your free time if you're curious. With one exception, I'm not taking time out of practices to show you more than a couple highlights.

"There's a week break between round one and the first set of death matches," Wymack continued. "Bad news is we won't know who we're up against until February. Good news: this year the Big Three are all in the odds bracket. They have to face each other in the third round. For the first time in six years one of them is getting knocked out before semifinals."

"Oh, damn," Dan said, startled. "That's lucky."

"My money's on Penn dropping," Nicky said.

"Don't," Kevin said before the others could place their bets. "It doesn't matter which one is eliminated; we are nowhere near ready to face any of them. How long is Neil benched?"

"A week," Neil said, a little resentfully. "Abby won't reconsider until next Tuesday."

"Generous," Dan said. "I'd have benched you for the entire first round."

"I'm fine to play," Neil said.

Kevin reached behind Andrew to smack the back of Neil's head. Every awkward ounce of empathy he'd managed yesterday was gone; he returned Neil's annoyed look with a fierce glower and a scathing, "I warned you once already not to lie about your health. We need you on the court, but not if you're going to drag us down with you. In the shape you're in now you'd be a complete waste of our time."

"I would not," Neil said. "Put me on the court and I'll prove it."

"Shut up," Wymack said. "When you're sporting fewer than

[36]

fifty stitches I'll consider letting you on my court again. If I catch you so much as looking at your gear before then I will bench you another week out of spite. Do you understand?"

"But—"

"Give me a 'Yes, Coach'."

"Coach—"

Neil forgot the rest of his argument when Andrew pinched his wrist. A bolt of fire popped through his fingers and he snatched his hand away as fast as he could. Neil flicked Andrew an irritated look, but Andrew didn't even look at him. Neil wrapped his arm around his stomach to get his hand out of Andrew's reach and sullenly turned his attention back on Wymack.

"Appreciate it, I think," Wymack said. "Andrew, how behind are you? I didn't see a fitness center listed with Easthaven's amenities."

"There wasn't one," Andrew said. "I improvised."

"Do I want to know?" Wymack asked, then answered his own question. "No, I don't, unless there's an impending lawsuit I should know about.

"Morning practices are at the gym again. Neil, until you're back on the court, you'll be meeting me here instead. I'll put you to work watching tapes and researching UT's defense. Tomorrow afternoon we're doing semester meet-and-greets with Betsy. You know the routine: you can't go with someone who plays the same position. Dan'll figure out the pairs and give you an allotted time during morning practice. Right?"

"On it," Dan said.

"Last order of official business from me is damage control," Wymack said. "We've got everyone's attention. A fierce season and ample tragedies mean we're the talk of the town, and this year people might actually root for the underdog. The board wants us to encourage that fever with more publicity. Expect more cameras at games, more interviews, and more nosiness in general. If I could ban some of you from ever opening your mouth in public, I would, but this is out of my hands. Attempt to behave yourselves without sacrificing your confident image. Think you can do that?"

"You're no fun, Coach," Nicky said.

"I will be a lot less fun if you make us look like fools," Wymack said. "But I'm not as worried about you as I am about our resident punching bag and his smart mouth. Anyone have ideas on how to make Neil look a bit less like a battered wife?"

"It's under control," Allison said, and looked to Neil. "You'll come to our room after the meeting."

"I was going to buy my textbooks today," Neil said.

"I wasn't asking," Allison said. "You can go when I'm done with you, unless you want to go out looking like that."

"We promise not to ask about Christmas," Renee said. Either she didn't see the annoyed look Allison shot her for killing their chance at getting good gossip or she chose not to acknowledge it. "It'll only take a couple minutes, I think."

Neil didn't trust Allison not to pry, but he trusted Renee to intervene on his behalf when that happened. "Okay."

"I need to get my stuff, too," Nicky said. "We can go when they're done with you."

Wymack nodded and surveyed his team. "Anyone got anything official to add?"

"We're going to need a shelf or something in here to put our championship trophy on," Dan said. "Can we rearrange again?"

"Board won't sign off on a purchase like that until we've at least made it through the second death match," Wymack said. "Nice try, though."

"Who needs the board's permission?" Allison said. "I'm going to buy it, because the board is too stingy. We deserve something obscenely expensive. Matt, measure the bed of your truck. I need to know what I can fit before I start looking for the right piece."

"Oh, to be young and filthy rich," Nicky said. "Must be nice."

[38]

Allison considered her manicure with lofty boredom. "It is."

Nicky rolled his eyes but didn't push it.

"Anything else?" Wymack asked. The sound of the main door opening heralded Abby's return and Wymack shook his head. "Never mind. Food's here. Stuff your faces and get out of my locker room. I'll be going over paperwork and scheduling if anyone needs me."

He hopped off his perch and vanished into his office. Abby covered the coffee table with food containers and passed out paper plates. When she was done she stayed only long enough to offer a quiet but warm welcome back to the Foxes. Neil thought it odd that she wasn't sticking around to ask about anyone's vacation, but the uncomfortable look she flicked Neil and Andrew on her way to Wymack's office made him think she was sparing their feelings. It was misplaced courtesy. Andrew wasn't likely to care if his teammates had better breaks than he did and Neil didn't begrudge them their happiness.

Lunch was a quiet affair. Neil unplugged his phone on the way out and Andrew wouldn't let him into the car until he powered it on. The team took two cars back to Fox Tower, and Neil followed the girls into their room. Allison had him sit sideways on the couch while she went through her suitcase. She brought a plastic bag with her and sat as close to him as she could. Neil watched as she unloaded makeup into the scant space between them.

"It would have been better if you'd come to the store with us," Allison said. It sounded like an accusation, even though they hadn't made Neil aware of their intentions. Neil wondered if he was supposed to apologize. Before he made up his mind Allison barged on. "It doesn't matter. I bought out the entire row. Something will match sooner or later. Look straight ahead and let me work. Don't speak until I ask you a question."

She lifted the small packets two at a time, one to either side of his face, and checked for the closest matching tones. Some she was able to discard outright. Others she set aside for a second inspection. Finally she was left with three, and she set to work covering up the bruises lining his throat and face. Renee and Dan came around behind the couch to watch her work. Neil didn't risk Allison's ire by looking up at them, but he could almost hear Dan grinding her teeth.

"Why?" Dan finally demanded. "What did he hope to gain? Why did he do it?"

"Dan," Renee said in quiet rebuke. "We promised."

"You promised," Dan said.

Neil would have let them fight it out, but it wasn't his decision Dan was challenging. "To get to Kevin," he said, and Allison lowered her hands from his face. Neil slanted a look at Dan. "Did you know? Kevin's been with the Foxes a year now, but he still has a room at the Ravens' Nest. Riko hasn't even thrown away his schoolwork. Interesting, isn't it? Riko threatens and dismisses Kevin at every turn, but he can't let go. He's as obsessed with Kevin as Kevin is with him.

"Now Kevin's starting to forget him," Neil said. "When we faced the Ravens last October, Kevin cared more about us than he did about having Riko standing at his back. He chose us over them that day, and that's unforgivable. Riko is King. He won't be dismissed or belittled or outplayed. So he took away the people Kevin was leaning on. He wanted us to fear him and to infect Kevin with those doubts."

Dan gave a rude snort. "What an incompetent asshole."

"Thank you," Neil said. Dan looked lost, so Neil said, "For not asking me if it worked."

"Of course it didn't work," Allison said. "You're not afraid of Andrew. Why would you be afraid of Riko? He's just another loudmouthed, spoiled child with anger issues. Now eyes forward and let me work. I didn't tell you you could look away."

Neil resumed a frozen position until she finished. She leaned back a bit to give him a scrutinizing once-over, then got up to grab a mirror from her desk. Neil's stomach churned as she brought it back to him. Neil took it from her outstretched hand but let it rest glass-down in his lap. Allison motioned for him to take a peek. Neil shook his head.

"If you say it's good, I'll believe you," Neil said.

"Not scared of Riko, but scared of your own reflection?" Allison crossed her arms over her chest and treated him to a pitying look. "You are one messed-up child. You come by that naturally or did your parents do that to you?"

Dan jumped in before Neil could react. "Looks great. Anyone gets too close they'll probably figure out you're wearing makeup, but I don't think anyone will ask. From back here I can't even tell. You'll just have to stop by here after morning practices to get dolled up for classes until the mess fades. Do you have nine o'clock classes this semester?"

"No, I cut it too close too often last fall." To Allison, Neil said, "Thank you. I wouldn't have even thought of trying this. It seems like a useful trick."

"It is. I learned it to keep the paparazzi off my back when I first started playing. I haven't needed it since then, but I never forget a good fashion tip." Allison lifted one shoulder in a shrug. "Take it for a test run and get your textbooks. Now, preferably. Dan is waiting to commandeer your room."

"It's not his room I'm interested in," Dan said.

Neil set the mirror to one side and got off the couch. "Leaving."

"Oh, and Neil?" Dan said when Neil made it to the door. Neil let his hand go slack on the doorknob and looked back at her. "If you want to talk about any of it, or anything, or," she gestured vaguely at the side of her head, maybe meaning Neil's abrupt change in looks, "you know we're here for you, right? Whatever you need."

"I know," Neil said. "Maybe later. Text me when it's safe to come back?"

"Maybe, maybe not."

Neil shook his head and left. He pulled the door closed

[41]

behind him and lingered in the hallway. He was tired and sore and not at all looking forward to his week off the court, but for a moment none of that mattered.

"We're okay," he said to the empty hall. "We're going to be okay."

The Foxes would be okay, at least, and that was more than enough.

CHAPTER THREE

Neil expected to feel jilted for being banned from the gym Thursday morning, but Wymack gave him one of UT's more interesting matches to watch. Wymack watched a different game in his office, and the two of them convened afterward to discuss players' styles. The girls picked him up from the stadium since Allison needed to work on his face again. It was faster this time now that Allison remembered what she was doing and had the colors figured out.

Classes were a blur; Neil spent more time worrying that people could see through Allison's makeup than he did actually paying attention to his teachers. It was a relief when his second class let out at one forty-five and Neil could escape back to Fox Tower. Matt was missing when Neil stepped into the suite. A glance at the class schedule tacked to the front of their fridge said he wouldn't be back until it was almost time to go.

Neil unloaded his backpack onto his desk. The bottom shelf of his desk still held last semester's math and Spanish books. He pried his math notes off the shelf, wiped dust off the binder, and sat down to review. Most of it was only dimly familiar, but the further he flipped the more it started coming back. Neil had a sinking feeling he knew how he was going to spend his weekend.

At a quarter to three Neil met up with Andrew's lot for a ride to the stadium. The Foxes usually traveled to practices in two groups. Today they took three cars, since they'd be going back and forth to Reddin Hall throughout afternoon practice. Andrew and Kevin had the first slots with Betsy Dobson and would head straight there, so Aaron and Nicky piled into the bed of Matt's truck with Renee. Neil didn't think he could climb that

[43]

high without pulling something, but he didn't have to worry. Allison stuffed him into her pink convertible as soon as he was within grabbing distance.

Neil braced himself for questions, but Allison didn't speak to him the entire ride. Neil thanked her as he got out, got a bemused look in response, and waited on the curb for the others to arrive.

Afternoon practice was as awful as he'd expected it would be. He took the disc Wymack offered him but stood lost in the hallway while his teammates changed out. He watched them head into the stadium for warm-ups and had to fight not to follow. Sitting down on the couch took every ounce of self-control he had, and he hoped the game would distract him. It worked only until the Foxes came back into the locker room to strap on their gear. Neil lost track of what was going on on-screen and stared through the wall instead.

"Focus," Wymack said somewhere behind him.

"I am," Neil lied.

"They just scored an impossible goal and you didn't even twitch," Wymack said.

Neil glanced back at the TV and saw the score had gone up. The crowd was going insane in the background. "I should be on the court."

"You will be," Wymack said. "Next week, when you're more healed. It won't kill you to sit out a couple days. It might kill you if you pull something and injure yourself beyond repair. I will definitely kill you if you eliminate us just because you're impatient. Look at it like this if you have to: your teammates are playing catch-up right now. You got two weeks of practice in over the holidays while they were goofing off and stuffing their faces. You're ahead of the curve."

"Kevin practiced," Neil said. "Matt said he was at the neighborhood court every day."

"That's one out of eight."

"They can afford to take time off. They're all better than I

[44]

am, and they have subs."

"They're more experienced and they have different strengths than you do," Wymack said. "But you're a hundred times better now than you were in May. Don't sell yourself short. Now focus. I'm going to need some good notes when you leave today."

Neil picked up his pencil again in silent acquiescence and Wymack left.

He was halfway through the second game before it was time to head to Reddin. This time he was going third and was paired off with Aaron. Neil drove, and somehow he resisted asking how long it'd been since anyone let Aaron ride passenger. There was nothing yet to gain from antagonizing Aaron.

It was too early for most of the student body to starting taking up space at the medical center, so Neil found a parking spot close to the door. They bypassed the general check-in and went down the hall to the counselors' quarters. Before Neil could ask which one of them was up first, Aaron continued to Betsy's office just out of sight. Neil sank onto one of the thick chairs to wait.

He didn't want to think about the session but didn't want to think about the Foxes practicing without him, so he went through his messages instead. Most were from Nicky: idle comments about things he saw in New York, questions about Millport, and scattered demands that Neil stop ignoring him. At least four messages consisted only of exclamation points. Renee sent greetings twice and Allison once, in a group text on Christmas Day.

Kevin messaged Neil only once, on the day Neil went to Evermore. Neil had missed it by only a few minutes; it was time-stamped for Neil's boarding time. Neil read the eight-word message four times: "Jean will help you if you help him."

Neil had sorely disliked Jean the first several days, and Kevin's message wouldn't have done him any good then, but he understood in retrospect. Jean was privy to the ugly truth about the Moriyamas, as he'd been sold to Tetsuji years ago to settle a debt with the head of the family. Jean hated his lot in life, but he was past the point where he could even think of fighting back. He wasn't a rebel; he was a survivor. He did whatever it took to get through the day.

Oftentimes that meant looking after Neil. Jean stood unflinching guard while Riko tore Neil apart again and again, but he was always there to pull Neil back to his feet afterward. They were each other's partners on the Raven court, which meant their successes and failures directly impacted each other. Jean was a questionable ally at best but he was the only Raven who'd looked out for Neil. It was selfishness, not kindness, but it had been just enough to keep Neil alive.

Neil had survived and made it out of there. Kevin had escaped when his life crashed down around him. Jean was still there, keeping it together as best he could. Neil wondered what it cost him to watch them both leave: if he thought them fools for defying the master or if a quiet part of him was jealous that they had a way out. Neil wondered if he cared. It was safer and smarter not to. If Jean wasn't willing to fight back, if he had nothing to fight for, there was nothing anyone could do for him.

A stray memory tugged at his thoughts, just out of reach. Neil tried to focus on it, but thinking about Jean had his mind spiraling back to Riko's abuse. Neil brushed it all aside and skipped through the rest of his messages. Dan and Matt had checked in several times. Aaron's single message was the last one anyone sent to Neil before the exchange of New Year's greetings.

"Don't tell Andrew about Katelyn," it said.

Katelyn and Aaron had sneaked around most of fall semester, avoiding each other at games and meeting up at the library between classes. Once Andrew was committed Katelyn had become a permanent fixture in their lives, having dinner with Aaron several nights a week and dropping by the dorm occasionally. It was strange thinking they were reverting to

[46]

secrecy and Neil idly wondered how Katelyn had reacted to the decision. Maybe Aaron told her how much Andrew disliked her. She might not be happy, but at least she was alive and safe.

The click of a door distracted him from his thoughts. Neil glanced at the time and closed his messages. Reluctance, more than pain, made him slow to get to his feet when Aaron returned. Betsy followed Aaron to the entryway and greeted Neil with a warm smile.

"Hello, Neil."

He followed her down the hall to her office and went past her to enter it first. The room looked the same as it had in August, from the perfectly-angled cushions on her couch to the crystal figurines lining her shelves. He sat on the couch and watched as Betsy closed the door behind her. She took a moment to mix some hot cocoa and looked over at him.

"I have some hot tea, if you would like. I remember you saying you don't like sweets."

"I'm fine."

Betsy sat opposite him. "It's been a while. How have you been doing?"

"The Foxes made spring championships, Andrew is back and sober, and I'm still starting striker," Neil said. "I don't have any complaints yet."

"Congratulations on qualifying, by the way," Betsy said. "I confess I don't understand much about sports, but you have very talented players on your team and your comeback last year was nothing short of brilliant. I think you're going to have an amazing run. Texas is a little far for me to travel, but I'll cheer you on for the home game against Belmonte. Are you ready?"

"No," Neil said, "but we'll get there. We don't have a choice. Last month we said we weren't going to lose a single spring game. We haven't changed our minds, but I think now that January's here we're realizing what we're up against and what it'll take to pull this off. We're going to face the best in the country, and we're only recent contenders."

[47]

"That's a mature way to look at it. It is also," Betsy spread her hands a bit as she searched for words, "very practiced. It sounds more like a soundbite you would give to a reporter than something you might admit to me. I hoped we might progress past such guarded statements. Remember that I am not here to cast judgment on anything you say."

"I remember," Neil said, and left it at that.

Betsy inclined her head and moved on. "You mentioned Andrew's return as a positive thing. I know you supported my decision to commit him last November. It is probably too soon to tell, but how are you handling the reality of his sobriety? Any concerns?"

"I'm not going to talk about Andrew with you."

"I'm trying to talk about you," Betsy said. "This session is about you."

"This isn't a real session," Neil said. "It's an informal meeting and I'm only here because Coach said we had to come see you once a semester. Neither of us benefits. You're wasting time on me that would be better spent with your actual patients and I'm missing out on practice."

"I don't consider this to be a waste of time, but I apologize that it's cutting into your time on the court." She gave him a couple moments to answer, then said, "Happy New Year, by the way. I forgot to say it. How were your holidays?"

There was the question he'd expected and dreaded. He didn't know what his teammates had told her. He wouldn't tell her the truth, but if he lied about it and they'd already told her, she'd start questioning everything else he'd said to this point. Neil juggled the possible consequences and decided to go for it. He was only required to see Betsy once a semester after all; this was the last time he'd have to sit down with her face-to-face. She could think what she liked of him.

"They were fine," Neil said.

"Does it ever snow in Arizona?"

"Now and then. They consider an inch and a half to be a

[48]

major snowstorm."

"Oh my," Betsy said. "I remember when we had a dusting a few years back. I passed a young woman on my way across campus. She was on her phone; she'd called someone just to tell them it was snowing here. She was so excited over such a paltry amount I wondered if she'd ever seen it before. I wanted to ask her where she was from, but it seemed intrusive."

There wasn't a question there, so Neil said nothing. Betsy said nothing either but sipped at her cocoa. Neil resisted the urge to look at the clock. He didn't want to know how little time had passed.

"Won't you talk to me?" Betsy finally prompted.

"What do you want me to say?" Neil said.

"Anything," Betsy said. "This is your time."

"Anything?" Neil said. When she gave an encouraging nod, Neil proceeded to tell her about the UT games he'd been watching. It was completely impersonal and definitely not at all what she'd been hoping for, but she didn't interrupt and didn't have the good grace to look bored. She drank her cocoa and listened like it was the most important story she'd heard all day. Somehow it made Neil like her even less, but he didn't stop.

Finally he was free to go. He cleared out of there, collected Aaron from the waiting room, and headed to the car. They were halfway to the stadium before Aaron spoke up.

"I didn't tell her."

They were the only two in the car, but it took Neil a moment to realize he was being addressed. He glanced over at Aaron, but Aaron was gazing out the passenger window.

"Neither did I," Neil said.

"She asked you about Andrew."

It wasn't a question, but Neil said, "Yes. You too?"

"She doesn't ask me anything anymore," Aaron said. "She knows there's no point. I haven't ever said a word to her."

Neil imagined sitting in stony silence while Betsy chattered away about this and that. It was at once inspiring and unsettling.

He didn't know if he could stomach a half-hour of that. "I wish I'd thought of that. I gave her a rundown of UT's merits instead."

"Predictable," Aaron said.

Neil wondered how Andrew killed time. While on his medication he'd been forced to have weekly sessions with Betsy. Neil didn't know if that would continue. He was more interested in how Andrew's view of Betsy was going to change. Andrew seemed oddly tolerant of her last year, to the point he'd admitted to getting texts from her outside of their sessions. Euphoric drugs probably made anyone easier to tolerate, though.

Neil stole the same parking spot he'd found the car in. He went back to his spot on the couch and Aaron continued to the locker room to get back into his court gear. Neil tried not to resent his good health and almost succeeded. The UT match was a good distraction from unwarranted irritation, but Neil lost track of the game when Renee and Allison passed through a couple minutes later. Neil watched their progress across the room, thought twice about it, then paused the game.

"Renee?"

They both stopped, but Allison didn't stick around for long. When she left Renee came and sat with Neil, close enough to offer silent comfort but far enough Neil could breathe.

"What did I say yesterday?" Neil asked her. "Why did you react like that?"

It didn't take her long to remember. "About the knives, you mean." When Neil nodded, she turned her hands over and considered her palms. "You remember I told you I used to be in a gang? There was a man there who went out of his way to hurt me. He liked knives and kept a half-dozen on him at all times. I couldn't defend myself by normal means, so I learned to fight with knives, too. I practiced for a year before I finally bested him.

"'Bested'." Renee contemplated the word choice for a few moments before saying, "He didn't survive the fight. Boss helped stage the body so we could pin it on a rival gang and I

[50]

was promoted. I kept the knives through my trial and my adoption. I wanted to remember what darkness I'm capable of— and what darkness I'm capable of surviving."

"You did what you had to do," Neil said. "If he lived he would have come back for you."

"I know," Renee said, soft. "There were other girls before I caught his eye; there would be girls after I left. But I didn't do it for the greater good. I did it because he wronged me personally and I didn't want to be afraid of him anymore. I regret what it did to me more than I regret the necessity of his death. I felt no horror when I watched him die. I was proud of what I'd done to him.

"I told Andrew what I did," Renee said. "The next day while I was at class he broke into my room and took my knives. When I asked for them back, he said I was lying to myself. If I wanted to remember, I wouldn't hide the knives in my closet like a shameful secret I couldn't revisit or let go of. They weren't doing me any good, so he said he would carry them until I needed them again.

"I let him have them because I trusted him not to use them," Renee said. "I thought he understood what they were supposed to be: not weapons anymore but a symbol of what we've overcome. I didn't ask him for his reasons. I knew he would tell me if he wanted me to know."

The obvious answer was Drake, but it didn't add up quite right. Neil turned it over in his head, working his way through it, and thought about the scars on Andrew's forearms. Who had Andrew survived: Drake or himself?

Neil wasn't going to share that idea with Renee, so he said, "So those knives he brings everywhere are yours?"

"Were mine," Renee said. "He was right; I don't need them anymore. If you need them, he will give them to you, and I will teach you how to use them."

She wasn't smiling anymore. Neil studied her calm expression and knew she meant it. She'd put her faith in

[51]

mankind and her Christian piety on hold and show him how to cut a man open throat to groin if he asked her to. Neil was starting to understand why Andrew liked her. She was crazy enough to be interesting.

"Thank you," Neil said, "but no. I don't want to be like—him."

He didn't say he'd used knives before; one couldn't grow up a Wesninski without having a blade pushed into his hand. Nathan didn't have the time or patience to teach his son but he'd put two of his people to the task. Luckily Neil left home before he progressed past cutting up hunks of dead animals.

"Of course," Renee agreed. She waited a moment to see if anything else was forthcoming, then got to her feet. "I shouldn't keep Allison waiting, but if you want to talk more later you know where to find me."

"Okay," Neil said. Renee made it as far as the door before Neil had to ask, "How is Andrew doing? Without his drugs, I mean."

Renee looked back at him and smiled. "Go see. I don't think Coach will mind."

Neil stayed where he was until the door closed behind her. He looked from his notepad to the paused game, then set his things aside and got to his feet. The sound of a ball popping off the wall greeted him as he stepped through the back door and he followed the path to the inner court. Wymack was standing near the home bench, watching his players scrimmage and taking notes. He had his back to Neil and the noise filtering through the court vents helped hide the soft pat of Neil's footsteps. Neil hung back a safe distance and watched his teammates.

They looked so small when they were down three players, but they played with the ferocity of a larger team. Dan and Kevin were paired up on offense against the three backliners, and despite being outnumbered they put up a tireless fight. Kevin even managed to out-step both Nicky and Aaron a couple times for shots on goal. Andrew deflected all of them, but it took a couple shots before Neil realized what he was doing. Instead of clearing the balls back down the court like usual, he was firing them back at Kevin. More specifically, right at Kevin's feet. Kevin had to execute some pretty nimble footwork to avoid tripping over the ball. Andrew did the same to Dan when she finally bulled past Matt for a shot of her own. She sidestepped it, but barely, and Matt had to catch her when she stumbled.

Wymack swore and turned to put his things down. As he twisted he spotted Neil, and he hesitated with his clipboard halfway to the bench. Neil expected a marching order back to the locker room. Instead Wymack snapped his fingers at Neil and jerked his thumb toward the court door.

"Tell your pet psycho to knock it off before he cripples someone."

"I don't think he'll listen to me," Neil said.

"You and I both know he will. Now get."

Wymack pounded on the wall, calling a pause to the scrimmage, as Neil headed for the door. Neil let himself onto the court and headed for the goal. Andrew slung his racquet across his shoulders at Neil's approach. Neil knew better than to call Andrew out with an audience, so he stopped as close to Andrew as he could and kept his voice down.

"Coach wants to know what you have against the offense line."

Andrew slid a look past Neil to the court wall. "He can ask me himself."

"Or you can answer me since I'm already here," Neil said. "There are only nine of us left. If we lose anyone else we're out of spring championships. You know that."

Neil waited a beat, but of course that wasn't enough to get a reaction. Andrew looked bored of this conversation already. Neil put a hand up in front of Andrew's face, neatly blocking his view of Wymack, and waited until Andrew looked at him again. "I want us to get to finals. I want us to be the ones who finally bring the Ravens down. After everything Riko's done to us, don't

[53]

you want that, too?"

"You say 'want' so freely," Andrew said, "when I have told you a thousand times before I want nothing."

"Probably because you're spending all your energy on not wanting anything," Neil shot back. "But if you can't grasp that simple concept, I'll put this in terms you do understand: this is a game we can't afford to lose. This is how we get to Riko. This is the only thing we can take from him that will actually hurt. Let's rip his rank out of his fingers and show him he had a reason to fear us all along."

"Do your teammates still think you're the quiet one?" Andrew asked.

"Our teammates," Neil said, with emphasis, "want this as much as I do. Stop cutting them off at the knees before they have the chance to try."

"I don't believe in giving people chances."

"I didn't until I came here," Neil said. "I took a chance on you when I decided to stay. You took a chance on me when you trusted me with Kevin. Is it really that hard to support them when they've been with you every step of the way?"

"What will you give me in exchange for my cooperation?" Andrew asked.

"Because revenge isn't good enough?" Neil asked. "What would it take?"

Andrew didn't have to think about it. "Show me your scars."

It was not what Neil was expecting, which was probably why Andrew asked for it. Neil opened his mouth to protest, but the words died in his throat. Wymack and Abby had already seen them, and the Foxes knew they were there. He'd put Andrew's hand to his ruined skin back in November to earn Andrew's trust. Neil had promised Andrew the missing parts of his truth if they survived the year. He hadn't thought Andrew would settle for a visual.

"When?" he said at last.

"We are going to Columbia tomorrow," Andrew said. "Now walk away and tell Coach to mind his pay grade. I will not let him get away with this a second time."

Neil didn't understand, but he nodded and left. The Foxes waited until the door was shut and locked before resuming play. The next time Kevin managed a shot on goal, Andrew cleared it all the way down the court. Neil had the feeling the Foxes would regret his intervention soon enough. This was definitely safer, but now Dan and Kevin had to chase the ball every time Andrew deflected it.

Neil went back to Wymack's side and relayed Andrew's message. He expected Wymack to brush off Andrew's threat without batting an eye. He wasn't expecting Wymack's amused huff and dry, "Just promise me this isn't going to be a problem."

"What?" Neil asked.

"I can't tell if you're being obtuse to fuck with me or if you're really that dumb," Wymack said. When Neil just stared blankly at him, Wymack rubbed his temples as if warding off a headache. "I would pity you, but Andrew's right. I don't get paid enough to get involved in this. Figure it out yourself—on your own time. You're supposed to be studying UT right now."

Wymack plucked up his clipboard and started scribbling notes. Neil looked from him to the court.

"Goodbye," Wymack said.

Neil swallowed his questions and headed back to the locker room.

-

The upperclassmen went out to dinner Friday after practice, but they swung by the dorms first to change into fresh clothes. Andrew showed up at Neil's room almost as soon as Matt had left, and he brought a bag of clothes with him. Neil still didn't understand why the cousins insisted he wear something new every time they went to Columbia, but he was past the point where he'd question it. He carried the bag into his bedroom to change. When he turned to close the door Andrew was right

[55]

behind him. Andrew said nothing but gestured to Neil's shirt.

Neil hesitated, then set the bag on Matt's bed and struggled out of his shirt. It was getting a little easier every day, but it hurt when he raised his arms too high and when he twisted he felt the pull at his stitches. He got his shirt over his head and to his elbows before Andrew got tired of watching him struggle and tugged the shirt loose. Andrew tossed it off to one side and didn't look to see where it landed. He was more interested in the scars and bruises covering Neil's front.

Andrew reached for the bandages on Neil's wrists, and Neil let him rip tape and gauze off. The scabs looked worse today than they had when he first landed in South Carolina. Abby was right; he needed to let his wounds air. Neil dragged his stare up from the ugly lines striped across his wrists to Andrew's face. Neil wasn't sure what he was looking for: a hint of Wednesday's violence or last semester's callous, cheerful dismissals. He got neither. Andrew looked a thousand years from all of this, detached and unconcerned.

On Neil's right shoulder was a burn scar, courtesy of getting smacked by a hot iron. Andrew put his left hand to it, fingertips lining up perfectly with the raised bumps the iron's holes had left behind. His right thumb found the puckered flesh from a bullet. Neil had slept in his bulletproof vest for almost a month after that close call, too scared to take it off. His mother had to bully him into shedding it long enough to wash up.

"Someone shot you," Andrew said.

"I told you someone was after me," Neil said.

"This," Andrew dug his fingers harder into the iron mark, "is not from a life on the run."

"My father gave me that. People came by asking questions about his work. I didn't say anything, but I didn't sit still enough, either. He hit me as soon as the door closed behind them. That's why I gave you 'Abram'," Neil said. "I don't want to give you my father's name because I don't want anyone to call me it ever again. I hated him."

[56]

Andrew was quiet a long time, then dropped his hand to the slashes across Neil's gut. "Renee said you refused our knives. A murder magnet like you shouldn't walk around unarmed."

"I'm not," Neil said. "I thought you were going to watch my back this year?" Andrew glanced up at him again, expression unreadable. He said nothing, so Neil pressed on with, "You're not actually a sociopath, are you?"

"I never said I was."

"You let them say it about you," Neil said. "You could have corrected them."

Andrew waved that off. "What people want to think of me is not my problem."

"Does Coach know?"

"Of course he does."

"Then your medicine...?" Neil asked. "Were those pills really anti-psychotics?"

"You ask a lot of questions," Andrew said, and left Neil alone to get dressed.

Neil found Andrew's lot in the hallway when he was done. Nicky gave a toothy grin of approval at how the new clothes fit. Aaron didn't so much as look at Neil. Kevin checked Neil's face for smudges in the make-up but said nothing. Andrew only waited long enough to hear the lock slide into place and started for the stairs. He had two cigarettes lit before he reached the second floor landing, and one he passed over his shoulder to Neil. Neil held onto it until they reached the car.

Nicky sent him an odd look as he opened the back door. "You don't smoke."

"No," Neil agreed, and rubbed the cherry out on the bottom of his shoe. He pocketed the other half of the cigarette for later. He got in the passenger seat before Nicky could ask anything else and tugged his buckle into place. The others weren't long in piling into the car, and Andrew had them on the road as soon as the last door was shut.

Neil would have been happy to never step foot in Columbia

[57]

again after what happened in November, but the others seemed unmoved. They pulled into the parking lot at Sweetie's like nothing bad had ever happened in this city and took the first booth available. Nicky rambled at length about his classes, but Neil couldn't focus on his words. He let them go in one ear and out the other and ate his ice cream in silence.

Eden's Twilight was as busy as usual. One bouncer sat on a stool checking IDs while the other guarded the doorway. The former actually hopped to his feet at the sight of Andrew's car at the curb. Neil hung back as Nicky and Aaron endured vigorous handshakes and back slaps. One of the bouncers said something to Aaron, voice low but expression intense. Neil assumed it was a promise of support in the upcoming trial, judging by Aaron's grateful nod. He looked back at Andrew, who was waiting in the driver's seat for a VIP parking pass, but Andrew was watching oncoming traffic instead of the spectacle at the door. Finally Nicky got a pass from one of the bouncers and brought it back.

Andrew drove off while the others headed inside. Neil followed Kevin through the crowd, pushing past overheated bodies and wincing a little at the bass crashing from the speakers. There weren't any tables open, so they ended up against the bar counter. It took no time at all for Roland to spot them and he almost dropped his cocktail shaker. As soon as he finished his orders he made a beeline for them.

"I'll be damned," he said. "I was starting to think I wouldn't see you again."

"As if we could stay away forever," Nicky said. "It just wouldn't have been the same without Andrew."

"Andrew's out, then?" Roland asked with obvious relief. "It killed us when we heard the news. I wish we could've done something, anything. You," he said, looking to Aaron, "are a hero. We've got your back here, understand? They try to make any of these bullshit charges stick and we'll march on the court. That guy got what he deserved and everyone knows it."

"Thank you," Aaron said.

[58]

Roland poured a round of shots. He'd seen Neil maybe a dozen times before and knew Neil didn't drink, but he put a shot halfway between himself and Neil in case Neil was feeling celebratory. Neil left it where it was and watched them drink. Roland had a second round ready to go by the time Andrew caught up with them. Andrew slid neatly into the narrow gap between Kevin and Neil.

"Welcome back to the land of the free," Roland said. "I'd say 'and the sober', but I know it won't last long. Cheers."

They downed their shots with ease. Roland started setting up their usual tray. He was half-done before a table finally opened up. Neil stayed behind with Andrew while the others went to claim it. Andrew drank Neil's shot when he saw it sitting there. Roland paused between drinks to refill it. This time he slid it a little closer to Neil.

"Let loose a bit. It's a special occasion," Roland said.

"It's the end of seven weeks' hard work," Neil said.

Andrew didn't waste his breath arguing. He drank Neil's second shot and Roland didn't try to pour Neil a third. When Roland was done mixing drinks, Neil cleared a path for Andrew to carry the tray. The others tore in, but Andrew went through his portion of the drinks slower than Neil had ever seen him. Neil assumed his tolerance was in the gutter after two months dry. He'd told Neil last year he always knew what his limits were. It made Neil wonder if Aaron and Nicky had ever seen Andrew drunk. Somehow he doubted it.

They knocked back cracker dust as a group, and Aaron and Nicky vanished. Kevin kept making inroads into the drinks. Andrew watched the crowd and sipped his drink at a snail's pace. Neil didn't know what to say to either of them, so he made himself busy. He traded the remaining full glasses on the tray for the empty ones littering the table and headed to the bar. Roland took it from him as soon as he was able. Neil folded his arms on the bar counter and watched Roland mix the next batch.

"So Andrew finally gave in, huh?" Roland said. "That looks

[59]

pretty bad."

Neil almost reached for his face, but Roland was looking at his wrists. Neil's new shirt was long-sleeved, but it was made of a thin material meant to breathe easy in a packed club. The ends had slid up his forearms a bit when he folded his arms. He tugged the hems back down, knowing it was too late to hide the half-healed lacerations. As he did so he realized that rumble in Roland's words was all checked laughter.

Roland gave an apologetic grin when Neil frowned up at him. "I'd wondered if being clean would cure that hands-off rule of his. Makes sense it wouldn't, now that we know about..." Roland shook his head and visibly forced his anger back. "I don't know whether to say 'thanks' for easing my curiosity or 'sorry' that sobriety has obviously exacerbated the problem. Just so you know, they make padded cuffs. You should look into them."

"The problem," Neil echoed, lost. "What hands-off rule?"

Roland looked startled, then confused. "You don't know? But then..."

"I got these in a fight," Neil said. "Why would Andrew do this to me?"

"Uh, you don't know," Roland said again, not a question anymore but a backpedal out of the conversation. "You know what, let's just forget I said anything. No, really," he said when Neil opened his mouth to argue. "Hey, here. Your drinks are done. I've gotta check on the rest of my customers."

He vanished before Neil could get more than a "What" out. Neil stared after him, but there were no answers here. He took the tray with unsteady hands and brought it back to the table. He wanted to send Kevin away, but Andrew would never let him get far without a guard. Luckily Kevin couldn't speak a word of German. Neil sat sideways in his chair, facing Andrew, and said,

"Why does Roland think you're tying me down?"

Andrew hesitated with his glass halfway to his mouth. He glanced down at Neil's hands where they were clenched on the edge of the seat between his knees. Neil didn't look to see if the

[60]

angry lines were showing again. He couldn't take his eyes off Andrew's face. At length Andrew put his full shot back on the tray. He didn't let go of it completely but tapped his fingers on the rim in an uneven beat. It seemed an eternity before he finally dragged his stare up from Neil's hands to his face.

"Presumably he thinks you're as bad at following directions as he is," Andrew said. "Roland knows I don't like being touched."

"That doesn't answer my question."

"It is the answer," Andrew said. "Rephrase the question if you don't like it."

"I want to play another round," Neil said. "What's outside Coach's pay grade?"

Andrew shifted in his seat to face Neil and propped his elbow on the back of his chair. He cradled his face in his hand and considered Neil. He didn't look at all bothered by the sudden interrogation but that calm did nothing to ease the gnawing in Neil's stomach.

"When Coach signed us, he promised to stay out of our personal problems. He said the board paid him to be our coach, nothing more and nothing less."

That answer wasn't much better. Neil wasn't sure he should keep pushing, but if he didn't get the truth now he knew he never would. "I didn't think I was a personal problem. You hate me, remember?"

"Every inch of you," Andrew said. "That doesn't mean I wouldn't blow you."

The world tilted a little bit sideways. Neil dug his shoes harder into the floor so he wouldn't fall over. "You like me."

"I hate you," Andrew corrected him, but Neil barely heard him.

For a dizzying moment, he understood. He remembered Andrew's hand over his mouth in Exites as he backed out of their conversation. He thought of Andrew yielding to his prodding and holding him up when Neil needed him most.

[61]

Andrew had called him interesting and dangerous and had given him keys to his house and car. He'd trusted Neil with Kevin because Kevin was important to both of them and he knew Neil wouldn't let him down.

Neil tried to piece it all together, but the more he pushed, the faster it fell apart. It didn't make sense. He didn't know what he was supposed to think. It could be a lie, but Neil knew it wasn't. Andrew was a lot of unpleasant things, but a pathological liar wasn't one of them. Honesty suited Andrew because he was an instigator at heart and his opinions were often unpopular.

It took Neil three tries to find his voice. "You never said anything."

"Why should I have?" Andrew lifted one shoulder in a shrug. "Nothing will come of it."

"Nothing," Neil echoed.

"I am self-destructive, not stupid," Andrew said. "I know better."

There was nothing Neil could say except, "Okay," but it didn't sound okay and he didn't feel okay. What was Neil supposed to do with a truth like this? He was going to be dead in four months, five if he was lucky. He wasn't supposed to be this for anyone, Andrew least of all. Andrew said all year long—had said it to Neil's face just this week—that he didn't want anything. Neil shouldn't be the exception to that rule.

Andrew downed his shot and dropped the glass carelessly back on the tray. He pried his cigarette pack out of his back pocket on his way to his feet and flicked it open to check the contents.

Neil should let him leave unchallenged, but he said, "It's your turn."

Andrew shook a stick into his hand and propped it between his lips. The pack was safely tucked away again before he looked at Neil. "I do not have to take it now."

Neil stared after him long after he'd disappeared into the crowd. He didn't realize Kevin was saying his name until Kevin finally pushed his shoulder to get his attention. Neil jumped like he'd been shot and jerked his attention to Kevin. Whatever Kevin saw on Neil's face, it was enough to kill his curiosity. Kevin slowly closed his mouth, withdrew his hand, and went back to drinking.

It was an hour before Andrew made it back to them. He didn't say another word to them that night and Neil was happy to give him his space. Aaron and Nicky eventually returned, drunk and exhausted, and they left together. The cousins' house wasn't far, but there weren't enough beds for all five of them. Kevin took the couch, so Neil curled up in a chair with a spare blanket.

It was hours before he could stop thinking long enough to sleep.

CHAPTER FOUR

On Monday Kevin started up night practices again, but he refused to take Neil along. On Tuesday afternoon Abby reluctantly gave Neil her blessing to return to the court, so long as he didn't get too rough in the scrimmages. Neil barely stuck around long enough to hear the okay before going for his gear. The Foxes were already on the court, since Abby had shown up almost two hours late to practice, but Dan called a halt to drills as soon as Neil thumped on the door. She and Matt greeted Neil's arrival on court with triumphant whoops. Nicky clacked sticks with him on his way to Kevin's side.

"If you can't play, don't," Kevin said.

"I know," Neil said. "If anything pulls I'll step off the court."

Kevin gave him a suspicious look but didn't argue.

It did hurt, almost immediately, but it was almost a relief to work out his sore muscles. Neil kept an easy pace because Abby and Wymack were watching him from the sidelines. When he had to finally stop and stretch he feared they'd pull him. They didn't, so he went back to the game with a vengeance. Afterward Wymack sat them all down in the locker room to go over the day's high and low points.

When he was done he looked at Neil and said, "Well?"

"I'm fine," Neil said. He leaned a little away from Kevin's death glare and said, "If I wasn't sore right now, I'd be worried, but it's not enough to be a problem. I can pass off the wall if overhand shots start pulling too hard on my stitches."

"Was that really so difficult to say the first time around?" Dan asked wryly.

"I did say it the first time around," Neil said. "I'm fine."

[64]

"The word you're looking for is 'hopeless' or 'obsessed'," Nicky said, grinning.

"All right," Wymack said. "Neil, you're at the gym tomorrow. Go easy for a few days, would you? Adapt the circuit as needed and let me know what doesn't work. Injure yourself here, not there." Wymack had to notice the dirty look Abby shot him, but he didn't acknowledge it. "That's it for today, then. Pack up and move out."

They washed up and headed back to the dorm. Dan came with Matt and Neil to their room. Neil took it as a hint to make himself scarce, but Dan beckoned to him when he turned to leave again. When she knew he understood she sat on the couch and hugged her knee to her chest.

"So it's back to life as usual," Dan said. "Us and them, I mean. It was fun last month, wasn't it? I liked our team dinners and nights out."

"Feels like we're right back where we started in August," Matt agreed.

"If we knew what Andrew had against us, we could try to fight it," Dan said. She drummed an agitated rhythm on her knee for a minute, then looked at Neil. "How'd you get him to stop tripping us up at practice the other day?"

Neil whittled it down the barest, easiest truth. "I asked."

"You asked," Matt said. It almost sounded like an accusation. "You said that about Halloween and Nicky's parents. Seriously, Neil. How do you keep talking him into doing things he obviously doesn't want to do? Is it bribery or blackmail?"

Dan flicked Matt an indecipherable look and said, "No pressure, Neil. No bullshit. Andrew's sober now and I know that's a game-changer. But can you bring them back to us?"

"I don't know," Neil admitted. "I can try. But," he continued, with a glance between them, "someone needs to work on Aaron. Nicky wants to be your friend and Kevin knows the team is stronger as a whole, but Aaron's almost as dead-set against us as Andrew is. That doesn't make sense, because siding

[65]

with Andrew means hiding Katelyn. If Aaron's willing to do that without a fight, this isn't just Andrew's decision. It goes back to the two of them."

Dan looked thoughtful. "Katelyn has to know something. No self-respecting girl would put up with this unless there was a really good reason. If she won't talk, you think you can wrestle something out of Aaron, Matt? You said he's been better since Christmas, right?"

"It's worth a shot," Matt said. "Coach give you our tutor schedule yet?"

"It's somewhere on my desk," Dan said. "As soon as I unearth it I'll text his hours to you."

"All right. I'll see if I can't hunt him down there."

"Let me try Katelyn first," Dan said. She shifted to pull her phone out of her pocket and tapped a quick message out. "I don't want Aaron telling her we're getting nosy." Matt nodded, but Dan was watching her phone like she could will a response from it. It didn't take long before it jingled. Dan went back and forth with Katelyn a couple times, then got to her feet. "All right. I'm going out for a bit. Might be a while, so eat without me. Wish me luck?"

"Luck," Neil said as Matt kissed her goodbye.

Neil and Matt ended up eating dinner with Renee and Allison in the girls' room. Allison's choice of movie was instantly vetoed, so Allison threw democracy out the window and put it in anyway. It was probably the worst thing Neil had ever watched, but at least it helped kill time. He was spared the last fifteen minutes of melodrama and limp acting because Kevin was ready to head to the court. They met Andrew at the car.

Andrew sprawled on the couch in the lounge while Kevin went ahead to change out. Neil hesitated, changed his mind and started after Kevin, and changed his mind again. He stood behind the couch, folding his arms across the back of it, and peered down at Andrew. Andrew had one arm folded under his

[66]

head and the other draped over his eyes to block the light.

"One of these days you might as well practice with us," Neil said. He wasn't surprised when Andrew didn't answer, but he refused to give up that easily. "Why'd you even start playing if you weren't willing to practice?"

"It was a bigger cage than the alternative."

That was one of the things reporters had liked harping about most when Kevin became a permanent fixture at Andrew's side: Kevin was raised at Evermore, surrounded by the best and practically born with a racquet in his hand, whereas Andrew learned Exy while he was locked up in juvie. Neil had a page-long article about it in his notebook. It was crassly titled "The Prince and the Pauper", and its focus was on how doomed their friendship was. The writer thought their attitudes toward Exy too incompatible and their backgrounds too different for them to stay together long.

Neil assumed Officer Higgins was the reason Andrew landed in one of the best juvenile facilities in California. It focused on rehabilitation through discipline and empowerment, which meant all of the inmates learned team sports. There wasn't enough room for a full-sized court, but an officer confirmed in an interview they had a half-court on the facility grounds. The best and best-behaved of the would-be Exy athletes went on occasional field trips to the community center and competed with neighborhood teams.

Neil didn't blame Andrew for thinking the court was a better place to be than a cell, but he doubted Exy was the only sport the facility offered. Andrew chose Exy for a reason. Neil would assume the aggressive nature of the game appealed to him, but Andrew was a goalkeeper. He got very few opportunities to indulge in mindless violence. He said as much to Andrew and got a faint shrug in response.

"The warden assigned it to me," Andrew said. "I couldn't play otherwise."

"They thought you'd hurt someone if you were loose on the

[67]

court?" Neil asked. Andrew didn't answer; Neil took his silence as confirmation. He tried imagining Andrew in any other position but couldn't see it. "I think it's better this way, with you as the last line of defense. You let us run ourselves into the ground and clean up behind us. You play the game like you play life. That's why you're so good at it."

Neil looked up when a door opened down the hall. Kevin came in search of him, already changed into his gear and looking annoyed by the delay. He stopped short when he realized they were talking. Kevin hadn't asked Neil yet what happened on Friday. Neil didn't know if he'd asked Andrew but he doubted Andrew would explain. According to Renee only she and Neil knew Andrew was gay. Neil had no idea how Wymack picked up on it.

"I'm coming," Neil said, but he didn't straighten.

Kevin held up a finger in a one-minute warning and left. Neil listened for the back door to close before looking at Andrew again.

"I'm not a striker by choice, either," he said. "I was a backliner in little leagues. Riko remembers because I scrimmaged with him and Kevin. He made me play defense with his Ravens over Christmas."

That finally got Andrew to lower his arm. "Little leagues, he says. I distinctly remember you telling people you learned to play in Millport."

"Partial truth," Neil said. "I knew how to play Exy. I just didn't know how to play offense. I didn't want to be a striker, but Coach Hernandez didn't have any room on his defense line. It was striker or nothing, and I wanted to play too badly to walk away. Now I can't imagine playing anything else."

Andrew said nothing for a while, then, "You're more a raccoon than a fox."

Neil stared. "What?"

"A raccoon," Andrew said, and mimed holding a ball in front of his face. "Exy is the shiny object of your sad little world.

[68]

You know you're being hunted and you know the hounds are closing in, but you won't let go to save yourself. You once told me you don't understand why a person would actively try to die, but here you are. I guess that was another lie."

"I'm not trying to die," Neil said. "This is how I stay alive. When I'm playing, I feel like I have control over something. I feel like I have the power to change things. I feel more real out there than I do anywhere else. The court doesn't care what my name is or where I'm from or where I'll be tomorrow. It lets me exist as I am."

"It is a court," Andrew said. "It does not 'let' you do anything."

"You know what I mean."

"I don't."

"Because you don't have anything, do you?" Neil said in quiet challenge. "Nothing gets to you like that. Nothing gets under your skin."

"He catches on at last," Andrew mused. "It only took him a year."

"What are you afraid of?"

"Heights."

"Andrew."

"If you make Kevin come looking for you, you will regret it."

Neil pushed away from the couch without another word and went to get changed. He tugged on his gear with more force than was strictly necessary, but he was still humming with annoyance when he stepped onto the court. Getting scolded for tardiness didn't help his mood any. Neil almost reminded Kevin that they didn't have a mandatory schedule for their extra sessions, but there was no point. They were here because they had work to do.

He went through the drills as hard and fast as he could, knowing he'd regret it in the morning. He didn't care. It was harder to think when everything hurt. Exhaustion finally killed the last of his annoyance and he wasn't feeling much of anything

[69]

by the time they left the court.

That lethargic peace lasted up until Neil left the shower and found Kevin sitting on a bench in the changing room. The stern look on his face said he wasn't waiting out of courtesy.

"Did you fix it?" Kevin asked.

"Fix what?" Neil asked.

"Don't act like an imbecile. If you are here, I expect you to be here," he said, emphasis on the last word. "The second your problems with Andrew interfere with our game they become our problems. Do you want us to win or don't you?"

"Don't lecture me like I don't know what's at stake."

"You told me to focus on the team," Kevin said. "That's what I am doing: ensuring you don't jeopardize its success."

"I wasn't jeopardizing anything. I was two minutes late because I asked Andrew to come practice with us."

"You were five, and don't ask him again. We do not need him there as a favor to us. He has to come of his own free will or it doesn't mean anything." Kevin got up and motioned sharply for Neil to follow. "We're leaving."

They collected Andrew from the lounge on their way out and split up in the hallway. Matt was already asleep, but he'd left his desk lamp on so Neil could find his way around. Neil changed out in its dim light. When he went to turn the lamp off on his way to bed, he found a scribbled note taped to the light switch.

"You were right," it said.

Neil put the note in his desk drawer and went to bed. There was no point wondering about it when they'd be awake in five hours, so he pushed his thoughts aside and willed himself to sleep. It seemed like he'd just closed his eyes when his alarm went off. Neil rolled over to turn it off and almost groaned at how sore he was. He'd have to scale it back at practice today or Wymack would ream him out.

Matt had his shoes on before he was awake enough to talk. He went still with the knots half-done and looked at Neil. "You were right. They made a promise. Aaron and Andrew, I mean. That's what Aaron told Katelyn, anyway. Aaron cut a deal with Andrew at juvie: if Andrew stuck with him until graduation, Aaron would stick with Andrew. No friends, no girlfriends, nothing. Aaron couldn't even socialize with his teammates."

Neil combed his fingers through his hair and tested the bandage on his cheek. "Aaron would have meant high school graduation. They renewed it when they signed a contract to play here."

"Now Katelyn's in the picture, but Aaron won't fight for her." Matt shook his head and finished tying his shoes. "Katelyn told Dan what Andrew did to Aaron's high school exes. If Katelyn's not afraid of Andrew, she's not safe from him. Is Andrew really that crazy that he'd lash out against someone so important to Aaron?"

"Aaron made a promise," Neil said, choosing his words carefully. "Andrew will make him keep it. It's not as crazy as it sounds."

Neil had almost forgotten how blind the upperclassmen were to the twins' issues. He hadn't figured it out until his second trip to Eden's Twilight, but now the cold war between them was achingly obvious. Katelyn's importance to Aaron was what put her in danger. If Aaron wouldn't fight for her, was it because he was too afraid to stand up to his brother or did he really think he had more to gain by playing along?

More importantly, why did Andrew agree to extend the deal? Was he still punishing Aaron for siding with their mother, or did he think enough time would make a difference? The latter seemed far-fetched, but Neil was inclined to believe it. When Drake left Andrew a concussed and bloody wreck in Columbia, the only thing that mattered to Andrew, the only person he needed to see, was Aaron. His own trauma was inconsequential; he'd cared about the blood splattered across Aaron's skin.

Andrew and Aaron had done this to each other, and they were locked in stalemate. They were unwilling to reach out and

[71]

unable to let go. November should have been the catalyst, but Aaron's arrest and Andrew's exile to Easthaven meant they'd recovered from that nightmare away from each other. Andrew had been back a week now, and Neil was positive the two hadn't talked about that night yet, same as they'd never talked through the reasons behind Tilda Minyard's death.

Aaron would ignore Neil if he brought it up and Neil didn't have a big enough secret to talk Andrew into reaching out to Aaron. Kevin wouldn't get involved and Andrew would just brush Nicky off if he tried. Wymack had promised to stay out of their personal problems, though he'd toed that line the other day for the sake of his team's safety. Renee might hold Andrew's attention long enough to plant a thought toward reconciliation, but Aaron had absolutely no interest in anything Renee had to say.

That left few options, and Neil had deleted Betsy Dobson's number out of his phone the same day Andrew programmed her in as an emergency contact. Aaron said he didn't talk to Betsy, but he had to have picked up on Andrew's attachment to her. Maybe he would let her mediate in a confidential setting. If he refused, Katelyn could give him the final push he needed. Getting Andrew to agree to it would be the real trick. Even if sobriety hadn't dimmed his opinion of Betsy, convincing him to open up to Aaron about all of this would be borderline impossible.

Idly he wondered if Betsy even knew the brothers had issues.

"Neil?"

Neil glanced up to see Matt hovering in the bedroom doorway. He hadn't even noticed Matt leave the room, too caught up in his thoughts. Matt looked a bit perplexed to find Neil right where he'd left him.

"You good? We gotta go."

If Neil was late to practice twice in a row Kevin would probably bench him out of spite. Neil scooped his keys off his dresser. "I'm good. Did Dan give you Aaron's new tutor schedule?" When Matt nodded, Neil said, "I changed my mind. I'll deal with him. I've got an idea."

Matt forwarded the text to Neil while Neil locked the suite door behind them. Neil felt his phone buzz in his pocket but let it sit unread on the way to the stadium. His screen was too small for anyone to read the message over his shoulder, but Nicky would want to know who was texting Neil this early in the day. Neil would have to get Betsy's and Katelyn's numbers later. If he was lucky Dan had both of them in her phone.

They spent morning practice doing strength circuits at the gym. Neil rode back with Andrew's lot but stopped by the girls' room to get his bruises touched up. He was looking better a week out of Riko's reach but he'd need to cover up for a couple more days. Long after everything healed Neil would have a bandage on his face, though, and he still hadn't told the upperclassmen what he was hiding from them. Neil thought about it as Allison worked on him. Andrew's lot and the staff knew, which meant there was no point in hiding it anymore.

"Allison," he said, a warning that he was about to move.

She drew her hand back a bit, and Neil reached up to the tape on his face. He didn't know where it was safe to touch, since his cheek felt cold all over from her concealer. Allison understood what he was trying to do, though, and swatted his hand out of the way. She snagged the edge of the tape with her long fingernails and pried the bandage off in one smooth move.

It took her a half-second to realize what she was looking at, and she was on her feet with a shrill, "Are you kidding me?"

Dan was in the kitchen scarfing down breakfast and Renee was in their bedroom, but Allison's outburst brought them running. Dan was on Neil's left, so she saw it first. She ground to a halt, but only for a second. A heartbeat later she was across the room and on the couch where Allison had just been sitting. Neil didn't know she could move so fast.

"This is a joke," Dan said, grabbing Neil's chin. "Neil?"

[73]

"He told me to transfer to the Ravens," Neil said. "He said I could finish this year with the Foxes but that I'd move to Edgar Allan this fall. They inked me in preparation and I couldn't stop them. I wanted you to know in case Riko says something about it. I'm still a Fox no matter what he says. I wouldn't sign his papers."

"Take it off," Dan said.

"It's permanent," Neil said.

"Nothing's permanent. Take it off. Matt will spot you the money."

"He will or I will," Allison said. "I don't want to see that on my court. Kevin's tramp stamp fouls the atmosphere enough."

"Kevin knew about this, didn't he?" Dan said, incensed. "He knew what Riko was going to do to you and he let you go anyway. The next time I see him—"

"You'll do nothing," Neil interrupted her. "Kevin didn't have the right to stop me."

"He let you go to Riko in his stead."

"No," Neil said. "Kevin didn't factor into any of that. He knew it wasn't about him."

Dan wasn't expecting that. Confusion took the edge off her anger. "You said Riko was trying to get to Kevin."

"I said Riko focused on me because of my relation to Kevin," Neil said. "I didn't say that's why I went. I just thought you should know about this before the season kicks off."

Dan let him get to his feet but seized his elbow before he could get far. Neil looked down at her, but she was staring across the room at nothing. It was a minute before she spoke.

"You never had any plans to go home for Christmas, did you? That whole mess about your uncle flying to Arizona—you made that up so we wouldn't ask too many questions or wonder why you weren't going to New York with Kevin."

There was no point denying it. "I did."

"I get that you don't trust us completely," Dan said. "I don't like it, but I think we've been pretty good at working around that all year. We haven't pushed you to give us more than you're comfortable with and we haven't asked why you're like this. So don't do this to us. Don't sit here and lie to our faces." She finally looked up at him, frustration pulling hard at the corner of her mouth. "We're your friends. We deserve better than that."

"If you always got what you deserved, you wouldn't be a Fox." Neil tugged out of her grip. She let him go without a fight, looking a little startled by that blunt rejoinder. Neil tried to stamp out the trickle of guilt but couldn't quite manage it. "I've never had friends before. I don't know how this works. I'm trying, but it's going to take time."

Time was something he didn't have, but that wasn't worth mentioning. Dan accepted his apology and promise with a weary nod, and they let him leave in peace. Neil stopped by his bathroom to put a new bandage over his tattoo. He still had time to kill before class, so he sat at his desk with his textbooks. He meant to review his notes from his previous lessons. Instead he drew fox paws across the pages until it was time to go.

Neil didn't text Dan until lunchtime, wanting to give her a couple hours to cool down. Either she'd forgiven him or she'd forgotten the morning's fiasco, because she responded almost immediately with the numbers he needed. Neil ended up programming both into his phone. Nicky had a habit of filling up Neil's inbox, and Neil couldn't afford to lose track of these ladies.

He reached out to Katelyn first. He must have caught her while she was in class, because it was almost an hour before she got back to him. It only took a couple messages to realize there was no good time in their schedules to get together today. She promised to make time tomorrow to hear him out, though, and that was good enough.

That afternoon Neil finally got the confirmation he was looking for: even though Andrew was off his drugs, he still had weekly sessions with Betsy. Neil knew what time Andrew's sessions started and assumed Betsy would have a small window without patients before Andrew showed up at her door. As soon as Neil knew Andrew was on his way to Reddin, he steeled his nerves and dialed Betsy's desk.

She answered on the second ring with a pleasant, "Dr. Dobson."

"It's Neil," Neil said, and continued before she could act surprised and pleased to hear from him. "I need a yes or no. If we can talk Aaron and Andrew into doing joint sessions with you, can you fix them?"

There was only a brief pause before Betsy said, "I will certainly try."

"Don't try," Neil said. "Don't guess. This is too important. Can you or can't you?"

"Yes." He could hear the smile in her voice: not amusement, but approval. "If you can get them here, I will take care of it. Neil?" she said as he was starting to move the phone from his ear. "I like the honest side of you."

Neil hung up on her.

-

It was too early in the year for the library to be crowded, so Neil had no trouble finding Katelyn. An oversized cup of coffee sat at her elbow and Neil was tempted to detour past the cafe for his own drink. He didn't want to look like he was staying, though, so he headed down the aisle to her table without stopping. A biochem textbook was pushed off to one side as she highlighted relevant portions of her notes. Aaron had the same book in his room, as he was studying biological sciences. Neil guessed their similar majors and overlapping classes was how they'd met outside of games.

Katelyn looked up at his approach and flipped her notebook closed. "Neil, hello! I know it's only been a few weeks but it feels like forever. How was Christmas?"

"It was fine," Neil said. "How was yours?"

"Oh my gosh, amazing." Katelyn clasped her hands in glee. "My sister finally found out she's having a boy, so I spent most

[76]

of my break buying things for him. Mom told me I'm going overboard but I know she's just as excited."

She'd told them last month that her sister was pregnant, but Neil hadn't held onto the details. He tuned her excited rambling out now, listening only for the key words that meant she was done detailing all her great finds and winter sales. It didn't take her long to remember they weren't here to catch-up, and she pulled herself together with a smile that was as sheepish as it was happy.

"So what's this about?" Katelyn asked. "You said you wanted to talk about Aaron?"

"Aaron needs help," Neil said. "I'm trying to get him some."

Katelyn sobered up in a heartbeat. "He's having nightmares again, isn't he? He said he was doing better. He promised that—" Katelyn gestured, frustration or helplessness, and pressed her fingers to her trembling lower lip.

"Nightmares," Neil echoed. It wasn't the turn he'd thought this conversation would take but he could guess what was tearing Aaron apart. "About November, you mean."

"He doesn't want it to bother him," Katelyn said. "He says Drake deserved worse than what he got. He says he's glad he did it. But wanting someone dead and actually being the one to kill them are two very different things. I'm willing to listen to him, and I want to do everything I can to help, but he doesn't hear me when I tell him it's okay."

"He needs to talk to Andrew," Neil said.

Katelyn gave a choked laugh. "He won't."

Katelyn knew what the upperclassmen didn't: that Aaron and Andrew could barely stand the sight of each other on a good day. Maybe she needed to know, since their fight was what was keeping her and Aaron apart. Neil favorably recalculated her odds of actually making it with Aaron in the long run.

"He has to," Neil said again. "They need each other. They just don't know how to take that first step. That's where you come in."

[77]

Katelyn searched his face for a minute, then said, "Why?"

"Why you?" Neil asked.

"Why you," she corrected him. "Aaron isn't..."

She was too nice to say it, but Neil had no problems filling in the blanks. "Aaron and I get along when we have to and avoid each other when we can. I'm not going to lie and say I'm doing this for his sake. I don't care whether he's okay in the long run. I care only about the team. We can't win without them. Does it really matter why I'm doing it so long as everyone walks away happy in the end?"

"It matters to me," Katelyn said. "I love him."

"So help me help him," Neil said.

Katelyn pressed her lips to a thin line as she debated. "I'm listening."

"Has Aaron ever told you about Dr. Dobson?" Neil asked. "She works at Reddin and she's the go-to shrink for our team. She's willing to run group sessions with Andrew and Aaron."

"Aaron's mentioned her before. He said she's a waste of time."

"Because he doesn't use her like he's supposed to," Neil said, neatly ignoring the hypocrisy in his accusation. "Luckily it doesn't matter what Aaron thinks. Dobson's seen both of them. She's treated Andrew for a year and a half now. If she honestly thought she couldn't reconcile them she would have said so. If we can get them both in her office at the same time, she can make them talk to each other."

"You want me to talk him into it," Katelyn concluded.

"You convince Aaron. I'll convince Andrew."

"Do you really think you can?"

"I have to," Neil said.

"But how?" Katelyn pressed. "I'm asking honestly, because I don't know how to talk Aaron into it. He wouldn't listen to me the last time I told him to get help."

"Then don't make this about him," Neil said. "Make this about you. You can fix this right here, right now. Stop being

[78]

collateral damage and make him fight for you."

"I don't think I can use 'us' against him. It isn't fair."

"But this is?" Neil gestured at her. "Look, there's no way I can convince Andrew overnight, so you've got some time to think about it. But when Andrew is ready, you have to pick your side. Try to pick the right one."

He got up and left, and she didn't call after him.

CHAPTER FIVE

Classes on January 12th were a complete waste of the Foxes' time. Neil's lessons were early enough in the day that he made it to both of them, but he didn't learn a single thing. His teachers' voices were white noise; the words they wrote on the board morphed to diagrams of plays. Neil held his pen at the ready but didn't write a single letter in his notebook. He'd have to borrow notes from a classmate later, but today none of that mattered. All that mattered was that they had a one-twenty flight out of Upstate Regional.

First serve was scheduled for seven-thirty, but Wymack wanted them on the ground in Austin two hours early. He didn't trust winter weather, he'd said. Neil was sure he'd jinxed them with that paranoia. It was pouring outside, cold and hard enough to feel like ice, and Neil worried their flight would be delayed. They had a small cushion, thanks to a ninety-minute layover in Atlanta, but Neil was still afraid. If they missed their first game of championships over something so stupid as the weather he would never get over it.

It was raining too hard for an umbrella to do any good, so Neil pulled his hood up and jogged back to Fox Tower. He slanted a look at the sky, hoping to see an end to the charcoal clouds, and was rewarded with rain in his eyes. Neil scrubbed a hand across his face and darted through a gap in traffic on Perimeter Road. An athlete on his way down the hill to class slipped and fell with a startled curse. He was back on his feet before Neil caught up with him, but Neil learned his lesson and slowed down. He hadn't survived Riko's cruelty to be handicapped by impatience.

The four CAUTION signs set up in the lobby were overkill,

[80]

but Neil still skidded a little on the wet floor. He caught the wall for balance and waved his wallet over the sensor near the elevator. His student ID was strong enough to trigger the lock through the leather. When the buttons lit up Neil pressed the Up arrow and got on the first car that arrived. There was standing water on the elevator floor, so he held tight to the rail until he reached the third floor. The carpeted hallway was stained from wet footprints. Neil added to the mess as he slogged for his room.

Dry clothes did nothing to make him feel warmer, so Neil sprawled on the couch with a blanket. He didn't remember falling asleep, but the sound of the door jarred him awake. Matt looked half a foot shorter than usual with his hair plastered to his skull. Despite his wretched state, he was grinning on his way in. He motioned at Neil to get his attention but didn't speak until the door was closed behind him.

"Just passed Allison," Matt said.

"Soaked?" Neil guessed.

"Understatement of the year," Matt said. "I think her umbrella broke. She's a hot mess. Told her I was going to take a picture of her for the yearbook and she threatened to cut my balls off with her fingernails. Five bucks says Dan'll have to push her out the door when it's time to leave again."

"She knows we need her."

"That mean you're in?"

"I don't bet," Neil said.

"Still? On anything?" Matt crossed the room to drop his bag by his desk. "We've got, what, sixteen ongoing bets now, and you don't want in on any of them? Well, fourteen that you're qualified to bet on. Some of the pots are getting pretty big and you're probably in the best position to win on a couple of them."

"Why fourteen?" Neil asked. "What happened to the other two?"

"Can't bet on yourself," Matt said. "That's cheating."

Neil tilted his head back to look at Matt. "I didn't know you were betting on me."

"We bet on everyone at one point in time," Matt said. "Did you know most of the team bet against me and Dan? They didn't think I'd have the courage to ask her and they knew she'd never give me a chance. She was kind of a man-hater when I met her. I want to blame it on her time at the strip club but I think it's mostly due to the guys Coach gave her to work with her freshman year. Even Allison told me not to try."

"You tried anyway," Neil said.

"For a year," Matt said. "Made Renee a small fortune when Dan finally gave in. She's the only one who bet on us. She's always the most willing to bet on lost causes."

Andrew had called Neil a lost cause last year, one hand over Neil's mouth to keep him from arguing. Looking back on it now, with all the missing pieces of that argument in place, Neil knew it wasn't really him Andrew was trying to shut up. Neil found the self-censure fascinating in retrospect. Renee would have told Andrew before then that she'd confessed Andrew's sexuality to Neil, and Andrew hadn't hedged his way around the truth when Neil asked for it this last Friday. What did Andrew think he was going to say last November?

It didn't matter; it shouldn't matter. Andrew didn't want anything to come of his attraction, and anyway, Neil wasn't allowed to let people that close. It was how he was raised. It was how he survived. He was lucky to be so detached now that the end was right around the corner. He'd broken every other rule his mother left him with. The least he could do was uphold one.

"That's why you bet on Andrew and Renee," Neil said, because he couldn't, wouldn't, think about this.

"Well, yeah," Matt said. "For a while there Renee was the only one outside of his little group Andrew would talk to. Renee said they had a lot in common and it was nothing serious, but then he let her drive his car. That's a GS, Neil. You don't loan that out to just anyone."

Neil waved a hand over his head to show the significance

[82]

passing him by. "I don't speak cars."

"I'm saying after he finished tricking it out, it cost almost six figures," Matt said.

Neil bolted upright and twisted around to stare at Matt. "Cost what?"

He knew Andrew blew most of Tilda's life insurance on it; Nicky once joked that Andrew picked whichever one would eat the inheritance up fastest. Neil hadn't asked how much money they made off her death but he'd known just by looking at the car it'd been a colossal waste of resources. Having a ballpark figure made Neil feel ill. His key ring suddenly weighed a ton and it was all he could do to not pull it out of his pocket.

"It's almost as expensive as Allison's Porsche," Matt said, "and he let Renee drive it just two months after meeting her. Do you blame me for putting money on them? Man, I was so sure that'd pan out."

The past tense was enough to distract Neil. "You changed your mind?"

"Sort of," Matt said. "But rules are rules. Once money's in the pot, you can't change which side you're betting on. You can bet against it in other pots, though, so I might make some of my money back. But hell, it's already after twelve. We gotta get moving. You want anything for the plane, I suggest you grab it now."

He was gone before Neil could ask what changed Matt's mind about Renee's chances. Neil let it go and grabbed his stack of notes on UT's line-up. Matt's grin was knowing, borderline pitying, when they met up to leave and he saw what Neil was holding. Neil pretended not to see and locked the suite door behind them. The girls waited for Matt to catch up with them, but Neil continued a few steps past them to Andrew's group.

Andrew's car looked like an entirely new monster as Neil approached it. He was feeling well enough to sit in back with Nicky and Aaron, but Kevin followed them in before Neil could suggest it.

[83]

In the time it took them to get from the dorm to the car and the car to the stadium, the Foxes were soaked. Allison hadn't bothered with an umbrella this time but had a second raincoat over her head to protect her newly-redone hair and makeup. She was dryer than any of them but she was still swearing at the weather as she stalked into the lounge. Wymack tolerated their rowdy arrival with his usual lack of patience and herded them down the hall to pack their gear.

They took the team bus to the airport because it was cheaper to leave one car in the garage than three. Being back at Upstate Regional made Neil think about his trip to West Virginia, so he focused on his teammates to keep his thoughts from spiraling down dark circles. It was a near-miss, at least until Wymack sent a searching look his way. Neil glanced at Wymack and chose not to think about Riko. Instead he thought about his homecoming, of Wymack dropping everything to pick him up and Wymack holding him together when he almost broke. The tightness in Neil's chest eased a little and he nodded an okay to Wymack's silent question.

They made it through check-in and security in good time and set off down the terminal in search of their gate. They were almost at the end, past the restrooms and a dozen shops. A cafe was halfway down, and the smell of coffee and warm pastries was almost enough to distract them. Wymack kept them in line with rude language and half-hearted threats.

The Vixens had beaten them to the airport and were camped out at the gate. Neil looked past them to the electronic sign about the desk. It read "Atlanta – 1:20pm", so the airline wasn't expecting a delay despite the weather. Neil chose to believe it only because their plane was already waiting outside.

The Foxes scattered at Wymack's okay, half of them to look out the window and the rest to dump their carry-ons on whatever empty chairs they could find. It took Neil only a moment to realize Andrew hadn't budged. Neil looked back at him, but Andrew was staring out the far window. Neil followed his gaze

[84]

and watched a plane rocket down the runway.

The others weren't close enough anymore to overhear, so Neil said, "When you said you were afraid of heights, you were joking, right?" He gave Andrew a moment to answer, then tried again. "Andrew, you can't be. What were you doing on the roof?"

Andrew didn't answer immediately, but the tilt of his head to one side said he was thinking about it. Neil didn't know if he was searching for words or just figuring out which ones he wanted to give Neil in explanation. Finally Andrew lifted a hand to his own throat and felt for his pulse. He tapped his finger along when he found it. It was going faster than it should. Neil blamed it on Andrew's surroundings.

"Feeling," Andrew said at last.

"Trying to remember fear, or trying to remember how to feel anything at all?" Neil asked, but Andrew didn't answer. Neil tried a different tactic. "If it makes you feel better, fewer than twenty planes crash every year and it's not always due to the weather. Sometimes pilots are just unreliable. I'm sure it's a quick death either way."

Andrew's hand went still. "What was his name?" He looked to Neil, who frowned confusion at him, and said, "Your father. What was his name?"

It almost knocked the breath out of him. Neil didn't want to answer, didn't want that name out in the air between them, but it was Andrew's turn in their game. He didn't have the right to refuse. He tried to take a little comfort in it, because Andrew wouldn't hit this low unless Neil's taunt had gotten to him, but Neil couldn't quite manage. He looked to the Foxes, made sure they were still out of earshot, and stepped closer to Andrew anyway.

"Nathan," he said at last. "His name was Nathan."

"You don't look like a Nathan."

"I'm not," Neil said through the stones in his throat. "I'm Nathaniel."

[85]

Andrew considered him a minute longer, then turned away without another word and went back to watching the runways. Neil retreated, needing breathing room to get that sick ache out of his veins. Nicky waved wildly to get his attention and motioned for Neil to join him. As soon as Neil was close enough Nicky slung a careful arm around his shoulders.

"Blatant favoritism," Nicky said. "You know he's said maybe ten words to me since we picked him up from Easthaven? I'd be jealous if I wasn't so against dying young. But anyway, we've got some time before takeoff. Want to come with us and grab some coffee?"

They ended up taking half the team and several of the Vixens with them to the cafe. Nicky said they were good on time, but none of them had counted on how slow the line would move. By the time they all made it back to their gate with their drinks, their flight was already boarding.

Neil kept a keen eye on Andrew as they joined the line, waiting for him to hesitate. Maybe Andrew noticed the attention, because he followed his teammates onto the plane with a bored look on his face. The act lasted up until they were all in their seats and the attendants were going through the safety features on the plane. The only thing Andrew had brought onto the plane with him was a pen. He turned it over and over in his hands while the attendants demonstrated how to use the on-board oxygen masks. Kevin, sitting between Neil and Andrew, didn't even bat an eye. Neil guessed he was used to Andrew being restless. Neil only knew what that fidgeting meant because Andrew had told him the truth when Neil asked what he was afraid of.

Neil glanced out the window, but the rain was so thick on the glass he could barely make out the wing of the plane. The lights were a blurry mess. Neil closed the shade as the attendants did a final walk-through of the cabin. Takeoff had never seemed a complicated process before, but Neil imagined how drawn-out it would feel to someone who didn't want to be airborne. Finally they were rolling down the runway, and Neil risked another look at Andrew.

Andrew's expression didn't change when the tires left the ground, but Andrew's pen went still for the entire ascent and he went tense. He was back at it as soon as they reached cruising altitude. He had to notice the looks Neil sent him, but he kept his heavy-lidded stare on the seat back in front of him.

They had time to kill in Atlanta, so as soon as Wymack confirmed their gate hadn't changed he let them wander the airport for an hour. Andrew's lot spent most of that time wandering from one store to another. Aaron picked up a book while Nicky loaded up on junk food. Andrew disappeared, but Neil finally spotted him near a glass case of figurines. It was an odd thing for Andrew to be distracted by, but Neil didn't have long to think about it. Kevin and Nicky were two seconds away from getting into it because Kevin was trying to put Nicky's snacks back on the shelf.

"It's not all for me," Nicky insisted, trying to wrestle out of Kevin's grip without dropping anything. "There's enough to go around."

"No one needs to eat this before a game," Kevin said. "Eat some granola or protein if you're that hungry."

"Hello, there's protein in the peanut butter," Nicky said. "Let go of me before I tell Andrew you're outlawing chocolate. I said let go. You're not the boss of me. Ouch! Did you seriously just hit me?"

"I'm walking away and pretending I don't know you," Aaron said.

"Traitor," Nicky called after him.

"Kevin, just let him go," Neil said. "It's not worth fighting over."

"When our defense is sluggish we all suffer," Kevin said.

"You aren't serious," Nicky said. "We've got how many hours until serve? This will all be out of my system by then. You can watch me take a shit if you don't believe me. I didn't think

[87]

you were into that kind of thing but—ha," he crowed when Kevin stomped off. He flashed Neil a triumphant grin, oblivious to the way the store clerks were staring at them. "I am a master at persuasion."

"Or self-delusion," Neil said.

Nicky's eyebrows shot up. "Oh my god, did you try to make a joke? Did it hurt a little? No, really," he said when Neil turned as if to leave him. "What put you in such a good mood?"

Turning put Andrew in Neil's line of sight again. Light flashed off the crystal figurine in Andrew's hand as he passed it to one of the cashiers. Neil was too far away to see what shape he'd settled on, but he didn't need to know. His thoughts were on a shelf of sparkling animals all set equidistant to each other. Surprise warred with relief and gave way to a hum of self-satisfaction. Neil didn't understand what Andrew saw in Betsy but he didn't care anymore. He was right to put his faith in her. She was going to patch the brothers up and the team would finally be whole. The Ravens wouldn't know what to make of them the next time they met on-court.

"Hey, Neil," Nicky said. "You ignoring me?"

"Just thinking about tonight," Neil lied. "I'll wait here while you check out."

Nicky shrugged and headed for the next open register. Andrew collected Kevin on his way back to Neil's side, and Aaron drifted back to them when Nicky called him. They headed back to the gate and settled down until boarding time. The skies over Atlanta were cloudy but dry. A quick board and all heads accounted for meant they got to leave a couple minutes early. Neil kept a discreet eye on Andrew until the plane leveled out, then turned his gaze out the window and thought of UT.

Neil had never dealt with baggage claim before, as he and his mother tossed out whatever wouldn't fit in a carry-on. It was an eye-opening and unpleasant experience. The same suitcases went around the conveyer belt so many times Neil started thinking the team's gear had been lost. The Foxes looked bored, not worried, so he kept that bit of panic to himself. He was rewarded a few minutes later when Allison's bag finally dropped down a chute and onto the belt. The rest of the bags weren't far behind hers.

"Load 'em up and line it up," Wymack said as he and Abby grabbed their own bags.

The Foxes trailed him to Ground Transportation, where Wymack had reserved a 12-seat passenger van. Their bags took up the entire trunk and then most of the foot room, but they managed to get the door closed and that was all that mattered. Wymack smoothed out a crumpled paper of handwritten directions, spared his notes the briefest of glances, and got them on their way. They stopped briefly at an Italian restaurant to wolf down chicken and pasta. Wymack grumbled about the bill, but his team knew better than to take him seriously.

The stadium was crawling with cops and fans when they arrived. Security guards helped Wymack find a place to park and the team was escorted to the locker room. They were early, so Wymack flicked on every TV he could find and went to check the crowd. The closest TV to Neil was playing highlights of last night's Class I games. Unsurprisingly, half of the moves worth rehashing were from the Ravens' fifteen-eight victory. Neil had watched their match between practices last night.

Thirty minutes out from serve they split up into the locker rooms to change. Neil was no longer surprised to find a complete lack of privacy in the men's changing room, but his teammates stayed out of the bathroom long enough for him to struggle into his gear. He left his helmet and gloves off since they still had plenty of time before serve and rejoined his teammates in the main room.

"Take them on a couple laps," Wymack told Dan. "Let them get a look at the place."

The University of Texas stadium was comparable to the Foxhole Court in size. The Longhorns and Foxes shared the same team colors, too, so the packed rafters looked familiar and comforting. Neil just had to ignore the crowd's challenging roar as they noticed the Foxes in their midst.

Dan stopped them after a mile, and they jogged back to the locker room to stretch it out. Abby had water waiting for them. Wymack was guarding the rest of their gear. Aaron and Nicky steered the stick rack out to the inner ring when it was time to take their spot on the benches. The Vixens had shown up and somehow found the section reserved for Palmetto State students. Dan had her team wave an energetic greeting to both the squad and their ardent fans. The Foxes were rewarded with enthusiastic cheers.

A few seconds later the Longhorns passed them in an infinite stream. The Foxes had come in their orange-on-white Away jerseys, and the Longhorns wore their white-on-orange Home uniforms. It was disorienting watching them go by on their laps; Neil hoped no one got confused in the heat of the moment. Even the smallest hesitation on the court could cost them a point.

When the Longhorns were ready they'd be on the court for drills, so the Foxes collected their racquets. Wymack gave them a few moments, then clapped his hands to get their attention.

"All right, listen up. It's time to get serious. These guys might look like friendlies in our colors but they're here for one reason only: to eliminate you right out of the gate. They are wannabe champions and they know what it takes to get to the next level. Your job tonight is to make them look like fools."

Abby scowled at him, but Wymack didn't even look at her. "We've been over their line-up a hundred times. You've read Neil's notes. I showed you what you needed to see. These guys are quick and dangerous but they are not impenetrable. The trick is holding center court. For the love of all things unholy, watch those dealers."

"I'll watch them limp off my court," Dan said.

"Do what you have to do," Wymack said, "but don't you dare get red-carded. That goes for all of you." He shot Matt a pointed look. Matt's grin did nothing to reassure anyone, but Wymack didn't waste his breath warning him a second time. "If you ladies start losing ground, call on defense to lend a hand. I don't care if it means putting one backliner on two strikers long enough to get some breathing room. The goalies are going to lock our goal down. Right?"

"We'll do our best," Renee said with a bright smile.

The crowd's screams escalated to an excited, feverish pitch. Neil assumed the mascots had shown up to rile the stands. He glanced past Wymack, still half-listening to the lecture, and followed pointing fingers. A bracketed VIP section was alongside the press box between the Foxes' benches and the Vixen squad. A couple bodyguards were checking the crowd for potential threats, but they moved back out of the way when their charges were comfortable. Neil's world slowed to a crawl at the sight of black tattoos and dark hair.

Wymack snapped his fingers in Neil's face. Neil flinched so hard he rocked back into Kevin. He darted a quick look up at Wymack, mouth open on an apology he didn't have the breath for, but Wymack didn't wait for it. He whipped around to scour the inner ring. It took him almost no time at all to spot Riko and Jean. When he turned back his expression was darker than Neil had ever seen it.

The Foxes saw them too, and Matt was the first to react with a furious, "What are they doing here?"

"I'll ask," Andrew said, and started that way.

Wymack hauled him to a stop before he could get more than a step away from the Foxes' huddle. "You are not allowed to kill anyone the first game of the season. Worry less about him and more about your offense line, got me? Focus, Kevin. You too, Neil. Neil," he said, louder. "Eyes on me."

Neil realized he was looking at Riko again. He dragged his gaze back to Wymack's face. Wymack looked angry, but Neil knew Wymack too well by now. That anger was born of genuine worry. Neil chose to interpret it as disappointment instead

[91]

because that was easier to motivate himself with. The Foxes needed him tonight. He couldn't let Riko get to him. Neil caught tight of every bad memory that was snarling at his ear and shoved it deep.

"I'm starting to think he likes me after all," Neil said with forced nonchalance.

Nicky's laugh sounded fake and his smile didn't reach his eyes, but at least he tried. "Who can resist a looker like you for long, right? You're lucky I'm taken, because damn. Maybe we can convince Erik to share me?"

"Would it kill you to leave the freaky shit off the court for once?" Aaron asked.

"If I have to watch you ogle Katelyn, you have to watch me lure Neil to the dark side."

"I do not ogle Katelyn."

"Okay, sure, you don't ogle. You long-distance pine, which is a thousand times more nauseating."

"You have two seconds to shut up before I send you all on laps," Wymack said.

Nicky subsided with a lightning-quick grin in Neil's direction. Neil managed a small smile back. The familiar bickering had taken the edge off the Foxes' outrage, and now the upperclassmen looked to Neil instead of Riko. Andrew made himself comfortable on Neil's left, a one-man barricade between Neil and the crowd. The next time Wymack looked at Neil, Neil nodded a silent okay.

"Where was I?" Wymack asked.

"Offense, I think," Neil said, and looked at Kevin. Kevin was staring white-faced at Riko, but Neil nudged him until he had Kevin's attention. "Fair warning: if they put Beckstein as my mark I'm going to have to do side passes all night. He's got a foot on me, so if he catches my stick on an upward swing it'll pull me too far and I'll tear something."

Kevin started to say something, but Andrew beat him to the punch with a calm, "Eight inches. He's only five-eleven."

[92]

Neil and Kevin pivoted to stare at Andrew. The flash of a grin on Wymack's face said he caught the significance of that remark and knew what it meant for the Foxes' chances tonight. The rest of the team blew right by without noticing. Dan said something to Allison about how to compensate for Neil's possible handicap. Neil knew he and Kevin were meant to be included in the conversation but he couldn't follow along.

Height was arguably the most critical detail on an Exy court. A player's height decided how long of a racquet they could wield and determined their reach. To most players, a general figure was good enough; it didn't matter if they were an inch or two off because they just needed an idea of what they were up against. They used the number solely to determine how tricky their mark would be to get around.

Neil and Kevin knew the exact height of every Longhorn backliner because they couldn't play the game without that information. Technical players like Kevin could use a man's height to map out his every weak spot. More importantly, he could cross-reference his own field of reach against his mark's and find the best places to push. That was how he got around defense so often.

Instinctive players like Neil knew where those gaps were without calculating angles and overlap. If Wymack gave Neil a pen and told him to draw a backliner's blind spot on a diagram, he couldn't do it, but once the game was going Neil could find it in a heartbeat. He wasn't good enough yet to take full advantage of that insight, but Kevin said a talent like that would have eventually secured Neil's spot on the US Court.

Andrew had no excuse for knowing Beckstein's height. For starters, Beckstein was a backliner. If the Foxes did their job right Beckstein shouldn't ever get close enough to goal to take a shot at it. More importantly, Wymack had only given out the Longhorns' heights once: when he'd first read the UT line-up out to his team. That statistic was printed on the round-one pamphlet Wymack handed out last week, but Andrew had stuffed that paperwork in his locker the first chance he got. Neil hadn't seen him take it out since.

Andrew had looked a thousand miles away when Wymack went over the Longhorns' roster, but he'd heard every word and he'd retained it. That perfect retention was what saved them in their match against Belmonte last fall. Wymack made a throwaway comment about penalty shots during the halftime rundown. The game didn't come down to penalties, but with so few seconds left on the clock and so much pressure on the Belmonte striker to tie the score, Andrew knew he'd go for what was familiar. He'd blocked an impossible shot without thinking twice.

Neil looked at Kevin, then Wymack, wondering why no one had told him Andrew had an eidetic memory, wondering if they'd even known. He couldn't help but give it another test. He mentally scrolled through the Longhorns' offense line and settled on a fifth-year striker. "How tall is Lakes?"

"Look it up," Andrew said.

"Humor me just this once," Neil said. Andrew started to turn away, so Neil hooked his gloved fingers in the netted head of Andrew's racquet and gave a careful tug. He tried again with an insistent, "How tall is she?"

"Five-six?" Matt guessed.

"Five-eight," Andrew said.

"Close enough." Matt shrugged apathy.

Neil let go of Andrew's racquet in favor of holding onto his own. "We're going to win."

"You were expecting us to lose?" Dan asked.

"No," Neil admitted. His lips twitched, and he knew from the hard pull at his mouth that he was wearing his father's smile. He pressed the side of his glove to his face, nearly crushing his teeth into his lips. He tasted blood before it was safe to drop his hand again. Neil leaned back a bit and looked past Andrew at Riko. "I'm just glad he's here to see it. Let's see if we can't rattle him."

[94]

"Let's," Wymack said. "Anyway, imagine I actually got through everything important I needed to say, because it's too late to finish it now. The court's open. We're on with the usual drills, ones and threes. I say this every time because you make me say this every time: keep the balls on our goddamned side of the court, Andrew."

The Foxes yanked on the last of their gear and headed on for a few drills. Neil was content to take it easy, more interested in judging the state of his body than one-upping his own goalkeepers. The sight of Riko had set every one of Neil's fading bruises to pounding, but now he barely felt a thing. The only thing that mattered was his team and the way they moved around him.

They had to leave the court for coin toss. Dan won them first serve and Wymack had a couple seconds before the line-ups were called to gather his team close.

"Remember," he said. "It's two out of three to advance and you can't afford to lose the first game of the season. Strikers, get three goals apiece or I'll register you for a marathon. Backliners, if you look like idiots you'll keep them company. Dealers: you've got this. Renee, play it like you know how. Andrew, keep the score at three or under for your half and I'll buy you as much alcohol as will fit in your cabinet."

The announcer called both starting line-ups to the court. Neil took his place on the half-court line and sent a final look Kevin's way. By some miracle Beckstein was on the court against Kevin. Kevin answered his glance with a nod. Neil was almost bouncing by the time the buzzer sounded.

For a while the game was an even back-and-forth. There were a couple collisions, a couple near-misses, and more than a few rude words exchanged. Wymack was right to warn them about the Longhorns' dealers. The girl Texas put in as a starter was fast and dirty. She and Dan shoved at each other almost nonstop. Even when the ball was on the other side of the court they rapped their sticks together in a constant check. How Dan

[95]

held out so long before snapping, Neil didn't know, but she lasted a good ten minutes.

The next time the ball went toward the dealers, Dan ducked, hooked her body under her mark, and flipped the girl clear off her feet. To add insult to injury, she offered the fallen girl a gloved hand back to her feet. The next second they were in each other's faces with jabbing fingers and strident tones. The referees made it halfway across the court to them, likely to card Dan for her dangerous body-check, before the other dealer punched Dan in her mouth. Dan threw her hands up and refused to retaliate. There was no point when she'd gotten what she wanted. Both dealers got yellow cards, and the referees restarted gameplay from a neutral position.

That almost-fight was the tipping point, and the rest of first half was brutal. Neil was sore all over by the time the bell rang for half-time but he didn't care how much his body hurt. Andrew had done what Wymack asked and given up only two goals. The Foxes, on the other hand, had already netted four. Neil followed his teammates off the court for half-time break, passed Wymack where he was giving breezy dismissals to the reporters, and paced the locker room until the feeling came back to his toes. Abby roped him into a quick check-up in the other room and Neil was too out of breath to wave her off.

The Longhorns went all-out in the second half, getting two players red-carded and five yellowed. Their underhanded playing style wore the Foxes thin, but the Foxes knew better than to fight back. A yellow card wouldn't get them benched, but two in a row would get them booted from the match and they had no one to spare. They kept their cool as best they could, toed a careful line on their own numerous transgressions, and harvested as many points as they could from penalty shots. In the end it was worth it, because the final score was seven-six, Foxes' favor.

When the Foxes filed off the court, Renee headed for Riko. She wasn't the sort to pick a fight, so Neil stopped to stare after her. Riko didn't take the hand Renee offered, but Jean did. The handshake lasted a little too long, but Neil didn't know which one of them was slower to let go.

Neil thought of Jean's odd reaction to Renee at the fall banquet, the lingering look and the uncomfortable introduction. It was the memory he'd been looking for last week when going through his messages at Reddin. Jean accepted Riko and Tetsuji's cruelty because he had no one outside of the Ravens. With nothing else to live for and no reason to fight, he bowed his head and focused on surviving. Renee was the first bright thing to catch his eye.

"He's interested in her," Neil said, not quite a question.

Kevin was watching them too. "It doesn't matter. It won't work."

Renee told Neil last fall that Ravens weren't allowed to date. Tetsuji didn't want his team distracted from the game. Renee knew that, but she was over there anyway. Neil might be over-thinking her intentions, but he was willing to exploit any angle they could find.

"Maybe not," Neil said, "but it could give us an edge. Do you still know his number? Give it to her and see what she can do between now and finals."

Dan and Kevin had agreed beforehand to handle the reporters post-game. Neil was happy to leave them to it and follow his jubilant teammates to the locker room, but he didn't make it far. He was probably eight steps from the bench before a reporter shouted after him.

"Neil, is it true you're marked for Court?"

The smart thing to do was keep going and pretend he hadn't heard over the sound of the furious crowd, but Neil ground to a halt. He stared straight ahead, weighing all the ways he could and shouldn't respond to that. Finally he turned back. Riko's presence meant Andrew was sticking close to Kevin, but Andrew's eyes were on Neil after a bold question like that. Neil tipped his head in silent question, and Andrew motioned for him to do as he pleased.

Neil undid the straps on his helmet and headed for the trio of reporters. Andrew took Neil's helmet as he passed, and Renee took it from Andrew as she headed to the locker room. Neil tucked his gloves under one arm and stopped beside Kevin.

"I'm sorry," he said. "Did you say something?"

"Rumor has it you've been invited to the perfect Court." The reporter thrust a microphone at him, her eyes on the bandage plastered to Neil's cheekbone with sweat and tape. "Care to comment on that?"

The first time someone asked about Riko's and Kevin's tattoos, Riko hadn't beat around the bush. He was the best striker in the game, he said, and he wanted everyone to know it. The story changed a little when Jean made his first public appearance with a "3" on his face. Riko was supposedly handpicking the future US National Team. He called it the "perfect Court", and even though it was unofficial and unbelievably arrogant, his talent and upbringing gave some credibility to the idea.

"Oh," Neil said. "You mean this."

He peeled the bandage off his face and let the reporters get a good look at his tattoo. One of the reporters snapped at her cameraman to get a close-up and Neil obediently tilted his face for a better view. He was smiling again and this time he didn't try to hide it. The reporters were too stupid, or too eager for a story, to read the threat in that expression. Kevin wasn't so blind and he hissed under his breath in tense French.

"Don't push him."

The urge to choke the life out of Kevin was as fierce as it was fleeting. Neil didn't waste his time looking at Kevin but addressed the reporters. "It's actually impressive, isn't it? I think it's the first time Riko's ever been wrong. He always seemed too thickheaded to admit when he'd made a mistake."

"You think he made a mistake marking you?" a reporter asked.

"You don't think you deserve the number?" another said at

the same time.

Neil affected surprise at their misunderstanding. "I don't think he deserves us," he said, and gestured between himself and Kevin, "but that's neither here nor there."

"What do you mean?"

"Look, I'm going to be honest," Neil said. "I know Riko's good. Everyone does. His uncle's name has gotten him pretty far in life and the Ravens have an impressive record. But Riko as a person is hard to respect. Up until December, I figured he was an egocentric maniac who was so desperate for his own glory he refused to see the potential in anyone else. He, of course, assumed I was a know-nothing from nowhere with no right to have an opinion.

"This Christmas we tried to meet halfway," Neil said. "Riko invited me to practice with the Ravens over the holidays so I could see the discrepancy between our two teams. This is what we walked away with." Neil gestured to the tattoo on his cheekbone. "He admitted he was wrong about me, and I promised to live up to his expectations. We're never going to be friends and we'll definitely never like each other, but we'll work around each other for as long as we have to."

"There was a rumor you might transfer to Edgar Allan."

"It was mentioned while I was there," Neil said, "but we both know it'll never happen. I'll never get where I need to be if I play with the Ravens. Besides, I could barely tolerate them for two weeks. I can't imagine playing with them for four years. They're horrible human beings.

"But you know what?" Neil said before the reporters could respond. "That's petty. I said I'd be honest, but that was a little too transparent. Let's say this instead: we promised the Ravens a rematch this spring, so I'll cheer them all the way to finals. If Riko didn't think we could meet them there, he wouldn't have marked me or flown halfway across the country to watch us play tonight. He knows we have a chance. He just hasn't figured out yet that we're going to win the next time we meet. Keep an eye

[99]

on us, won't you? It's going to be an exciting year.

"Good night," he said when they started to ask him questions. He turned and headed for the locker room like he didn't hear them calling after him.

Dan's delighted laughter said she was following him, but he didn't look to see if Andrew and Kevin were with her. The locker room door banged closed behind them, muffling most of the noise from the crowd, and Neil caught the tail-end of Kevin's sour complaint. Neil's temper flared hot again and this time he didn't choke it back. He turned and shoved Kevin into the door as hard as he could. Kevin had the better part of a foot on him and could easily take Neil in a fight, but he was too startled to defend himself. Dan gaped at Neil. Andrew, who'd attacked Matt for hitting Kevin, took a neat step out of the way. Neither of them was going to interfere, so Neil tuned them out in favor of Kevin.

"Enough," Neil said, in fast and furious French. "Don't ever try to censor me again. I am not going to let him dictate how I end this."

"You are going to bring him down on all of us," Kevin shot back. "You don't think."

"You aren't thinking either. You can't be afraid of him anymore."

"It is not a switch you turn on and off. You of all people know this." Kevin finally pushed Neil off him, but he didn't try to get past Neil. "You did not grow up with him. You do not get to judge me."

"I'm not judging you. I'm telling you it's past time to stand your ground. What's the point of any of this if you're still his pet at the end of the day? If you really believed in us—if you really believed in yourself—you'd push back."

"You don't understand."

"I don't," Neil said hotly. "You have a way out. You have a future. So why won't you take it? Why are you so afraid to take it?"

[100]

Just like that his anger was cracking, breaking apart of the weight of premature grief and too much need. The way Kevin's expression faded from irritated to intent said he heard that hoarse edge in Neil's words. Neil struggled to hold onto his rage and bulled on.

"When I first found out about the Moriyamas, I stayed because I thought you had a chance. One of us had to make it and I wanted it to be you. But you still believe in that number on your face. What's so important about being second-best?"

Kevin looked at Andrew, not that Andrew could follow any of this argument. It turned out it wasn't a bid for help, because Kevin said, "When we tried to sign Andrew to the Ravens, he said the same thing. He said I didn't interest him because I made a career of coming second. I don't want this, but I'm not like you." The look Kevin shot Neil was frustrated, but the anger in it was more self-directed than anything. "I have always been Riko's. I know more than anyone what happens when you defy a Moriyama."

"You know," Neil agreed. "But they already took everything away from you. What else do you have to lose?"

Kevin didn't answer. Neil gave him a minute, then turned away. Wymack was waiting at the end of the hall with his arms crossed and an unlit cigarette dangling from his lips. He quirked a brow at Neil as Neil headed his way.

"I don't know if you recall, but we won," Wymack said. "Any particular reason you're trying to kill the good mood?"

"Just a difference of opinions," Neil said, as calmly as he could manage. He hesitated halfway through the changing room door and looked back at Wymack. "Oh, and sorry in advance about the press. In my defense, they started it."

"Christ alive," Wymack said. "What did you do this time?"

"He called Riko a Class I douchebag," Dan said. "Not in so many words, but I think they got the message."

Wymack dug a thumb into his temple. "I should have asked for hazard pay when I took this job. Out, out, out. I'm not

[101]

dealing with your attitude problem until I've had a couple drinks. That goes for the rest of you, too. Get out of my sight and get cleaned up. If you're not on the van with your gear in twenty minutes I'm leaving you here. And hey," he said before they could scatter. "Good job tonight."

He said they only had twenty minutes, but Neil wasted ten of them in the shower. He turned the water on too hot and didn't care that it scalded his skin. He wrote his name on the tile walls with his fingertips, over and over and over until his hand went numb.

CHAPTER SIX

The Ravens handled Neil's insults with rude grace. Their only official comment on the matter was that they couldn't care less what a loudmouthed amateur had to say about them. Neil was a little surprised they stopped there and didn't mock his miserable December performance. Belatedly he realized they couldn't throw him under the bus when he'd come back to South Carolina with Riko's number on his face. It would undermine Riko's estimation of his worth. Neil went to bed feeling more than a little smug.

The fans were less tolerant, and their retaliation started before sunrise Saturday. Pounding on the door startled Neil awake. He looked at the clock first, the dim window second, and scrubbed a hand across tired eyes. The pounding stopped, but Matt's phone started ringing a couple seconds later. Matt rolled over and blindly slapped a hand about for his phone. The pounding started up again, so Neil slung his legs over the side of the bed and went down his ladder.

Voices in the hallway were loud enough to carry through the door, muffled but angry. Neil didn't recognize any of them, but as he pulled the door open he definitely heard the word "cops". Neil opened his mouth to ask what was going on, but Dan slipped past him as soon as she could fit through the doorway. Neil watched her make a beeline for the bedroom, then leaned into the hall. Doors were open most of the way down, but only a couple athletes stuck around to rant at each other. The rest aimed for the stairwell like their lives depended on it.

Neil closed the door and went after Dan. She'd shaken Matt awake and was talking as Neil walked in: "—trashed the cars."

Matt rolled out of bed and onto his feet in a heartbeat. Neil

[103]

boosted himself up his ladder enough to grab his keys from under his pillow. Matt slowed just long enough to throw a jacket on over his pajama pants and pull his shoes on. He slapped his jacket pockets until his keys jangled in response. By the time Neil found his shoes Matt was already gone with Dan close behind him. Neil locked the door and ran after them, catching up on the stairwell. Matt jumped the last flight and slammed the back door open.

Neil didn't know what was worse: the sight or the smell. A layer of raw meat, broken eggs, and rocks covered the parking lot and stuck to the athletes' cars. Some cars got by with a couple dings and scratches; others had cracks and holes in their windows and windshields. Enraged athletes swarmed the parking lot, half of them on their phones, the others raging at the state of their vehicles. Someone had already been inside long enough to get a bucket, and she was steadfastly scrubbing beef off her hood. Squad cars and campus security were on the scene, with a dozen officers taking statements and pictures.

Any thought that this wasn't his fault died when Neil spotted Matt's truck. Someone had taken extra time to wreck it. Every window on the cab had been busted clean out, leaving only glittering spikes of glass around the frames. The tires were long-deflated from wild slashes. New dents were pounded into the frame from whatever tool the rioters had used on the windows. Allison's car was in the same sorry shape two spots down from Matt's. She stood by the trunk with her arms folded tight across her chest and her face a stony mask. She looked up at their approach, followed Matt's blank stare to his truck, and cut a hard look at Neil.

"The hell," Matt said in a strangled tone. He reached for his truck but drew up short, not wanting to actually touch the mess. "How did no one hear them?"

"They saved the windows for last," Allison said. She jerked her chin to indicate the men standing across the row from them. "Paris called the police when he heard glass break, but he

[104]

couldn't get down here fast enough to see any faces. Just a lot of cars peeling out of here, he said. At least four, maybe five."

"Oh, Jesus." Matt made another aborted reach for his truck, then settled for raking his hands through his hair. Dan pressed herself up against his back and wound her arms around him. He held tight to her wrists. "Are we really going to do this again?"

"I'm sorry," Neil said.

Allison curled her lip at him in scorn. "Shut up. No you're not. You're not," she insisted when Neil opened his mouth to argue. It sounded less like an accusation and more like an order, so Neil reluctantly subsided. "Have you forgotten who has to paint you back together every morning? If you'd let them steamroll you yesterday after all of this," she flicked her fingers up at her own face, "I would hate you."

"You told them the truth," Dan said. "It's not your fault they don't like it."

"I don't want this fight coming back on you," Neil said.

"Too late for that now. But whatever," Allison said. She was going for lofty, but Neil could still see the anger in every tense line of her when she surveyed her car again. "They want to break my toy? So what? I'll buy another one. Maybe I'll buy two. Fuck them if they think this will hurt me."

"Hey," Matt said, low but urgent.

Neil followed the unsubtle jerk of his chin to the back door. It apparently was Renee's job to break the news to Andrew, because Renee was now leading Andrew down the back steps into the chaos. Andrew's car was further back in the parking lot and a couple rows over, but Andrew followed Renee to the upperclassmen first. Andrew stopped at Neil's side to inspect the damage. Neil in turn studied his face, but there was nothing to see. Andrew looked as unimpressed with this as he did with everything else.

Renee hooked an arm through Allison's and gave her hand a short squeeze. "I'm sorry."

"Has anyone called Coach yet?" Neil asked.

"He called us," Dan said. "The cops are notifying all the coaches and getting them down here to help corral us. He should be here any minute."

Andrew hummed and turned away. Allison nudged Renee in silent permission to abandon her for Andrew, but Renee glanced over her shoulder at Neil. Neil nodded and went after Andrew. He'd only been out here a couple minutes, but the crowd in the parking lot had tripled in size in that time. Despite Allison's tart support, Neil couldn't look anyone else in the face. These athletes had done nothing to earn the Ravens' disfavor. They were collateral damage, suffering now because Neil couldn't keep his mouth shut.

It'd never bothered him before. Caring about the Foxes was unexpected but easily explained due to long exposure. Feeling guilty over these strangers' misfortunes was new and uncomfortable. Every strident voice was a knife on Neil's nerves and he hated it. Luckily—or not—they reached Andrew's car then and Neil could stop thinking about everyone else for a minute. Neil looked up from the asphalt when Andrew stopped, and his mouth fell open in silent disbelief.

The Ravens' fans hadn't stopped with Andrew's tires and windows, and they hadn't settled for simple dings. It looked like they'd taken a sledgehammer to the entire frame, pounding fist-deep craters throughout the entire vehicle. Red spray paint across what was left of the mangled hood screamed "Traitor". The front seats were shredded, as were the back, as far in as people could reach their knives through the nonexistent windows. Someone had burst compost bags in the backseat; everything from leftovers to coffee filters and chicken bones were piled a foot deep on the cushions. On top of the reeking mountain was a dead fox.

An anguished wail jarred Neil from his shock. He shot a quick look to his left and saw Nicky had shown up with Aaron and Kevin in tow. Nicky looked devastated as he took in the car's wretched state; Aaron looked like he'd been sucker punched. Kevin had a hand over his nose and mouth to block out the smell but his green eyes were wide. It took him only a moment to notice Neil's attention, and the look he sent Neil was a clear, "I warned you." Neil clenched his teeth and tore his gaze away.

Nicky stumbled over to the car and pressed unsteady hands to the misshapen hood. "No, no, no," he said piteously. "What did they do to you, baby? What did—is that a dead animal? Oh, Jesus, Aaron, there's a dead animal in our car. I'm going to be sick."

Aaron inched closer and leaned over to look inside. He cursed at the sight waiting for him and was quick to retreat. He hid his nose in the crook of his elbow as he gave the car another once-over, then glowered at Neil. Neil knew what was coming before Aaron even dropped his arm to speak.

"You just had to open your mouth, didn't you?"

"I'm sorry," Neil said. "I thought he'd come at me. I didn't think you'd get caught up in it."

"Right," Aaron said snidely. "Seth was a one-off, then?"

Neil flinched so hard he took a step back. He opened his mouth to argue, but he couldn't defend himself against an accusation like that.

It turned out he didn't have to. He hadn't realized the upperclassmen had come around to check on them, but Allison was past Neil in a heartbeat and she backhanded Aaron hard enough to nearly knock him down. She might have taken another swing, except Andrew moved like lightning. He caught her wrist to wrench her arm up behind her back and gave a violent twist to slam her to her knees. As she fell his other hand came up and seized the back of her neck. It forced her head down when she landed and kept her from getting up again. Allison tried to say something but managed only a sick choke under his fierce grip.

Renee was almost as fast; maybe she'd started moving when she realized Allison was going for Aaron. She didn't waste

[107]

her time tackling Andrew but threw herself atop Allison's fallen form. She wrapped her arms around Allison, comfort and support or a fierce warning to stay still, and stared up at Andrew's blank face. Somewhere behind them someone was calling, "Whoa, whoa," as he noticed the short but vicious scuffle, but Neil was more aware of Renee's quiet but insistent,

"Andrew, it's just Allison. Okay? It's just Allison."

"It is not 'just' anyone when she lays a hand on what's mine," Andrew said. "Let go."

"You know I won't," Renee said. "You told me to protect them."

"You failed," Andrew said. "You should have been faster."

"Damn it, Andrew," Matt said, with a ferocity that was more fear than anger. Matt looked like it was killing him to stay put. Neil was glad for that self-control; there was no telling what Andrew would do if Matt challenged him right now.

Dan stood white-faced and frozen at Matt's side, her wide eyes on Allison. Nicky was too afraid to go after Andrew, so he slowly dropped to his knees and slid a hand across the asphalt. He curled his fingers around Allison's and gave her hand a tight squeeze. Neil looked to Kevin, who'd gone still as stone, then Aaron. Aaron's expression was torn, a heavy mix of outrage at Allison and fear over what his brother might do. Neil didn't know what side of the fence he'd come down on but Neil couldn't rely on him to intervene.

"Andrew," Renee said. "Give her back to me."

They were drawing too much attention now. In another moment someone was going to step up where the Foxes wouldn't, and Andrew would react to that threat in the worst possible way. Neil had maybe ten seconds to make this right and no idea where to start. Andrew wasn't worried about hurting Allison, so Neil couldn't exactly appeal to his better nature. The last time Andrew looked a breath away from killing someone Neil had used Kevin as a distraction. That wouldn't work this time, but maybe—Neil hesitated, then gave up second-guessing.

"That's enough," he said in German. He was close enough to grab Andrew, but Andrew had warned him he didn't like being touched. He held his hand out over Renee's head instead and waited for Andrew to flick it a hooded look. Satisfied he had Andrew's attention, Neil said again, "That's enough, Andrew."

"You don't get to decide that."

"If you hurt her, you disqualify us," Neil said. "The ERC won't let us play with eight people."

"Your single-mindedness is as nauseating as always."

"You promised," Neil insisted, bending the truth until it almost broke. "You said you'd stop cutting them off at the knees. You said you'd cooperate at least until we destroyed the Ravens in finals. Were you lying to me?"

"I didn't promise that," Andrew said.

"You promised to have my back this year," Neil said, "and I told you where I was going. It's all the same at this point whether you want it to be or not. So do you have my back or don't you? Andrew," Neil insisted when Andrew didn't answer fast enough. "Look at me."

Andrew's mouth gave a violent twitch, a grimace he forcibly repressed, and he finally looked up. The darkness in his stare almost took Neil's breath away. Fast on the heels of shock was a bolt of triumph. Andrew had been back from Easthaven for almost two weeks, and this was the first sign that there was anything real going on behind that blank mask. Neil would have preferred to see the real Andrew under safer circumstances, but knowing he could be reached was a desperate relief.

"Fuck you," Andrew said.

The edge in his voice had every hair on Neil's arms standing on end. Neil held Andrew's stare, silently daring that anger to break against him instead of Allison.

"Do you or don't you?" Neil asked again.

"I made him a promise, too," Andrew said. "I won't break his to keep yours."

Neil didn't understand, but Aaron was finally startled into

[109]

choosing a side. "Andrew, that's—" He faltered, and Neil wished he dared look away from Andrew to see Aaron's expression. Every hint of anger had vanished from Aaron's voice; he sounded almost lost. Andrew didn't look at him, but the slight tilt of his head toward Aaron said he was listening. "No, Andrew. No. It's all right. I'm all right. It didn't even hurt."

Neil filed that away to ask about later. He was afraid he already knew what the answer would be. He hoped he was wrong, because if he found out Aaron really was that stupid he was probably going to choke the life out of him.

Andrew stared at Neil for another endless moment, then relaxed his death grip on Allison and let her collapse, gasping, to the asphalt. With the immediate threat out of the way Neil expected retribution from Dan or Matt. He put his hand out toward them to warn them off just in case. He couldn't stop them if they really wanted to get past him, but luckily they obeyed his silent order to stay put.

At their feet Renee buried muffled reassurances against Allison's hair. Allison's response was too hoarse to understand but she let Renee help her to her feet. Renee turned her away and guided her to Dan and Matt. They were quick to take her in their arms, holding her up between them. Renee stood back a bit, a quiet but physical barricade between the upperclassmen and Andrew. Neil risked a glance at Aaron. Aaron was staring at Andrew like he'd never seen him before.

When Dan was sure Allison was all right, she shot Andrew a look that should have flayed the skin from his bones. "You asshole. You could have seriously hurt her!"

"You do not have the right to act surprised," Andrew said. The fury was gone from his eyes; his expression was back to its dead slate and his shoulders were relaxed. He sounded bored again, like none of this had happened or mattered. "That is the second time in as many weeks one of you has forgotten yourself. You should have learned your lesson the first time. You do not get to take offense when you force my hand."

[110]

"This isn't—"

A booming voice cut Dan off. "What the fuck is going on here?"

Neil's heart almost punched a hole through his ribcage. He'd been so intent on Andrew he hadn't heard Wymack's approach. He darted a look over his shoulder but had to quickly look away from the anger on Wymack's face. Wymack raked his team with a glare and waited for them to recover. Dan was the first to find her voice again.

"Nothing," she said, a heated and obvious lie. "Just rethinking every time we defended our decision to recruit the monsters."

"Hey," Nicky said, too uncomfortable to sound offended. He winced when Dan glowered at him but persisted with, "Andrew might have overreacted, but he has a point. She did start it."

"Don't even try to justify it," Matt said. "You don't return a punch with a broken neck."

"Where you come from, maybe not," Andrew said.

"The real world?" Matt said, heavy with sarcasm.

"Don't," Andrew said, with a calm Neil didn't believe for a second. Andrew tapped his finger to his lips twice, warning Matt to silence, and pointed at him. "A privileged child like you has never seen the real world. Don't speak of it like you understand."

"Enough," Wymack said, and snapped his fingers at the upperclassmen. "Where are you parked?" Dan gestured over her shoulder, too angry to answer aloud. Wymack pointed. "Go wait with your cars. I'll be there in two seconds. Go, I said." He waited until they'd squeezed between cars to get back to their row, then turned a stony stare on Andrew's lot. His gaze landed on Neil last. "No one answered my question. What the fuck is going on?"

There was no point lying when the upperclassmen were going to tell Wymack everything, so Neil summed it up as succinctly as he could. "Allison hit Aaron, so Andrew hit back."

[111]

Wymack closed his eyes pinched the bridge of his nose. He was obviously trying not to snap on them, not wanting to reignite an awful situation, but it took an age before he dropped his hand. "Andrew, we are going to talk about this. No, I am going to talk about this and you are going to listen. Today, but not now. After the rest of this chaos has been sorted out. Do you understand?" Wymack gave Andrew a minute to acknowledge that, then said, "I didn't hear you."

"You'll talk, I'll listen," Andrew said, and even Neil wasn't sure if he was agreeing or summarizing Wymack's demands.

"I'm going to check on them," Wymack said. "I'll be right back. When I come back, we are going to focus on the real problem and the real enemy. Is that clear?"

"Crystal," Nicky said weakly.

"Yes, Coach," Neil said.

Wymack stomped off, and Andrew's lot waited in silence for his return. Neil looked between Andrew and Aaron. Andrew, like Nicky, had turned his attention back on the mangled car. Aaron was still looking at Andrew as if the answer to the universe was just out of reach. Kevin had stayed out of the way during the entire fight, but now he finally edged forward and took up a post at Andrew's side.

Wymack was gone for a while, but he eventually made it back to them. He'd meant it when he said they were putting the Foxes' fight on hold. He didn't say another word about Andrew's violence or Allison's safety. Instead he gave Andrew's car a long look and shook a cigarette into his hand. Andrew put an expectant hand out as soon as it was lit. Wymack handed it over without hesitation and lit himself another.

"Well," Wymack said, "at least you upgraded your insurance policy last year."

"Fat lot of good that does us." Nicky jammed his hands in his pockets and toed the car's bent bumper. "This mess can't be fixed. Even if they ripped out and replaced the entire interior, I couldn't get back into it without getting the heebie-jeebies. Did you see the dead fox, Coach? They put a dead animal in our car. Ugh."

"Pigs," Aaron said.

Neil was lost for the second it took him to notice the cops. They were only two cars down from Andrew's now. Neil didn't tense up at the sight of them, but it was a near thing. He dragged his stare away without trying to be obvious, but the view wasn't much better in the other direction.

"Cameras, too," he said.

At some point the police had cordoned off the parking lot and made a checkpoint for the arriving coaches. Two press vans were stopped outside the line and reporters were snapping shots of the dismal scene.

The cops made it to them a few minutes later. One made a slow lap, jotting down the license plate number and presumably writing out descriptions of the extensive damage. On his second lap he had a camera out, and he shooed the Foxes out of his way with an impatient hand so he could get good shots. The other cop swept them with a tired look, pen poised above his notepad, and said, "Whose car is this?"

"Ours," Nicky said, raising a hand. "Well, it's in Andrew's name, but I'm on the insurance policy too. We're cousins, see. Nicky Hemmick and Andrew Minyard, room 317. You need the registration or anything, I can tell you where to find it, but I'd really rather not reach in and get it for you. Look inside the car and you'll understand why. No, really, look inside."

The cop spared a glance for the car but said nothing about its sorry state. Neil guessed he'd stopped caring about sixty angry athletes ago. All he said was, "Did you see or hear anything unusual last night or this morning?"

"Friday night on a college campus," Nicky said with an apologetic shrug. "You learn to tune things out if you want to get any sleep. Besides, our room faces the front of the building."

"What about you?" the cop asked Aaron.

"No," Aaron said.

[113]

The cop looked to Andrew last. Andrew gazed back in unimpressed silence and took a slow drag off his cigarette. Nicky only gave him a couple seconds before answering for him. "He found out when I did. Renee stopped by and woke us up when she heard the news. Uh, Renee's our teammate." At the look the cop sent him for speaking up, Nicky shrugged. "Yeah, sorry. Andrew doesn't talk to cops. It's a long story and completely irrelevant. What else do you need to know?"

The cop only had a couple more questions, some of which he aimed at Andrew despite Nicky's warning, the rest of which he split between Nicky and Aaron. Andrew stopped paying attention to the interview before long and let his gaze wander. Nicky filled in the gaps as quickly as he could, and eventually the cops moved on.

A couple insurance agents showed up from local offices to get a firsthand look at the mess and touch base with whichever athletes were their clients. The woman representing Andrew's agency must have brought a cheat sheet with her, because she greeted the cousins by name and expressed sympathy for going through this a second time. While she chattered and took notes and pictures of her own, tow trucks rolled onto the scene and began the slow process of hauling every car to repair shops.

"We're footing the bill for rental cars and vans for a week," Wymack said when she trotted off to her next client. "I'll get the two we need sometime today. It might take the shop a while to get around to you," he gestured, indicating the enormity of the task awaiting the local crews, "so let me know as soon as you get an ETA. I can extend the cars if I have to."

"Yes, Coach," Nicky said.

"You good here for a minute?" Wymack asked, and at their nods went in search of the rest of his team.

There wasn't much left to do then but wait. It took the cops over an hour to get through everyone and the tow trucks longer to make a noticeable dent in their workload. Wymack came back when the cops were done talking to Allison and Matt. The

[114]

upperclassmen weren't far behind him, to Neil's surprise. Dan and Matt still looked a little angry, but they all looked more tired than anything. Allison made a point of meeting Andrew's gaze, a silent declaration of defiance and fearlessness.

"Andrew and I are going to pick up some lunch for everyone," Wymack said. "Any preferences?"

Neil doubted anyone was hungry after drowning in the parking lot stench all morning, but no one was going to pass down free food. They took an unenthusiastic vote and Andrew followed Wymack away. The Foxes were left staring after them in awkward silence. Finally Neil risked a look at Allison. He opened his mouth, needing and wanting to say what he should have said months ago, but all this time later he still didn't have the right words.

"Thank you," Allison said stiffly.

It was so undeserved Neil was stung into saying, "I'm sorry."

It was woefully inadequate for what he'd cost her, what he'd cost all of them by deciding to stay, but it was all he had. The look Allison sent him said she knew what he was trying to apologize for. She pursed her lips, like she wasn't sure what response she wanted to waste on him. Before she could make up her mind Dan spoke.

"We knew when we signed you there were going to be problems," she said, looking from Aaron to Nicky. "We took you in despite the rumors and the protests because we believed in you. We've defended you and stood by you and forgiven a lot of shit no one else would have understood. We've tried to be your teammates and tried to be your friends and have reached out to you over and over and over again.

"But there is a line here where it all stops. If you ever cross it again we are done. You will not, will not," she said again with fierce emphasis, "hurt another person on this team again. Do you understand?"

Nicky's characteristic cheer was gone. He looked almost

[115]

defeated as he glanced between Dan and Allison. "I understand, and you're right, but I'm sorry. I can't promise anything. Andrew's—Andrew. We can't predict him or control him."

"He can," Matt said, jerking his chin at Neil. "Why can't you?"

"Fewer survival instincts?" Nicky guessed, but his attempt at humor fell flat.

"More," Neil corrected, knowing Nicky wouldn't understand.

Matt turned on Neil, expression intense. "Even Renee wasn't getting through to him. What did you say to him to make him stop? If you're not there next time, someone else needs to know how to talk him down from the edge."

Neil couldn't explain without getting into things that weren't their business. "Don't let there be a next time."

"Neil, I'm serious," Matt said.

Neil shook his head. "So am I."

"Allison," Kevin said. "Did he hurt you?"

Allison knew Kevin too well to think he was concerned for her well-being. She sent him an impatient glare and didn't answer. Kevin interpreted the silence how he liked and sent a considering look at Neil. After a moment he reached out and covered Neil's tattoo with his thumb. The result made him frown, not in disappointment but confusion, and Kevin dropped his hand again. Neil waited, but Kevin said nothing.

"We're going in," Dan said, and the dejected Foxes trudged inside.

Aaron, Kevin, and Nicky disappeared into their room. Neil put a hand in the doorway before Nicky could close it behind them. The women were following Matt to his room further down, but it only took them a moment to realize they'd lost Neil. Neil held up a finger to promise he'd be right over and slipped past Nicky. Nicky closed and locked it as soon as Neil was safe inside.

Aaron dropped into one of the beanbag chairs and didn't

[116]

bother to look up when Neil stopped in front of him. Neil shoved his hands in his pockets so he wouldn't use them on Aaron and sank to a crouch. Aaron curled his lip at Neil, unapologetic and defiant. Neil clenched his hands into fists. He tried counting to ten in his head but only made it to six.

"Tell me you're not that stupid," Neil said.

"This isn't your room," Aaron said. "Get out."

"What did he promise you?" Neil demanded, ignoring that. "He didn't say he'd keep you safe. If he had he wouldn't have let Kevin stay last year. So who did he promise to protect you from?" He gave Aaron a minute to cooperate before guessing. "He moved back in the house and found out your mother was beating you. He said if you couldn't defend yourself against a woman he'd have to. Didn't he? All you had to do in exchange was stick with him until graduation."

"It doesn't matter."

"Obviously it does," Neil snapped. Aaron scowled but gave up denying it. "You've always known why he killed your mother. Why did you make me spell it out for you?"

"No," Aaron argued immediately. "That had nothing to do with me. He made that promise his second night home with us, but he waited five months to kill Mom. You didn't see the bruises she left on him when she thought he was me that night."

"Andrew didn't care that she hurt him. He cared that she hurt you. It only took him that long because accidents take time to plan."

"You don't know that."

"I do. So would you if you'd paid attention to how he treated you in Columbia," Neil said. "You knew before I did why he turned on Allison today. The only one who can stop this is you. Figure out what you have to do—what you have to forgive—to make him let you go."

He slammed the door behind him on his way out but stood frozen in the hallway. He knew better than to go back to the upperclassmen in a mood like this. This wasn't the time or place

[117]

for it, not with the team already so fragile, but Neil's temper had never had good timing. He wasn't even sure who he was angrier at: Aaron, for being so impossibly blind, or himself, for not putting the pieces together sooner. It didn't help that he was still mad at Nicky and Kevin for being so useless.

He couldn't calm down, so he did the only thing he could: he took the stairs to the ground floor and went for a run. He wasn't aiming for the court but he inevitably wound up there. He dropped his keys by the home bench when he passed and ran the stadium steps. Halfway through he finally outran his thoughts. He stopped feeling, stopped being "Neil", stopped being anything but a body in motion. He walked it off afterward in the inner ring. Every shuddering breath was too hot in his strained lungs, but Neil finally felt normal again.

He collected his keys on his way out and locked up behind himself. It was a slow walk back to Fox Tower and he took the stairs to the third floor. Matt was on the couch in their room, Dan to one side and Renee to the other. Allison had claimed one of the desks. They all looked to the door when he walked in and from the looks on their faces Neil got the feeling he'd interrupted an important conversation. He held up a hand on his way to the bathroom, a silent apology for bad timing and a promise he was going to be out of earshot in the shower momentarily.

"Lunch is in the fridge," Matt said. "Coach dropped it off while you were gone."

Neil had forgotten all about it. "Thank you."

He opened his closet to dig out clothes but hesitated at the sight of his safe. He crouched to run his fingers over the lock, thoughts spinning a million miles an hour. He wondered how much the insurance company would cover toward repairs for his teammates' cars. Even if it couldn't cover everything, Allison and Matt had enough money to pick up the rest. The cousins didn't have that kind of cash, and their car was nearly as expensive as Allison's was. Nicky had already predicted they'd get bad news back on it.

[118]

The tap of a shoe on thin carpet distracted him. He leaned back out of the closet to look. Allison was standing in the doorway, expression guarded and arms folded across her chest.

Neil still didn't know what to say to her, but he had to try. "I'm sorry. He didn't deserve it."

Allison was silent for an eternity, then said, "You already said it. If we got what we deserved, we wouldn't be Foxes." His words sounded callous when applied to Seth's death. Neil winced, but Allison shrugged and looked away. "Maybe it's better like this. If he'd done it to himself, I'd live knowing I'd never gotten through to him. At least this way there's someone else to take the blame."

"Andrew told you about Riko?"

"I've known since it happened," Allison said. "The monster stopped by Abby's house before the funeral to ask me about Seth's medicine. He told me his theory to make sure I got back on the court."

Neil thought about Allison returning to the game too soon after Seth's death and the way Andrew stopped by her side on his way to goal. He'd thought it suspicious at the time that Andrew would offer any sort of support. Maybe Andrew had been reminding her to get angry.

Allison stopped speaking to Neil for weeks after Seth's overdose. Neil thought her withdrawal was because of her grief. He'd welcomed the cold shoulder, unsure how to approach her with his guilty conscience. If she'd always known Andrew's theory, though, she'd always known Neil was partly to blame. Maybe that was why Andrew got involved: he'd already taken Neil under his protection by then, so he needed to make sure Allison wasn't going to be a problem for them.

Somewhere along the way she'd forgiven him and Neil hadn't even realized it.

"I should have said something sooner. I just didn't—" Neil gestured, helpless and lost and awful. "I don't know how to talk to people about the important things."

[119]

"We noticed." Allison shrugged like it was no big deal when they both knew it was. "You're a real piece of work. One of these days you're going to tell me why."

She went back to the other room, leaving Neil alone with his thoughts and secrets.

CHAPTER SEVEN

Neil was on his way out of the bedroom after his shower when his phone buzzed. He patted his pockets, found them empty, and dug his cell phone out from under his pillow. Two messages were waiting for him, one from Nicky timestamped almost an hour ago and the more recent one from Katelyn. Katelyn's was just a desperate "What happened???" that Neil didn't waste his time answering.

Nicky's was a heads-up that Andrew was back. It seemed redundant, since if Wymack had brought them food of course he'd have dropped Andrew off as well. Knowing Nicky, it was a veiled plea to get involved and make sure everything was okay. Neil stuffed his phone in his back pocket and left his room without a word to anyone. Nicky answered his knock within seconds and didn't have to ask why Neil was there.

"He took a bottle and left again," Nicky said. "Don't know where he went."

There wasn't far Andrew could go with an open bottle of liquor in hand and no car. "With Coach?"

"Don't think so," Nicky said. "Aaron left, too, right after you did."

Neil didn't care what Aaron did. He nodded and left, and Nicky didn't call after him. Neil took the stairs up to the roof and fought the knob the way he'd seen Andrew jar it loose. It only needed a couple tries before he got it open, and he stepped out onto the windy rooftop.

Andrew was sitting on the back end of the roof this time. The handle of vodka at his knee looked empty from here, but Neil saw sunlight flash off a little bit of liquid as he headed for Andrew. Neil quieted the instinctive thump of his heart as he got

[121]

so close to the edge and helped himself to a spot just out of Andrew's reach. He looked out at the ruins of the parking lot. There were still a dozen cars left, but a crew was already scrubbing the asphalt clean. The police were gone, leaving one of campus security's teams behind to supervise, and the press had vanished.

Andrew flicked his pack of cigarettes at Neil. "Give me one good reason to not push you off the side."

Neil shook a stick out and lit it. "I'd drag you with me. It's a long way down."

"I hate you," Andrew said, but it was hard to believe him when he sounded so bored by the concept. Andrew took a swig from the bottle and swiped his mouth clean with a thumb. The look he slanted Neil was both unimpressed and unconcerned. "Ninety percent of the time the very sight of you makes me want to commit murder. I think about carving the skin from your body and hanging it out as a warning to every other fool who thinks he can stand in my way."

"What about the other ten?" Neil asked.

Andrew ignored that. "I warned you not to put a leash on me."

"I didn't," Neil said. "You put that leash on yourself when you told me to stay no matter what. Don't be mad at me just because I was smart enough to pick up the other end of it."

"If you pull it again I will kill you."

"Maybe when the year is up, you will," Neil said. "Right now there's not a lot you can do about it, so don't waste our time threatening me."

"I don't think it was the money," Andrew said, and elaborated at Neil's questioning look: "Why they chased you so long. I imagine at some point they realized it was far more important to hurt you than to recoup anything they'd lost."

"So you say, but you still won't hit me."

Andrew stubbed his cigarette out between them. "The time is fast approaching."

[122]

Neil studied his face, looking for a hint of the earlier fathomless anger and finding nothing. Despite Andrew's unfriendly words, his expression and tone were calm. He said these things like they meant nothing to him. Neil didn't know if it was a mask or the truth. Was Andrew hiding that rage from Neil or from himself? Maybe the monster was buried where neither of them could find it until Neil crossed another unforgivable line.

"Good," Neil said at length. Tugging a sleeping dragon's tail sounded like a good way to die a painful death, but Neil would be dead before Andrew's protection wore off. "I want to see you lose control."

Andrew went still with his hand halfway to the vodka. "Last year you wanted to live. Now you seem hell-bent on getting killed. If I felt like playing another round with you right now, I would ask why you've had a change of heart. As it stands, I've had enough of your stupidity to last me a week. Go back inside and bother the others now."

Neil feigned confusion as he got to his feet. "Am I bothering you?"

"Beyond the telling."

"Interesting," Neil said. "Last week you said nothing gets under your skin."

Andrew didn't waste his breath responding, but Neil counted it as a victory. He tossed his cigarette into the wind and went back inside alone. He took the stairs to the third floor but didn't make it more than a couple steps down the hall before the elevator opened. Looking back was instinctive. Neil had one second to recognize Aaron and another to register the fury on his face. Then Aaron slammed into him like a freight train and crushed him up against the wall.

Neil took a glancing blow to his cheek and a harder punch in the mouth before he wrestled Aaron off of him. Neil landed a good hit high in Aaron's gut as Aaron jumped him again, and then heavy hands ripped them away from each other. Neil darted

[123]

a quick look around at the intervention. The fight had drawn a quick crowd from the nearest rooms. He knew these faces from passing them enough times in the hallway and stairwell; he knew their names and teams despite his best efforts to not learn anything about them.

Aaron made a violent attempt to get free, then settled for glowering at Neil across the hall. Neil tested his own restraints, found them equally unforgiving, and prodded the inside of his mouth with his tongue. He'd chomped his cheek when Aaron punched him and the first swallow wasn't enough to get rid of the taste of blood.

"Cool it," Ricky warned them, with his hands out toward both of them. "We've got enough trouble to deal with right now without your bullshit."

"We're good," Neil said.

Aaron wasn't keen on letting other people into his business, so Neil expected him to play along until they were alone. He underestimated how angry Aaron was. Instead of waiting for privacy Aaron tore at him in furious German.

"Fuck you! What the fuck did you tell her?"

The harsh sounds caught the other athletes off-guard, giving Neil enough time to respond. There was only one "her" that could get Aaron this riled. Neil regretted not answering Katelyn's text but he just shrugged nonchalance at Aaron. "Why, did she finally make up her mind? What happened, you showed up at her door to complain about the car and got an ultimatum in response?"

"You should know!"

"Hey," Ricky said. "Calm down, we said."

Neil ignored him. "I told her to make a stand. I never went back and asked her if she found her spine. For what it's worth, I did it before I found out how specific Andrew's promise was. I might have been a little more considerate if I'd known how stupid you were."

"You had no right to drag her into this!"

[124]

Dorm doors weren't made to be soundproof, and the loud German finally got the Foxes' attention. Nicky was the first out into the hallway, but the upperclassmen weren't far behind him. Soccer players stepped aside to let them closer, but Dan and Matt held back to watch. Neil expected a lecture, but Dan looked from one to the other and said nothing. Neil didn't know if she was too surprised they were making a spectacle to intervene or if she was still mad at Aaron for whatever role he'd played in Allison's close call.

Nicky got as close to Aaron as he could and sent a bewildered look at Neil. "Do I want to know?" he asked in German.

Aaron made another rough attempt to get free. This time Amal let him go, though he kept his hands out in case Aaron went after Neil again. Aaron took a half-step back instead, like he couldn't stand to be this close to Neil. "Katelyn's refusing to see me or talk to me until Andrew and I get counseling."

Nicky's jaw dropped, but he sounded more admiring than anything. "Damn, Neil."

Aaron shot him a livid look. "Don't you dare take his side."

"Why not?" Nicky asked. "It's not like you've ever let me take yours."

Aaron shoved Nicky aside and stomped for his room. Nicky grimaced at Neil and went after him. Kevin was standing in the doorway, but he stepped into the hall to let them by. He hadn't understood a word they'd said, but the hard pull of his mouth was displeased. Neil stared back at him, trying to silently convey how little he cared about Kevin's bad mood.

Dan motioned to the athletes hanging onto Neil. "Thanks. We'll keep an eye on them."

Neil was released into her custody and the small crowd slowly dispersed. Dan gestured for Neil to take the lead, so he headed for his room with Matt and Dan on his heels. Renee and Allison were inside still, and they watched Neil's return with interest.

[125]

Neil wasn't hungry, but eating gave him something to do. It also made him easier to corner. Dan propped her hip against the counter and watched him rummage through the fridge. She was trying to outlast him, Neil thought, but Neil wasn't going to be the first to speak. He popped his takeout container into the microwave, twisted the dial, and returned her heavy stare. Dan managed the silent treatment only until the timer dinged.

"Are we going to talk about this?" she asked.

"You might want to avoid Aaron for a couple days."

"That was already the plan," Dan said. "What the hell is going on?"

"I'm doing what you asked me to do," Neil said. "I'm fixing them."

"That's not what it looked like."

Neil shrugged, poked his noodles, and restarted the timer. "If a bone isn't healing straight, you have no choice but to break it. They'll be fine."

Matt leaned against the doorframe and arched a brow at Neil. "That's not exactly reassuring. From you 'fine' could mean anything from 'I'm going to hitchhike across the state' to 'I'm beaten to a bloody pulp but I can still hold a racquet'."

"Did you bet on them?" Neil asked. Realizing Matt couldn't follow his train of thought, he said, "Aaron and Katelyn."

"Everyone except Andrew bet on them," Matt said. "It's not a matter of them working out. It's a matter of when."

Neil considered that. "Then they'll be fine."

Dan didn't look convinced, but she left him to eat in peace and took Matt with her. Neil spent the rest of the afternoon staring at his textbooks instead of getting any real work done. Dinner was delivery because Allison didn't want to see anyone in the dining hall, and dinner was followed by complicated card games and a lot of shots.

Dan, Matt, and Allison played like the only way to win was to be the first one tanked. Allison was the first one to nod off, but Matt and Dan didn't last much longer. Allison claimed the couch, so Dan and Matt stumbled into the bedroom to share Matt's bed. Neil straightened the mess they'd made of the living room while Renee fetched an extra blanket from the girls' room. She was back in time to clear away the last of the trash. They washed sticky glasses side by side in the kitchen and were finishing up when Renee spoke.

"Thank you," she said, "for reaching him when I couldn't."

Neil glanced at her. "He asked you to protect them?"

Renee nodded. "Kevin told Andrew the truth about the Moriyamas first. Andrew knew letting Kevin stay could mean serious consequences for the rest of us. He was willing to protect his own against the backlash, but he didn't care enough to fight for the rest of us. He gave them to me instead." She tipped her head to indicate her sleeping friends and held a glass up for inspection. "One of the first things I asked him last June was who was keeping you. He said he'd know after a night out in Columbia."

Neil took the cup back and gave it a second scrub. "He regrets keeping me now, I'm sure."

"Andrew doesn't believe in regret; he says regret is grounded in shame and guilt, neither of which serves any real purpose. That being said, I tried taking you off his hands at one point." When Neil looked at her in surprise, Renee affected an innocent look that for once was not entirely convincing. "Andrew refused on the grounds he wouldn't wish you on anyone except a mortician."

"Drama queen," Neil muttered.

Renee gave a quiet laugh and traded him a hand towel for the glass. Neil dried his hands and passed it back. Renee hung the towel off its hook on the front of the fridge and stepped out of the kitchen to survey the living room.

"Will you be all right here?" Renee asked.

Neil cocked his head to one side, listening for noises from the bedroom, and heard only silence. "I'm fine."

He saw her out, locked the door behind her, and headed to

[127]

bed. Morning came too soon, and with it came more bad news. Wymack called them early to say the campus was defaced. Black paint covered buildings and sidewalks in thick sloshes and the pond was stained bright red from dye. Rude graffiti tarnished the white outer walls of the Foxhole Court. Wymack didn't want the team stopping by to see it but didn't want them hearing about it secondhand, either. The facilities department was out and about trying to restore everything as fast as possible. Wymack vowed to shred campus security as soon as he got them on the phone.

The second wave of vandalism brought the press running back, and a reporter finally got close enough to Wymack to put a microphone in his face. Wymack was too smart to go after the Ravens, so he settled for attacking the fans.

"I think it's pathetic," he said. "What good do these cowards think they're accomplishing by lashing out at us like this? All they're doing is bringing negative attention and publicity to the team they're trying to defend. It's past time the Ravens spoke out."

Edgar Allan's president, Louis Andritch, responded within the hour and made an obligatory appeal to Raven fans to cease such "unruly" behavior. Tetsuji Moriyama released a harsher statement shortly afterward, condemning the attacks as both insulting and unnecessary. It sounded suspiciously supportive until Moriyama finished with, "You cannot house train a dog by beating it a day late; it is not smart enough to correlate action and punishment. You have to discipline it the moment it misbehaves. Leave it to us to correct them on the court."

Dan seethed the rest of the day, but Moriyama's words got through to the fans. Monday dawned with no new disasters. Neil almost regretted it, because without outside distractions the team was free to focus on their internal problems again. Dan and Matt spoke to Neil but ignored the rest of Andrew's group. Allison acted like nothing had happened but noticeably stayed out of Andrew's reach. Aaron didn't so much as look in Neil's direction

[128]

and wouldn't talk to anyone, Nicky included. Neil expected him to speak up when Neil caught a ride with them to practice, but maybe Aaron was trying to keep Andrew out of the fight for as long as possible.

Kevin griped about the rampant discord for forty minutes of afternoon practice, then gave up chewing out his teammates and rounded on Neil. "If you cost us our game because you couldn't keep your mouth shut—" He didn't finish that threat, assuming Neil could fill in the blanks himself. His expression only darkened when Neil waved him off. "This is not the time for your attitude. Stop causing unnecessary problems before you ruin anything else."

Neil weighed all the possible responses to that and settled on the simplest: "Fuck you."

Kevin shoved him like he could push sense into Neil. Neil shoved back with everything he had and sent Kevin careening into Matt. Luckily Matt had been watching the short argument. He stumbled under Kevin's sudden weight but didn't fall and grabbed Kevin to stop him from going after Neil. Neil pointed his racquet at Kevin in warning and strode for half-court. He knew Kevin tried coming after him because he heard Matt's fierce warning to knock it off. By the time Neil reached the half-court line Dan had gotten involved. It took several minutes of angry threats to calm Kevin down, but the questionable peace only lasted because Kevin and Neil resorted to ignoring each other.

As soon as they were dismissed for break Neil went to the locker room for a drink. Wymack followed him up and stood just inside the back door. He planted his hands on his hips and stared Neil down across the room.

"I'm really interested to know how this went from an us-and-them feud to an all-out war," Wymack said. "Popular opinion is it's your fault. That true?"

"I had good intentions," Neil said.

"I don't care what your intentions were," Wymack said. "We

[129]

can't afford to lose Friday's game, not after what they did to us and especially not after what Coach Moriyama said. I don't know if you've noticed, but we're not exactly in winning shape right now."

"I know," Neil said. "I'm sorry about the timing, but I'm not sorry for anything I said."

"I don't want your apologies. I want this fixed as soon as possible," Wymack said.

"Yes, Coach."

Neil started for the door to return to the inner ring, but Wymack put a hand out to stop him and said, "Speaking of timing, how's your mental clock doing? Does having a set schedule again help any?"

"Not as much as having them all here does," Neil said. "I'm not alone enough to get lost."

"Good," Wymack said. "Now come on. Let's see if we can't salvage this mess."

Neil followed him back to the inner ring. His teammates had dispersed in his short absence. Matt, Dan, and Allison had claimed one of the Vixens' benches. Kevin stood alone near the court wall, Wymack's clipboard in hand, and rummaged through the day's notes. Nicky lounged on the steps leading into the stands, and Neil spotted Aaron about twenty rows up. Andrew and Renee were making their usual laps around the inner ring and hadn't gotten far.

Neil didn't feel like dealing with anyone else yet, so he went after the goalies. Renee spotted him as they rounded the first corner and motioned for Andrew to wait. Neil had excuses ready if they asked why he was invading their space, but Renee greeted his arrival with a brilliant smile and Andrew acknowledged him with an unconcerned glance. They set off again at a lazy pace as soon as Neil caught up.

Neil had wondered what the two talked about when they were away from everyone else. The last thing he expected was for them to be discussing Exy. Renee wanted to switch which halves they played now that Andrew wasn't limited by his withdrawal. Their opponents were going to get more challenging every week and Andrew was the stronger goalkeeper. She wanted him to pick up the slack when their teammates wound down in second half. Andrew accepted her suggestion without argument, and Renee moved on.

What started as a normal conversation quickly spiraled out of hand, and Neil had no idea how they went from the construction work on the far side of campus grounds to a likely starting point for World War III. There had to be a correlation between the two, but as hard as he wracked his brain he couldn't find one. Eventually he gave up, because trying to make sense of the jump meant he couldn't actually listen to their argument. Renee expected it to start over resources, particularly water shortages, whereas Andrew was convinced the US government would get involved in the wrong conflict and draw vicious retaliation. There wasn't enough time left in break for either one of them to win the other over, and since Neil wouldn't play tiebreaker they set the debate aside for another day.

Wymack called his team to the Home bench and restarted practice with a blistering pep talk. He got through to the upperclassmen first. When he cast them onto the court for scrimmages Dan swallowed her resentment long enough to pull Aaron and Nicky aside. She and Matt had a couple ideas they wanted the backliners to try, so they held an impromptu powwow on the first-fourth line. Aaron listened because he had to, but he didn't look at Dan and didn't say anything.

Tuesday was fractionally better, and that was only because Dan's group was making an active effort to get along with everyone. Aaron was unmoved by their act, Nicky clung desperately to any hint of warmth he could get, and Andrew was his usual uninterested self on the outskirts. Kevin spent an hour tearing into the cousins, then directed all his angry energy at whipping the upperclassmen into shape. He spared only a few caustic words for Neil, and Neil wasted no words at all on

[131]

Kevin.

When Wymack dismissed them for break Andrew immediately set off down the length of the court wall. Renee glanced at Neil. Neil wasn't sure it was an invitation until he turned toward her and got an approving smile. He was keenly aware that they were attracting attention as they set off after Andrew, but Neil didn't look back at anyone. There was a good chance the others didn't want him hanging out with the goalies, and it wasn't because it meant he and Kevin were still on the outs. The Foxes might be leery of Andrew and Renee's friendship, but there was over three hundred dollars in the pot on their would-be relationship working out. Neil distracted them from each other.

Neil harbored no such illusions about Renee's chances. Besides, Renee did a good enough job distracting herself. She faded out of the conversation several times to check her phone and tap out quick messages. Neil picked up a little of the slack because they were planning evacuation routes and critical supply stops in case of a zombie invasion. Surviving on the run was Neil's forte and, even though it was a ridiculous scenario, it was interesting to see how his priorities compared with theirs. Renee stressed the importance of collecting survivors, which Andrew shot down immediately.

"You wouldn't go back for anyone?" Renee asked.

Andrew turned his hand over. "I can count them on one hand."

"I think Coach would be good in a fight," Renee said as they passed the benches again. Wymack glanced their way, hearing his name, but only needed a moment to realize they weren't talking to him. "He's got a weapons permit, too."

"He sold the gun when I kept breaking into his apartment," Andrew said.

"What about Abby?"

"What use is she to me?" Andrew asked. "You can't bandage a zombie bite and she wouldn't let us execute the

[132]

infected. Besides, Coach wouldn't let her leave his sight. Let him keep her safe as long as he can."

Renee conceded the point with a nod, and the conversation moved on to less crazy ideas. It stuck with Neil, though, and he tuned out their next debate. He wondered what he'd do if an invasion really happened. Neil was used to cutting all ties and hitting the ground running. Chances were it'd be instinctive to abandon all of them if the undead put in a ravenous appearance. It wasn't exactly an uplifting realization, but Neil could accept the ugly truths about himself.

"Oh," Renee said, checking her newest message. "Excuse me."

She cut away from them and went up the stairs, phone already at her ear. Andrew slanted a look at Neil as they continued on without her. "Jean," he said. "Care to explain that?"

"I didn't know Kevin passed his number along," Neil said, looking over his shoulder. Renee didn't go far, just up a couple rows where she could make her call in relative privacy. Andrew said nothing, so Neil shrugged. "He seemed interested in her when we saw the Ravens at the banquet. I'm hoping she can weaken his blind loyalty." Neil thought about it a moment longer, then said, "Maybe that's why Matt stopped betting on the two of you?"

Andrew didn't answer, and they finished the lap in silence.

Since Andrew's weekly therapy was no longer mandatory and the Foxes were down to two cars, Andrew skipped his Wednesday afternoon session with Dobson. Neil remembered he hadn't talked to Andrew about his insurance policy yet and he made a mental note to pull Andrew aside at some point. He thought he could sneak time in on break, but the conversation was never at a lull when they passed the benches and Neil couldn't exactly drive Renee off mid-sentence. His chance didn't come until they were back at Fox Tower.

"Andrew," he said when they piled out of the rental car. Nicky rocked to a stop and sent him a curious look. Kevin and

Aaron didn't wait but followed the upperclassmen to the dorm. Neil shook his head at Nicky and, when that subtle dismissal didn't work, said, "We'll be up in a minute. Keep an eye on them."

Nicky grimaced and turned away. "Easier said than done."

Neil watched until the last of the Foxes disappeared inside, then scanned the parking lot with a slow look. The school had done a good job of putting the place back to order; the only sign that anything bad had happened was that there were fewer cars than usual. The presence of a few trucks and SUVs said some athletes had already started getting their vehicles back, but at least half the cars were unfamiliar.

"Have you heard back from the shop?" Neil asked, dragging his attention back to Andrew. "Matt got a call this morning saying his truck would be ready for pickup tomorrow. Allison should have hers back Saturday morning. Can they fix yours?"

Andrew flipped his phone open, pressed a couple buttons, and handed it over. Neil waited, mystified, until Andrew's voicemail started playing on speaker. A mechanical voice announced Tuesday's date, and a sobering message followed. The damage was even more extensive than it'd appeared; the garbage in back had hidden whatever the Raven fans did to the backseat cushions, and none of them had looked in the trunk before the car was towed. The shop wanted Andrew to call them back to talk about his options and discuss what it would take to restore the car to its former glory.

Andrew hoisted himself onto the rental car's trunk and dug a pack of cigarettes out of his pocket. He lit two and traded Neil one for his phone. Neil cupped a hand around his to shield it from the breeze. He studied Andrew's face as Andrew put his phone and cigarettes away, but Andrew gave no sign he was bothered by the bad news.

"You're going to have to replace it," Neil guessed. "If the insurance company won't cover a replacement for your car, take

[134]

the difference from me. You know I have enough for it."

Andrew slid him a cool look. "I'm uninterested in your charity."

"It isn't charity," Neil said. "It's revenge. It wasn't my money in the first place, remember? I told you my father skimmed it from the Moriyamas. If you take some for your car, you're making Riko replace what his fans destroyed."

"Revenge is a motivator only for the weak-willed," Andrew said.

"If you believed that you wouldn't be planning how to kill Proust."

The doctor's name still tasted like acid, burning Neil's tongue and throat, but it wasn't enough to put a dent in Andrew's calm expression. Andrew gazed at him in silence for what felt like an eternity, then propped his cigarette between his lips and motioned Neil closer. Neil was sure he was stepping forward into a knife for bringing Proust up again, but he obediently closed the short space between them. Andrew caught the back of Neil's neck in a bruising grip to keep him from retreating. He pulled Neil's head toward him and blew smoke in Neil's face.

"This is not revenge," Andrew said. "I warned him what I would do to him if he touched me. This is me keeping my word."

He waited a beat to make sure Neil understood, then let go. The next time he raised his cigarette to his mouth Neil took it from him. Neil broke it between his fingers and let it fall to the asphalt by their feet. Andrew watched the halves roll away from each other and turned an unimpressed look on Neil.

"Ninety-one percent," Andrew said.

"Just take the money," Neil said. "You bought the last car with someone's death. You can buy this one with someone's life—my life. That money was going to buy my next name when I ran away from here. Thanks to you I don't need it anymore."

"Your life has a price tag you are already paying," Andrew reminded him. "You cannot barter away the same thing twice."

[135]

"You've lost the right to call me difficult," Neil said. Andrew shrugged that off, so Neil said, "Make a new deal with me."

Andrew tipped his head to one side, considering that. "What would you take for it?"

"What would you give me?" Neil asked.

"Don't ask questions you already know the answer to."

Neil frowned at him, lost, but Andrew didn't waste his breath explaining. He held his hand up between them and turned it palm-up. When Neil just looked at it, Andrew motioned to Neil's hand. Mystified, Neil mimicked the gesture. Andrew took the cigarette from his unresisting fingers and stuck it between his lips. It had nearly burnt out with no breath to keep it alive, but Andrew coaxed the flame back to life with a long drag.

"That was mine," Neil said.

"Oh," Andrew said, unconcerned.

Neil didn't care enough to take it back, so he watched Andrew smoke. Andrew held his gaze and said nothing. He was waiting, Neil guessed, for Neil to come up with a suitable trade. Neil had no idea what he was supposed to ask for, but he knew there were a hundred ways to mess this deal up.

Common sense said push for a reconciliation with Aaron, but if Andrew got backed into that truce neither brother would enjoy it. Neil should ask for something that would strengthen the Foxes, like permission to restart the group dinners and movies they'd had in Andrew's absence. He hesitated because it felt like a waste of a chance. Halloween had been surprisingly easy to talk Andrew into. Not surprisingly, Neil realized, because hadn't Kevin said it last fall? "When you know what a person wants, it's easy to manipulate them," he'd said. Neil just hadn't known until this year what—who—Andrew wanted.

Neil shook that off as counterproductive. His mind went from Halloween to Eden's Twilight to Sweetie's, and Neil finally figured it out. "I want you to stop taking cracker dust."

"And he says it isn't a righteous streak," Andrew mused,

more to himself than to Neil.

"If it was righteousness I'd ask you to give up drinking and smoking, too," Neil said. "I'm only asking for this one thing. It doesn't have any effect on you anyway and it's an unnecessary risk. You don't need a third addiction."

"I don't need anything," Andrew reminded him, right on cue.

"If you don't need it, it'll be easy to give it up," Neil said. "Right?"

Andrew thought it over a minute, then flicked his cigarette at Neil. It singed the material where it bounced off his shirt. Neil ground it out under his shoe when it hit the asphalt. The cool look he flicked Andrew was wasted; Andrew's gaze had already drifted past him in search of something more interesting.

"I'm going to take your temper tantrum as a yes," Neil said. "I'll bring the money by your room tonight."

"Will you?" Andrew slid his stare back to Neil's face. "Rather, can you? Aaron doesn't want you in the room anymore, Nicky says. Something about you inviting yourself to fights that aren't your concern?" He waggled his hand in a so-so kind of gesture. "This phone tag nonsense has left the message a little unclear. Perhaps you'll explain to my face why you're suddenly so interested in my brother's life."

"I'm not," Neil said.

"Without the lies," Andrew added.

"I'm not," Neil said again. "I can't stand him, but we're out of time. I told you last October we can't make it to finals if we're a fractured mess. You two are holding us back. I had to start with one of you. Since everyone bets on Aaron and Katelyn, I thought he'd fight you for her."

"Wouldn't that be an interesting change of pace," Andrew said. "See also: a waste of energy and effort. He might try, but he won't win."

"You have to let him go."

"Oh," Andrew said, as if this was news to him. "Do I?"

[137]

"You'll lose him if you don't," Neil said. "He'll keep pushing Katelyn away if you tell him to, but he'll resent you for it. He'll count down the days until graduation and when it comes you'll never see him again. You're not stupid. I know you can see it. Let him go now if you ever want him to come back."

"Who asked you?"

"You didn't have to. I'm volunteering my opinion."

"Don't," Andrew advised him. "Children should be seen and not heard."

"Don't dismiss me for lying to you then ignore me when I tell the truth."

"This is not truth," Andrew said. "Truth is irrefutable and untainted by bias. Sunrise, Abram, death: these are truths. You cannot judge a problem with your obsession goggles on and call it truth. You aren't fooling either of us."

"If you ask for half the truth, you'll only get half the truth," Neil said. "It's your fault if you don't like the answers I give you, not mine. But as long as we're talking about obsession and Aaron's life, what are you going to do about his trial? She's going to be here for it, isn't she? Cass, I mean," Neil said, though he was sure Andrew knew who he was talking about. "You're going to have to face her."

"Seen and not heard," Andrew reminded him.

He sounded bored, but Neil knew a warning when heard one. Neil let it slide and went back inside.

CHAPTER EIGHT

For once Neil woke up before Matt's alarm sounded. He lay still for a minute, then rolled over and switched his own alarm off. He flipped his phone open to stare at the date. It was Friday, January 19th. "Neil Josten" was supposed to turn twenty on March 31st. Today Nathaniel Wesninski turned nineteen years old. Neil had never made a habit of celebrating his birthday, but each one he was alive for deserved a moment of silence. He rubbed his thumb over the date on his small screen and made a wish that they'd win against Belmonte.

Neil knew he went to his classes, but he didn't learn anything. He wrote down what his teachers said but didn't absorb a single word. He stuffed his notes into the bottom of his bag, ate a flavorless meal alone at the athletes' dining hall, and returned to Fox Tower. He passed a couple volleyball players in the stairwell who wished him enthusiastic luck and remembered to thank them. He thought he thanked them, anyway. He didn't know. He couldn't focus when he was thinking about the game.

The Foxes didn't have afternoon practices when they had home games, so Neil had a lot of time to kill. He tried studying but got nowhere, then tried napping to no avail. By the time they left for the stadium an hour out from serve he was going crazy.

The locker room smelled faintly of bleach and window cleaner. Neil had never understood the point of cleaning the locker room before a game, but a small crew came by every day. The smell was usually gone by the time the Foxes showed up for practices, but Neil assumed game day campus traffic had slowed them down. It explained why Wymack was sitting on the entertainment center instead of holed up in his office, though. Wymack claimed he was allergic to cleaning materials. Abby thought it an uncreative excuse for the unkempt state of his apartment, but Wymack stubbornly maintained his story.

Wymack watched his team go by, likely hoping for a sign they'd made peace. Each practice that week had gone a little better than the one before, but they weren't quite where they needed to be. Neil and Kevin started talking again on Thursday because there was only so long they could ignore each other. While the upperclassmen couldn't yet forgive Andrew for his violence they accepted it out of a misplaced sense of necessity. They still thought of him as a half-cocked sociopath, incapable of regretting his actions or understanding their anger.

Aaron, on the other hand, was an unmoving stone of loathing in the Foxes' midst, a speed bump tripping them up as they tried to find their feet again. Neil didn't know how much longer to tolerate such immature animosity before giving Aaron another hard prod. He wished Nicky had more influence over his cousins, since their rooming situation meant Nicky had more chances to lean on them. Even Kevin would be an acceptable ally, but Kevin only defied Andrew when it came to Exy. He wouldn't get involved in their personal problems.

There wasn't time to worry about it anymore tonight; Neil would have to sort it out over the weekend. He pushed the brothers from mind and followed the men into the changing room. He twisted his combination into the lock on his gear locker and pulled the door open. There was a split second of unexpected resistance, then a sharp pop of something breaking.

And then—blood.

It exploded in his locker, triggered by the door opening, and Neil recoiled as it cascaded over everything inside. The smell of it was so thick it clogged his throat and choked him. Neil's shock only lasted for a white-hot second before panic took over. He dove at his locker, grabbing for his uniform and gear. It was too late and he knew it, but he had to try. His jersey squelched in his hands like a swollen sponge, spurting blood all over his fingers. He dropped it and scrabbled for his helmet. His fingertips grazed hard plastic but couldn't latch on before Matt grabbed him.

"No," Neil said, but Matt hauled him away from his locker. "Wait!"

He dug his feet in, but the tread of his shoes were soaked and slid across the ground. The blood had hit the bottom of his locker and was now spilling onto the floor in a swiftly-spreading puddle. Hanging from the top of his locker was an empty plastic bag, rigged to tear open when the door pulled too wide. It looked big enough to hold at least two gallons; it was more than big enough to destroy every single piece of gear Neil owned.

"Nicky," Andrew said, "get Coach."

Nicky bolted. Neil elbowed Matt as hard as he could. Matt cursed as he lost his grip on Neil. Neil ran back to his locker, skidding a little as he got closer. He had to catch himself on the neighboring locker to keep from falling. As soon as he had his balance he frantically unloaded everything piece by piece. He couldn't tell his Home and Away jerseys apart anymore. Even the padding on his armor was wrecked. Neil picked his helmet up and turned it to watch blood slide off the hard plastic face guard.

"Neil?" Matt asked.

Neil dropped the helmet to the pile at his feet and punched the back of his locker. His fist hit plastic instead of metal, and Neil wrenched the broken bag off its hook. When he turned to throw it Andrew caught his wrist. Neil hadn't even heard Andrew cross the room toward him. Neil stared at him and through him, heart pounding in his temples.

"It's ruined," Neil said, voice ragged with an awful rage. "It's all ruined."

Wymack burst into the room with Nicky on his heels. The sight of so much blood stopped him short for a moment before he strode for Neil. "Is that yours?"

"Coach, my gear," Neil said. "It's—"

"It's not his." Andrew let go of Neil and went back to his own locker. "He's fine."

[141]

"Peroxide," Neil said. "Does Abby have any in her office?" When Wymack just looked at him, Neil started for the door to find some himself. Wymack put an arm in his way to stop him. "I need to clean my clothes before the blood sets or I won't have anything to wear tonight."

"And I need you to derail that one-track fucking mind of yours for two seconds and focus on the fact that you are covered in someone or something's blood. Are you okay?"

"Andrew already said I'm fine," Neil bit out.

"I'm not asking Andrew," Wymack said. "I'm asking you."

"Here, I've got an extra towel," Matt said, and dug one out of his open locker. He hurried to the bathroom to soak it in the sink but jerked to a stop as he was turning back to them. His startled voice echoed off the bathroom walls. "What the hell?"

Neil knew better than to look, but he went anyway. Wymack and Andrew were right behind him. Neil followed Matt's gaze to the far wall and felt his stomach bottom out. Written in blood across the tile was a bold message: "Happy 19th Birthday, Jr.".

Neil's head filled with static and screams. The strident mumble in the background was out of place and it took Neil an eternity to realize that sound was coming from his teammates. He understood their anxious tones, but he didn't understand a word they were saying. Fear trailed icy claws over his stomach and crawled up his throat. Neil closed his eyes for two seconds and breathed. He couldn't deal with this now. He couldn't; he wouldn't.

He grabbed the fledgling sense of panic and buried it deep, the same way he'd smothered his broken heart long enough to burn his mother's body. He would have to react to this later, but if he did it now with all of the Foxes as his witnesses he was going to lose everything.

The world came back into focus in jagged pieces, just in time for Neil to hear Wymack mutter something about calling the police. Neil grabbed his elbow before Wymack turned away

[142]

and squeezed so hard he felt bones creak.

"Coach," he said, as calmly as he could. "You're going to have to leave them out of this one. Okay? Let's just get through the game. I'll clean this up afterward. No one else has to know."

"Give me one good reason not to cancel the game and pull security in here," Wymack said.

"I can't give you that yet," Neil said, slanting a look at him. "I told you to wait until May."

He willed Wymack to remember the promise he'd made on New Year's Eve when Wymack challenged his lies and scars. He hadn't told Wymack he was on the run, but he'd cut it close enough Wymack should have put the pieces together. Neil needed him to remember that now and figure out the obvious: Riko's men wouldn't have left evidence behind, but Neil had prints all over the place.

Wymack said nothing but studied Neil with a disquieting intensity. Neil let go of Wymack and took the wet towel from an unresisting Matt. His lungs felt like they were pulling tight as he crossed the room to his birthday message. He breathed shallowly so as not to set off his gag reflex and scrubbed the letters off the wall. There were enough clean patches on the towel afterward for Neil to wipe his hands off. He came back to the others and dropped the towel in the sink to worry about later.

"Neil," Matt said.

Neil didn't want to hear it. "Change out, Matt."

He went back into the main room and considered his locker. It didn't take long to realize none of his teammates were moving. Matt was still frozen by the sinks. Wymack and Andrew stood in the bathroom doorway. Aaron, Kevin, and Nicky were by their lockers. Neil could feel all eyes on him. He felt like the truth was written on his skin for all of them to see. The message only said "Junior" but he expected someone to call him by his name.

Neil looked around at them and focused on the one most likely to help him salvage this. "Kevin," he said, and continued in French. "Get them moving. We've only got forty minutes until

[143]

serve."

"Can you play?" Kevin asked.

"I'm pissed off, not injured," Neil snapped. "I'm not going to let this keep us from winning tonight. Are you?"

Kevin considered him for a moment, then turned a caustic look on their teammates. "Get moving. We have a game to win."

"You're joking," Matt said, coming up behind Andrew and looking between the strikers. "You're really going to ignore the fact that this," he stabbed a finger in the direction of Neil's locker, "just happened? Neil, you look like a Carrie stunt double. You don't even want to get security up here while the scene's still fresh?"

"No," Neil said. "I don't."

"You're joking," Matt said again.

Neil looked at him. "Riko is an egotist and an asshole. He wants us to react to this. If we do, he wins. Don't give him that satisfaction. Pretend this never happened and focus on the Terrapins."

It took Wymack only a few more moments to pick his side. "No one's changing in here. Get your gear and get out. You can have the girls' room when they're done with it. I will give you one chance tonight," he said when Neil looked at him. "If I think your head isn't in the game, I will pull you so fast you'll get whiplash and Dan will take your place. Do you understand me?"

"Yes, Coach," Neil said.

Wymack glanced at the mess one more time, looking a little like he hated himself for siding with Neil. Finally he shook his head and dug Neil's clothes from the small mountain on the floor. "I'll get Abby cleaning this. Someone loan Neil another towel."

"Thank you," Neil said.

"Shut up," Wymack said, and stormed out.

A terrible silence descended in the locker room. Finally Andrew crossed the room to his locker and finished unloading his gear. That was the trigger the others needed, apparently, because they took their things and left. Nicky gave Neil one of his spare towels on his way out. Matt was the last to go, and he hesitated when he realized Neil wasn't moving.

"I'll wash up in here," Neil said, and gestured at his wretched appearance. "I don't want to track this any further than I have to."

Matt accepted that without argument and left Neil in peace. Neil looked at his locker, then resolutely looked away and went to wash up. He stared at the ground as he showered and watched the red slowly fade from the water. Even when the water ran clear he felt like he was dying inside. He washed three times before finally giving up.

As soon as the water cut off, Wymack called to him from out of sight. "Matt went back to Fox Tower to get you some boxers and socks. I brought the spare gear in but you'll have to figure out which ones fit best. I'll bring back your uniform when it's clean. Sit tight until then."

"Yes, Coach," Neil said.

He listened for the door to close behind Wymack and dried off in his stall. The Foxes had a couple sets of backup gear leftover from years when the line was a little bigger. Renee had scrounged armor from there when subbing in as a backliner this past fall. Most of the gear was adjustable, but only to a certain degree. It took Neil trial and error to pick a complete set from the pile Wymack had left him. Then there was nothing to do but wait.

It felt like forever before Matt made it back; game night traffic made the short trek to Fox Tower much longer than it should have been. Neil was jarred from his dire thoughts when someone knocked. He slid off the bench and went to investigate. The gear he'd put on made it impossible to fit the towel around his body. Instead of wrapping it around him, he held it up by his neck and let it hang down his scarred front.

Neil opened the door just far enough to realize it was Matt in the hallway and was startled into saying, "You knocked?"

[145]

Matt looked at him oddly. "Abby said she still has your uniform."

It wasn't the first time the Foxes had gone out of their way to accommodate Neil's privacy issues, but they usually had time to think it through. Matt was late for warm-ups because of Neil and shaken by Riko's awful trick. Despite that he'd remembered not to barge in.

"Thank you," Neil finally said, and took the clothes Matt squeezed through the doorway. Matt had brought him an entire outfit so he'd have something to wear after the game. The thought of Matt going through his things made his skin crawl, but Neil fought off that instinctive fit of nerves.

"No problem," Matt said. "Need anything else?"

"A clear shot at Riko and no witnesses," Neil said.

Matt grinned like he thought Neil was joking and left. Neil closed the door behind him and tugged on his underwear and socks. He carried his shoes to the bathroom and rinsed them off in the sink. There was only so much he could do. Blood had soaked into the liner inside. Neil could wear them tonight, but he'd have to replace them as soon as possible. Neil could pull his shorts on over his shoes, so he toed into his shoes and tied them. He paced the locker room, watching the clock so he wouldn't look at the blood.

Finally Wymack showed up with his uniform. "We did what we could, but we're going to have to get you a complete new set. I'll order it tonight and get it here express."

He handed it over and set to work rolling his sleeves up. Neil had gotten blood on his shirt when he grabbed Wymack's arm. It took Wymack a bit of tugging to hide all of it. Neil thought he should apologize, but he didn't think Wymack would let him. Instead he squeezed excess water from the hem and sleeves of his jersey.

"It's as dry as we could get it," Wymack said, looking up at the splatter of water against the floor. "Matt brought back one of the girls' hair dryers, but Abby didn't want to use it for fear of

[146]

setting the stain."

"If anyone asks, I'll tell them it was a pre-game prank," Neil said. "It's technically the truth."

Neil finished getting dressed. Wymack gave him a once-over, deemed him fit for public scrutiny with an unconvincing nod, and shooed Neil ahead of him out of the locker room. This close to serve the team had already finished warm-ups and stretches. Neil took a couple laps on his own while Wymack ran his team through a pre-game spiel. Wymack was done by the time Neil came back, and Neil abruptly became the center of attention.

"Are you sure you're okay, Neil?" Dan asked.

"I'm sure we have a game to win," Neil said. "Worry more about that and less about me."

The referees let them on-court for drills. Neil focused on his every move so as not to think about anything else. By the time starting line-up took their places for serve, Neil was so lost in himself and tonight's game he'd almost forgotten what transpired in the locker room. The ghost of it still clung to him, even if he wouldn't acknowledge it, and it egged him to go harder and faster. Kevin didn't warn him to scale back, and they crashed into their backliner marks with an unusual aggression. Neil had a yellow card before the halftime break. He expected Wymack to use it as an excuse to pull him, but Wymack said nothing about it when he took his team back to the locker room.

Neil thought he smelled blood but knew it was impossible. There was too much space between the changing room and the foyer, and the stench of his teammates' sweat and deodorant clogged the air.

"Where's Abby?" Dan asked, and Neil realized he hadn't seen her since serve.

"She had to go on campus for a bit. No one get mauled in her absence." Wymack gestured to the cooler. "Everyone drink up and stretch out. We don't have a lot of time."

The Foxes played second half like they had everything to

[147]

lose. Neil used the passing and shooting skills Kevin had taught him and slipped in some of the defensive footwork he'd learned with the Ravens. When he had to call to Kevin he did so in French. He didn't say a word to his backliner mark, no matter what the man said to him. He didn't have the breath for senseless snark and he needed every ounce of his flagging energy to get through the game. He knew the silence was getting to his mark, judging by the growing sharpness in the other man's tone. Neil didn't acknowledge him except to push against him and past him.

Matt was a dominating force on the far side of the court. Nicky was still the weakest link on the defense line, but Andrew balanced him out with ruthless efficiency. When Aaron came on, he and Andrew played together as if nothing was wrong. Neil didn't know if they closed ranks because of Riko's interference or if the game was enough to distract them from their personal problems. For now Neil didn't care what the reason was so long as they cooperated.

With eight minutes on the clock the Foxes started to slow down. They'd gone too hard too early. As long as they could hold their ground, they'd be okay, because they had a two-point lead, but Neil wanted another point to revitalize the team. He and Kevin were up against fresh backliners, though, and the defense cut them off at every turn. Neil knew Kevin was as frustrated as he was, because Kevin was starting to toe the line of unacceptable checking. Neil snapped a warning at him when they lost control of the ball again. Kevin snarled something rude back.

Two minutes later, the Foxes got the surge they needed. A Terrapin striker got around Matt and raced at the goal. Matt couldn't quite catch up, but he managed a glancing blow when the striker went to shoot. The striker stumbled, racquet twisting in an attempt to hold onto the ball, and got one step too close to the goal. Andrew was outside of his box in a heartbeat, and he body-checked the striker hard enough to floor him. The striker

[148]

stayed where he was for a good five seconds, too dazed to get back up again. The game didn't wait for him. Matt went after the ball with a war cry and flung it up the court to Allison. The next time Neil took a shot on goal he made it, and the Foxes rallied.

The Foxes won, eight-five, and the crowd almost blew the roof off with their racket. The Foxes took their celebration to goal because Andrew wouldn't come to them. Nicky and Renee had hooked him into the partying last season because he was too sick to fight back. Now Nicky made as if to pounce on him and Andrew pointed his racquet at Nicky in warning. Nicky thought better of it and hung off Aaron instead. Andrew stayed a disinterested spectator on the outskirts while the Foxes jumped and yelled a few feet in front of him. Somehow Kevin got around everyone else to say something to Andrew. Neil couldn't hear it over his teammates' noise, but Andrew's dismissive gesture said he wasn't concerned with Kevin's approval.

They shook the Terrapins' hands as quickly as they could and booked it off the court. Wymack and Abby were waiting for them, Wymack with a toothy grin and Abby all smiles. Wymack's glee only kicked Dan's excitement up another notch, and she ran at the crowd to rile them. Nicky and Matt tore off after her. Wymack let them go, knowing the reporters would rope them in as the easiest targets, and ushered his Foxes to the locker room. Neil made it all the way to the foyer before he remembered the mess that was waiting for him.

"Do you have a mop I can use?" Neil asked.

"Shut your face," Wymack said. "You're not dealing with that right now. We just won."

"Eight-five," Allison said, as if Neil had already forgotten. The edge in her voice betrayed how angry she still was about all this. Neil didn't flinch at the next words out of her mouth, but it was a near thing. "I guess you can consider that your birthday present from the team."

"Allison," Renee said.

"No." Allison stabbed a finger at Renee to cut her off but

[149]

kept her eyes on Neil. "I've hit the limit of what bullshit I'll tolerate this week, let alone this year. I need to know how much worse this pissing contest between Neil and Riko is going to get."

"We are going to talk about this," Wymack said, "but not until everyone's here. Go get washed up. We're going in turns again. Ladies first." He watched them leave and waited until the changing room door closed behind them. "I'm instating a new team rule where everyone is required to be happy after a win. You downers are going to suck the life out of me before my time."

Wymack looked at them, but Kevin was watching Neil and the twins were back to ignoring one another. Wymack threw his hands up in defeat and left. The room descended to tense silence until Dan showed up with Nicky and Matt in tow. The three still looked enthused from the win and their interviews, but being around their moody teammates killed their cheer. Dan hesitated only a moment before continuing to the changing room without a word. Nicky came and propped his shoulder against Neil.

"So we totally just bagged our two out of three. Next week's win is gonna be the icing on the cake." Nicky flicked Kevin a meaningful look as if demanding he join in the conversation. "Then it's on to the first death match. Chances of us playing someone interesting?"

"Zero," Kevin said. "All of the interesting teams are in the odds bracket."

"All except us, you mean." Nicky gave him a moment to agree, then heaved an exaggerated sigh when he didn't. "You're so biased. Just don't forget whose team you're on. If we end up facing USC, you'd better be rooting for us."

"I'll consider it," Kevin said.

The Ravens and Trojans were fierce rivals, but Kevin was an unrepentant USC fan. Neil wasn't surprised, since USC had one of the best teams in the nation. They were famous for their sportsmanship and they'd spearheaded the movement to keep the

[150]

Foxes in the running last fall. They were worth Kevin's attention and favor.

"Jerk," Nicky said. "I'm telling Coach you like Coach Rhemann more."

"Tell him," Kevin said. "If Coach is worth his position he knows the Trojans are better than the Foxes are. They always have been and always will be."

"Biased," Nicky muttered again.

Dan came to get them when the women were done, and the men took over the changing room. Neil stood under the spray and checked under his fingernails for blood. He found none, but for a minute he swore he smelled burning flesh.

Neil was the last one dressed, as usual, and he found his teammates waiting for him in the lounge. Wymack was standing in front of the entertainment center with his arms crossed over his chest. Abby was hovering in the doorway. Neil was tempted to continue past her outside and skip this conversation entirely. He doubted anyone would let him get away with it, so he sat beside Andrew on the couch.

Wymack waited until he'd gone still before starting. "First off: the massacred elephant in the room. Massacred birds, rather. I called in a favor with the faculty and got Abby access to the microscopes in the science labs. We needed to make sure that wasn't human blood."

"That's morbid," Nicky said.

"But necessary considering who we're dealing with." Wymack shook his head. "The last thing I want is to put you all at risk. The court is supposed to be a safe place for you, but I've failed to protect you. I have half a mind to install cameras in here in the public areas, but I won't do that unless everyone agrees. If we do rig something up, the only ones who will see those tapes are the people in this room right now. I want people in our business as much as you do.

"Which leads me to my second point: Neil asked us to leave the authorities out of this," Wymack said, looking each of his

[151]

Foxes in the face. "I respect him enough to allow that, but it's not up to just me. Are you going to be okay with that?"

"You're really just going to let Riko get away with this?" Dan asked.

"He wouldn't have done this if he thought he would get caught," Neil said.

"Maybe we can't get him, but we could get his middlemen," Matt said. "No one's perfect. Everyone leaves a trail."

Aaron spoke up then, and his callous accusation made Neil's blood go cold: "You'd know all about that, wouldn't you, Junior?"

Neil flicked a quick look at Aaron's dark expression and braced for the worst. When it came, though, it was worse than he expected.

"They'll never find proof that Riko was involved in this," Aaron said, "but they might find you, right? That's what this is all about, isn't it?" Aaron gestured at his own face, indicating Neil's abrupt change in appearance. "Your looks, your languages, your lies—you're running from something or someone."

That biting demand was a sucker punch, knocking the breath from Neil's lungs and crushing his stomach to his spine. The silence that followed felt infinite. Neil was sure his teammates could hear his heartbeat; it was pounding so loud he felt it on every inch of his skin. Their stares were piercing enough to peel up every disguise he'd ever worn.

Finding his voice was an act of desperation. Keeping it calm took every ounce of energy he had left. "You know, I expected low blows and backstabbing from the Ravens. I thought Foxes were better than that. No," Neil said when Aaron opened his mouth again. "Don't you dare take your issues with Andrew out on me. I know you're mad at me for getting Katelyn involved, but you're going to have to get over that."

"You dragged her into my business. I'm dragging them into yours. Not as much fun when someone does it to you, is it?"

Aaron asked.

"You're so stupid," Neil said. "I invited myself to your fight because I wanted to help you two. You're doing this because you think it's going to hurt me. There's a pretty critical difference there. On the bright side, you being an asshole at heart means I was right about your chances." Neil tipped his head to one side and eyed Aaron. "You do understand by now that your cowardice is what's keeping you and Andrew apart, right?"

"I am not a coward."

"You're a spineless asshole," Neil said. "You let the world happen to you and don't bother to fight back. You let other people dictate how you can live your life and who you can spend your time with. Remind me why you put up with your mother's abuse for so long. Did you actually love her despite her madness, or were you just too afraid to walk away?"

"Neil," Dan said, shocked. "That's not—"

"Fuck you," Aaron said. "I'm still waiting for an answer to my question."

"And I'm still waiting for a thank you," Neil said. He slanted a look at Andrew. "From both of you, to each other. You're even now, aren't you? So why can't you just wipe the slate clean and start over? Why do you have to drag it out another three years when you can fix it right now?"

"You don't know anything," Aaron said, low and acidic.

"You don't want me to be right," Neil guessed, "because if I am it's your fault she's dead."

Andrew finally joined the argument. "No. It is always going to be her fault."

"She didn't kill herself, Andrew," Aaron said, savage with grief.

Andrew flicked him a cool look. "I told her what would happen if she raised her hand again. She had no right to look so surprised."

"Oh, Jesus," Matt said. "Did you just—?"

Wymack pinched the bridge of his nose and exhaled noisily.

[153]

"Could you at least let us leave the room before you confess?"

Aaron glanced from Wymack to the upperclassmen, then turned back on Andrew. Neil half-expected him to take Wymack's warning as an order to silence. Instead Aaron switched to German and said, "That's not why you did it. Don't lie to me."

"She was nothing and no-one to me," Andrew said. "Why else would I have killed her?"

It took Aaron a minute to find his voice again. He still sounded angry, but there was a muted edge to his, "You wouldn't even look at me. You wouldn't say a word to me unless I said something first. I'm not psychic. How was I supposed to know?"

"Because I made you a promise," Andrew said. "I did not forget it just because you chose not to believe me. I did what I said I would do, and fuck you for expecting anything else."

There it was again: a hint of that infinite anger at Andrew's core. Aaron opened his mouth, closed it again, and dropped his eyes. Andrew stared at his brother's bowed head for an endless minute. Aaron had given up the fight, but every passing second seemed to put more tension in Andrew's frame. Neil watched Andrew's fingers curl against his thighs, not into fists but a mimicry of crushing the life from someone, and knew Andrew's temper was nearing a breaking point.

He put his hand up between them, trying to block Andrew's view of Aaron, and Andrew cut a vicious look at him. A heartbeat later Andrew's expression went dead. Neil regretted his intervention immediately. No one could let go of that much rage that easily; Andrew had simply buried it where it could hurt only him. It was too late to take it back, so Neil dropped his hand to his lap in defeat.

"Is that it, Coach?" Neil asked.

"No," Allison said. "As enlightening as this little diversion was, it doesn't answer the original question. What does Riko have on you?"

Lying at this point wouldn't work, considering Aaron's bold

[154]

accusations. Neil opted for honesty in its simplest, most unhelpful form: "He knows who I am."

It took them a moment to realize that was it, and Matt prompted Neil with, "Uh?"

"Neil's family has a reputation," Kevin said, unexpectedly coming to Neil's defense. Neil looked at him, willing him to silence even as he tried to keep his expression as neutral as possible. Kevin didn't return his stare, but all he said was, "Riko is trying to use it against Neil."

"Is it going to be a problem?" Dan asked.

"No," Neil said.

Allison arched a brow at him and gestured over her shoulder, presumably toward the wrecked changing room. "Are you sure about that?"

"Yes," Neil said, but no one looked convinced. Neil weighed his words carefully, looking for the right balance between truth and lies that would get them off his back. "Riko knows who I am because our families operate in similar circles, but he is a Moriyama in name only. He doesn't have the resources to do more than threaten me."

"Damn, Neil," Matt said. "Your parents must be something else if even Riko's got to follow the rules. Aaron was right, then? This is what you're supposed to look like?"

"Yes," Neil said.

"But why lie about your age?" Matt asked. "I don't get it."

"I don't want anyone tracking me back to my family," Neil said. "The harder it is for people to put two and two together, the better. Being eighteen in Millport meant my teachers and coach didn't have to consult my parents for anything. Telling you the truth meant having to explain why I lied in the first place, and I'm not used to trusting people. I don't want you to judge me for my parents' crimes."

"As if we have room to judge anyone," Dan said, and Neil shrugged a silent apology. She looked like there was more she wanted to say, but somehow she stifled her curiosity and let it

[155]

go. She looked to Matt first, then to Allison and Renee. When no one had anything to add, Dan said, "Yeah, I guess that's it for now, Coach."

Wymack nodded. "Cameras okay with everyone? Yes? I'll have them up over the weekend. We'll talk about their locations and the game on Monday afternoon. Before then figure out what you have to do to resolve these personal issues," he said with a meaningful look at Aaron. "Don't any of you dare bring these attitudes to my court ever again. Understand?"

The Foxes mumbled assent, and Wymack motioned for them to clear out. "Dismissed. Drive safe."

It was chaos outside the stadium. Drunken fans hollered and ran about like madmen; the rest of the crowd danced and sang triumphant cheers. Policemen were out in full force trying to control the mess. Security guards kept an eye on the Foxes until they made it to their cars. Aaron went right past the rental car and climbed into the back of Matt's truck. Nicky started to say something, but Andrew sparked his lighter an inch from Nicky's face in silent warning. Nicky silently climbed into the backseat with Neil and spent the ride staring at his lap.

Traffic around the stadium was bumper-to-bumper, so the Foxes' cars got separated as they edged into traffic. Matt beat them to the dorm. By the time the others caught up, Aaron was long gone. Neil watched Andrew usher Kevin and Nicky into their room before heading to his own. Matt followed Neil, and Neil tried to be surprised that the girls were right behind him.

The soft buzz of his phone distracted him, and Neil tugged it out of his pocket. There was a new message in his inbox. He didn't recognize the number or the area code. He understood the message even less: "49". Neil gave it a minute, but nothing else was forthcoming. He deleted the text and put his phone away.

"Neil," Dan said, and waited until Neil was looking at her to continue. "Thank you. For the truth, I mean. I know that's not all of it, but I know you didn't let us in by choice. We're ready to listen when you're ready to talk. You know that, right?"

"I know," Neil said.

She squeezed his shoulder in silent but fierce support. "And thank you for... well, whatever you're doing with Andrew and Aaron. I'm not entirely sure I understand what happened tonight but I know it was important."

"Important?" Matt echoed. "Are we going to talk about the fact that Andrew killed their mother? I thought she died in a car accident. That's what everyone's always said."

"She did die in a car wreck," Neil said.

"I said accident," Matt said, with emphasis. Neil gazed calmly back and said nothing else, so Matt asked, "How did you find out?"

"Nicky told me months ago," Neil said.

"Just like that," Matt said dubiously. "You've always known what he's capable of, but you said he's never given you a real reason to be afraid of him. What the hell are your parents into, if you can glide past murder like it's no big deal and get in Riko's face all the time?"

Neil shook his head and was saved by Renee's gentle, "Perhaps Neil trusts Andrew's reasons. Andrew admitted to murder, yes, but he also said he did it for his brother's sake."

"It was premeditated," Dan said. "That isn't defense. He could have called the police or social services or gotten Nicky's parents involved."

"People with our backgrounds are not inclined to trust the police," Renee said. "It probably never occurred to Andrew that they were a viable option."

"And look at what happened last November," Neil added. "Andrew's always known Luther wouldn't protect Aaron."

Dan looked between them, disbelieving. "You condone this?"

Renee spread her hands and gave her friend a reassuring smile. "We cannot understand the situation entirely, Dan. We will never know Andrew's frame of mind at the time or how bad life with her was for them. All we can do is make a choice:

[157]

believe that he was protecting Aaron or condemn him for taking the most extreme path. I would rather go with the former. Wouldn't you? It is encouraging and comforting to think he wasn't acting out of malice."

"Next you'll say it's sweet," Allison mocked her.

"Please don't," Dan said, with a small grimace. "My stomach's weak enough as it is right now."

Neil waited to make sure that was it, then said, "I'm going to bed."

None of them tried to stop him. Neil shut himself in the bedroom, changed out, and crawled into bed. His thoughts threatened to tug him down to dark places, so Neil silently counted as high as he could in every language he knew. It did nothing to help him sleep, but it at least kept the demons at bay for a little longer.

CHAPTER NINE

When the sun came up Neil gave up pretending to sleep and got out of bed again. He went for a run along Perimeter Road and pointed his feet toward the Foxhole Court when the turnoff came. The usual security guards were making their rounds. Neil trusted them less today than he had yesterday, now that he knew how easy it was to get past them, and made a wide loop around them. He let himself in with his keys and flicked on the lights as he headed to the changing room.

He pushed open the door, already rolling up the sleeves of his sweatshirt, and hesitated halfway into the room. The mess was gone, and the floor was spotless. Neil looked over his shoulder, but the place had been dark when he'd shown up. He was the only one here. He crossed the room to his locker and tugged the lock undone. His locker was clean and empty.

It was half past seven, which meant Wymack had been up for hours. Neil straddled one of the benches and called him. Wymack answered on the second ring by saying, "I don't know what amazes me more: that your phone is actually turned on or that you're awake this early on a Saturday morning."

"Coach, the changing room is clean."

"Yeah, I know. Abby and I took care of it last night after you left."

"I'm sorry," Neil said. "I was going to clean it this morning."

"Didn't I tell you not to worry about it?" Wymack demanded.

"You told me not to deal with it yesterday," Neil said.

"Whatever," Wymack said. "You can make it up to me later. Actually, what are you doing now that I've ruined your morning plans? Nothing?" He waited for Neil's affirmative and said, "You can sort through files with me instead. I'll lug them over and grab breakfast on the way. Or did you eat already?"

"Not yet," Neil said. "I'll wait here."

Wymack hung up. Neil looked at his open locker again, then migrated to the lounge to wait. He walked the length of the walls, studying the photographs Dan had put up over the years. Neil never saw Dan add to it, but the collection had grown to include a couple dozen shots from this year. The majority were of the upperclassmen, since Dan rarely had a chance to catch her younger teammates off the court, but Neil spotted several from Halloween and a couple stray pictures of their team dinners in November and December.

Right near the corner was a picture Neil didn't recognize at all: a shot of Neil and Andrew standing alone. They were bundled up in their matching coats and staring each other down barely a breath apart. It took Neil a moment to place it; the people packed into the background didn't look like a game crowd. The windows finally gave it away. Dan had taken this at Upstate Regional Airport on their way to play against Texas. Neil hadn't even realized she'd been watching them.

Neil had gotten caught in a couple of her group pictures, but this was the only one up that had Neil's natural looks. Dan had even caught Neil on his right side, so the bandage over his tattoo wasn't showing. This was a picture of Nathaniel Wesninski; this was the moment Neil gave Andrew his name. Neil reached out to tear the picture down but stopped as soon as he caught hold of the edge.

He'd come to Palmetto State to play, but he'd also come because Kevin was proof that a real person existed behind all of his lies. In May both Nathaniel and Neil would be gone, but in June this picture would still be here. He'd be a tiny part of the Foxhole Court for years to come. It was comforting, or it should be. Neil didn't think comfort should feel like such a sick knot in his stomach.

[160]

Luckily for him Wymack showed up then. He had a brown paper bag hanging from one hand and a box stuffed with papers in his arms. Neil got the door behind him so Wymack could put his things down. Wymack looked around the lounge a moment, then put the TV on the ground and shoved the entertainment center closer to the couches as a makeshift table. Neil watched him lay out folders in four stacks. When Wymack tossed the empty box aside, Neil opened the closest folder for a peek. It was a profile sheet with an unfamiliar picture on it.

"Potential recruits," Wymack explained. "We need six minimum."

"Six," Neil echoed as he knelt opposite Wymack. "You're doubling the line?"

"Not by choice," Wymack said. He pulled bagel sandwiches and juice from the brown bag and split the haul with Neil. "It was one of the conditions of us staying in the game when Andrew got locked up. The ERC doesn't like how close we've cut it this year and they don't want to keep bending the rules for us. I promised it'd never happen again. That means filling up on subs next year."

Wymack checked each stack, then pushed one toward Neil. "The girls are all going to be fifth-year seniors, so we need at least three bodies training to replace them. In total we're looking for two strikers, two dealers, a backliner, and a goalie. Find me some potential in the strikers and we'll narrow it down later."

"Shouldn't Kevin be doing this with you?" Neil asked.

"You choose the first cut," Wymack said. "He'll do the second. I'll make the final call."

Neil looked at the stack of files in front of him. At length he opened the top one and started to read through pages of statistics: fitness, scoring trends, ratios, and so on. He wasn't entirely sure what he was looking for, but he had an idea by the time he made it to the third striker. The third striker was consistently good, but the fourth was more interesting because there was measurable improvement. Discs were taped to the

[161]

inside back cover of every folder, likely containing clips of the players' brightest moments.

He split the files into two stacks, the most promising and the maybes, and went back through both piles when he was done. He thought the second round would be faster now that he'd seen everyone's information, but he second-guessed himself on every one. Wymack would probably finish every other position by the time Neil made up his mind, but when Neil sneaked a glance in his direction Wymack wasn't much further along than he was. Wymack's gaze wasn't even moving. He wasn't reading statistics; he was studying the player's picture like it could tell him everything he needed to know.

Neil looked back at the open file in front of him and tried to see what Wymack saw. Maybe Wymack could read pain in people like Neil could read anger; where Neil saw a girl's unshakeable calm maybe Wymack saw a vacant stare and defeated shoulders. Neil wondered if Wymack had seen anything in his high school snapshot or if he'd just trusted Hernandez's assessment that something was wrong. He'd like to think he had a good poker face, but Wymack was rarely fooled by it anymore.

"Problem?" Wymack asked.

"No," Neil lied, and went back to the task at hand.

It took half the morning to get through the would-be strikers, but Neil finally had a stack ready for Kevin and Wymack to pore through. Wymack set it on the ground by his knee and put the rejected files back in the box.

"Anything else?" Neil asked.

"Free to go," Wymack said. "You need a ride?"

"I'm fine," Neil said.

"Uh-huh," Wymack said without looking up. Neil let it go and gathered their breakfast trash. He was almost to the garbage can before Wymack spoke up. "By the way, I'm making you vice-captain next year."

Neil's heart lodged in his throat. He twisted to stare at Wymack, but it took two tries to find his voice. "You're what?"

"Dan's got to leave eventually," Wymack said. "She needs a replacement."

"Not me," Neil protested. "You should be asking Matt or Kevin."

"Talented players with more experience," Wymack allowed, "but they don't have what this team needs. Do you know why I made Dan captain?" Wymack glanced up at Neil and waited for Neil to shake his head. "I knew the moment I saw her she could lead this team. It didn't matter what her teammates thought of her; it didn't matter what the press thought of her. She refused to be a failure so she refused to give up on this team. That's what I needed to get the Foxes off the ground.

"You're the only one here who can succeed her," Wymack said. "Didn't you notice? They're uniting around and behind you. That's something special. You're something special."

"You don't even who know I am."

"The hell I don't," Wymack said. "You're Neil Josten, nineteen year-old recruit from Millport, Arizona. Born March 31st, five-foot-three, right-handed, stick size three. Starting striker for my Foxes and most improved freshman striker in NCAA Class I Exy.

"No," Wymack said, getting louder when Neil started to interrupt. "Look me in the eye and tell me if you think I care who you used to be. Hm?" Wymack stabbed a finger up at his face, then jabbed it into the table. "I care about who you are right now and who you can be going forward. I'm not asking you to forget your past, but I am telling you to overcome it."

"I can't captain them," Neil said. "I won't."

"This isn't a democracy," Wymack said. "You don't get to vote on what you do or don't want to do. I make the rules and you get to deal. And you are going to deal with it. You need this as much as they need you. Give me one good reason why you'd try to turn this down."

"I—" Neil said, but he couldn't say "I'm dying". He couldn't tell Wymack he wouldn't live long enough to take the position.

"I have to go."

He was afraid Wymack would argue, but all Wymack said was, "See you Monday."

Neil thought he'd breathe easier once he got out of the stadium, but his chest was still too tight when he stumbled out onto the sidewalk. He stared at the empty parking lot, heart pounding in his temples. The thought of going back to Fox Tower and facing his teammates right now made his stomach hurt, but there was nowhere else to go. He should run it off, burn himself down to fumes until he couldn't think or feel anymore, but Neil's feet stayed planted on the sidewalk. Maybe they knew he wouldn't stop if he ran now.

He sank to the curb to buy himself time, but his thoughts kept twisting in anxious circles. Neil felt a half-second from losing his mind, but then Andrew said his name and Neil's thoughts ground to a startled halt. He was belatedly aware of his hand at his ear and his fingers clenched tight around his phone. He didn't remember pulling it from his pocket or making the decision to dial out. He lowered it and tapped a button, thinking maybe he'd imagined things, but Andrew's name was on his display and the timer put the call at almost a minute already.

Neil put the phone back to his ear, but he couldn't find the words for the wretched feeling that was tearing away at him. In three months championships would be over. In four months he'd be dead. In five months the Foxes would be right back here for summer practices with six new faces. Neil could count his life on one hand now. On the other hand was the future he couldn't have: vice-captain, captain, Court. Neil had no right to mourn these missed chances. He'd gotten more than he deserved this year; it was selfish to ask for more.

He should be grateful for what he had, and gladder still that his death would mean something. He was going to drag his father and the Moriyamas down with him when he went, and they'd never recover from the things he said. It was justice when he'd never thought he'd get any and revenge for his mother's

[164]

death. He thought he'd come to terms with it but that hollow ache was back in his chest where it had no right to be. Neil felt like he was drowning.

Neil found his voice at last, but the best he had was, "Come and get me from the stadium."

Andrew didn't answer, but the quiet took on a new tone. Neil checked the screen again and saw the timer flashing at seventy-two seconds. Andrew had hung up on him. Neil put his phone away and waited.

It was only a couple minutes from Fox Tower to the Foxhole Court, but it took almost fifteen minutes for Andrew to turn into the parking lot. He pulled into the space a couple inches from Neil's left foot and didn't bother to kill the engine. Kevin was in the passenger seat, frowning silent judgment at Neil through the windshield. Andrew got out of the car when Neil didn't move and stood in front of Neil.

Neil looked up at him, studying Andrew's bored expression and waiting for questions he knew wouldn't come. That apathy should have grated against his raw nerves but somehow it steadied him. Andrew's disinterest in his psychological well-being was what had drawn Neil to him in the first place: the realization that Andrew would never flinch away from whatever poison was eating Neil alive.

"I don't want to be here today," Neil said.

"We were almost to the interstate," Andrew said.

It was the most half-hearted invitation to come along that Neil had ever heard, but Neil didn't care. Andrew had turned around and come back for him without hesitation. That was more than enough reason to get up and go with him. Neil climbed in behind the passenger seat and stared out the window. Kevin glanced back at him but said nothing, and Andrew got them moving before his door had even slammed all the way closed.

They didn't ask what was wrong, so Neil didn't ask why they were taking I-85 toward Atlanta. They were the longest two

[165]

hours of Neil's life, but the silence and the illusion of escaping Palmetto State University helped Neil pull his head back together. By the time they made it to Alpharetta he'd sunk to a comfortable numbness. Last night's sleeplessness started to catch up with him and he let himself nod off. He woke when Andrew's phone rang, but Andrew was only on the call long enough to say, "Don't." A couple minutes later they pulled into a dealership. Kevin got out as soon as Andrew parked. Andrew killed the engine and tossed his keys in the now-empty passenger seat.

"Get out or stay here," Andrew said. "Those are your only choices."

Running wasn't an option, he meant. Andrew knew why Neil had called him. "I'll stay."

Andrew got out and slammed the door behind him. Neil watched him disappear through the front doors in search of a sales rep, then closed his eyes and fell asleep again. When he woke there was a metallic black beast parked alongside the rental car. Neil wasn't any smarter about cars now than he'd been at the start of the year, but every curve of this one screamed expensive. Neil assumed Andrew did with this purchase what he'd done with the last: simply looked for whichever car would burn through his budget the fastest. It was a perplexing quirk for a man who claimed to have no attachments to his material possessions.

Andrew opened the back door and looked across the backseat at Neil. "Kevin?"

Neil scrubbed the sleep out of his eyes and undid his buckle. "Let him ride with you. I have nothing to say to him."

Andrew shut the door again, and Neil moved up to the driver's seat. Andrew pulled out of the lot first and Neil followed him to the interstate. They stopped at a gas station with a fast food joint attached. Neil wasn't hungry, but he filled the largest available cup with coffee while they ate. He sat in the adjacent booth to sip on it and stare into space. Kevin glanced at him occasionally as they ate but said nothing, likely attributing his odd mood to yesterday's fiasco. Andrew gazed out the floor-to-ceiling windows at his new car.

The ride back felt shorter than the ride out to Georgia had been, even though they had to pass Palmetto State and drop the rental car off in Greenville. The rep checked the car for new damage, turned the engine on long enough to see how much gas was in the tank, and had Andrew sign off on a couple forms. Then there was nothing to do but return to campus. Neil thought he'd been away long enough to be okay, but the first sight of Fox Tower out the window left him feeling tired.

They took the stairs up, and Neil didn't stop at the third landing. The soft tap of footsteps said Andrew was following him, but the hall door banged closed as Kevin headed for his room. Andrew caught up with Neil when Neil stopped to fight the rooftop access door. He had two cigarettes out and lit before they were even outside. Neil took his and carried it to the front end of the roof. He sat as close to the edge as he could get, hoping that jolt of fear would distract him from his dire thoughts, and looked out at the sprawling campus.

Andrew sat beside him and held something up. Neil looked, but it took a minute before he understood what Andrew was offering him. The dealership had given him two keys for his new ride, and Andrew was giving the second one to Neil. When Neil took too long to take it from him, Andrew dropped it on the concrete between them.

"A man can only have so many issues," Andrew said. "It is just a key."

"You're a foster child. You know it isn't," Neil said. He didn't pick the key up but pressed two fingers to it, learning the shape and feel of this newest gift. "I've always had enough cash to live comfortably, but all the decent places ask too many questions. There are background checks and credit checks and references, things I can't provide on my own without leaving too much of a trail. I squatted in Millport. Before that I stayed in decrepit weekly hotels or broke into people's cars or found

[167]

places that were happy being paid under the table.

"It's always been 'go'," Neil said. He turned his hand palm-up and traced a key into his skin with his fingertip. He'd toyed with Andrew's house key so many times he knew every dip and ridge by heart. "It's always been 'lie' and 'hide' and 'disappear'. I've never belonged anywhere or had the right to call anything my own. But Coach gave me keys to the court, and you told me to stay. You gave me a key and called it home." Neil clenched his hand, imagining the bite of metal against his palm, and lifted his gaze to Andrew's face. "I haven't had a home since my parents died."

Andrew dug a finger in Neil's cheek and forcibly turned his head away. "Don't look at me like that. I am not your answer, and you sure as fuck aren't mine."

"I'm not looking for an answer. I just want—"

Neil gestured helplessly, unable to finish that plea. He didn't know what he wanted; he didn't know what he needed. The past twenty-four hours had kicked his feet out from under him and Neil still couldn't find his footing. He didn't know how to make that ache go away or how to silence the voice whispering "Unfair" in his ears.

"I'm tired of being nothing," Neil said.

Neil had seen this look on Andrew's face once before, when he and Andrew called a truce in Wymack's living room last summer. Neil fed him half-truths to buy his acceptance, but it wasn't vague descriptions of his parents' crimes and deaths that got through to Andrew. It was his bone-deep jealousy of Kevin, his loneliness and desperation. After everything they'd been through these last few months, Neil finally knew what this look meant. The darkness in Andrew's stare wasn't censure; it was perfect understanding. Andrew had hit this point years ago and broken. Neil was hanging on by a fraying thread and grabbing at anything he could to stay afloat.

"You are a Fox. You are always going to be nothing." Andrew stubbed his cigarette out. "I hate you."

[168]

"Nine percent of the time you don't."

"Nine percent of the time I don't want to kill you. I always hate you."

"Every time you say that I believe you a little less."

"No one asked you." With that, Andrew caught Neil's face in his hands and leaned in.

Nicky's drugged assault aside, Neil hadn't kissed anyone in four years. The last girl was a scrawny French-Canadian who'd held him with just her fingertips and kissed like she was afraid of smudging her tacky-bright lipstick. Neil couldn't remember her name or face anymore. He remembered only how unsatisfying the illicit encounter had been and how furious his mother was when she found them. That awkward peck wasn't worth the punishment that had followed.

This was nothing like that.

Andrew kissed him like this was a fight with their lives on the line, like his world stopped and started with Neil's mouth. Neil's heart stuttered to a stop at the first hard press of lips against his and he reached up without thinking. His hand made it as far as Andrew's jaw before he remembered Andrew didn't like to be touched. Neil caught hold of Andrew's coat sleeve instead and knotted his fingers in the heavy wool.

The touch was a trigger. Andrew leaned back just enough to say, "Tell me no."

Neil's lips were sore; his skin was buzzing. He felt winded, like he'd survived a half-marathon. He felt strong, like he could run another five more. Panic threatened to tear his stomach to shreds. Common sense said to refuse this and retreat before they both did something they'd regret. But Renee said Andrew regretted nothing, and Neil wouldn't live long enough for it to matter. He hadn't figured out which way to lean before Andrew pried Neil's hand off his coat.

"Let go," Andrew said. "I am not doing this with you right now."

He practically shoved Neil's arm away from him and leaned

[169]

back out of Neil's space. He picked up his crumpled cigarette butt, decided in a glance it wasn't salvageable, and dug his pack out of his pocket again. Neil watched him until it was lit, tracking the new tension in Andrew's shoulders and the violence in his short movements. He thought he should say something, but he didn't know where to start. Andrew's kiss and abrupt retreat were equally bewildering.

Andrew managed only one drag before he crushed his second cigarette beside the first. He lit a third anyway, but Neil reached out and took it from him. It was a good sign, maybe, that Andrew didn't react to the theft. Neil set the stick beside his own dropped cigarette and looked back at Andrew. Andrew chucked his pack off to one side and tucked his knee to his chest.

Neil should let it go, but he needed to understand. "Why not?"

"Because you're too stupid to tell me no," Andrew said.

"And you don't want me to tell you yes?"

"This isn't yes. This is a nervous breakdown. I know the difference even if you don't." Andrew dug his thumb into his lower lip like he could erase the weight of Neil's mouth and fixed his stare on the horizon. "I won't be like them. I won't let you let me be."

Neil opened his mouth, closed it, and tried again. "The next time one of them says you're soulless I might have to fight them."

"Ninety-two percent," Andrew said, "going on ninety-three."

It wasn't funny—none of this was—but that response was so obnoxious and so typically Andrew that Neil couldn't help but smile. He forced it off his face before Andrew noticed and looked out at the campus again.

For the first time that day, maybe for the first time that rocky week, he could breathe without feeling like his chest was pulling too tight. As his tension seeped away, the weight of Neil's exhaustion came back, but this time it was genuine

[170]

tiredness. He hadn't slept last night and had only snatched an hour's rest in the car. Sleeping now would throw the rest of his weekend off, but Neil didn't care. He scooped Andrew's key up and got to his feet.

"Hey," he said, but Andrew didn't look at him. "Thank you."

"Go away before I push you off the side," Andrew said.

"Do it. I'd drag you with me," Neil reminded him, and left Andrew to his thoughts.

By some miracle his room was empty. Neil still closed the bedroom door before changing into sweats. He set his alarm to wake him around dinnertime, then pushed it back when his thoughts kept him up for another hour. He dragged his hand out from under the blanket and unclenched his fist to inspect his newest possession. The key's teeth had left indents along the flesh of his thumb. Neil worked the key onto his key ring beside Andrew's old car key and watched them sway without really seeing them.

Neil gave up fantasizing shortly after his mother beat his interest in intimacy out of him. He still had needs, but he dealt with them with no more attention than he might afford hunger or thirst. Maybe refusing to want anything else was a coping mechanism. He couldn't have it, so there was no point resenting its absence. Paranoia helped reinforce that mindset over the years until keeping people at arm's length was the only logical thing to do.

Befriending the Foxes was inadvisable but inevitable. Kissing one of them was unthinkable and went against everything he knew. Neil hadn't meant to toe that line or invite Andrew across it. Chances were he wouldn't have to worry about it, considering Andrew's rather vocal dislike of him and his serious boundary issues. Andrew wasn't like Nicky, who would wheedle and argue and protest if Neil said it was a bad idea. If Neil turned him down flat Andrew would never ask why or bring it up again. It'd be like nothing ever happened, and Neil could live out the last few months of his life in peace.

[171]

But was this peace or cowardice, and was this survival or avoidance? Neil could tell himself all day long what the smart thing to do was, but if he really cared that much about what was smart he wouldn't have come here in the first place. He would have left when he found out the Moriyamas were criminals or when Riko called him by his real name or when Riko dared him to trade his safety for Andrew's. Neil had been doing one stupid thing after another all year long and this had turned into the best year of his life.

That wasn't reason enough to accept this, but Neil wasn't willing to reject it, either. Time wasn't something he had a lot of, but it was going to take more than these frazzled moments to figure it out. Neil knew he wasn't in the right state of mind to decide one way or another. He stuffed his keys under his pillow and rolled onto his other side like that would change what had just happened. He told himself not to think about it right now, but his mouth still remembered the weight of Andrew's lips and that made his hair stand on end.

He distracted himself the only way he knew how, counting as high as he could in every language he knew. He didn't remember falling asleep, and he didn't know how long he was out before his phone hummed at him. The new message in his inbox was from an unfamiliar number, and all it said was "48". Neil deleted it and would have passed out again if not for the muffled sound of a TV in the next room. Neil searched for the strength to face the upperclassmen and found it closer than it'd been this morning. With a quiet sigh he kicked his blankets off, shut his alarm off, and climbed down from the loft.

Dan sat tucked against Matt's side on the couch. She snatched up the remote and cut the TV off as soon as she spotted Neil in the doorway. "We wake you?" she asked, and even though Neil shook his head said, "Sorry."

"I shouldn't sleep this late in the day anyway," Neil said.

He went to get a glass of water from the kitchen. He expected them to go back to whatever he'd interrupted, but when

[172]

he returned to the living room the TV was still dark. There was a silent conversation in the looks Matt and Dan sent each other. Neil didn't know which one of them won, but Matt shook his head and looked across the room at Neil.

"We wanted to throw you a birthday party," Matt said. "It doesn't seem right having a birthday and doing nothing for it. Renee thought it was a bad idea, though, to the point that she called Andrew for backup. He took her side."

Neil remembered a phone call waking him up as they turned into Alpharetta. Andrew had only listened for a moment before saying "Don't". Neil quietly took back every suspicious thought he'd had about Renee. Her serene veneer would probably always have him second-guessing her, but she understood the little things when it mattered most.

"Thank you, but they're right," Neil said. "I'd rather pretend it didn't happen."

"What if we skipped the party and just bought presents?" Dan asked, and sighed when Neil shook his head. "Fine, but if we let this go we're going to do something crazy on March 31st. Deal?"

"Define crazy," Neil said.

Dan smiled like he hadn't spoken. "Deal?"

"Deal," Neil said.

"Good," Dan said. "Now come on."

Neil joined them on the couch, and they turned their show back on. He might have forgotten about the text that woke him up if he didn't get a "47" message from a new number the following evening. Neil looked down at his phone in consternation as he realized someone was sending him a countdown. He pushed his schoolwork aside in favor of the calendar hanging from the kitchen fridge. He counted days with his fingers, flipping pages until he found March. For a moment he thought he'd get to Neil Josten's birthday, but he landed on Friday, March 9th. It was an odd day to end on. It was the last day before Palmetto State University's spring break. There was a

[173]

game that night, but it wasn't one of championships' two death matches.

Neil checked his phone again, debating whether or not to respond. In the end he deleted the text and went back to conjugating Spanish verbs.

-

The rest of the Foxes didn't find out until Monday morning that Andrew had replaced his wrecked car. Nicky trailed Neil across the parking lot, yammering away about a project he should have finished by today but was only halfway done with. When Andrew stopped walking, Nicky did too, but since Nicky didn't see the rental car he kept talking. He stopped when Andrew opened the driver's door. Nicky looked, did a double-take, and nearly fell down when he jumped back.

"No way!"

His yelp got the others' attention, and Matt was predictably the next to react. He bolted past Neil to stare at the car. "What are you doing with a Maserati?"

"Driving it," Andrew said, like it should be obvious, and got in the driver's seat.

Matt reached for the hood with both hands but didn't touch it, like he thought his fingerprints might ruin the perfect exterior. The blatant awe on his face had Neil looking to Andrew. Andrew met his gaze through the windshield but didn't hold it for long. He reached for the door to close it, but Matt darted around and put his hand in the way. He leaned over to look inside, owl-eyed and rapturous. Nicky had fewer reservations about putting his hands all over the new ride and he made a slack-jawed lap of the car.

"But when—?" Matt asked. "And how—?"

Allison was less tactful. "Did he steal it?"

Dan hissed at her to keep her voice down, but Allison shrugged her off.

Matt beckoned to Andrew. "Start it up! Let me hear it."

Andrew twisted the key in the ignition, and the car came to

[174]

life with a quiet roar. Matt threw his hands up and spun away like he was orchestrating a symphony. Andrew closed his door, so Matt wheeled back to Dan, sputtering facts and statistics that went way over Neil's head. Neil glanced at Aaron to gauge his reaction. Aaron looked torn, as if he wanted to be awed by the prestigious ride but couldn't let go of his resentment enough to be excited.

Kevin was rarely impressed by wealth thanks to his upbringing, and he'd been there when Andrew bought the car. He didn't have the patience to put up with his teammates' antics and he swept them all with an annoyed look.

"Don't make us late for practice."

"Whatever!" Nicky said, but he scrambled into the backseat. He'd taken to riding in the middle seat so he could keep Aaron and Neil away from each other. He didn't waste his time buckling but leaned between the front seats to stare at the dashboard. He was ooh-ing and ahh-ing when Neil and Aaron got in. Andrew tolerated it for a couple seconds before shoving him out of the way with a hand on his face. Nicky was too excited to be bothered. Instead of complaining, he said, "But seriously, Andrew. Where did you get this thing?"

"Georgia," Andrew said.

Nicky sighed but didn't ask again.

Andrew and Aaron still weren't talking, and Aaron and Neil stayed out of each other's way whenever possible, but the rest of the Foxes filled in the gaps as best they could. Riko's cruel prank last Friday brought out an unnecessary but well-meaning protective streak in the upperclassmen. Even Kevin made an effort to be more tolerable, maybe because he'd seen how shaken up Neil was on Saturday.

Neil could have told them all he was fine, but they were playing together better than they had in a week and he didn't want to rock the boat. The Foxes had one more game to get through for the first round. Their back-to-back wins meant they'd secured their spot in the death match, but they weren't willing to take it easy this week.

Neil tried stuffing Exy into every scrap of free time he had. He brought SUA tactics and line-ups to class with him to hide under his textbooks, and he met Kevin at the dining hall for lunch to argue plays. Despite the active effort he made to focus on Friday's game, his thoughts kept derailing without warning. Whenever Andrew crossed the room, Neil's gaze followed. Every time Neil took his keys out of his pocket and saw the newest addition to his set he remembered Andrew's kiss. He looked at Matt and Nicky to see if he saw them any differently, but nothing had changed. Neil didn't know what that meant, but he knew this still wasn't the time to figure it out. He should wait until next week, when the Foxes had a week off before the death match.

The perfect distraction from himself came on Wednesday, when Kengo Moriyama collapsed at a board meeting and was raced to the hospital in an ambulance. Wymack always kept the news on for background noise when he was working at the stadium, so he messaged his team a heads-up the second he heard. Neil was pretty sure there were microphones in Riko's face before Kengo was even checked in, and if he didn't hate Riko so much he'd be disgusted by the reporters' heartless enthusiasm.

He found snips of the interview online at the library computers between classes. Riko tolerated most of their prying questions with good grace and a calm demeanor, but the ugliness showed when he was asked if he was on his way to the hospital. The reporters knew full well that Kengo and Riko were estranged; they just didn't understand the severity of the separation. Kevin once told the Foxes Riko had never met his father or brother. The Moriyama family had no time to waste on second-born sons, so Riko was shipped to Tetsuji as soon as possible after birth.

The look Riko turned on the woman should have melted the microphone she was holding. "You are aware we have a game

[176]

tomorrow. My place is here with my team. If the doctors are worth their degrees they will return him to full health whether or not I am there to see it happen."

Neil got out his phone and texted Kevin. "Do you think it's serious?"

"It better not be," was Kevin's first response, and then, "Riko still believes he can win his father's attention with his fame. If the lord does not recover, Riko will take his anger and grief out on everyone around him."

Neil considered that, then said, "Good thing you're not there anymore."

"Jean still is," Kevin answered, and Neil knew better than to comment.

Neil's replacement gear showed up Thursday. Friday's away game against Arkansas meant an all-day drive. They were on the Fox bus before the sun came up and they stopped every four hours at rest stops. Neil finished his homework and studies with too much time to spare and got sick of his book halfway through. He knew SUA's line inside and out, so there was no point in reviewing it. He was tired from boredom, but not tired enough to sleep.

Kevin and Nicky were fast asleep and Andrew was staring out his window at nothing. Aaron was ignoring them as usual. Neil gave up on them as a source of entertainment and headed to the front of the bus, where the upperclassmen were caught up in a lively conversation. They didn't ask why he'd strayed from his usual seat but absorbed him into their group without hesitation. It didn't make the ride feel any shorter, but it was significantly less mind-numbing. How Wymack slept through their noise, Neil didn't know. Willpower, he guessed, because Wymack still refused to hire a driver and didn't want his Foxes staying in Arkansas overnight. He was bringing them back to South Carolina right after the game.

They got into town around six central time, two hours before serve. Dinner was at a local buffet, where they

[177]

desperately inhaled enough calories to get them through the game, and they had enough time afterward to walk slow laps around SUA's court. When the gates finally opened to let the crowd in, Wymack sent his Foxes to get ready.

SUA didn't play with the speed or aggression UT and Belmonte had brought to the court, but they were the most communicative team Neil had faced. They were constantly shouting back and forth to each other, calling openings and tracking each other's marks. They put up a fight, but they weren't awful about it. SUA had already lost out to both UT and Belmonte; winning against the Foxes wouldn't save them or their dignity.

By halftime the results from the other night's match were in: UT had slaughtered Belmonte and would proceed to the death match. Having a rival knocked out gave the Foxes the second wind they needed and they dominated the court through second half. The Foxes won by a comfortable margin, took their time washing off afterward, and were back on the bus by eleven. Neil found a message waiting for him when he turned his phone back on: "42".

He typed out a "Go away" but deleted it immediately. The last thing he wanted to do was encourage whoever was taunting him by acknowledging the messages. Neil shut his phone off again instead and went to celebrate with the upperclassmen.

CHAPTER TEN

A week without a match didn't lessen the intensity of their practices any, but Wymack built in a little elbow room where he could. It wasn't consideration but necessity: he'd made the first round of cuts with his stack of would-be Foxes and needed his team's help to narrow it down. The girls took to the task with enthusiasm Neil hadn't expected. He thought choosing their own replacements would be a bittersweet reminder they were graduating in a year. If any of them were aware that their time was running out, though, they gave no sign of it.

Less surprising was Kevin's scornful rejection of every file Wymack had to offer him. He insisted Wymack put out a second request, to which Wymack demanded Kevin be a little more accepting of strikers who hadn't been raised to be champions. Neil didn't have the experience or insight to argue with Kevin, but he quietly clung to one of the choices he'd made and refused to let it go. Kevin tried wrenching it from his hands only once before writing Neil off as a know-nothing and rounding on Wymack again. Abby stepped in when the argument got too loud and banished Wymack and Kevin to opposite ends of the locker room.

On Tuesday Kengo was released from the hospital. If he wasn't Riko's father, he might have made it home without question or fanfare, since Kengo Moriyama passed as just another wealthy businessman. As it was there were a couple reporters waiting on his doorstep. Kengo answered their questions with stony silence and let his assistants clear a path for him. HIPAA laws kept anyone from figuring out what had put him in the hospital in the first place, but he appeared to have recovered, so eventually the press gave up and moved on.

On Wednesday afternoon Andrew had his weekly session with Betsy Dobson, which meant his group would catch a ride with Matt. Kevin and Nicky were waiting for them in the hallway when Neil followed Matt out of their dorm room. Aaron was nowhere in sight. Neil locked the door behind him and looked to Nicky.

Nicky shook his head. "He said he was catching a ride with Andrew today."

"To the court?" Dan asked.

Neil considered Nicky's wide-eyed expression and guessed, "To Dobson's. Aaron wants to sit in with him."

"No shit," Matt said, startled. "You think so?"

"Crazy, right?" Nicky asked. "I said I didn't know Andrew agreed to it, and Aaron said Andrew didn't know what he was planning. Aaron hasn't come back yet, so either he's dead in the parking lot or he pulled it off. Guess he got tired of Katelyn avoiding him? Speaking of, one of these days I want you to tell me how you roped her into it."

"I asked," Neil said.

"There goes that 'asked' thing again," Matt said. "Does it mean something different where you come from?"

"Most of the time, yes," Neil said.

The unexpected honesty startled a laugh from Matt. Without Andrew and Aaron's antagonism throwing up roadblocks, it was easy for the Foxes to mingle. They went down the stairs a mixed group. Nicky checked the parking lot for signs of Aaron's gruesome demise and hoisted himself into Matt's truck with a wild grin when he found none. Despite that glee he was fast to volunteer Neil as spokesman when Wymack needed an explanation for Aaron's absence. Wymack responded by assigning the Foxes extra laps. Neil expected at least Nicky to grumble about it, but Nicky was so floored by his cousins' questionable progress he shouldered the work without complaint.

Andrew and Aaron had to notice the intense scrutiny they

were subjected to upon their eventual arrival, but neither one acknowledged the attention. The Foxes weren't suicidal enough to ask how it'd gone. Andrew looked unruffled, but Aaron's expression was downright vicious.

Wymack looked from one to the other. "Is this going to be an ongoing thing? I need to know how to plan around you."

"No," Andrew said.

Aaron flicked him an irritated look. "Yes."

"Okay," Wymack said, and that was that.

-

They didn't have a game on Friday, but the ERC finally posted the following week's line-up. Six teams from the evens bracket were proceeding to the death match, compared with eight from the odds. The Foxes would face the University of Vermont Catamounts at home. UT was up against Nevada and Washington State would take on Binghamton. In the odds bracket, the Big Three had miraculously avoided drawing each other's names. They'd all proceed to the third round, along with whichever team won the Oregon-Maryland match. There would be another week-long break between the death match and round three.

A free weekend meant they should have spent the night drinking in Columbia, but Aaron's stunt on Wednesday dragged the twins' cold war down to a whole new level. According to Nicky, Aaron was only at the dorm long enough to sleep or change clothes. Nicky assumed Aaron spent the rest of his free time with Katelyn. Neil hoped he was wrong. Katelyn might be willing to talk to Aaron again now that he'd put his foot down, but Andrew had a promise to keep and more reason now than ever to lash out at her. If Katelyn was smart she'd lie low for a couple weeks.

They couldn't go to Columbia without Aaron, so Nicky dragged Neil to their room instead. Aaron was missing, but Nicky and Andrew claimed the beanbag chairs and teamed up in a horror game. Neil had brought his backpack, but the creepy music and occasional on-screen scream were perfect excuses to not attempt any homework. He looked to Kevin, who unplugged his headphones from his laptop and motioned over his shoulder to the bedroom. Kevin grabbed the computer, so Neil fetched a notepad and closed the bedroom door behind them.

Kevin had a subscription to an Exy streaming site. He searched for Vermont's most recent game and turned the screen so they could both see. Neil took notes, Kevin absorbed what he could from watching, and they compared insights afterward. UVM had an imbalanced team: an intimidating defense backing up a mediocre offense line. Neil and Kevin would have their hands full, but at least their fractured backliners would have an easier time of things.

One game turned into two and would have become three if Nicky hadn't come looking for them. It took Nicky only a second to realize what they were doing and he flicked a dismayed look between them.

"You aren't serious. It's Friday night and this is how you're entertaining yourselves? Give me a break! Think about something else for a while, would you? Like ice cream. I thought we were going down to Columbia. My body's been ready for some ice cream all day long. I've been gypped and I demand compensation."

"That's not our problem," Kevin said.

"I'm making it your problem," Nicky said. "Neil, you're coming with me to the store."

"Go by yourself," Kevin said.

"Great idea," Nicky said. "Tiny flaw, though: I'm not on the insurance policy anymore and don't have a key to the new ride."

"You what?" Neil asked, startled.

Nicky shrugged and didn't explain. "Let's go, Neil. The games will still be there tomorrow. I'm here right now, I'm hungry, and I'm tired of you ignoring me in my own room."

Kevin opened another game and paused it so it could buffer. "Andrew can take you."

[182]

"I'm not talking to you anymore," Nicky said. "I'm talking to your mini-me."

"I," Neil started, but faltered when his phone buzzed.

He could guess what it was, but there was a chance it wasn't. He pulled his phone out of his pocket and flipped it open to read today's contribution to the countdown: "35". Neil gazed down at it in silence. If Neil believed in signs, this would be proof he should stay here with Kevin. They could get another match in before they had to crash for the night. One more game and he'd probably have names and numbers memorized. They had less than three months until finals. The Foxes couldn't afford a single misstep between here and there.

Neil looked up, ready to turn Nicky down, but Andrew had come up beside Nicky in the doorway. Neil looked at him and thought about Nicky's worried appeal last fall, the warning that one day Exy wouldn't be enough on its own. It could be a safe haven from his thoughts and a reason to get up and the inspiration to fight harder. It could mean the world to him, but it couldn't be everything. It couldn't fill in the broken pieces of him the way the Foxes did. It wouldn't drop everything to get him from the airport or come back for him without question or call him "friend". Neil built his life around Exy after his mother died because he needed something to live for, but Neil wasn't alone anymore.

Maybe he'd regret this on Monday when he was a thousand steps behind Kevin at practice, but it wasn't like Neil would ever catch up to him anyway. Neil snapped his phone shut and looked at Kevin. "What kind do you want?"

Kevin stared at him. "You're not leaving," he said, not quite a question.

"If we get into another one, we'll be up too late tonight. Pick a flavor."

Kevin didn't respond; maybe he was too disappointed in Neil to take the question seriously. Neil didn't care anymore what Kevin thought of him. Like he'd reminded Kevin the other

[183]

week, Kevin's journey didn't stop in May. He could spend every night watching endless replays and tactics because he had all the time in the world to spare.

Neil tucked his phone into his pocket and got to his feet. "Text Nicky when you make up your mind."

Nicky looked beside himself with glee over winning the tug-o-war. Neil let that self-satisfaction trump Kevin's attitude and led Nicky down to the car. Nicky chattered about Erik for most of the drive to the grocery store. Nicky was planning on spending most of May in Germany. His short reunion with Erik over Christmas break just made Nicky miss him more than ever, and Nicky was counting down days until they could see each other again. He was a little worried what Andrew and Aaron might do in his absence, but he trusted Neil to keep them both alive until the dorms reopened in June.

Kevin still hadn't messaged Nicky by the time they reached the ice cream aisle, so Nicky gave in and called him. Neil half-expected Kevin to ignore Nicky's call, but Kevin wasn't so sour with them that he'd turn down a free snack. Nicky paid for the pints before Neil could offer to get his own, and they headed back to the dorm with their haul.

Kevin was nowhere in sight but the bedroom door was closed again. Neil assumed he'd resumed watching matches alone. It bothered Neil for a moment that Kevin wasn't willing to wait for him, but he refused to regret his decision. Nicky grabbed spoons from the kitchen and distributed pints to their hungry owners. Neil checked his expression when Nicky came back from dropping Kevin's off, but Nicky just rolled his eyes at Neil and grinned again. Nicky tossed the empty plastic bag in the general direction of the garbage can and surveyed his DVD stand with his fists on his hips.

After a minute's serious study, Nicky complained, "There's nothing to watch. I'm going to scour Matt's collection."

He said it definitively, but he waited a beat in case Andrew shot that idea down. Neil looked from him to Andrew, who was

[184]

rolling his pint between his hands to soften it. When Andrew said nothing, Nicky vanished. Neil locked the door behind him and carried his ice cream to Andrew. He knelt on the floor near Andrew's beanbag chair and listened. He didn't hear the sound of a game coming from the bedroom, but Kevin's headphones weren't on his desk anymore. Neil set his ice cream and spoon to one side and turned a searching look on Andrew.

"Question," Neil said, but it took him a few moments to figure out the right words. "When you said you don't like being touched, is it because you don't like it at all or because you don't trust anyone else enough to let them touch you?"

Andrew glanced at him. "It doesn't matter."

"If it didn't, I wouldn't ask," Neil said.

"It doesn't matter to a man who doesn't swing," Andrew clarified.

Neil shrugged. "I don't because I've never been allowed to. The only thing I could think about growing up was surviving." Maybe that was why this was in that gray area of what was acceptable. It didn't matter that Andrew was a would-be sociopath or a man; the idea of Andrew was so intertwined with the idea of Neil's safety that this too was a means of self-preservation. "Letting someone in meant trusting them to not stab me in the back when terrible people came looking for me. I was too afraid to risk it, so it was easier to be alone and not think about it. But I trust you."

"You shouldn't."

"Says the man who stopped." Neil gave Andrew a few moments to respond before saying, "I don't understand it, and I don't know what I'm doing, but I don't want to ignore it just because it's new. So are you completely off-limits or are there any safe zones?"

"What are you hoping for, coordinates?"

"I'm hoping to know where the lines are before I cross them," Neil said, "but I'm open to drawing a map on you if you want to loan me a marker. That's not a bad idea."

"Everything about you is a bad idea," Andrew said, as if Neil didn't already know that.

"I'm still waiting for an answer."

"I'm still waiting for a yes or no I actually believe," Andrew returned.

"Yes."

Neil took the pint from Andrew's unresisting fingers, stacked it on top of his, and leaned in. He stopped shy of actually kissing Andrew, not daring to touch him until Andrew gave him a green light. Andrew's expression didn't change but there was a subtle shift in his body's tension that told Neil he'd gotten Andrew's attention. Neil lifted a hand but stopped it a safe difference from Andrew's face. Andrew caught hold of his wrist and squeezed in warning.

"It's fine if you hate me," Neil said.

It was the truth, if a bit of an understatement. So long as Andrew was only physically attracted to Neil, this was safe to experiment with. Neil's death wouldn't be more than a faint inconvenience to Andrew.

"Good," Andrew said, "because I do."

For a second Neil thought Andrew would push him away and be done with this. Andrew did push, but he followed Neil down. The short carpet was rough against Neil's knuckles where Andrew pinned his hand over his head. Neil couldn't complain when Andrew was an unyielding weight on top of him. He started to reach for Andrew again but stopped himself halfway there. Andrew snagged that hand too and held it down out of the way.

"Stay," Andrew said, and leaned down to kiss him.

Time was nothing. Seconds were days, were years, were the breaths that caught between their mouths and the bite of Neil's fingernails against his palms, the scrape of teeth against his lower lip and the warm slide of a tongue against his. He could feel Andrew's heartbeat thrumming against his wrists, a staccato rhythm that echoed in Neil's veins. How a man who viewed the

[186]

world with such studied disconnect could kiss like this, Neil didn't know, but he wasn't going to complain.

Neil had forgotten what it was like to be touched without malicious intent. He'd forgotten what body heat felt like. Everything about Andrew was hot, from the hands holding him down to the mouth steadily taking Neil apart. Neil finally understood why his mother thought this was so dangerous. This was distraction and indiscretion, avoidance and denial. It was letting his guard down, letting someone in, and taking comfort in something he shouldn't have and couldn't keep. Right now, Neil needed it too much to care.

It didn't—couldn't—last long, because Kevin was in the next room and Nicky was just two doors down, but Neil's mouth was numb and his thoughts buzzed to incoherency by the time a thump said Nicky had walked into the locked door. Neil fought back a flash of irritation as Andrew pushed himself up and away from Neil. Neil tried to call to Nicky to wait a moment, but he didn't have the breath to speak.

Andrew studied Neil's expression for a few seconds, then got to his feet and started for the door. Neil pushed himself up with unsteady hands and retreated to Kevin's desk with his ice cream. Getting the plastic safety seal off was the hardest thing he'd done all year, but at least it gave him an excuse to not look at Nicky. Nicky grumbled about being locked out of his own room as he came through the doorway, but by the time he made it to his beanbag chair he'd already forgotten it in favor of the movies he'd borrowed.

"Look, you guys get to vote this time," Nicky said, like he was doing them a huge favor. He rattled off titles and lead actors. Neil let the list go in one ear and out the other. He recognized most of the actors' names after living with the Foxes for so long, but he didn't know any of the movies. He didn't care right now, anyway, and it didn't take Nicky long to catch on. "Hello, Earth to Neil. You even listening to me?"

Neil looked at the half-moon marks he'd left on his palm.

[187]

"You choose."

"You two are the least helpful people in the entire universe," Nicky complained, but it took him only a second to make up his mind. The case snapped opened and closed as he popped the DVD out. Neil listened to beans crunch as Nicky got comfortable in his chair. Neil didn't hear Andrew getting settled again, but he didn't trust himself enough to look and see where Andrew was. "Come on, Neil!"

Neil couldn't come up with an excuse to stall longer. "I'm coming."

The overhead lights cut off then, which meant Andrew had stayed by the door after letting Nicky in. Thinking that Andrew needed space and time to regroup the same way Neil did almost wrecked Neil's attempts to get his neutral facade back together. The chilly ice cream was a little more helpful at sucking the heat from his skin, so Neil held tight to it and got up from the desk. There wasn't room to sit between the beanbag chairs and he couldn't look like he was avoiding Andrew, so he sat on the floor to Andrew's left.

Nicky got the movie started as soon as Andrew joined them. Neil watched it so he wouldn't stare at Andrew, but if someone asked him later what it was about he wouldn't be able to tell them. He was sure he still felt Andrew's heartbeat on his skin when he went to bed a few hours later.

-

Neil had survived more than a few hectic weeks growing up, but the week leading up to the Foxes' first death match was almost enough to rattle even him. His teammates' stress levels were through the roof and Neil couldn't help but be affected by their quiet panic. Dan tried playing it cool, but Neil could hear the strain in her voice as she directed her team at practices. Allison harped at the fractured defense line any chance she got, and Kevin was awful to all of them. Matt was marginally better at keeping his act together, but the further into the week they got the more restless and anxious he seemed.

[188]

Even Renee was feeling it, though she hid it well. When her friends were around she was the perfect rock to lean on, as encouraging and pleasant as always. It was a different story when she was walking laps on break with just Neil and Andrew. She admitted to nothing, but she looked a little more tired every day. Neil knew better than to ask her if she was all right. She might feel obligated to put on a smile for him, too, when what she really needed was time to catch her breath and soothe her own nerves.

It took Neil a couple days to realize it wasn't the Foxes draining most of her energy. Renee rarely said anything on their walks anymore, too intent on what was happening on her phone. The occasional unhappy twitch at the corner of her mouth said her text conversations with Jean weren't going well.

Afternoon scrimmages had all of them walking away bruised and sore. Kevin and Neil pulled out all the stops to get around their teammates, and their backliners pushed back as hard as they could. Despite the aches Neil took home with him, the only thing he could think about over dinner was getting back to the court that night.

When Neil drove Kevin to the court Wednesday night, he said, "We should have brought Andrew with us."

"No," Kevin said. "I told you: he must come with us of his own volition. It means nothing if he agrees for our sake."

"I know what you said," Neil said, "but we need more practice against a guarded goal."

"It would not do us any good," Kevin said. "Your target is not the goalkeeper: it is the goal itself. Goalkeepers change every week. No two have the same strengths or styles. Why obsess over besting one man when it has no effect on the rest? Perfect your own performance and it won't matter who is in goal."

"I'm just saying—"

"Continue arguing with me and you will be practicing alone tonight."

Neil scowled out the windshield and went quiet. Despite his annoyance, Neil thought about Kevin's words the remainder of the drive. He couldn't make sense of them, but he refused to ask Kevin to explain. Goalkeepers weren't invisible obstacles. They were the last line of defense for their teams and usually the most agile players on the court. Scoring wasn't just landing a ball within the marked goal lines; it was getting the ball to that point in a way the goalkeeper couldn't predict or deflect.

It still bothered Neil the next day, so he asked the Foxes' goalies about it on break Thursday afternoon. Renee turned her phone over in her hands as she considered it. Andrew didn't even acknowledge the question.

"It's an interesting idea," Renee said, "and it seems to be working for him. Asking someone to change his mindset and approach is a tall order, though, especially so late in the season. Then again," she said after a moment, "you did change racquets mid-season."

"A racquet is one thing," Neil said. "I don't think I can do this."

"If you don't want to, don't," Renee said, as if it was that simple to turn Kevin down. "If you want to try, we will help you any way I can."

"No," Andrew said before Neil could answer. "Stop copying him."

"I'm trying to get better," Neil said. "I can't improve on my own."

Andrew flicked him a bored look and said nothing else. Neil gave him a minute then planted himself in front of Andrew when he realized Andrew really wasn't planning on elaborating or explaining. Renee quietly put her phone away and looked between them. Her gaze lingered on Neil, but Neil didn't return it. He searched Andrew's calm expression for answers.

"Why shouldn't I copy him?" Neil asked.

"You are never going to play like he does," Andrew said. Before Neil could take that as an insult against his potential,

Andrew continued. "He is a fool whose style is numbers and angles. Formulas and statistics, trial and error, repetition and insanity. All he cares about is finding the perfect game."

"Is that so bad?"

"Don't ask stupid questions."

"Don't make me."

"A junkie like you can't be that cold," Andrew said.

"I'm not a junkie."

Andrew just looked at him, so Renee broke in with a careful, "I think he means to say Kevin is very analytical, whereas you're passionate. You both care about winning, but not in the same way."

Andrew said nothing to confirm or deny that interpretation, so Neil stepped out of his way. Andrew continued on, done with this conversation. Renee remained behind with Neil but said nothing else. Neil gazed after Andrew as he considered their take on it. If Andrew was right, Kevin didn't care about goalkeepers because he was a technical player. His focus was on perfecting impossible shots and tricky angles. He played against himself, not the goalkeeper, so the goalie was always an afterthought.

Andrew was right. Neil couldn't play like that. Learning Kevin's tricks was necessary to his development as a player, but Neil could never implement them the exact same way on the court. Neil was too aware of the obstacles and his thrill came in outsmarting his marks. He liked being the better, faster player. He liked frantic plays, close calls, and heart-stopping goals. It didn't have to be pretty or perfect so long as they won in the end.

Understanding took the edge off last night's lingering tension. As Neil relaxed he realized Renee was still watching him. She smiled when Neil looked at her and tipped her head a beckon to come along. They started after Andrew and walked their last lap in comfortable silence.

-

When the Foxes hit the court February 9th, no one was expecting the fight they brought to it. Forty-five minutes into the game, the Catamounts were trailing by three points. On the TV in the Foxes' locker room, the sportscasters were shaking their heads in amazement.

"I'm with you on this one, Marie. I'm not entirely sure who we're looking at now or what they did with last year's Foxes, but they've completely blown me away."

Neil glanced at the TV as he stretched. The two were reporting live from inside the Foxhole Court, a few feet from the Foxes' empty benches. It was hard to hear them over the noise from the stands, especially when Rocky Foxy the mascot went wheeling by.

"Quite honestly, I never expected them to finish the season," Marie said. "The number of setbacks they've endured this year is unbelievable and I was sure they'd bow out in November. It's a serious credit to this year's line-up that they've made it this far. This is the first Fox roster that actually embraces teamwork."

"Indeed," her male counterpart agreed. "This is the kind of synchrony you expect from top-notch schools. A few weeks ago we all laughed when freshman Neil Josten said the Foxes were raring for a rematch with the Ravens. No one's laughing now. If they can keep this momentum and keep playing like they are tonight, they stand a real chance of proceeding to semifinals."

"Ten minutes left of halftime," Marie said. "The score is six-three. It's going to take some serious footwork for the Catamounts to recover. We're less than an hour from seeing if the Foxes can secure their first death match victory. Let's take a look at some highlights from the first half, and then—"

Dan turned the TV off and stood in front of the dark screen. Matt gave her a minute, then touched her shoulder to get her attention. She answered his questioning look with a wry smile.

"It's weird hearing them say good things about us," she said.

"It took them long enough," Allison huffed.

"It took us long enough to earn their consideration," Renee

pointed out, not unkindly.

The seniors exchanged a long look, exhausted and triumphant. The Foxes' first line-up had crashed and burned two steps out of the starting gate, and halfway through the season they'd been the laughingstock of the sport. The girls came to Palmetto State University knowing it'd take work to salvage that sour reputation and knowing Wymack was their only ally. Exy was a co-ed sport but women were vastly outnumbered in the NCAA. Even fewer made it to major leagues and professional teams. The school board approved the three on Wymack's say-so but their own teammates made their lives a living hell. Despite every loss and every roadblock, they'd made it, and now they were finally getting the nod they deserved.

"All right," Dan said, turning away from the TV.

Her gaze lingered for a moment on the newest addition to the locker room: a mahogany stand in the corner near Andrew and Neil's picture. She'd said last month she wanted a stand for their eventual championship trophy. Neil thought she'd been talking big to inspire the team, but apparently not. Allison found the perfect one yesterday after dinner. When Neil and Kevin came to the court to practice last night they'd found the upperclassmen getting the stand situated.

Dan smiled, short and fierce, and looked around at her teammates. "I'm in the mood to completely ruin the Catamounts' night. Anyone with me?"

"Let's do it," Matt said with a toothy grin. "What've you got for us, Coach?"

Wymack ran down the first-half pointers as quickly as he could and led them back to the court when the warning buzzer sounded. UVM came out as strong as they could at serve, angered by first half's results and spurred on by their coaches' halftime rants. They were an entirely new monster, but Neil squished his flicker of panic. Losing his cool here would only destroy the Foxes' chances. He focused only on what he and Kevin could control and trusted his teammates to handle their side of court.

Twenty minutes into second half, the score still hadn't budged. Neil and Kevin couldn't get around their fresh backliners, and the UVM strikers couldn't get past Andrew. The game hadn't been friendly before but as tempers flared and patience thinned, play got a little rougher. Neil was used to a bit of back-and-forth shoving with his marks as they waited for the ball to come their way, but this aggressive pushing had him skidding across the floor. Neil gritted his teeth and pushed back, but his backliner had a half-foot and forty pounds on him; he wasn't going anywhere without some violence.

A fight was coming; they all knew it. It was just a toss-up as to which player snapped first. Surprisingly—or not—it was Andrew.

After smashing another ball up-court, Andrew beat his racquet against the wall and called Nicky. Neil only had a half-second to see Nicky wheel toward the goal; the ball was on its way to Kevin and that was more important than what was happening at the far end of court. Kevin couldn't get past his backliner and was in a bad angle to pass to Neil, so he flicked the ball to Dan. Dan shouldered her mark out of the way and raced up the court to buy the strikers room. She heaved the ball to the far wall so it'd rebound to the strikers. Neil and Kevin raced for it, but the goalkeeper took a running leap to get the ball first. He popped it up toward the ceiling at a steep angle and it came back down at mid-court between the dealers and Foxes' defense.

Nicky's mark started for it, and Nicky swept his legs out from under him with his racquet. Such a blatant foul brought the entire game to a screeching halt, at least until Nicky's striker found his feet again. He came at Nicky with fists flying, but Andrew was already there. He thrust his racquet out lengthways between them and used it to shove the furious striker away from his cousin. The striker was almost stupid enough to take a swing at Andrew instead, but Matt and his mark intervened.

By then the referees were on court, and Nicky blew them a kiss when he was handed his red card. He sailed off the court like a triumphant champion, both fists high in the air and grinning ear to ear. Aaron came on to replace him, and the teams prepped for a foul shot. Neil was smiling as he took his place. He glanced down the line at Kevin. Kevin was already braced to run, confident in Andrew's ability to defend the shot.

Andrew did, and like always, he fired the rebound where Neil could get it. Neil tore off up the court like his father was on his heels, and there was nothing his striker could do to stop him. A glance at Kevin showed his mark was too close for a safe pass. Neil snagged the ball and passed it to himself instead, hitting the ground low where it'd bounce off the wall a few feet from goal. The goalkeeper took a swing for it, but Neil was just quick enough. He grabbed the ball, twisted his racquet out of the way in the nick of time, and fired at the goal. He was going too fast and was too close to the wall to stop, but he had just enough space to turn. He crashed shoulder blade first, back and helmet next, and grunted as the breath was crushed from his lungs.

Neil didn't care about the pain; the goal was red and the buzzer was deafening in his ears. He stumbled away from the wall, using his racquet as a cane until he found his balance again, and gasped air back into his aching body. The goalkeeper snarled something rude at him, but Neil tuned it out with the ease of long practice. His teammates caught up with him on his way across the court. Neil clacked sticks and accepted their excited congratulations, but all that mattered was getting through them to the goal. Neil didn't have a lot of time left before the referees could dock them for stalling play, so he jogged the rest of the way to Andrew.

"Nicky's not a fighter," Neil said. "You told him to take a swing."

"It was getting boring," Andrew said.

Neil grinned. "Now are you having fun?"

"That part was vaguely interesting," Andrew said. "I can

[195]

take or leave the rest."

"It's a start," Neil said, and headed to half-court.

Ten minutes later, Kevin exploited the Catamounts' rattled nerves and scored. The Catamounts didn't score again at all, though they tried with a ferocity borne of desperation. Andrew stopped every shot on goal and bounced a couple rebounds off the strikers' helmets just to rile them further. The stands were in an uproar the entire last minute on the clock. With five seconds left in the game Dan threw her racquet aside and took a running leap into Matt's arms.

The buzzer sounded on an eight-three win. They'd dominated the first death match and were on to round three for the first time ever. Dan had Matt's helmet off by the time the Foxes caught up to her and kissed him to the roar of crowd. Kevin and Aaron clacked sticks and exchanged triumphant looks.

Neil was dimly aware of the subs tearing across the court toward them, but he looked past them to where Andrew was standing alone in goal. He'd already set his racquet aside and was busy undoing his gloves. He had to know this was a historic night for the Foxes, and Neil knew he could hear the crowd losing its mind, but Andrew was unhurried and uninterested. Whatever had inspired him to intervene earlier was long gone. Neil hadn't honestly expected this to be the game that finally got through to Andrew, but that didn't make it easier to see him regress.

Nicky was a perfectly-timed distraction, barreling into Aaron and Neil nearly hard enough to take them off their feet. He hooked his arms around their shoulders and gave them a back-cracking squeeze.

"Can you believe it?" he asked, amazed. "We are such hot shit sometimes!"

Allison gave Neil's shoulder a thump on her way past them to Dan and Matt. Renee snagged Kevin for a quick hug before looping arms with Allison and Dan. Dan was laughing, giddy

[196]

with impossible success. Matt left them to each other and slung an arm around Kevin's shoulders. Neil looked from one happy face to another, savoring and memorizing this moment.

Andrew missed the half-court party, but he showed up in time to follow his teammates past the Catamounts' line-up. Wymack, Abby, and two cameras were waiting for them when they filed off the court. Dan flashed the cameras a toothy grin before hugging both Wymack and Abby. Neil joined his teammates in waving up at the stands but was quick to abandon the girls to the reporters' microphones and questions.

Wymack was waiting for them in the lounge when they were all showered and dressed. He did a quick headcount and nodded when he found all nine accounted for. "Remember when I told you not to make plans for tonight?" He jerked his thumb at Abby. "We're going to her place. That's 'we' as in everyone." He sent a significant look at Andrew's group. "Consider this a mandatory team event. Abby's already agreed to cook for us, and I spent most of the morning stocking her cabinets with booze."

"Was that a vote of confidence or plans for a consolation party?" Dan asked.

"Doesn't matter," Wymack said. "Let's go. I'm starving and I really need a cigarette."

Security guards helped them to get to their cars. Traffic made the ride to Abby's five times longer than it should have been, but the Foxes were in too good of moods to really care.

Abby's fridge was full of covered dishes she'd prepped earlier in the day. She popped a couple pans in the oven while Wymack and Dan poured drinks. Kevin stayed in the kitchen when Wymack and Dan started talking about the night's game. Matt commandeered the sound system in the other room. Nicky and Allison argued with all of his choices and each other, but they didn't sound serious so Neil didn't intervene. Aaron had claimed a chair by the window and was watching them with a distant look on his face. He shot Neil a dirty look when he realized Neil was watching him, but Neil waved him off and went in search of the absentee goalkeepers. He didn't waste time going down the hall, since the only rooms back that way were bedrooms, but went out onto the front porch.

Andrew was sitting on the hood of his car with Renee standing in front of him. Renee glanced at the house at the sound of the door and motioned for Neil to join them. When Neil was halfway there, though, Renee turned away from Andrew and headed up the sidewalk. She flashed Neil a smile on her way by but said nothing. Neil wondered what he'd interrupted and whether or not he should apologize. He didn't have time to make up his mind before Renee disappeared inside. Neil took the spot she'd just abandoned and studied Andrew's blank face.

"We won," Neil said. He waited, but of course Andrew didn't respond to that. Neil tried to stamp out his frustration but couldn't stop all of a sigh. "Would it kill you to let something in?"

"It almost did last time," Andrew said.

He said it matter-of-factly, but Neil still winced when he realized his misstep. He reached out but stopped his hand a careful distance from Andrew's arm. Andrew's long sleeves and bands hid his scars but Neil remembered how they felt under his fingers.

"This is different," Neil said. "The only one in your way now is you. You really could be Court one day, but you can't get there if you won't try." Neil waited, but Andrew stared wordlessly back at him. Neil could win a stare-down with almost anyone else, but he didn't have the patience to fight Andrew tonight. "Andrew, talk to me."

"You sound like a wind-up doll with only one topic," Andrew said. "I have nothing to say to you."

"If I talk about something else, will you talk to me?"

Andrew quirked a brow at him. "Can you talk about something else?"

That stung. Neil opened his mouth to snap something back, but words failed him. The small talk that kept their teammates

[198]

entertained so easily meant nothing to either of them. Neil didn't want to talk about movies and classes with Andrew. He wanted to talk about tonight's unprecedented win. He wanted to talk about their chances of breaking through round three for another death match. He wanted to talk about the look on Riko's face when the Foxes faced them again in May. He wanted to savor this win, not write it off as something trivial and uninteresting.

The front door opened. Nicky held onto the doorframe but leaned out to call to them, "Drinks are ready! You coming or what?"

Andrew pushed Neil out of the way and slid off the car. "Too late."

Neil was too disgruntled to stop him. He stayed by the car until Andrew caught up to Nicky, then finally set off toward the house. Halfway across the lawn his phone went off. Neil was annoyed enough to answer tonight's "28" in his inbox with an "Enough".

No one responded.

CHAPTER ELEVEN

The rules changed in round three. Up until now a team's chances depended solely on its ability to win as many games as possible. From here through finals, the emphasis switched to points. The three schools that had survived the evens-bracket death match would face off against each other over the next three weeks. Whichever two teams netted the most points between the games would proceed to the second elimination round. Technically a team could lose both games and still advance, but that hadn't happened in years.

Because of the odd number of teams, the Foxes would play Nevada home on February 23rd, have the following week off, and face off against Binghamton in an away game on March 9th. The week between the death match and Nevada's game was a rest week, but the Foxes weren't willing to take it easy. They were as inspired by as they were terrified of their win on Friday, and they didn't want to lose momentum. Luckily for them there was no way they could slow down. Wymack kept them ramped up until Thursday.

A TV crew came by the Foxhole Court Thursday afternoon to film a segment on the Foxes for their NCAA show. Neil thought Kevin would argue, since the interviews and filming meant practice was a stop-and-start broken mess, but Kevin knew how badly the Foxes needed good publicity. Neil had almost forgotten how pleasant Kevin could be when there was a camera in his face. Neil stifled the urge to call Kevin out on his act and avoided the microphones as much as possible.

Neil couldn't escape the spotlight forever. Wymack and Kevin both watched over the reporter's head when Neil was finally singled out for an interview. Neil answered Kevin's

[200]

warning stare with a placid look and attempted to remain civil for as long as he could. It was easy at first, since most of the questions were about the Foxes' progress. It was inevitable they'd finish up with a question about Riko and the Ravens. Neil tried for something neutral, but the interviewer took a good-natured jab at his newfound discretion.

"The last time I said something no one wanted to hear, my school got vandalized," Neil said. "I was trying to prevent collateral damage this time. But you know what? You're right. I can't afford to be quiet. Silence means I condone their behavior, and that's a dangerous illusion. I'm not going to forgive or tolerate them just because they're talented and popular. Let me answer that question again, okay?

"Yes," Neil said. "I am a thousand percent sure we are going to face the Ravens in finals this spring, and I know for a fact we are going to win this time. And when the nation's best loses to a nine-man 'know-nothing' team—when they lose to a team their own coach likened to feral dogs—Edgar Allan is going to have to change things up. Personally I think they should start by demanding Coach Moriyama's resignation."

The noise Kevin made wasn't human. The interviewer and his cameraman both shot startled looks over their shoulder at him. Kevin didn't stick around long enough for them to ask but bolted down the hall out of sight. Wymack, despite having complained numerously and at length about Neil's attitude problem, flashed his teeth in a fierce smile. Neil answered the interviewer's curious stare with a blank look and waited for the signal that he was done. As soon as the camera was off he headed back to the court. Unsurprisingly, Kevin ignored him the rest of the day.

Neil had a feeling practice that night would be chilly and silent. Matt drew the same conclusion and wished Neil a cheery good luck before heading out to a late dinner date with Dan. Neil locked the door behind him, checked the clock, and spent the next half hour toiling through math problems. He was on the last one when there was a single rap at his door. It wasn't Kevin's imperious knock or Nicky's enthusiastic rat-tat-tat, but the upperclassmen wouldn't drop by when Matt and Dan were both out. Neil pushed his schoolwork aside and went to investigate.

Andrew stood in the hallway, hands stuffed inside the front pocket of a dark hoodie. Neil opened the door wider and stepped out of the way. Andrew glanced past him before entering the room. Neil guessed he was looking for an audience, so explained, "Matt went out with Dan for a couple hours. Are you coming with us to the court?"

"Entertain yourself tonight." Andrew invited himself the kitchen and opened the fridge. "Kevin is too drunk to curse your name, much less stand up and hold a racquet."

"He what?" Neil asked, but Andrew didn't waste his breath repeating it. Neil looked down the hall like he could somehow see Kevin in his wretched state. "Coward."

"Don't sound surprised," Andrew said. "It is nothing new."

"I thought I'd gotten through to him last time," Neil admitted. He closed the door and propped his shoulder against the kitchen doorframe. "On a scale of one to ten, how bad do you think this will get?"

"How bad can it?" Andrew returned. "Riko can't kill you yet, and Moriyama already told the Raven fans to stay out of it."

"They could still disqualify us somehow," Neil said. "They got their showdown last October. Since they don't think we can make it to finals there's no reason for them to tolerate us any longer."

"They don't have a choice anymore. If the Ravens don't let us run our course there will always be room for doubt and speculations. The Ravens can't share their throne with what-ifs. They have to be supreme victors." Andrew gave that a moment to sink in before saying, "I'm undecided."

"About our chances this spring?" Neil asked.

Andrew held his hands palm-up between them. "The thought that you've unintentionally conned them into this corner is intolerable, as it means you're stupider than even I gave you credit for. If you did it knowingly, however, you're cleverer than you've led me to believe. That means the Ravens aren't the only ones you're playing with. One of these is the lesser evil."

"Not everything's a con," Neil said. Andrew didn't answer, but Neil read his calm expression as disbelief. Neil considered defending himself and decided it a waste of energy. Andrew wouldn't believe him anyway. "Which one is the lesser evil?"

"I'm undecided," Andrew said again.

"That's helpful," Neil muttered. "You could just ask."

"Why bother?" Andrew asked with a slight shrug. "I'll figure it out eventually."

Andrew stole a beer from the fridge and worked the tab back and forth. Neil watched him for a moment before looking across the room at his desk. He was annoyed with Kevin for canceling practice, but he knew a free evening was a lucky break. He had a math test next week and a paper due tomorrow that he hadn't started yet. Midterms weren't far away and Neil's grades were straddling their usual shaky line. This was the perfect night to play catch-up.

A metal tab bounced off his cheek. Neil looked back at Andrew and was suddenly keenly aware of Matt's absence. It'd been over a week since Andrew pushed Neil down and kissed him. They hadn't been alone long enough to do anything since.

He didn't know if Andrew saw that understanding on his face or if Andrew had just wanted his undivided attention. Andrew set the beer aside without taking a sip and closed the fridge door with his foot. It took two steps to close the small space between them and Andrew stopped as close as he could get without actually leaning against Neil. His fingers were cold from the can when he curled them around Neil's chin.

"Yes or no?" Andrew asked.

"Yes," Neil said.

Andrew sent a significant look down at Neil's arms where they were folded across his chest. It took Neil a moment to catch

[203]

on, and then he dropped his arms and stuffed his hands in his jeans pockets. Andrew waited until he'd gone still before kissing him. Neil stopped thinking about classes, Exy, and Kevin's liquid spine and let Andrew kiss him senseless. He was cotton-headed and unsteady by the time Andrew pressed his other hand flat against Neil's abdomen. Every nerve ending from his chest down seemed to twitch in response. Neil clenched his hands into fists like that would keep them where they were and let Andrew back him into the wall.

His phone hummed as he received his daily countdown, and pressed against the wall it sounded obnoxiously loud. Andrew let go of Neil's chin and fished the phone out of his back jeans pocket. He leaned back a bit as he held the phone up in offering. Neil half-expected him to open it and was relieved Andrew didn't. Neil took his phone and tossed it out of their reach without bothering to open the text. He knew what day it was; he knew how little time was left. He didn't care to see it, especially right now.

Andrew watched the phone bounce off the couch and skitter across the carpet. It was a toss-up whether or not he'd ask. Neil kissed his neck, hoping to distract him, and was rewarded with a startled jolt. That was enough reason to do it again. Andrew pushed his face away, but they were standing too close together for Neil to miss the way he shivered. Andrew kissed him before Neil could say anything about it.

Andrew pushed him harder into the wall, mapping him out through his shirt from shoulders to waist and back again. He'd had his hands on Neil's bare skin just a couple weeks ago when he saw Neil's scars, but this felt completely different. This was Andrew learning every inch and edge of him. His hands had never felt this heavy or hot before. Every press and demanding slide of his fingers sent heat curling through Neil's veins. It made Neil restless, made him anxious, made him lean a little deeper into Andrew's kisses and made him too aware of the denim trapping his hands at his hips.

[204]

Neil couldn't remember the last time he'd put hands on someone. It wasn't the girl in Canada—maybe the girl before. For the first time he considered touching Andrew like that and learning Andrew's body the way Andrew was memorizing his. He wanted to find the places that made Andrew give ground.

He hadn't said that aloud, but as if on cue Andrew followed Neil's arms down to his wrists and poked his fingers into Neil's pockets. He was making sure Neil's hands were still there, Neil guessed, so Neil twisted his hands deeper in response. Andrew caught hold of his wrists and squeezed to stop him. After a moment's consideration he pulled Neil's hands free and held them up by his head.

He kissed Neil like he wanted to bruise his lips and leaned back to fix Neil with an intense stare. "Just here."

"Okay," Neil said, and dug his fingers into Andrew's hair as soon as Andrew's grip went slack. It wasn't much but it was a desperate relief having something to hold onto. Maybe that low rush in his gut was from being trusted enough to reach out at all. Neil would figure it out later. All that mattered now was how easy it was to pull Andrew in for another kiss.

Andrew slowly let go of his wrists and placed a hand flat on Neil's chest. They stood like that an age, Andrew testing Neil's control and Neil content to kiss their mouths numb. Andrew's hand between his legs was an unexpected weight. Neil didn't realize how tight he twisted his fingers in Andrew's hair until Andrew bit his lower lip in warning. Neil grumbled something incoherent and forcibly loosened his death grip. He thought he tasted blood, but it was a fleeting tang quickly forgotten as Andrew got his button and zipper undone.

Andrew wasn't gentle, but Neil didn't want him to be. Neither of them had the constitution for tenderness. This was ruthless, almost angry, Andrew's hand taking Neil as far and fast as he could go. Neil tried pulling Andrew closer, but Andrew kept a hand flat on Neil's chest to keep space between their bodies. Neil barely managed Andrew's name before Andrew

[205]

pushed him over the edge and kept going. Andrew smothered his frantic gasp with a last hard kiss and finally let go of him.

They stood cheek-to-cheek a minute, an hour, a day, Neil's heart pounding in his temples and overloaded nerves shuddering. Coherent thought came back in lazy, fractured pieces and the first thing Neil was really aware of was how tight Andrew's fingers were digging into his chest. Neil tried to look down, but Andrew gave him a short shove in response.

"What about—" Neil started.

Andrew cut him off with a low, "Don't."

"You can't go back to Kevin and Nicky like that."

"I said be quiet."

"You said 'don't'," Neil said.

Neil flexed his fingers in Andrew's hair, fixing his grip so he could tug Andrew into a short kiss. Andrew tolerated it for only a moment before leaning back. He wiped his hand on Neil's shirt before tugging at Neil's wrists. Neil obediently let go of him and didn't miss the way Andrew watched him lower his hands. Neil didn't know if he could get them back in his pockets without brushing up against Andrew, so he tucked them behind his back instead. Andrew eased back out of Neil's space and dropped his hands.

"Go," Andrew said.

"Where?" Neil asked.

"Anywhere I can't see you," Andrew said.

Neil wouldn't live long enough to understand all the broken layers of Andrew's sexuality, but he at least knew better than to be offended by that dismissal. He waited until Andrew was far enough back that he could step away from the wall without bumping into him. The room was set up so his desk was partially out of sight from the door, but Neil went to the bedroom instead. He dug the knuckle of his thumb into his swollen lower lip and winced a little at the sting. He peeled his shirt over his head, bundled it up to hide the mess, and stuffed it into his laundry basket. He traded his jeans for sweats, scrounged up an old tee to

[206]

wear, and leaned against his bed to wait.

Before long he heard the sink cut on. Neil waited until it stopped, then went in search of Andrew. Andrew had his back propped against the fridge as he drank his stolen beer. He didn't look up when Neil appeared in the doorway and if he noticed the once-over Neil gave him he didn't acknowledge it. He drank his beer in silence, looking calm and clean like nothing had happened, and Neil watched until he crumpled the empty can in his hands. Andrew left the can on the counter for Neil to deal with and turned toward the door. Neil stepped aside to let him out and Andrew left without a word. Neil locked the door behind him and put the can in Matt's small recycle bin.

He went back to his desk, but he got nothing else done that night.

-

Neil spent Friday night in Andrew's room, but he only watched one match with Kevin. The rest of the night was spent half-buried in a beanbag chair with an oversized controller in his hands. Nicky was a surprisingly patient teacher as he walked Neil through his favorite game, but the copious amounts of alcohol he was drinking made his instructions steadily more unclear. Neil was ready to call it a night by two in the morning, but Nicky was wired from sugary mixers and another pint of store-bought ice cream.

Andrew spent most of the evening smoking on his desk and staring into space. He disappeared into the bedroom around three and kicked Kevin out so he could sleep. Kevin put his laptop back on his desktop, turned the TV down to near-mute, and went to bed. Nicky waited until the door closed behind him before turning the sound back up a bit. He grumbled loudly as he got comfortable again. Despite his protests, he tuckered out not even half an hour later. He dropped his controller to one side and looked at Neil.

"Wait." It took Nicky two tries and a bit of drunken flailing before he could get out of his beanbag chair and on his feet. He stumbled out of the room, rummaged around so loudly Neil knew he had to be waking Andrew and Kevin up, and came back with a blanket. He dropped it in an unceremonious pile on top of Neil and threw his hands up in an exaggerated shrug. "Might as well sleep here! Dan and Matt are probably doing the straight-person nasty. We'll get breakfast tomorrow morning."

He pointed at Neil, stabbed his finger a couple times in silent emphasis, and wheeled away again. Neil waited until the bedroom was quiet before getting up. He stood for a moment by the beanbag chair, debating, then turned off the light and came back. It was easy to straighten the blanket out, easier to get comfortable, and he was asleep in minutes.

A bell woke him up the next morning, but it took Neil's tired brain a moment to recognize the sound as a phone alert. His phone vibrated in his pocket a second later. Neil scrubbed a tired hand across his eyes and stifled his yawn against his fist. A strident trill in the next room was Nicky's phone sounding off. That meant the bell was Kevin's phone, left out here the night before, because Andrew was as likely as Neil was to have the sound turned off on his phone.

A mass text like that had to be from Wymack. Neil groaned a bit in protest but dug his phone from his pocket. Wymack's morning message was short but more than enough to wake him up: Kengo Moriyama was hospitalized again.

Neil sat up and kicked his blanket aside. He cut the TV on, turned the volume down to a murmur as fast as he could, and flipped through channels. Kengo wasn't important enough to make the regular news, but it was sure to be mentioned on the sports news station Wymack watched every morning. Andrew padded out of the bedroom as Neil finally found the right channel. He spared Neil only a brief glance on his way to the kitchen. Neil had to turn the TV up a bit when Andrew ran the sink to brew coffee, but there wasn't much point straining to hear when he'd caught the tail-end of the clip.

There was no new news yet, but Neil knew there'd be an

update as soon as someone made it out to Castle Evermore to harass Riko for a comment. Neil wondered if one of Kengo's people would tell Tetsuji and Riko or if it wouldn't even occur to the main family to inform them. Maybe Riko would find out when someone put a microphone in his face again. It amused Neil, but only for the moment it took his thoughts to wheel to his father.

Nathan was incarcerated, but he was Kengo's right-hand man. Someone would have told him Kengo was ill. It was questionable whether or not Nathan would care. Neil couldn't picture it, but if Nathan was even a fraction as loyal to Kengo as his people were to him, he would be pacing grooves in his cell floor right now. Maybe Nathan would never see Kengo alive again; maybe he'd be released and find himself serving Ichirou instead. Neil wondered what impact Kengo's death would have on the Moriyama family but he couldn't even begin to imagine it. He had no honest idea what the main family was capable of orchestrating. Riko had an alarming amount of pull and he was working with just scraps.

Andrew returned and crossed the room toward him. Neil watched his approach and felt queasy with guilt. The deal he'd struck with Andrew now looked as heartless as it'd been desperate. He hadn't been convinced Andrew could take on a monster like Nathan, but he'd been willing to let Andrew try. He hadn't cared what it would cost Andrew so long as it bought him time to play with the Foxes.

Andrew turned the TV off on his way by. "It is too early to obsess."

"This is important."

"To whom?" Andrew asked as he sank into the second beanbag chair. "It doesn't change our season and Riko is too stupid to harvest pity points. So who cares?"

Neil opened his mouth to argue and found he didn't have a good answer. Andrew pointed at him as if Neil's silence proved his point, and Neil shut his mouth again without a word. Andrew

[209]

shifted around a bit until he was more comfortable and closed his eyes. Neil looked from him to the darkened screen, then turned on his side on his lumpy chair so he was facing Andrew. Andrew cracked open an eye at the noise but closed it when Neil settled down. Neil contented himself with watching Andrew instead.

Andrew wasn't looking, but maybe he felt the weight of Neil's stare, because after a couple minutes he said, "Problem?"

"No," Neil said, but even he heard the lie in it. "Andrew? Last summer you made me a promise. I'm asking you to break it."

"No," Andrew said without hesitation.

"You said you'd stick with me if I kept Kevin south, but Kevin doesn't need me anymore. He chose us over the Ravens because as a whole we're finally worth his time. There's nothing else I can give you in exchange for your protection."

"I will think of something."

"I don't want you to," Neil said. "I need you to let me go."

"Give me one good reason," Andrew said.

"If I'm hiding behind you I'm still running," Neil said. "I don't want to end the year like this. I want to stand on my own two feet. Let me do that. None of this means anything if I don't."

Andrew stared at him in silence. Neil didn't know if he was weighing the truth of Neil's words or silently rejecting them. He wanted to push Andrew for a solid answer but knew it'd backfire. Andrew took his promises and his word too seriously. Convincing him to renege was going to take more than one attempt and if Neil pushed too hard Andrew would know something was wrong. Neil closed his eyes and scrunched deeper in the beanbag chair. He hoped Andrew would read it as his willingness to wait for a decision.

The dorm room was comfortably quiet. Kevin and Nicky had slept through the messages, so the only real noise was the quiet gurgle of the coffee maker. It beeped when it finished brewing the pot. Neil considered getting up for a mug and decided it could wait another minute.

He didn't mean to doze off, but the next thing he knew he was jolting awake to the sound of Nicky's alarm clock. The obnoxious beeping went on forever before Nicky finally stirred enough to cut it off. Bedsprings creaked as Nicky rolled over, and the room went quiet again. Neil looked to the clock over the TV, which put the time at half-past nine. It was definitely time to get up if he wanted to have a normal schedule today, but Neil was comfortable.

Andrew was still curled up in the other chair, but the noise had woken him as well. He met Neil's bleary-eyed stare a moment before going back to sleep. It was implicit permission to keep being lazy, so Neil closed his eyes and drifted off again.

-

The week leading up to Nevada's match was an exhausting blur, but Neil loved almost every moment of it. Mornings were practices with his teammates, his days were wasted on the necessary evil called school, and his afternoons were spent at the court. The Foxes no longer looked askance at him for walking laps with the goalkeepers on break. After dinner with the upperclassmen Neil and Kevin headed back to the stadium for drills.

It was the routine he was used to, with one critical addition. Neil went back to the dorm with Kevin and went down the hall as if going to his own room, but as soon as the door closed behind Kevin he made an about-face and went back to the stairwell. Andrew was waiting for him on the rooftop, usually with a cigarette in one hand and a bottle at his knee. The nights were still cool enough to warrant jackets but Andrew's body heat burned most of the chill away.

They didn't talk at night, maybe because they'd talked at practice or maybe because it was late and they were only stealing a few minutes before much-needed sleep, but night was where Neil had the most questions. They niggled at him when Andrew pinned him against chilly concrete and worked hot hands under his shirt. Being curious about Andrew wasn't anything new, but the gnawing importance of these answers was. Kissing Andrew changed things even if Neil knew it shouldn't.

He wanted to know where all of the lines were and why he was the exception. He wanted to know how Andrew was okay with this after everything he'd been through and how long it'd taken him to come to terms with his sexuality after Drake's abuse. Why and when and how only complicated things, because wondering about these developments made him wonder about everything else. He could have used their secrets game to justify prying, but Neil didn't want to fight for every piece and parcel. It would take too long and he was running out of safe things to trade. It was better to just keep his mouth shut and not think about it.

His control only lasted until Thursday. Renee's foster mother had just closed on a house, and it was all the upperclassmen could talk about at dinner. Renee wanted to go home and help her move that weekend. Matt was willing to get tickets for himself and Dan if she needed help. Neil didn't understand their enthusiasm until he remembered how sedentary their childhoods had been. Dan had lived in the same place for fifteen years and Matt stayed with his father until high school. Allison had summer and winter homes and traveled a lot with her parents, but she'd never actually moved.

It stayed with Neil all through evening drills and his shower afterward: not so much because it was odd but because it was a perfect shortcut past his and Andrew's game. As soon as Neil left Kevin at his room that night Neil took the stairs up to the roof. Andrew was where he was every night now, sitting cross-legged near the front ledge. His cigarette was a too-bright blur against the rest of the shadows and seemed to pulse when Andrew took a drag off it. Neil stole the cigarette as he sat down beside Andrew and turned it over in his hands. Andrew blew smoke in his face in response, so Neil flicked ash at him and made as if to stub the cigarette out. Andrew pinched his wrist and took the stick back.

"Upperclassmen are going out of town this weekend," Neil said. "Renee's mother is moving and it's apparently the most interesting thing to happen around here in months. I can't imagine what it'll be like when they all graduate and have to move." He waited a beat even though he knew he wouldn't get a response. "I know Nicky's going back to Germany when he graduates, but what will happen to his house? Is he selling it or giving it to one of you?"

"Ask him," Andrew said.

Neil ignored that. "Do you want to stay in South Carolina?"

Andrew lifted one shoulder in a shrug. "Planning that far ahead is a waste of time."

Neil hugged a knee to his chest and followed Andrew's gaze out to the campus. The trees lining the hill between Fox Tower and Perimeter Road blotted out most of the streetlamps, but there were lampposts every twenty feet on the campus sidewalks. It was after midnight but Neil saw at least a dozen students out and about.

"Maybe I'll go to Colorado," Neil said. "It'd be an interesting change of pace, anyway. I've mostly stuck to the coastal states."

"Not California," Andrew said, not really a question.

Neil didn't know if Andrew was humoring his best attempt at having a conversation about something other than Exy or if he was genuinely curious. Neil didn't really care. Andrew's disconnect—learned or forced—meant they probably amounted to the same thing in Andrew's book. That Andrew responded at all and prompted him to elaborate was victory enough.

"I went through California on my way to Arizona but didn't stay. I liked Seattle, I think, but..." Neil remembered the thick crunch of a pipe against his mother's body. "I couldn't live there again. I couldn't retrace my steps to any of those places."

"How many is 'any'?"

"Twenty-two cities," Neil said, but didn't say he'd spread them across sixteen countries. Andrew still thought Neil had hit

[213]

the road alone all those years ago. A child couldn't go back and forth across the world without help. "Longest stay was that year in Millport. Shortest was one week with my uncle."

"Am I supposed to believe he's real?" Andrew asked. "You told Nicky you would see him over Christmas. You lied."

"Uncle Stuart is real," Neil said. "He was the first person I went to when I ran away, but he's a gangster, too. I didn't feel any safer with him than I did at home so I left again. I still have his number, but I've never been desperate enough to call him. I don't know what his help would cost me." Neil looked at Andrew. "Did they move you a lot?"

"Twelve houses before Cass," Andrew said. "They were all in California."

"Were any of them good?" Neil asked.

Andrew stared Neil down a minute, then stubbed his cigarette out and reached for his drink. "None of the ones I remember were."

Neil didn't want to know how far back Andrew's memory stretched. "So California and South Carolina. You've really never been anywhere else except when traveling for a game?" Andrew only shrugged in dismissal. Neil thought it over for a bit, then said, "Spring break's coming up. We could go someplace."

"Go someplace," Andrew echoed, like it was a foreign concept. "Where and why?"

"Anywhere," Neil said, and amended, "Anywhere at least three hours from campus. There's no point in going someplace closer than that. It won't feel like a vacation. The only trick is figuring out how to pry Kevin away from the court."

"I have knives," Andrew reminded him. "That doesn't answer the 'why'."

Neil couldn't explain where the idea had come from, so he said, "Why not? I've never traveled just for the sake of it, either. I want to know what it's like."

"You have a problem," Andrew said, "wherein you only

[214]

invest your time and energy into worthless pursuits."

"This," Neil flicked his finger to indicate the two of them, "isn't worthless."

"There is no 'this'. This is nothing."

"And I am nothing," Neil prompted. When Andrew gestured confirmation, Neil said, "And as you've always said, you want nothing."

Andrew stared stone-faced back at him. Neil would have assumed it a silent rejection of Neil's veiled accusation if Andrew's hand hadn't frozen midair between them. Neil took the bottle from Andrew's other hand and set it off to one side where they couldn't knock it over.

"That's a first," Neil said. "Do I get a prize for shutting you up?"

"A quick death," Andrew said. "I've already decided where to hide your body."

"Six feet under?" Neil guessed.

"Stop talking," Andrew said, and kissed him.

Neil went to bed far too late that night, and morning came much too early. He half-dozed through all of his classes and caught a quick nap before the game. It was a good thing he did, because Nevada was a brutal opponent and a harsh wake-up call. This round the Foxes were up against the two other schools who'd survived the evens' death matches. The sudden jump in skill and difficulty nearly knocked the Foxes off their feet. It was made infinitely harder by Nicky's absence. His red card against UVM meant he was benched for the entire game. Luckily Renee was willing to reprise her role as a backliner sub, and Andrew guarded his goal like every point scored was a personal offense.

It was enough, but just barely. They ended the game in a six-up tie, and championships didn't allow for overtime. Draws were settled by shootouts. Nevada had seven strikers to cycle through whereas Neil and Kevin would have to keep alternating. Neil's heart was thunder in his ears as he followed Kevin to far-fourth. He inhaled as deep as he could and let it out slowly, willing his nerves to wait until later.

"It isn't the game we should have played, but this is an acceptable outcome," Kevin said when he saw the tight look on Neil's face. Neil shook his head, not understanding. "We are ending tonight with nearly the same number of points and Nevada plays again before we do. We will know before we face Binghamton how many points we must score to proceed."

"I guess," Neil said, unconvinced.

The Tornadoes took the first shot and scored. Kevin scored on his first attempt, and the next Tornado striker scored as well. Neil landed his ball home against the goal and looked to Andrew. Andrew slammed the next striker's shot all the way down the court, and Neil could breathe again. He looked at Kevin, who smiled in vicious triumph as he stepped up to the line. His next shot landed in the bottom corner of the goal, and the Foxes won the game by one point.

-

Thursday night's practice was canceled on account of the night's line-up. The odds bracket had their last games tonight, with Edgar Allan against Maryland and Penn State against USC. Only two teams from each bracket would proceed to the fourth round, which meant one of the Big Three was getting eliminated tonight. It was the first time in six years one of them was going home before semifinals, and Kevin needed to see it happen. Somehow the entire team got roped into it, and they all stayed at the stadium after Wymack dismissed them for the day.

Some clever scheduler made sure the Ravens and Trojans were the hosting schools. The time zone difference meant the Foxes could watch both games back-to-back. Wymack ordered them pizzas but didn't stick around for the matches. He'd nailed down which six players he wanted to recruit and was busy figuring out travel arrangements. He was hoping to have all of them signed by the time the Foxes got back from spring break. Neil was glad his player had made the cut, but he felt quietly guilty for not pushing Wymack into getting a third striker.

Dan kicked Wymack off his computer long enough to use his printer. She came back with four signs and a roll of tape, and she hung the papers above the TV. They were each team's cumulative points going into tonight's matches. Kevin barely glanced at them while the Raven match was on, but as soon as the USC-Penn State game started he kept darting quick looks up at them. Neil knew Kevin was a Trojans fan, but he hadn't realized how diehard Kevin was about it. Kevin watched the game like a poor result would be the death of him. Neil almost wished Penn State would win just so he could see Kevin throw a temper tantrum.

By the time the Trojans and Lions hit halftime Neil had forgotten all about Kevin. He'd been so wrapped up in the Foxes' season and the Ravens he'd forgotten how spectacular the rest of the Big Three were. These teams played like they were professionals. They didn't have the Ravens' spotless record but they were only a half-step behind Edgar Allan. Kevin had warned them weeks ago the Foxes weren't ready to face these schools. For once his callous dismissal felt like a gentle understatement.

He wasn't the only one who found it a sobering sight. Dan muted the commercials, tapped the remote against her thigh in a nervous rhythm, and said, "So we definitely need to step it up, guys."

Kevin frowned at her. "Even if you'd stepped it up when I told you to a year ago, you would have no chance of beating them. There is nothing at all you can do this late in the year. They are better than we are and they always will be."

"Do you get off on being such a Debbie Downer?" Nicky asked.

"Denial does none of us any good," Kevin said. "We struggled against Nevada. How do you honestly expect us to make it past the Big Three?"

"California's overdue for a big earthquake," Nicky pointed out. "That'd take care of USC, at least."

[217]

"That's a little extreme, don't you think?" Renee asked.

"We need something extreme at this point," Allison said.

Renee's expression was calm and her tone steady, but Renee didn't need to look disappointed in them for them to get the message. "The Trojans had our backs when we needed them most. Do you really want them to suffer just so we can profit?"

"It's just not fair," Nicky said, shying away from her gaze. "Us getting this far and putting up with so much and then losing here, I mean."

"We haven't lost yet," Dan said, "but we will lose if you give up right out of the gate."

Kevin started to say something Neil knew would be negative and dismissing. Neil reached behind Andrew and popped Kevin in the back of the head to shut him up. Matt choked on a laugh and tried unsuccessfully to pass it off as a cough. Kevin froze for a startled second, then sent Neil a scathing look.

"No one wants to hear that right now," Neil said.

"If you hit me again," Kevin started.

Andrew cut in with a casual, "You'll what?"

Kevin shut up but didn't look happy about it. Allison gestured to Dan. Neil saw it only in his peripheral vision, not enough to tell what she did, but when he glanced over there Dan was making a face at her friend. Matt slung an arm around Dan's shoulder and gave her a short squeeze. It could have been unrelated, but the smile Matt couldn't quite fight off was more smug than sympathetic. Neil looked to Renee to see if she understood, but he couldn't get any hints from her serene expression.

"You know," Matt started, but Dan turned the volume back on before Matt could finish. He grinned at her, amused instead of offended, and let it drop.

Halftime was over a few minutes later, and the Trojans and Lions went back at it with new line-ups and terrifying skill. Another point from USC took a little of the tension from Kevin's shoulders, but he didn't relax until USC finally won. With an astounding thirty-seven goals between their three round-three games, the Trojans were following the Ravens to the second set of death matches.

"You could look less happy about this," Nicky said when he saw Kevin's satisfied smile. "We're going to have to face them."

"They worked for this," Kevin said, with a cool look in Neil's direction.

Dan rolled her eyes and cut the TV off, and the Foxes finally called it a night.

CHAPTER TWELVE

Unfortunately for the Foxes, Binghamton University was less than eight hundred miles from home. It was considered too close to waste money on airfare, so they were out of bed by five and on the road before six. Between lunch, unavoidable bathroom breaks, and the rush hour traffic they were sure to hit on the way up the coast, it was destined to be a long ride. Neil didn't even have any schoolwork to distract himself, as they'd just survived a week of midterms. Next week was spring break, so none of Neil's teachers had sent him home with assignments.

At the four-hour mark the upperclassmen made a strident case to upgrade the bus next season with a TV. Wymack feigned not to hear them, but he couldn't tune them out forever. Finally he promised to look into it if they won finals. The Foxes knew Wymack-speak well enough to know it was a "yes" no matter how this season ended. It didn't help their boredom today, but it was something to look forward to for next year.

Six hours in, they stopped for an early lunch, and Dan got Kevin talking about the Binghamton Bearcats on the way across the parking lot. Kevin hesitated in the aisle, torn between arguing the merits of the night's opponents with his teammates and staying within Andrew's protective circle. His indecision effectively blocked the Foxes' foot traffic, since he'd been second onto the bus behind Andrew. It took Andrew only a minute to realize he'd lost Kevin. He gave a dismissive gesture, so Kevin slid into the seat behind Dan and Matt. Aaron and Nicky claimed the bench right behind him. Neil doubted they were that interested in what Kevin had to say; it was more likely they were bored out of their skulls and desperate to socialize.

There was an open spot on Kevin's bench, plenty of room

for Neil to join them. Kevin wasn't saying anything he and Neil hadn't gone over at their night practices, but Neil should still listen and glean whatever advice he could. Besides, it wouldn't take long for Nicky to pull the conversation off-course and the Foxes would be a good distraction from this endless ride.

Staying up here with them, though, meant leaving Andrew alone for the second half of the trip. Neil knew he likely wouldn't notice or care that he'd been abandoned, but for some reason the thought rankled him. Neil had spent his entire life drifting by on the outskirts, looked over and looked past. It'd made him happy, or so he'd thought, because being ignored meant he was safe. He hadn't realized how lonely he was until he met the Foxes.

"Neil?" Dan asked when she saw Neil wasn't moving.

Kevin frowned at Neil like he had no honest idea why Neil wasn't already sitting down with him. For a moment Neil felt trapped, stuck between what he wanted and what he needed, what he'd never have or be and what he had but couldn't keep. It sent an unexpected bolt of panic through his chest and Neil jerked his gaze away.

When he started for the back of the bus, Kevin tried to call him back with an annoyed, "Get back here."

Neil didn't look at him or slow. "No."

The seat cushion creaked and Kevin's shoe hit the floor with a too-heavy thud. Neil knew Kevin was coming after him, sick of Neil's distractions and back-talking, but a half-second later Kevin snapped at someone to let go of him. Neil knew neither Aaron nor Nicky would have thought to intervene. Matt was the likeliest defender, but Neil didn't care enough to look back and confirm it.

Kevin settled for fussing at Neil in French: "Remember that you gave me your game. You don't have the right to walk away from me when I am trying to teach you."

"I gave my game to you so we could get to finals," Neil sent back, "but you said yesterday you don't expect us to make it

[221]

there. You've given up on us, so I'm taking my game back. I don't owe you anything anymore."

"Stop acting like a spoiled child. Tonight's game rides on how well you and I perform. You need to hear this more than anyone does."

"I've heard it all before," Neil said. "Leave me alone."

Neil claimed Kevin's abandoned seat, second from the back and right in front of Andrew's. Dan only waited a couple seconds to see if anything else was forthcoming before prodding Kevin's attention back to their aborted conversation. It took a few tries before Kevin stopped fuming long enough to cooperate. Neil waited until they started speaking before pulling his phone out of his pocket.

Every night since his real birthday he'd gotten a number texted to him. Today's sobering "0" had arrived during lunch. Neil didn't know what to make of it or what to expect next. It was as anticlimactic as it was nerve-wracking. He wanted to erase the message as he had every single one before it, but when his phone prompted him for confirmation he snapped the phone closed instead. He put his phone away again, turned backward in the seat, and pushed up onto his knees to look down at Andrew.

Andrew ignored him, but Neil didn't mind. He was content for now to look, arms folded over the back of his seat and chin propped on a forearm. He didn't know what he was looking for. Andrew looked as he always had, and Neil knew his face as well as he knew every iteration of his own. Despite that, something seemed different. Maybe it was the sunlight streaming through the window, making Andrew's pale hair shine brighter and his hazel eyes seem almost gold. Whatever it was, it was disorienting. A wordless question buzzed under Neil's skin, leaving him restless and out-of-sorts.

"Hey," Neil said, because maybe if Andrew looked at him he'd figure it out.

It took a moment, but Andrew finally slid a calm gaze his way. Andrew only tolerated the staring another minute before

[222]

saying, "Stop."

"I'm not doing anything."

"I told you not to look at me like that."

Neil didn't understand, so he let it slide. "Is it exhausting seeing everything as a fight?"

"Not as exhausting as running from everything must be."

"Maybe," Neil allowed. "I told you I'm working on that."

"Work harder."

"I can't unless you let me go," Neil said, quiet but firm. "Stand with me, but don't fight for me. Let me learn to fight for myself."

"You never explained that change of heart."

"Maybe I got tired of seeing Kevin bend. Or maybe it was the zombies." When Andrew just stared at him, Neil shrugged and said, "A few weeks back you and Renee argued contingency plans for a zombie apocalypse. She said she'd focus on survivors. You said you'd go back for some of us. Five of us," Neil said, splaying his fingers at Andrew. "You weren't counting Abby or Coach. Since you trust Renee to handle the rest of the team, I'm guessing the last spot is for Dobson."

He knew Andrew wouldn't answer that, so he dropped his hand and said, "I didn't say anything then because I knew I'd look out for only me when the world went to hell. I don't want to be that person anymore. I want to go back for you."

"You wouldn't," Andrew said. "You're a different kind of suicidal. Didn't you figure that out in December? You're bait. You're the martyr no one asked for or wanted."

Neil knew he wasn't that good of a person, but all he said was, "Only one way to be sure, right?"

"You'll regret it."

"Maybe, maybe not."

Andrew looked away. "Don't come crying to me when someone breaks your face."

"Thank you."

Neil tipped his head to one side to rest his cheek on his arm

[223]

and looked out the window. They were crossing Virginia, barely over halfway to their goal. East coast interstates offered boring views clogged with endless cars and uneven asphalt. Neil thought of the coastal roads he'd taken through California, the ocean on one side, the world on the other, and towns too small for stoplights. Neil lifted his hand and checked his fingernails for blood. There wasn't any, of course, but for a moment he thought he smelled it.

"I've been through here," Neil said, because something, anything, needed to fill the silence before his thoughts ran away from him. Andrew looked at him again, which Neil took as wordless permission to continue. He told Andrew about the cities he'd been through, their back alleys and tourist stops and sketchy city buses. Most of his memories were stained with tension and fear, but he didn't have to water that down with Andrew. Neil just had to cut out every mention of his mother.

It was strange sharing this history with someone else. Neil grew up looking over his shoulder, but he'd always been looking for his father. There was rarely a reason to think back on his day-to-day life. It passed the time, though, and Andrew let him ramble. He never once took his eyes off Neil's face or looked like he was mentally tuning out of the conversation.

Eventually Neil got Andrew to open up a bit about his transition to Columbia. The first thing Andrew did after their mother was out of the way was take care of Aaron's addictions. He stocked the upstairs bathroom with canned food and barricaded Aaron in there until he finished withdrawal. Luckily they had a house, not an apartment, so there were no neighbors close enough to hear Aaron's best attempts at breaking out.

When Nicky moved in to keep an eye on them he started as a host at Sweetie's. He found out about Eden's Twilight from the customers he chatted up and, after going out of his way to befriend the bouncers and Roland, snagged a gig there as a bar-back. Eventually Nicky got Aaron and Andrew part-time jobs in the kitchen washing dishes and doing basic food prep. The more comfortable the staff got with the odd twins, the easier it was to talk drinks out of them. It wasn't until they went off to college that they had to get those drinks at the bar counter like the rest of the club's clientele.

The bus decelerating got Neil's attention, and he looked out the window as Abby took an exit ramp to a busy street. A travel center was two stoplights down, one half packed with diesel pumps and big rigs, the other half crowded with regular traffic. Abby found them a parking spot on the trucks' side and killed the engine. Neil was confused to be stopping again so soon, but a glance at his watch showed he'd lost almost three hours talking with Andrew. They were now only two and a half hours out from Binghamton.

"Last stop before campus," Wymack announced, and the front half of the bus cleared off.

Wymack stood at his seat until everyone but Neil and Andrew was gone. He looked at them like he wanted to say something, then held up his hand in a forget-it gesture and exited the bus. Neil watched out the window as his teammates disappeared inside. He was still full from lunch, but old habits said to take advantage of any pit stop.

Before getting up, though, he said, "I really want to know when Coach figured this out."

"It isn't a 'this'," Andrew reminded him.

Neil didn't roll his eyes, but it was a near thing. "I really want to know when Coach figured out that you want to kill me only ninety-three percent of the time."

"He didn't know before I left," Andrew said.

But he'd known as soon as Andrew returned, it seemed. Neil remembered Wymack's sly trick at practice in January, when he'd used Neil to rein Andrew in. Neil hadn't even known then, so it wasn't like he could have slipped up when he was with Wymack for New Year's. Neil thought back, looking for the first hint that Wymack suspected something was going on with them, and straightened a bit in startled realization.

[225]

"Yes, he did," Neil said. Last November Neil put Andrew's hand to his ravaged skin and asked Andrew to believe in him. Somehow Wymack had seen right through Neil's crushing guilt and Andrew's grudging trust. It was more than a little unsettling. "When they took you away he asked me when 'that' happened. I just didn't know then what he meant. How did he see it when Aaron and Nicky still can't?"

"Coach doesn't care for rumors and bias," Andrew said. "He sees what is, not what people want him to see."

Like he'd seen through Andrew's supposed dysfunction, Neil guessed. Aaron and Nicky, on the other hand, still believed Andrew was a borderline sociopath incapable of having normal human relationships. Nicky put money on Renee and Andrew because everyone else did, but even he admitted he didn't want it to work out.

"Are you ever going to tell them?" Neil asked.

"I won't have to," Andrew said as he slid out of his seat. Neil would have reached out to stop him, wanting to hear the rest of that, but Andrew wasn't leaving. Instead he helped himself to the other half of Neil's seat. Neil turned to face him as Andrew explained. "Renee says the upperclassmen are betting on your sexuality. They're split down the middle."

Matt had said they were betting on Neil, but this wasn't what Neil expected them to be putting money on. He floundered a moment, unsure how to react, but said at last, "It's a waste of time and money. They'll all lose. I've said all year I don't swing and I meant it. Kissing you doesn't make me look at any of them differently. The only one I'm interested in is you."

"Don't say stupid things."

"Stop me," Neil returned. He buried his hands in Andrew's hair and tugged him in for a kiss. It was easy to forget this endless ride and tonight's game with Andrew's hand on his thigh and teeth on his lip. Andrew pulled away too soon and got to his feet. Neil knew this wasn't the time or place, but that didn't stop him from feeling cheated.

[226]

They finally got off the bus and went inside for drinks. Wymack only let his team wander for a couple minutes before shepherding them across the parking lot back to the bus. The rest of Andrew's lot stayed up front for the last few hours. Neil stole Kevin's seat again but couldn't think of anything to say. The silence was surprisingly comfortable, so he propped his head against the window and napped the last hours away.

The Binghamton University campus was decked out in green and white for the night's game, and the stadium parking lot was packed with more people than cars. If there were any Fox fans in the crowd, Neil couldn't find them. Police were on hand in reflective vests, directing traffic and monitoring alcohol use. Neil studied the tailgating parties they passed. Everyone seemed to be in high spirits. The Bearcats beat the Tornadoes last week seven to six and were ready for another victory tonight.

Nevada had fourteen points for round three, and the Foxes currently stood at eight. To proceed to next round's death match, they had to get at least seven points tonight. The Bearcats were a better-balanced team than Nevada was, but the Foxes were cautiously optimistic. They'd had a great game against Nevada and a week off to rest, and Nicky was back on the court with them tonight.

Guards opened the gate for Abby to drive through, and she parked alongside the Bearcats' buses. Wymack ushered his team off, counted heads as they disembarked, and got the storage compartment open. They unloaded the gear and let campus police escort them out of the parking lot and to the door. They had the better part of an hour to kill before they were allowed in the inner ring for warm-ups. Neil spent it reading and rereading the Bearcats' line-up. When Kevin caught him at it he took the papers away and gave him a verbal review instead. He might be mad at Neil still, but the game was more important than their fight.

Neil followed his teammates onto the court for first serve. He thought about USC and Edgar Allan and let his grim

[227]

determination give him speed and strength. He threw himself against the Bearcats' defenses again and again, pushing himself to the edge of exhaustion and coming dangerously close to getting carded more than once.

At halftime Wymack threatened to skin him alive if he picked up a red card, but Dan nodded encouragement as soon as Wymack moved on. She understood what Neil did: no one could afford to scale it back yet. They were two points behind going up against a fresh line-up. So long as they scored three points this half, they'd advance, but Neil didn't want to lose tonight. He'd promised the Foxes they weren't going to lose any games this spring. For once Neil didn't want to be lying.

A warning bell urged them back to court, and starting line-up took their spots by the door. Aaron and Andrew were the last two in line, but Aaron shifted out of the way at Neil's approach. Neil barely noticed. He knew the last minute to second half was ticking down on the screens overhead because the stands were in an uproar. He was dimly aware of the court to his left and his tense teammates lined up behind him. The only thing that really mattered was Andrew, who stood unaffected by all of this chaos.

For the first time Neil appreciated Andrew's apathy. In a stadium gone mad and with too much on the line tonight, Neil finally saw Andrew as the crucial eye of the storm. Because Andrew refused to get caught up in this, he was the only person on the court with a cool head.

"Last month you shut the Catamounts out," Neil said. "Can you do it again tonight?"

"The Catamounts were a wretched team," Andrew said. "They brought that ridicule on themselves."

"Can you or can't you?"

"I don't see why I should."

Neil heard the click of a lock coming undone and knew the referees were opening the door. Andrew wasn't moving yet, but Neil still put an arm in his path to keep him where he was. He pressed his gloved hand to the wall and leaned in as close to

[228]

Andrew as he could with all of his bulky gear on.

"I'm asking you to help us," Neil said. "Will you?"

Andrew considered it a moment. "Not for free."

"Anything," Neil promised, and stepped back to take his place in line again.

Neil didn't know what he'd gotten himself into, but he honestly didn't care, because Andrew delivered exactly what Neil wanted him to. Andrew closed the goal like his life depended on it and smashed away every shot. The Bearcat strikers took that challenge head-on. They feinted and swerved and threw every trick shot they had at Andrew. More than once Andrew used his glove or body to block a ball he couldn't get his racquet to in time.

That might have been enough, except Andrew didn't stop there. For the first time ever he started talking to the defense line. Neil only understood him in snatches, since there was too much space and movement between them, but what he caught was enough. Andrew was chewing out the backliners for letting the strikers past them so many times and ordering them to pick up the pace. Neil worried for a moment what they'd do with Andrew's rude brand of teamwork at their backs, but the next time he got a good look at Matt, Matt was grinning like this was the most fun he'd had in years.

It took all of second half for the Foxes to catch up, and with one minute left on the clock Kevin scored to put them in the lead. The last sixty seconds of the game were a blur of violence and threats as the Bearcats tried to draw even. The final buzzer sounded on a Fox win, and the teams were fighting before the sound petered off. Neil didn't know who started it; he shot a triumphant look down the court to Andrew and stared when he saw the Bearcat strikers tangling with Nicky and Matt. Allison and her dealer mark got dragged into it when they went to intervene.

Kevin started that way, but Neil ran to grab him. If Kevin got pounced Andrew would get involved and the violence would

[229]

escalate to unforgivable levels. He dragged Kevin around the brawl instead so Andrew could see he was all right. Wymack and the Bearcats' three coaches helped the referees untangle their players. The teams skipped the customary post-game handshake in favor of stomping off the court. Since Wymack didn't waste his breath yelling at them, Neil guessed the Foxes hadn't thrown the first punch.

It was Neil's turn to help Dan with the post-game press. Andrew caught Neil's eye and tipped his head toward the locker room. He was respecting Neil's decision to stand alone and wouldn't hover while Neil said his piece. Neil answered that trust with a small smile, and Andrew turned away. Neil would have watched him go, but Dan redirected his attention where it needed to be right now.

They were asked all the usual questions: how were they feeling, how excited were they to advance, what did they think of the Bearcats' performance, and so on. Dan was happy to ramble away at length, which nicely balanced out Neil's more reserved responses, and they survived the interview intact. Dan slung an arm around Neil's shoulders as they headed for the locker room and tipped her head to one side to rest her helmet against his.

She didn't say anything, but she didn't have to. Neil could practically feel her excitement radiating off of her. They'd made an incredible comeback tonight and continued their perfect streak. One game stood between them and semifinals. All they had to do was win their rematch against the Bearcats in two weeks and they were in.

The showers were going when Neil made it to the men's room. The Bearcats, like the Foxes, had actual stalls erected in both bathrooms, so Neil didn't have to wait on everyone else to finish before washing up. He carried his clothes to one of the open stalls and let the hot water work every ache out of his exhausted body. By the time he was done and getting dressed again, the locker room was empty. Neil packed his bag and slung it over his shoulder.

He was halfway to the door when his phone hummed. His first thought was it was a text, but his phone kept buzzing. He stopped to pull it out of his pocket and flipped it open. The screen lit up with the incoming number and Neil's stomach bottomed out. He didn't recognize the phone number, but he didn't have to. He knew that 443 area code.

Baltimore was calling.

"Don't run."

The sound of his voice startled him. He hadn't meant to speak. His muscles screamed with barely restrained tension; he was braced to bolt but somehow he held his ground. Neil fought to relax, but his blood was pounding in his temples.

He knew this wasn't his father calling. It couldn't be; it wouldn't be. It was Riko or one of Riko's lackeys playing a sick joke. Riko would know by now that the Foxes had made it to the fourth round. His attempt to rattle Neil with that countdown had failed. Neil knew that was the logical explanation, but it still took him until the fourth ring before he could answer.

"Hello?"

"Hello, Junior. Do you remember me?"

Neil's heart lurched to a sick halt. It wasn't his father or Riko, but he would know this voice anywhere. It was Lola Malcolm, one of his father's closest people and one of the two who'd tried teaching Neil how to wield a knife so many years ago. She'd been in and out of their house so many times Neil had thought for a while she lived there with them. She posed as Nathan's personal assistant, but her job was to get rid of the bodies Nathan's circle created. She was worth her weight in gold. Not a single one had ever turned up again.

Neil tilted the phone away from his ear and took a long, slow breath. It didn't help. His lungs were full of shards of ice, chilling him to the bone and cutting him up from the inside out. It was an age before Neil found his voice again and he couldn't keep a thick edge from it.

[231]

"I didn't give you this number, Lola."

"So you do remember me," she said. "Now you see, that's bad, because if you remember me, you remember who you are and where your place is."

"I made my own place."

"You don't have that right." She gave him a beat to respond, but Neil had nothing. "Are you listening? It is time to go. If you make this difficult for us, you will regret it for the rest of your very short life. Do you understand?"

Neil wanted to be sick. Lola trashed bodies; she didn't often make them. That was what the rest of Nathan's people were for. Neil remembered faces better than he remembered names, but he could guess who Lola had brought with her. Lola's business partner of choice was her brother Romero, and where Romero went Jackson was never far behind. The three were Nathan's inner circle. They answered only to Nathan's right-hand man DiMaccio and Nathan himself.

Neil could have tried outrunning one of them. He wouldn't make it past three. For a moment he was so scared he couldn't breathe, but fast on the heels of fright was an irrational and wild anger. He was halfway to winning Andrew's trust, a weekend from his first vacation, and one month from semifinals. There were only four matches left in championships. Neil was so close to everything he wanted and Lola was here to steal it away.

"Put a hand on me and you'll regret it," Neil said.

"Oh, what's this?" Lola said, entertained. "Has the baby finally inherited a spine? Your father will be glad to hear it."

"My—" Neil choked on it. "He is in Seattle. You'll never get me that far."

"He is in Baltimore," she corrected him. "His parole hearing was on your birthday. They had to notify his family when his case came up. You must have missed the memo, being dead and all, so I'll fill you in. They made a final decision last week, and the feds swung it so he'd get released back to Maryland this morning. They're hoping being back in familiar territory will make him careless." Neil could hear the savage smile in her words. "Don't worry, kid. They'll never know you stopped by. I'll make sure of it."

Neil blinked and saw that zero on his eyelids. He was out of time. For a moment Neil felt the weight of Andrew's mouth against his. He dug his fingers into his lower lip and tried to breathe around them.

"You don't honestly think you can take me away from here," Neil said. "My team will know I'm missing and they won't get back on the road without me."

"They don't have a choice. We can't kill them," Lola said, "but we can hurt them. You'll see."

"No," Neil said, but Lola hung up. Neil called her back, but it went straight to voicemail. She'd cut her phone off already. Neil swore and snapped his phone shut with unsteady fingers. He gave his hands a vicious shake like he could knock the trembling out of them, but those quivers were bone-deep. His mind raced a thousand miles an hour, grabbing at every exit strategy and dismissing every single one that ended with him running.

He'd promised Andrew he'd hold his ground here, but he couldn't do that if it meant catching his teammates in the crossfire. The only way to save his team was to do the last thing Nathan's people expected of him. He'd run and lied and hid all his life. Telling the truth to save himself, to save his team, was completely out of character. Neil had wanted to do it when the season was over, but he couldn't afford to wait any longer. The Foxes could sit tight here until the feds showed up to take them all into protective custody.

Neil hurried out of the changing room and down the hall. A security officer stood at the end of the hall, looking in on the Foxes where they were celebrating in the lounge. Neil made it halfway there before the man realized someone else was coming. Neil froze when the officer looked his way and Neil got a good look at his face. Jackson Plank was in the locker room with his team. A second later Romero Malcolm stepped into view in a similar getup. Retreating from them was instinctive, but Neil grabbed at the wall to stop himself before he got far.

Romero let his hand rest casually on the gun hooked to his belt. Neil flinched and gave a fierce shake of his head. Romero turned away from him to face the Foxes. Neil had no problems interpreting that warning and he put his hands out in a desperate plea to stand down. Jackson flicked Neil only a cursory glance before returning his attention to the oblivious team.

"If we're all accounted for, we should head out," Jackson said.

"We're still waiting for Neil," Nicky said, and Jackson gestured down the hall in Neil's direction. Neil swallowed against the stone in his throat and tried to school his expression into something calm. He continued down the hall on feet that wanted to carry him anywhere but here. Nicky jumped to his feet when Neil stepped into the den, grinning ear to ear. "Hey, Neil! We were starting to think you'd drowned in there."

"I'm sorry," Neil said.

Nicky waved it off, thinking Neil was apologizing for the wait, and went to grab his bag. Neil watched them gather their things, looking from one face to the other and trying to savor these last impossible seconds. Wymack watched over them all from the corner, an unlit cigarette hanging from the corner of his mouth and a triumphant smirk still twitching at his lips. Abby was repacking her bag; she'd likely been checking on the scrapes her team picked up in the brawl.

The five feet between Neil and his team could have been five thousand miles. Looking at them all, Neil was as sad as he was proud. He was destroying their chances of making it through the season, but the girls still had one more year. They'd be bitterly disappointed by the near-miss but they were fighters. They'd come back swinging next year and they wouldn't let anything stop them.

He was sorry to leave them with all of his lies, sorry they'd have to get the truth from Kevin after the fact. They were all right here with him still but he missed them with a ferocity that threatened to turn him inside-out.

Only Andrew saw the strain in Neil's mask. He crossed the room to stand in front of Neil, a silent demand in his stare. Neil wanted to answer that, but he didn't know how. German was the obvious answer because it would afford them a little bit of privacy, but Romero and Jackson didn't understand German. They wouldn't know what he was saying and they would have to react like he was spilling every dark secret. Neil couldn't allow that. He didn't want to leave Andrew with nothing, but what could he possibly say?

"Thank you," he finally said. He couldn't say he meant thanks for all of it: the keys, the trust, the honesty, and the kisses. Hopefully Andrew would figure it out eventually. "You were amazing."

He meant it for Andrew's ears only, but Allison was close enough to overhear. She sent Matt a significant look. Neil saw it in his peripheral vision but didn't take his eyes off Andrew to see Matt's reaction. He didn't want to look away, as if by holding Andrew's gaze he could somehow save this moment. Then Wymack was motioning for them to head out and Neil had no choice but to turn his back on his teammates.

They left the stadium in a line, Romero in front and Jackson in back. Neil had been closest to the exit, so he was right behind Romero. He hated being that close to his father's man but he liked thinking his body was a shield between Romero's cruelty and his unsuspecting team. He tried to keep his stare on Romero's back, but he kept looking for Lola in the crowd. Only half of the fans had headed home for the night. The rest were having a post-game party on the stadium lawn. The smell of alcohol was so thick Neil could almost taste it.

The Foxes' fans were lined up to one side of the walkway, and they cheered the team's arrival. They were swiftly drowned out by vile insults from the other side where the Bearcats' fans stood. The Foxes ignored both sides and kept moving. Even Nicky was smart enough to keep his mouth shut, not wanting to rile the bitter fans further, but it didn't matter in the end. They were halfway to the parking lot when a bottle came flying out of nowhere. Aaron's florid curse a few spots back said it'd hit him, and Andrew shot a deadly look at the crowd. A shoe was hurled next, then another empty beer bottle.

More police shoved their way toward the team, yelling for order and pointing fingers. They might have succeeded in restoring order, except the next thing thrown was someone's cooler. Dan dodged in the nick of time, and it crashed into a drunk fan on the Foxes' other side. There was a furious outcry from the man's friends that was swiftly picked up by the crowd at their back.

Romero caught Neil's wrist in an iron grip. Neil dug his phone out of his jeans pocket with his free hand and stuffed it into the netted end pocket of his duffel. He just made it when the crowd's tension hit a breaking point. Students and fans went at each other's throats with the Foxes caught in the middle. Bodies crashed into Neil hard enough to take him off his feet, but Romero hauled him up and away as fast as he could. Neil dropped his racquet and let his bag get ripped from his shoulder. Andrew and Kevin knew he'd never let go of these things willingly. It wouldn't tell them where he'd gone, but they'd know he hadn't left them by choice.

Somewhere between the riot and the parking lot Romero lost his reflective vest. As soon as Neil's shoes hit asphalt Neil started struggling, but Jackson was right behind them. He yanked Neil's arm up behind him so sharply he almost dislocated Neil's shoulder. Neil gasped at the white bolt of pain that shot through his back.

"You won't get away with this," Neil said, voice strained. "My teammates will know I'm missing. They can't leave New York without me."

"They'll be busy for a while," Romero said. "Your coach

[236]

will spend half the night trying to figure out which ER the lot of you were taken to. By the time he realizes you're gone it'll be too late."

They pushed him into the backseat of a highway patrol car. Lola was waiting for him on the far cushion. Neil stared dumbly at her, at a face that had aged but would always be familiar. The toothy smile that curved her mouth too wide, threatening to split her face in two, was the same as it'd always been, and Neil instinctively recoiled from her. There was nowhere for him to go with a locked door at his back and a protective grate between him and the front seats.

"Junior's all grown up," Lola said as Romero and Jackson got in the front seat. It was bumper-to-bumper traffic around the Binghamton campus, but Jackson set their lights flashing and drove on the shoulder. "How unexpected. Rumor has it you're some sort of rising star? It is a strange world we live in, but you won't have to worry about it much longer."

Romero half-turned in the passenger seat and looked through the grate. "You tell them?"

"Do I look stupid to you?" Neil asked. "Of course I didn't."

Lola pressed her thumbnail to the tattoo on his cheek. "But at least one of them knows, hmm? You're not the only branded one."

"Kevin remembers me, but he's the Ravens' pet. He knows better than to say anything."

"I hope that is the truth," Lola said. "You know what we will do to them if you are lying."

"I've spent eight months with a camera in my face. If I'd told someone, you would have heard about it by now. You wouldn't have needed this to track me down." Neil gestured at his face. "Did you give Riko a finder's fee?"

Romero snorted in disdain. "We gave his uncle a courtesy call that we were taking you."

That easy dismissal only made Neil feel worse. He had a sinking suspicion Riko hadn't been behind the bloody birthday

[237]

surprise or the countdown after all. Lola said Nathan's parole hearing had been that same day. His circle knew he'd get out. Now Neil wondered if their presence was what had Riko keeping his distance from the Foxes this spring. Did Tetsuji warn Riko not to draw attention to himself while Nathan's men were on the prowl? Tetsuji and Riko were Moriyamas, but they were not the family the Wesninskis served and protected.

Lola grinned. "He was pretty pissed, but what could he do about it? Kengo couldn't give two shits about you right now."

"Because he's sick," Neil said, not quite a question.

"Sick, he says," Lola said, and thumped the side of her fist on the grate to make sure her brother had heard that. "'Sick' is a cold or an STD, child. This isn't 'sick'; this is the end of the road. His kidneys are failing. I give it a week tops before Ichirou's crowned new high king. I'll pass on your condolences and congratulations. You won't be alive to deliver them yourself.

"Speaking of which, it's tradition for me to tell a man what I plan on doing with his pieces," Lola said, and she proceeded to tell him in great detail how she was going to take his corpse apart.

Neil tried not to listen, but he couldn't tune out her cruel words. He put every ounce of strength he had left into keeping his fear from showing on his face. He couldn't keep his hands still, but he could at least hide them in his pockets. He didn't want her to know she was getting to him. It wasn't like a brave front would save him, but they'd been waiting for this moment for nine years. The least Neil could do was rob them of as much satisfaction as possible.

It was only a couple miles to I-81, and the car they'd acquired for this job let them hit the interstate at ninety miles an hour. Jackson cut the police lights on and off depending on whether or not cars were in his way. Even at such speeds it was almost three hours from Binghamton University to Baltimore.

Two miles into Maryland they pulled off to the shoulder behind an abandoned car. Jackson stayed with the patrol car, but

Romero and Lola walked Neil to the Cadillac. Neil was pushed into the passenger seat. Romero put his gun in Neil's face before Neil could even think of making a break for it. He was pretty sure he was supposed to be delivered to Nathan alive, but Neil's mother had taught Neil how many places one could shoot a man without killing him. Neil watched Lola cuff his ankles to the seat's rails and barely refrained from kneeing her in the face.

Lola climbed into the backseat behind him and pulled Neil's arms around back of his chair. She cuffed his hands together and clicked them as tight as she could. As soon as she closed her door Romero got them on the road again. Neil kicked his legs a bit, testing his range of movement, but was quickly distracted by the press of sharp, cold metal against his fingertips.

Neil reflexively tried to clench his hands into fists. Lola laughed and dug a thumb into the pressure point of his wrist. When his fingers loosened she slid her blade between his fingers and palm. The scrape of the edge against his fingers was encouragement to open his hand again. Lola tapped the tip to the webbing between his fingers, hard enough to be a threat but not quite hard enough to break the skin. She got bored of the teasing before long and cut a shallow line along the base of his fingers.

Neil tugged hard at the cuffs, trying to yank his hands out of her reach, but there was no give in the metal. For a blinding moment it reminded him of Christmas break at Evermore, and Neil's wavering control cracked a little further. "Stop it."

"Stop me," Lola returned, and cut a stinging line down from the base of his finger to the thick flesh of his thumb. She covered his hand with burning lacerations before moving on to the next one. When she was done she slid over and leaned between the front seats. She traced Neil's tattoo with the tip of her blade. "We read all about your feud with Riko. What a convincing act! In another life you could have been an actor. Tell me, did you really think his collar would protect you from us?"

"It doesn't matter."

"It does. I can't take you before your father with such a

stain on your face. Rome?"

Romero reached for the dashboard. Something clicked as he pressed it, and Neil scanned the array of buttons for a hint of what he'd done. It wasn't the radio, and none of the lights were on to indicate he'd clicked on the heater. That left only one possible solution, but Neil refused to believe it. Denial didn't change facts: soon enough the dashboard cigarette lighter popped free of its lock with a metallic cling. Romero pulled it out and held it up.

Neil leaned away from it with a heated, "You're sick."

Lola wound her arm around the back of his chair so she could hold her knife to the right side of his face. The blade cut a paper-thin line from his mouth to the corner of his eye. Neil went still at that warning and watched as Lola took the lighter from her brother. She gave it an experimental twirl and tipped it where she and Neil could see the red-hot coils inside. Lola nodded approval and favored Neil with one of her wide smiles.

"What do you think?"

Neil thought he was two seconds away from losing his cool. "I think fuck you."

"Don't flinch," she said, and pressed the lighter to his cheek.

She said not to move, but there was no way Neil could obey. Agony exploded in his face, knifing down his jaw to his throat and eating its way through his eye. The smell of charred skin only made the blinding pain worse and Neil couldn't hold his ground in front of it. Heat ate a fierce line through his other cheek as he retreated right into Lola's waiting knife. He felt it like a distant memory, an insignificant tickle against the inferno. Lola followed him when he retreated, keeping the lighter in place, but pulled back after a second to inspect her handiwork. Neil knew she put the lighter away because he saw her do it, but he still felt its metal and fire on his skin. Every passing second just made it worse until Neil's stomach was roiling inside of him.

"Better," Lola said, and dug her fingernails into his raw skin just to make him cry out again. "Don't you think?"

[240]

Neil didn't have the breath to answer. Every breath he gulped in was frantic and shallow, too short to make it to his lungs, just thick and quick enough to choke on. He twisted his head out of her reach and remembered her knife too late. He tore a second line down his cheek and hurriedly hunched forward instead. He couldn't go far with his hands locked behind the chair, but he had to try. Blood streamed slow and steady down his face, hot against his lips before it dripped off his chin and mouth to his thighs. He tasted it when he gasped for breath.

The lighter clicked again. Neil heard it like a gunshot and flinched.

"I know your father's going to ask, but I have to know now," Lola said. "You listening, Junior? Hey." She thumped his back with the hilt of her knife. "Where's the bird, hm? We've had some time to dig around since we figured out where you were, but there's no sign of her anywhere. Tetsuji says you told them she's dead. He was sure you were telling the truth. Me, I'm not so trusting."

"She's dead," Neil choked out.

Lola grabbed a fistful of hair to yank him upright. She'd put her knife aside so she could hold him with both hands, and her free hand clenched around his throat so tight he could barely breathe. She pulled him back against his chair, pinning his head to the headrest. Romero plucked the lighter out again, and Neil put up a desperate fight.

"She's dead," he said, almost wheezing through Lola's brutal grip. "She died two years ago after he beat her in Seattle. Do you think she'd have let me go to Palmetto if she was still alive? I signed up because I had nothing left."

"Do we believe him?" Lola asked Romero.

"Might as well be sure," Romero said.

"Right that," Lola said, and held fast to Neil so Romero could crush the lighter to his face once more. Lola's strangling grip on his throat meant the best Neil could manage was a pained whine. He thrashed mindlessly against his restraints. Lola

[241]

was speaking again, but he couldn't understand her over the roar in his ears. His world narrowed down to the fire in his face.

Romero put the lighter away, but he pushed it in all the way so it'd reheat. Lola loosened her grip enough that Neil could breathe but didn't let go completely.

"Try again, Junior," Lola said. "Answer me and make me believe you. Where is Mary?"

"She's dead," Neil said, voice raw with pain. "She's dead, she's dead, she's dead."

Lola looked to her brother. "You believe him now?"

Romero lifted his shoulder in a noncommittal shrug. Lola considered Neil again, then smacked his burned face as hard as she could. She leaned further forward between the seats to get the lighter when it was ready and retreated back to her original cushion with it. Having the lighter behind him out of sight was worse than the pain they'd already put him through and Neil fought to yank his hands free. He tore his wrists open on unyielding metal but he couldn't stop.

"Don't," he begged. "Lola, don't."

"I've got questions," Lola said, voice oddly muffled. Neil guessed she was holding the lighter handle between her lips, because she used both hands to roll his sleeves up. She ran her hands down his bared forearms, fingernails scratching faintly at his skin. She withdrew a moment later, and her voice sounded normal when she spoke next. "Let's start with your teammates again. Tell me everything you told them."

Time stopped as Lola burned and cut a path up Neil's arms. Neil clung to a version of the truth that would protect the Foxes but no matter how many times he said it she wouldn't stop. Eventually he stopped answering altogether, afraid he'd slip up in his pain and panic, and saved his energy for breathing. Every grimace and silent cry pulled the burns on his face, and salty tears were acid on his ruined cheeks.

He didn't want to think about this, didn't want to feel this, so he thought about the Foxes instead. He clung tight to the

[242]

memory of their unhesitating friendship and their smiles. He pretended the heartbeat pounding a sick pace in his temples was an Exy ball ricocheting off the court walls. He thought of Wymack holding him up in December and Andrew pushing him down against the bedroom floor. The memories made him weak with grief and loss, but they made him stronger, too. He'd come to the Foxhole Court every inch a lie, but his friends made him into someone real.

He'd hit the end of his rope before he wanted to and he hadn't accomplished everything he'd hoped to this year, but he'd done more with his life than he'd ever thought possible. That had to be enough. He traced the outline of a key into his bloody, burnt palm with a shaky finger, closed his eyes, and wished Neil Josten goodbye.

Lola finally stopped and left him limp in his restraints. She said something, but he couldn't understand her through the buzzing in his ears and he didn't care, anyway. His natural choice in fight-or-flight mode had hit a brick wall hard enough to break every bone in his body. That left only one option, so Nathaniel Wesninski let the last few miles fly by unnoticed. He catalogued every throbbing point on his body and mentally ordered them by severity. The worst injuries were the ones on his face, but the mess Lola made of his hands was the most inconvenient. It'd be hard to fight back when even the slightest twitch of his fingers made his hands ache.

They pulled into the parking lot of a sketchy hotel. Only half of the outdoor lamps were working. Nathaniel was willing to bet the security cameras were equally defunct. He gazed out the window and waited to see what came next.

What came was a police car, and it backed into the spot beside them. Nathaniel didn't recognize the baby-faced officer who got out the passenger side or the seasoned cop that came around the hood a few seconds later. The older man gestured, and the younger cop went to pop the trunk. Romero climbed out of the car and went to exchange a few quiet words with them. He nodded satisfaction and opened the passenger door. He unlocked the handcuffs from Nathaniel's ankles only long enough to untangle him from the rails. As soon as the metal snapped shut again, Lola undid the cuffs on his wrists. Romero hauled him out of the car by his shirt and locked his hands together again.

Nathaniel flicked a cool look at the cops, who were studying him with blatant interest and zero remorse. "How much do my father's people pay you to break your oaths?"

"More than the state does," the older officer said. "Don't take it personally."

"I have to," Nathaniel said, voice hoarse with pain and hatred. "It's my life."

The only thing in the trunk was a small toolbox, so there was plenty of room for him. He couldn't climb into the trunk himself when he was bound like this, but the cops helped Romero hoist him in. Lola took Romero's offered gun and climbed in after him. She wound herself around his battered body, holding him close, and cocked the gun in warning. Nathaniel answered her smile with a blank stare.

"We're good," Lola said, and Romero closed the trunk. Nathaniel closed his eyes against the pitch black that threatened to swallow him whole. Lola smiled against his cheek and bit at his burns. She slung a leg across his and hooked the heel of her shoe between his ankles. "You could almost be my type if you weren't so young, hmm? You look just like your father."

The inviting rock of her hips against his made his skin crawl. "And you look like a strung-out whore."

"Feisty still." She sounded appreciative, not insulted, and scratched hard lines down his injured arms. "Not for much longer."

Doors slammed as the cops got back in. The world rocked beneath them as they pulled out of the parking lot. He counted eight stops before the cops started talking. He couldn't understand their voices through the thick cushion of the backseat, but a few moments later the sirens cut on and the cops

[244]

picked up pace.

"Oops," Lola murmured against his ear. "Seems there's been an incident at your father's house. Perhaps some vandalism from lowlifes unwilling to have him back in their neighborhood, fools who buy into the conspiracy theory that he killed his beloved wife and child."

"People you paid to create a disturbance tonight," Nathaniel guessed, "so police could stop by unquestioned."

"Ten points to Junior," Lola said.

Nathaniel's childhood home was a five-bedroom house in the Windsor Hills neighborhood a couple miles northwest of downtown Baltimore. As far as the community knew, Nathan was a former successful day trader who'd given up stocks in favor of investing in businesses around the city. His interest rates were steep, but he never turned down an application. It didn't matter who asked or what the amount was. If a company couldn't repay him within the requested time frame, he simply bought it out and moved on.

At last count he owned a dozen businesses of varying trades and had deals with a dozen more. The front let him go anywhere in the city he needed, but also explained why he could stay home for weeks at a time. The feds investigated Nathan's holdings more than once, but Nathan was too smart to do any of his real business with companies he owned in his own name.

Nathaniel knew they were getting close because of the noise. Police lights always drew an interested crowd. That told him two things: whatever happened to the house was big enough to attract attention and they weren't the first officers on scene. If the feds were sitting on Nathan, they were going to have a lot of bodies to watch tonight.

The car bounced a little as it started up the curved drive to the house. The further up they went the quieter it got as they left behind spectators in favor of working police. Tension made the driveway feel endless, but finally the car rolled to a stop. Doors slammed behind the two cops as they went to investigate.

[245]

Nathaniel waited for Lola to make a move, but she was seemingly content to lie still a while longer.

At last Lola's phone chirped. She reached over Nathaniel to mess with something. The toolbox, he guessed when he heard metal click open. Plastic crinkled and Lola propped herself up on her elbow in front of him.

"If you fight me, I will cut you off at the knees."

Sarcasm would only illicit the worst response, so Nathaniel gritted out, "Just do it."

The sickly sweet smell that filled the car made his stomach churn, and everything in him ordered him to struggle. He held still and let her clamp a drenched cloth over his nose and mouth. Numbness started in his fingertips and swiftly overtook the rest of his body. He heard a car door open, and he thought someone was putting the backseat down, but he couldn't hold onto consciousness long enough to be sure.

"Go," Lola said, voice nasal as she pinched her nose shut, and everything fell away.

CHAPTER THIRTEEN

Coherent thought came back in jagged pieces. He was aware of cold stone beneath his cheek and the sight of his uncuffed hand lying limp in front of his face, but none of it held any real significance for him. Lola had lined the back of his hand with crosshatches and burned angry circles into his knuckles. Another burn mark stained the tender flesh between his thumb and index finger. The burns were starting to ooze, but drying blood smothered most of the mess. Nathaniel was impressed by Lola's cruelty for the fuzzy minute it took his mind to remember how much pain he was in.

He groaned and carefully sat up. He was in the cellar, which meant they'd come in through the garage. An underground tunnel led from one to the other, installed for the sole purpose of moving the occasional body. Nathaniel and his mother had escaped through it nine years ago. It was only fitting that he was returned home the same way.

Lola was halfway across the room. She'd turned a wooden chair around and was straddling it. One arm was folded along the thin back. The other hung limp at her side. She still had Romero's gun on her, and her finger rested close to the trigger. Whoever had helped her get Nathaniel inside from the car was long gone. One of the cops, Nathaniel guessed, who had to rejoin the chaos outside to maintain appearances.

"Going somewhere?" Lola asked.

Nathaniel brandished his hands at her. "These are going to get infected if I don't clean them soon."

"I wouldn't worry about it if I were you."

"You're not me," Nathaniel said, and got to his feet.

An industrial sink was built into the far wall. It didn't have a mirror. He was glad he couldn't see his face, but it would have made this easier. He washed his hands first, hissing through clenched teeth. It hurt so bad he wanted to stop, but he made himself rub soapy water into his burns. By the time he rubbed wet hands over his face his fingers were trembling and his stomach was quaking with pain-induced nausea. He had nothing to dry off on afterward, since his clothes were dirty with sweat and streaks of blood. He held his arms out to air dry instead.

"How much longer is this going to take?" Nathaniel asked.

"The waiting, or the killing?" Lola asked. "The latter might take a while. It's not normally his style but you've caused us so much trouble and money I think he'll make an exception."

"You could have just let us go."

"Don't say such childish things."

Nathaniel sat down to wait. It was an hour before the police finished taking statements from Nathan's security and photographing evidence of the vandalism. He knew they were finally gone when a door opened at the top of the stairs. Lola was on her feet in a heartbeat. Nathaniel's heart kicked into overdrive, but with Lola's interested stare on him he couldn't afford to look afraid. He locked a calm expression on his face and watched death come downstairs for him.

Two years behind bars hadn't aged his father a bit. Aside from a couple lost pounds Nathan Wesninski looked the same now as he always had. The house was a garish demonstration of his wealth, but Nathan didn't waste his time dressing up. He saw no need for fancy clothes when he liked getting dirty at work. He came down the stairs barefoot, wearing dark gray jeans and a black button-up shirt. His sleeves were rolled up to his elbows, and he had his hands in his pockets as he reached the landing. Cool blue eyes settled on Nathaniel, and Nathaniel had to look away.

Lola wasn't much safer to look at, but Nathaniel didn't want to look at the monster who'd accompanied Nathan downstairs, either. Patrick DiMaccio was Nathan's live-in bodyguard. He carried himself like he could take on half the world bare-handed, an arrogant swagger backed by three hundred pounds of steroid-fueled muscle. He'd never laid a hand on Nathaniel or Mary, maybe knowing he could kill them with one careless hit, but Nathaniel knew how dangerous he was. He was deathly loyal to Nathan, and Nathan trusted him unequivocally. DiMaccio would have been charged with keeping the circle strong in Nathan's absence.

"On your feet," Nathan said. The sound of his voice was enough to turn Nathaniel's stomach to jelly. "You know better than to sit in my presence."

Nathaniel told himself to stay put, but he was already getting up. Lola laughed at that easy obedience and made a circle of the room so she could stand behind Nathaniel.

"Hello, Junior," Nathan said.

Nathaniel's jaw worked. He didn't dare speak; he didn't know what he would say. Nathan padded across the room toward him. It took everything Nathaniel had left to hold his ground. Nathan stopped in front of him, so close Nathaniel could smell his cologne. Nathaniel stared at the top button of his shirt like it could somehow save him from all of this.

Nathan's hand settled on his shoulder it what could have been but wasn't a reassuring gesture. Nathaniel braced himself for the inevitable blow, but his knees still buckled when Nathan punched the burns on his cheek. Nathan caught him by his throat as he fell. Nathaniel choked and scrabbled to find his feet again. He knew better than to grab his father for balance. He knew what his father would do if Nathaniel touched him.

"I said hello," Nathan said when Nathaniel was upright again.

Nathaniel's lips moved, but no sound came out. It took two more tries before he managed a quiet, "Hello."

"Look at me when I'm talking to you."

A scream felt like it was going to tear his throat open where he was keeping it bottled inside, but Nathaniel forced his stare

[249]

up to Nathan's face.

"My son," Nathan said. "My greatest disappointment in life. Where is my second greatest?"

"Mom is dead," Nathaniel said. "You killed her. Don't you remember?"

"I would remember," Nathan said. "I would have savored the memory while counting down days to finding you again."

"You broke her," Nathaniel said. "She only made it as far as the California border."

Nathan slid a hooded stare past Nathaniel at Lola, who said, "I believe him."

Nathan nodded, accepting her judgment, and cupped Nathaniel's battered face in his hands. He squeezed so hard Nathaniel thought the gashes on his face would split further. Nathaniel's hands flew up instinctively but he jerked them back away from his father at the last possible second. Nathan gave a thin smile at that close call and shook Nathaniel so roughly his neck popped in protest.

"Who told you that hiding in plain sight was a viable option? You had to know I would find you eventually."

"You should have let me go," Nathaniel said. "You sold me. I wasn't your problem anymore."

"The transaction was never finalized. Tetsuji did not agree to take you because you were not around long enough to convince him. That means you still belong to me," Nathan said. "You made a liar of me to people who are not to be lied to. Do you know what I'm going to do to you?

"I'm not entirely sure just yet, myself," Nathan said when Nathaniel could only stare numbly up at him. "I've had a couple years to think it over but now that the time has come I'm indecisive. I might skin you alive. I might take you apart one inch at a time and cauterize the wounds. I think no matter what I choose we are going to start by slicing the tendons in your legs. You're not going to run away this time, Nathaniel. I'm not going to let you."

[250]

"Fuck you," Nathaniel spat at him, voice sharp with horror.

Nathan pushed Nathaniel away from him and held his hand out. DiMaccio crossed the room toward him. In one hand he held Nathan's ancient, dull axe. In the other was Nathan's cleaver. Nathan turned at DiMaccio's approach and considered the weapons with interest. Nathaniel took advantage of his distraction and tried to bolt, but Lola was expecting it. She jumped on Nathaniel from behind and wound her arms around him. She couldn't hold him forever but she didn't have to. She slowed him long enough that DiMaccio could hand off a weapon and thunder past Nathan.

He scooped Nathaniel off the ground with a fistful of shirt, unmoved by the fists that rained down on him. Lola let go and neatly stepped back, and DiMaccio heaved Nathaniel at the closest wall. Impact smashed the breath of Nathaniel and he fell awkwardly to the floor. He caught himself with his hands, which was an awful mistake, but he didn't have the breath to cry out. He was so dizzy he felt ill, but movement in the corner of his eye got him moving. Metal flashed a scarce inch from his face as Nathan took a swing. Terror got Nathaniel on his feet faster than his body wanted to move and he retreated from his father's cleaver.

Nathan didn't chase him. He gave his cleaver an experimental wave, as if reacquainting himself with its weight, and tested its blade against his thumb. He must have just sharpened it, because blood welled up almost immediately.

Nathaniel's last nerve broke. He couldn't get past Nathan and DiMaccio, which meant taking his chance with Lola's knife and gun. He spun and ran for her. The wild smile on her face said she'd expected this resistance. She braced herself for the inevitable collision, knife out and ready to do some terrible damage. She slashed at him as he got closer. Nathaniel twisted away from the blade, nearly spraining his ankle in his hurry. Lola's gun was in his face a second later and knowing she couldn't pull the trigger didn't stop him from ducking.

She came at him, knife hand up for another swipe, and Nathaniel punched her in the throat. He barely heard the terrible choking sound she made through the crackling pain in his ears. Every cut and burn on his hand was screaming in protest. He clenched his fingers tighter and took another swing. Lola dodged, but barely, and left a hot stripe up his chest with the tip of her blade. Nathaniel was now between her and the door, and he threw the bar up to unlock it. Lola grabbed his hair before he could open the door but Nathaniel didn't care how much hair he lost. He surged forward anyway, refusing to let go of the knob.

"Move," Nathan said right behind them.

He was talking to Lola, but Nathaniel threw himself to one side too. Nathan's cleaver came down right where he'd been standing. Metal screamed as he scratched a line down the door, and Nathan turned a hot look on his fallen son. Nathaniel scrambled backwards, hope dying a vicious death in his chest. Nathan stomped toward him, done playing cat and mouse. Nathaniel tried getting to his feet, but a boot in his ribcage sent him sprawling. A fist to the face killed his next attempt and then Nathan was sitting on top of him with his cleaver to Nathaniel's throat.

DiMaccio came up behind them and offered Nathan's axe. Nathan put it to Nathaniel's neck next so he could carve shallow lines in Nathaniel's burned face with his cleaver. "Maybe we'll do both," he said, casual like he was debating the next day's weather. "Skin you an inch or two at a time and carve the flesh out from underneath. If we do it right, you might last all night. Patrick, have them toss us down the blowtorch. It should still be in the drawer by the oven."

"No," Nathaniel said, but DiMaccio went to the base of the stairs to call up.

"Lola," Nathan said, and Lola came immediately to his side. She wasn't smiling anymore. The look she turned on Nathaniel was venomous and she pressed careful fingers to her bruising neck. Nathaniel wanted to take some satisfaction in

[252]

having wounded her, but all he felt was fear. Nathan didn't look up from his son's face but said, "Would you like the pleasure of crippling him?"

"No," Nathaniel said again, but Lola crouched out of sight. Nathaniel kicked his legs out to the other side away from her. The axe wasn't sharp enough to cut his throat open without serious effort, so he ignored the way the weight of it made him gag and struggled as best he could. Nathan tolerated it until Nathaniel actually grabbed him, and then he lay his cleaver across the bridge of Nathaniel's nose.

"If you do not sit the fuck still I will gouge your eyes out."

Nathaniel froze, but he was trembling so hard it was a wonder he didn't shake his father off. "Please," he whispered, unable to stop himself. "Please don't."

"Can I?" Lola asked, excited all over again.

"We'll slit your ankles, then your knees," Nathan told Nathaniel. "And if you try to crawl away I will take your arms from you too. Do you understand?"

DiMaccio was back. He set the blowtorch down at Nathan's side. Nathaniel wanted to scream, but if he screamed now he'd really lose it and he wouldn't be able to stop. His eyes burned, maybe from the blood, maybe from panic held at bay by desperation. He clung to what remained of his self-control with bloody fingertips, knowing it wouldn't do him any good but unable to let go.

"Please," he begged again. "Just let me go, just let me go, I'm not—"

"Lola," Nathan said, but he didn't get to finish.

The cellar door opened from the outside, and a swarm of strangers came in shooting. Silencers helped muffle the sound somewhat, but in such a closed space Nathaniel still felt every pop like a bite against his skin. Lola was the closest to the door, and her body jerked as bullets tore countless holes through her. Nathan disappeared, hauled to questionable safety by DiMaccio. Nathaniel tried to lie still, not wanting to draw attention to

[253]

himself, but he looked to his father as more people poured into the room.

His father was completely shielded by DiMaccio's larger body, and he was yelling to his men for help. His guards rushed down the concrete stairs, but the unending burst of gunfire drowned out their footsteps. Someone grabbed Nathaniel and pulled him across the floor away from his father. Nathaniel lashed out instinctively, but his attacker didn't fight back. Nathaniel was dumped in a corner and subsequently abandoned.

Staying put seemed a good idea with so many bullets flying. Nathaniel curled his battered body up as tight as he could and shielded his head with his throbbing arms. It was an eternity before the house went still and silent. Nathaniel slowly lowered his arms and looked around.

Nathan was kneeling in the middle of the room with four guns aimed at his head. He started to get to his feet, but someone knocked him back down with the butt of a rifle. Nathan responded with an unintelligible snarl. One of the men guarding the door whistled a signal down the tunnel, and footsteps echoed faintly in the corridor.

A man stepped into the room, and Nathaniel stopped breathing. He would know that face anywhere. Nine years had taken a severe toll on Stuart Hatford, but Nathaniel still saw his mother in Stuart's lined face. Stuart answered Nathan's scowl with a glacier stare. He had his gun out halfway to Nathan, but a woman intercepted him and jerked her chin in Nathaniel's direction.

Stuart followed her gaze, and surprise took the edge off his white fury. "Bloody hell. Nathaniel?" Nathaniel was too stunned to speak, but he managed a small nod. Stuart pointed the gun in Nathan's direction but kept his stare on his nephew. "Where is Mary?" Nathaniel couldn't find his voice, so he shook his head. Stuart's expression shuttered; his glimmer of hope disappeared as quickly as it'd come. "Don't look. This will be over in a moment."

[254]

"How dare you," Nathan said savagely. "You defy Moriyama by coming here and killing my men. You are a dead man walking. You don't have the power to—"

Stuart didn't let him finish. Nathan's body jerked as two bullets punched holes into his chest. Nathaniel watched, wide-eyed and disbelieving, as blood splattered his father's throat and rushed down his shirt to stain his jeans. Nathan's body fell backward from the force of impact and hit the floor with a wet smack.

Nathaniel pressed a shaking hand to his mouth, then clamped his other hand over it. It wasn't enough to smother his ragged keen.

"I told you not to look," Stuart said.

That wrenching feeling in his chest wasn't grief, but a need so fierce Nathaniel thought it would kill him. His world was crumbling around him and he was falling. Nathaniel couldn't breathe, much less explain that terrifying exhilaration. He didn't fight when two of Stuart's men hoisted him to his feet.

Stuart crossed the room to stand in front of him. Nathaniel stared past him at his father's corpse. Stuart's hand on his chin forced his attention to his uncle's face. Stuart gave Nathaniel an intent once-over, checking his wounds with a furious gaze.

"He can ride with me," one of the women said.

"He is our only ticket out of here," Stuart said. "We will leave him behind. For now," he added before Nathaniel could react. He clenched his fingers tighter on Nathaniel's face and gave him a small shake. "You will listen to me and do exactly as I say. They only let us come here unchallenged because we promised we would take him alive."

Nathaniel finally found his voice. "The Moriyamas?"

"No," Stuart said, so harsh Nathaniel leaned away from him. "Do not speak that name tonight. You cannot pull them into this. They were not expecting their Butcher to die and we only have a small window in which to win their favor. We are giving you to the FBI as a distraction. You need medical attention, and we cannot yet take you where we need to go. This is the only way you survive. Do you understand?"

His father was dead. Nathaniel would agree to anything right then. "I won't tell them."

Stuart nodded. "Then we are leaving."

They helped him down the tunnel to the garage. The stairs up were dangerously steep and narrow, and the opening at the top was barely big enough for a man's body. Stuart's people vanished out the open garage door as fast as they could go, but Stuart stayed behind a moment with Nathaniel. Nathaniel stared out at the darkness, looking for the feds who had to be watching all of this from a safe distance. For now the street was calm and empty, but there was no way the neighbors had missed that shootout. In another minute, maybe two, the neighborhood would be crawling with police and the press all over again.

Stuart guided him to his knees and put his hands behind his head. "We will come back for you when we can. I promise."

Then he was gone, disappearing into the night after his team. Nathaniel stayed on his knees and bowed his head to wait. It didn't take long. Feds melted out of the shadows like ghosts, guns out and dressed head-to-toe in tactical gear. Nathaniel was too small to be his father, but the cover of darkness helped the illusion. They didn't realize anything was wrong until they yanked him to his feet with rough hands and strident voices. Nathaniel finally tipped his head up to look at them, and the agent closest to him trailed off mid-sentence.

"You're too late," Nathaniel said, even as someone radioed EMS to rush on-scene. "My father is dead."

"Your father," the agent said stupidly. Six men tore off down the hole so fast they almost fell, and Nathaniel heard their boots echoing off the tunnel wall as they ran to check the house. He didn't realize he'd looked down at the opening until the agent snapped gloved fingers in his face. Nathaniel met his searching look with a cool stare, and the man repeated, "Your father?"

"My name is Nathaniel Wesninski," he said, "and my father

is dead."

It wasn't at all funny, but a second later he was laughing. It sounded hysterical but he couldn't stop. Hands caught his shoulders and pushed his head down. A gruff voice ordered him to breathe but Nathaniel couldn't. He grabbed at his knees for balance. Pain lanced up his arms from his abused hands but he couldn't let go. The adrenaline of an unexpected firefight and the relief of being alive were breaking him apart, and Nathaniel finally lost the battle with his unsteady stomach. Someone held onto him while he retched onto the concrete floor. Nathaniel spat in a vain attempt to get the sour taste out of his mouth.

The hand on his shoulder tightened. "I'd rather not cuff you in the state you're in, but I will if I have to. Are you going to be a problem for us?"

Nathaniel struggled to look up and focus on the man's face. "I've been a problem for nineteen years. I'm too tired to be one tonight. Just get me out of here."

An ambulance pulled up to the curb. It'd gotten here fast enough Nathaniel guessed it'd been waiting down the street out of sight. Despite his reassurance, he had a three-agent escort down to the paramedics. They had the stretcher out and on the street by the time he made it there, and Nathaniel lay down on it without a fuss. They strapped him in for the ride and lifted him into the back. An agent rode with them; Nathaniel assumed more would follow. He didn't care anymore. He closed his eyes and let the paramedic get to work.

-

When Nathaniel opened his eyes again, he was on his back in a hospital bed and soft sunlight was filtering through the curtained window. Ropes of plastic tubing streaked out from underneath his blanket and the drugs made his head feel like cotton. He was awake, but pleasantly detached from the pain.

He had two guests he didn't recognize, but he knew in a glance they were feds. They had that air of smug authority men often carried when they thought themselves more powerful than

[257]

they were. One sat on a stool to his left. The other had claimed the better of two chairs near the foot of the bed and was going through paperwork. The door was closed to give them privacy but Nathaniel assumed someone was standing guard outside.

A handcuff locked one of Nathaniel's bandaged wrists to the bed frame. Nathaniel rattled it and said, "Really?"

"We're not taking any chances," the closer man said. "As soon as the doctors clear you we're moving you to our field office. But don't think you have to wait for an official setting to talk to us. We're ready to hear everything you have to say. Special Agent Browning," the agent said belatedly, and gestured to his partner. "This is Special Agent Towns. We're going to be your handlers."

"My handlers," Nathaniel repeated. "I am not your property."

"But you are in our custody."

"Are you arresting me?"

"Right now we're acting in good faith and assuming we will have your full cooperation. If we need to take a more aggressive approach, we will do so. We've got a string of offenses we could charge you with, starting with the fake IDs in your wallet and escalating to your mother's current whereabouts. Just let us know if we've got to play hardball."

Nathaniel made a rude noise. "You couldn't at least use an Exy idiom? I hate baseball."

"Right now what you do or do not hate is of little concern to us," Towns said. "We only care about the truth."

"I'll trade you truth for truth," Nathaniel said. "My teammates were caught in a riot last night. The Palmetto State Foxes," he elaborated, though he was sure the agents had pieced at least that much together since picking him up at his father's house. "Were they hurt?"

"Eighty-six people ended up in the hospital, including three of your teammates," Browning said. "They were treated and summarily released. Minor injuries. They were lucky. A couple

[258]

people ended up in the ICU."

"We made contact with Coach Wymack shortly after you were admitted here and asked him to bring his people for questioning," Towns added. He checked his watch and said, "They should be wrapping things up soon. When we're done with them they are free to return to South Carolina."

He didn't say "without you", but Nathaniel heard it in his tone.

"It's your turn," Browning said. "Where is your mother?"

Nathaniel told them about running into his father in Seattle and the vicious attack they weren't fast enough to escape. He told them about fire and sand and burying her on the coast. It was brutally unfair that she hadn't lived long enough to see Nathan die, but Nathaniel kept that bitter misery to himself.

"All this time you were hiding out in Seattle?" Browning said, sounding annoyed by their oversight.

"No," Nathaniel said. "That was just the last real stop before Arizona."

"What came before Seattle?"

"I want to see my teammates."

"What came before Seattle?" Browning repeated.

Nathaniel pressed his mouth into a hard line and stared at the ceiling. Browning tolerated the silent treatment for a few minutes, then started talking. He laid out everything they were willing to offer Nathaniel if his cooperation was worth their while: immunity from all charges, a fresh start in the Witness Protection Program, and the chance to tear apart his father's circle. When Nathaniel remained unmoved by such generous offers, Browning turned to threats instead. What they had on Nathaniel so far was enough cause to lock him up, and they'd eventually dig up the dirt they needed to throw away the key.

"I want to see my teammates," Nathaniel said when Browning finally took a breath.

"Be reasonable," Towns said. "Don't make this harder for yourself than you need to."

[259]

"You think this is hard? Look what I've been through. Surviving you is easy." Nathaniel tipped his head to one side and fixed Towns with a cool look. "But can you survive me?"

"Are you threatening a federal agent?"

Nathaniel smiled so hard his burns ached. "I wouldn't dare. What I should have said was: can you survive my family? My parents are dead, but my uncle remembers me. More importantly, he remembers that you gave him permission to take on my father last night. Since when do suits cut deals with gangsters?"

"I don't know what you're talking about," Browning said, with a cool neutrality Nathaniel didn't believe for a second.

"Whatever," Nathaniel said. "I'm going to nap."

They didn't argue, so he closed his eyes and drifted off. He woke some indeterminable time later when a nurse came in to check his injuries. All the painkillers in his system meant nothing as she cleaned the burns on his hands and arms. Nathaniel clenched his teeth so hard he thought he'd break them and fought the urge to kick her away from him. She gave his stitches an approving nod and promised to have the doctor stop by later. She closed the door on her way out.

It was impossible to sleep again when his nerves were screaming alarms in his ears. Nathaniel flexed his fingers instead, checking his range of motion. Lola had burnt him to hurt him, not maim him. Maybe she'd feared too much melting skin would wreck the coils and kill her fun. He knew from the nurse's reactions his face hadn't gotten off so lightly, but he didn't want to see a mirror yet. Nathaniel was as furious as he was nauseous just thinking about it.

Before the latter could win out Nathaniel looked up and said, "I want to see my teammates."

"And I want coffee," Browning said. "You two good here?"

Towns nodded. Browning checked his pockets for his wallet and left. Nathaniel gave his handcuff a couple experimental tugs just to see how Towns responded. Towns was unimpressed by that faint attempt at rebellion and went back to his files. They ignored each other until Browning came back. Browning sat quietly until his coffee was gone, then perused one of Towns' discarded stacks. After an hour of this, he made another attempt at getting through to Nathaniel.

"Feel like cooperating yet?"

"I still don't see my teammates, so no," Nathaniel said. Browning made a dismissive gesture. Nathaniel yanked at his cuffed hand again. "Look: these are the people I chose to stay with even knowing I couldn't stay for long. I picked them over my own safety. So give them back to me and I'll answer anything you ask."

"You only think you want to see them," Towns said. "Remember that they just found out who and what you are. If they still want anything to do with you, I'll eat my hat."

Nathaniel opened his mouth, closed it again, and looked away. His teammates had accepted the vague confession Aaron forced out of him, but knowing his family was awful and dealing with the reality were two entirely different things. Maybe Kevin had had time on the ride from New York to tell them how the Wesninskis and Moriyamas were connected, in which case they now knew how much danger he put them in by signing Wymack's contract.

He'd promised them his family wasn't going to be a problem for them, but he'd gotten them hurt and was going to cost them championships. They might hate him, they might fear him, and they would likely never forgive him, but Nathaniel couldn't leave them like this. He hadn't gotten to say goodbye yesterday. He had to say it today, before the feds pushed him so deep the light would never again reach him.

"In fact," Towns continued, "they're probably already on the road south. It wouldn't have taken long to get their statements, and there's nothing else we need from them yet."

"You're wrong," Nathaniel said. "They can't leave without Andrew, and Andrew won't go anywhere until he talks to me."

[261]

"You don't know that."

"Yes, I do." Even if it was just to tear Nathaniel apart for hiding this from him, Andrew would wait as long as it took. He wasn't the sort to leave things unfinished. Nathaniel knew that, believed that, with every fiber of his being. It was enough to soothe the sting of Towns' callous warning. "You can take me to him, or you can let me rot silently in a cell somewhere. Those are your only options."

Finally Browning got up and went into the hall. Nathaniel heard his strident tone through the wood, but he couldn't understand Browning's words. Towns watched his partner closely when Browning returned, and Browning answered by scribbling a note on Towns' clipboard. Nathaniel resisted the temptation to throw his thin pillow at them and eased onto his back again instead.

They didn't say anything else to him, so Nathaniel let his thoughts drift. The hours to his discharge stretched endless and miserable. When the doctor stopped by to give him advice about how to treat his injuries, Nathaniel cut her off with a rude, "I don't need your help."

The doctor, likely used to ornery patients, signed the bottom of Nathaniel's chart without another word. She looked to the agents and said, "They can sign you out at the desk down the hall. They'll have his medicine ready for you."

Browning nodded but waited for the doctor to leave before unlocking the handcuff that bound Nathaniel to the bed. He and Towns put the rail down so Nathaniel could slide off the mattress. Towns handed over a bag, and Nathaniel dumped a set of dark sweats onto the bed.

"Where are my clothes?" Nathaniel asked.

"Taken as evidence," Towns said.

Towns went to stand by the door. Browning stayed close, but he half-turned away from Nathaniel. If Nathaniel tried anything, he'd see it in his peripheral vision, but it was still a smidgen of privacy. The hospital gown Nathaniel wore was

[262]

unfastened, which he was immensely grateful for. He didn't think he could deal with knots and strings until his hands were better. He shrugged the gown off and eased into his new clothes as carefully as he could. His hands were burning by the time he was done. He held them close to his stomach, knowing it wouldn't help at all but needing to try and quench that fire somehow.

Browning cuffed his hands in front of him, then pulled his hood down over his face. "Thanks to your father's neighbors, the press knows someone was taken from Nathan's house last night. The major channels don't have a name yet, but they won't need it. You've spent too much time on TV this last year. People will recognize your face the second they get a glimpse of it."

"Is there enough of it left to recognize?" Nathaniel asked.

"There's a mirror around here somewhere if you want to see."

"I'd settle for your opinion," Nathaniel said.

"It'll heal eventually," Browning said, which was neither here nor there.

They led him down the hall. Towns signed them out and picked up a white bag that rattled. Painkillers and antibiotics, Nathaniel assumed. Burn cream if he was lucky. Towns gave it to him to carry, and they took an elevator down. Browning called ahead as they reached the ground floor and got an all-clear. Nathaniel didn't look up to see if there were reporters lurking around for photographs. He kept his head tilted as far down as he could and hoped the hood was bulky enough to shield his face.

An SUV idled at the curb. The back door opened at their approach and Nathaniel climbed in. Towns got in the far back, so Browning took the seat at Nathaniel's side. Browning slammed the door and made a short call from his phone just to say, "We're on the way. Get it out of sight before we get there."

The woman in the passenger seat flicked Nathaniel a curious look over her shoulder. He slid his gaze away and stared

[263]

out the tinted windows. He recognized streets and buildings as they drove. In a terrible, impossible way, this somehow felt like home. Nathaniel wanted to claw that feeling out of himself and burn it. The Foxhole Court was the only home he needed; the Foxes were his family. He didn't want any of this to have a hold on him anymore. How sad, how strange, how stupid, that he could run so far and still end up back here in the end. He couldn't stand the sight of the city, so he tipped his head back and closed his eyes.

He couldn't sleep, but at least he could daydream his father's death over and over again. That was almost enough to make him smile, and eventually it thawed the chill from his veins.

CHAPTER FOURTEEN

Nathaniel expected to be carted straight to their office for questioning, but the SUV turned into a hotel parking lot. The place was crawling with feds. Men stood on the sidewalk, smoking and attempting to look casual, but Nathaniel's skin crawled at the sight of them. The ladies sunning by the pool were equally offensive despite their attempt to be inconspicuous. The woman by the vending machine was a toss-up, but Nathaniel was inclined to think badly of everyone in his sights.

As soon as the car stopped Nathaniel turned an expectant look on Browning. Browning put a finger in his face. "You have twenty minutes or until they throw you out of their lives, whichever comes first. Then you are coming with us and you are going to tell us everything we want to know. Do I make myself clear?"

"They," Nathaniel said. "They're here? I don't see the bus."

"I don't want the press seeing it here and putting it all together yet, so I had your coach move it. I said, are we clear?"

"Clear," Nathaniel said, and pulled the hood down over his face again. "Get out."

"Your winning personality makes me rethink this entire thing," Browning said, but he got out of the car.

They took him up rickety metal stairs to the second floor. A woman lounged against the balcony railing with a cellphone to her ear. She pushed her hair over her shoulder and flicked her fingers in the same move. Browning guided Nathaniel to the appropriate door and knocked. The door opened half a foot, but Nathaniel couldn't see anything past a hefty suited body. The man standing guard scowled down at Nathaniel before turning an annoyed look on Browning.

"I don't like it."

"Noted. Watch him a moment, Kurt," Browning said. Kurt stepped aside and pulled the door open. Browning strode past him, clapping as he went to get everyone's attention. Even on the balcony he was loud enough for Nathaniel to hear every word. "Listen up, people. You've got twenty minutes. Let's keep this orderly and have only one person up at a time."

Kurt obviously expected the Foxes to submit without a fight, because he dropped his arm and let Nathaniel through. He should have waited a bit longer, as Nathaniel's teammates started arguing almost immediately.

Dan's outraged voice carried the easiest when she snapped, "Twenty minutes? You've got to be joking. Why do—oh my god," she broke off when Nathaniel stepped into the room. The rush in her voice wasn't anger or disgust, but terror-fueled relief. "Oh my god, Neil. Are you okay?"

Nathaniel opened his mouth, but words failed him. Last night he knew he'd never see any of them again. Having them back was a salve on every one of his aching wounds, but he was keenly aware he was just here for goodbye. It would kill him to walk out of here.

He owed them explanations and apologies, but he didn't know where to start. All he could do was look from one stunned face to another. There was a hollow look on Kevin's face and dark bruises on his throat. Nicky was a disconsolate mess near the window. Allison and Renee sat on the far bed with two black eyes and a couple dozen bruises between them. The spots on Allison's arm were obviously left by fingers. Nathaniel hoped Allison beat up whoever was stupid enough to grab her so hard, but maybe Renee had handled that for her. One of Renee's hands was bandaged and she wore a brace on her other wrist. Aaron sat halfway down on the same bed, and for once even he looked more upset than angry when he looked at Nathaniel.

Matt and Dan were on the nearer bed. Matt had a white-knuckled grip on Dan's shoulder like he'd had to stop her from

[266]

charging Browning. Matt had taken a severe beating in the riot and still had ice packs strapped to both hands. His shirt was filthy and torn in two places, and Nathaniel could see ugly bruises through the gaps. Abby stood between the beds, her first aid kit open on the blankets near Matt's right hip, but she dropped the antiseptic she was holding when she saw Nathaniel.

Abby's mouth moved, but Nathaniel didn't hear a word she said. Browning said the Foxes only suffered minor injuries and that none of them had ended up in the ICU, but only seven of them were here. Wymack was out moving the bus, but that left one person unaccounted for.

Nathaniel's blood went cold, and he couldn't keep the alarm from his voice when he started to ask, "Where's And—"

There was a crash behind Nathaniel, the unmistakable sound of a body slamming into wood. He turned as Andrew forced his way into the room with Wymack right on his heels. Kurt grabbed at Andrew but lost his grip when Wymack shouldered past him. Nathaniel had only a second to see the handcuffs locking Andrew and Wymack together, and then Browning reacted to the violent entrance by reaching for his gun.

Nathaniel grabbed Browning's arm with both hands and yanked as hard as he could. He only meant to slow Browning down and pull him off-balance, but the agony that shot from Nathaniel's fingertips to his elbows almost took him off his feet. He let go without meaning to and hunched over like that would somehow make the pain go away. Crushing his hands to his stomach didn't help, but Nathaniel needed to shield them somehow.

"Don't," he said through clenched teeth.

He thought he said it, anyway; he couldn't hear himself through the white noise roaring in his ears. The weight of a hand on the back of his neck said he'd bought Andrew enough time to reach him. Nathaniel didn't remember closing his eyes, but he forced them open again. He tried straightening, but Andrew

[267]

caught his shoulder and shoved him to his knees. Nathaniel went without argument and cradled his wrecked hands in his lap. His hands felt so terrible he expected to see blood soaking through his bandages, but the gauze stayed white and clean.

"Leave it," Wymack said.

He sounded so angry Nathaniel knew Wymack wasn't talking to him or Andrew. He guessed Browning or Kurt was moving to haul Andrew out of the way before he hurt Nathaniel further. Either the feds trusted his judgment or they couldn't get around Wymack to get to Andrew, but Andrew knelt in front of Nathaniel unchallenged. Nathaniel turned his hands over and looked up.

Andrew's expression was deceptively calm, but there was iron in his grip when he seized Nathaniel's chin. Nathaniel let him look his fill because it gave him time to study the bruises lining Andrew's face. The worst of the lot was a dark, narrow streak running down over his cheekbone from the corner of his right eye. The force of impact left half of Andrew's eye red with blood. An elbow, Nathaniel thought, that had come way too close.

"They could have blinded you," Nathaniel said. "All that time fighting and you never learned how to duck?"

A stony stare was his only answer. Andrew let go of him so he could tug Nathaniel's hood out of the way. He dragged a finger along the lines of tape keeping the myriad of bandages in place as if looking for the best place to start. He tore the gauze off Nathaniel's right cheek first, exposing the striped lines left by Lola's knife. He favored the stitches with a cursory glance before moving on. The tape on Nathaniel's other cheek hurt like hell coming off, since it pulled the skin around his burns, and Andrew froze with his hand a few scant inches from Nathaniel's face.

Andrew's expression didn't change, but there was a new tension in his shoulders that didn't bode well for anyone in the room. Andrew had dropped the first bandages as useless, but

[268]

these ones he slowly set on the floor by his knee without taking his stare off Nathaniel's face. Since Nathaniel was kneeling with his back to the room, Wymack was the only other person who could see the mess Lola made of his face. Nathaniel didn't dare look up at him, but Wymack's fierce, "Christ, Neil," said the burns looked as bad as they felt.

A bed creaked as one of the Foxes got up. Wymack jerked his free hand in an emphatic order to stay put and said, "Don't."

"One at a time," Browning reminded them.

Andrew pressed two fingers to the underside of Nathaniel's chin to turn his head. Nathaniel let himself be guided and said nothing while Andrew looked his fill. When Andrew dropped his hand and clenched it in Nathaniel's hoodie, Nathaniel risked looking back at him. There was violence in Andrew's eyes, but at least he hadn't shoved Nathaniel away yet. That had to count for something.

"I'm sorry," Nathaniel said.

Andrew's fist went back, but he didn't take the swing. Nathaniel knew it wasn't because that was the hand cuffed to Wymack; Andrew's arm actually shook with the effort it took to not knock Nathaniel's head off his neck. Nathaniel said nothing to tip the balance either way. At length Andrew uncurled his fingers and let his hand hang limp from the cuff.

"Say it again and I will kill you," he said.

"This is the last time I'm going to say it to you," Kurt said, coming up beside Wymack with a dark look on his face. "If you can't stow that attitude and behave—"

Nathaniel shot a warning look at him and cut in with, "You'll what, asshole?"

"The same goes for you, Nathaniel," Browning said. "That's your second strike. A third misstep and this," he twirled his finger to indicate the Foxes, "is over. Remember you are only here because we are allowing it."

Andrew shifted as if to get up and Nathaniel knew he was going to shut Browning up for good. Nathaniel knew better than to touch Andrew yet but he got as close as he could and framed Andrew's face between his bandaged hands. Andrew could have easily pushed him aside, but after a short pause he got settled again. Nathaniel flicked him a quick look, grateful for that compliance, before leveling another icy stare at Browning.

"Don't lie to a liar," Nathaniel said. "We both know I'm here because you have nothing without me. A pile of dead bodies can't close cases or play the money trail with you. I told you what those answers would cost you and you agreed to pay it. So take this handcuff off of Andrew, get your man out of our way, and stop using up my twenty minutes with your useless posturing."

The silence that followed was brittle. Browning was weighing his options, or at least acting like he was. Nathaniel knew this could only end one way. If the FBI had let the Hatfords into the country uncontested they had to be desperate for some resolution. No one could prove—yet—that Nathan had killed Mary Hatford, but the Hatfords' hatred for Nathan wasn't a secret and they'd reacted to his parole by booking tickets across the Atlantic. It didn't take the FBI's brightest to know their visit wouldn't be friendly.

Finally Browning gestured. Kurt's face was a thundercloud as he dug keys out of his pocket. Wymack turned to make it easier for him. Andrew didn't watch as the cuff came off, but he flexed his fingers a few times to test his freedom and dropped his hand to his thigh. Browning took Kurt with him to wait just inside the door. They radiated displeasure and distrust and the look Browning sent his watch was pointed, but Nathaniel didn't care. Satisfied they were out of the way at last, he turned his full attention on Andrew again.

"So the attitude problem wasn't an act, at least," Andrew said.

"I was going to tell you," Nathaniel said.

"Stop lying to me."

"I'm not lying. I would have told you last night, but they

[270]

were in our locker room."

"They who?" Browning asked.

Nathaniel switched to German without missing a beat. He was pretty sure he earned a dirty look from Browning for that trick, but he wouldn't take his eyes off Andrew to look. "Those weren't security guards that came for us. They were there for me, and they would have hurt all of you to get me out of there. I thought by keeping my mouth shut I could keep you safe." Nathaniel still had his hands up by Andrew's face, so he lightly tapped a thumb against the bruise at Andrew's eye. "I didn't know they'd staged a riot."

"What did I tell you about playing the martyr card?" Andrew asked.

"You said no one wanted it," Nathaniel said. "You didn't tell me to stop."

"It was implied."

"I'm stupid, remember? I need things spelled out."

"Shut up."

"Am I at ninety-four yet?"

"You are at one hundred," Andrew said. "What happened to your face?"

Nathaniel swallowed hard against a rush of nausea. "A dashboard lighter."

He winced at the awful sound Nicky made. The groan of a quickly-shifting mattress almost swallowed up Aaron's ragged curse. Nathaniel looked back without thinking, needing to see who was on the move, and saw Aaron had rolled off the bed to go stand with Nicky. Turning meant the others got a look at his burned cheek. Kevin recoiled so hard he slammed into the wall behind him. He clapped a protective hand over his own tattoo and Nathaniel knew he was imagining Riko's reaction to this atrocity.

This time it was Dan stopping Matt from getting up, her knuckles white against his dark shirt and her head turned away. Matt started to fight free but settled for a hoarse, "Jesus, Neil.

[271]

The fuck did they do to you?"

Abby had kept her distance long enough, it seemed. She came around the bed, wide-eyed and frantic, but only made it to the corner before Andrew realized her intentions. He caught hold of Nathaniel to turn his face forward again and shot Abby a look so vicious she stopped in her tracks.

"Get away from us," Andrew said.

"Andrew," Abby said, quiet and careful. "He's hurt. Let me see him."

"If you make me repeat myself you will not live to regret it."

Nathaniel had never heard that murderous tone from him. It made his hair stand on end but somehow eased some of the lava in his chest. It was Nathaniel's fault Andrew's self-control was in shreds, but it was also for his sake. Andrew's bottomless rage would never hurt Nathaniel, and that made all the difference in the world. Nathaniel gave Andrew's hair a cautious tug. Andrew resisted the first two attempts but finally let Nathaniel drag his attention back where it needed to be.

"Abby, I just got out of the hospital," Nathaniel said without looking away from Andrew. "I'm as good as I can be right now."

"Neil," Abby tried.

"Please," Nathaniel stressed. He didn't hear her step back but he knew she did by the way Andrew's death grip on his skull relaxed. Nathaniel kept one hand buried in Andrew's hair but finally lowered the other. In quiet German he said, "Did they tell you who I am?"

"They didn't have to. I choked the answers out of Kevin on the way here." Andrew ignored the way Nathaniel gaped at him and said, "Guess you weren't an orphan after all. Where is your father now?"

"My uncle executed him," Nathaniel said, wondering. He crossed a precarious line and pressed two fingers to Andrew's chest over his heart. The memory chilled him to the bone, and he couldn't suppress all of a shudder. "I spent my whole life

[272]

wishing he would die, but I thought he never would. I thought he was invincible. I can't believe it was that easy."

"Was it easy?" Andrew asked. "Kevin told us who he worked for."

Nathaniel didn't think either agent could understand them, but names were hard to disguise in any language. He was glad Andrew was smart enough to not say the Moriyamas' name aloud. "My uncle said he was going to them to try and negotiate a ceasefire. I don't know if he's strong enough to bargain with them, but I'd like to think he wouldn't have risked it without real ground to stand on. Promise me no one's told the FBI about them."

"No one's said a word to them since they said we couldn't see you."

Nathaniel's heart skipped a beat. The heat that gnawed at his chest was an ugly mix of gratitude and shame. He tried to speak but had to clear his throat before trying again. "But why? I've done nothing but lie to them. I willingly put them all in danger so I could play a little longer. They got hurt last night because of me. Why would they protect me now?"

"You are a Fox," Andrew said, like it was that simple, and maybe it was.

Nathaniel dropped his eyes and worked his jaw, fighting for a center he was quickly losing hold of. He barely recognized his own voice when he said, "Andrew, they want to take me away from here. They want to enroll me in the Witness Protection Program so my father's people can't find me. I don't want—" he started, but that wasn't fair. "If you tell me to leave, I'll go."

He didn't say it would kill him, but he didn't have to. Andrew hooked his fingers in the collar of Nathaniel's sweatshirt and tugged just enough for him to feel it. For a moment Nathaniel was months away from this moment, standing in the darkened front hall of Andrew's house for the first time with a warm key digging into his palm. It felt like coming home, and it was enough to take the edge off his fear.

[273]

"You aren't going anywhere," Andrew said: the same words, the same promise. He was speaking in English again, and Nathaniel understood why when he heard Andrew's next words. Andrew was playing instigator and inviting the Foxes to the fight. "You're staying with us. If they try to take you away they will lose."

"Take you away," Dan echoed. "To where?"

"Are we talking about 'away for some questioning' or 'away for good'?" Matt demanded.

"Both," Browning said.

"You can't have him," Nicky said. "He belongs with us."

"When people find out he is still alive they will come for him," Browning said. "It is not safe for him here anymore, and it sure as hell isn't safe for you. It is better for everyone if he disappears."

They understood better than he ever would, since Kevin had already told them of the Wesninski-Moriyama alliance. They'd been dealing with Riko's madness for a year now thanks to Kevin, and they looked wholly unimpressed by Browning's warnings.

"What part of 'go to hell' do you need us to explain to you?" Allison asked.

"We're all legal adults here," Matt added. "We've made our decision. Unless he wants to stay with you, you'd better bring Neil back to us when you're done with all your questions."

"'Neil' isn't a real person," Browning said, fed up with their willful ignorance. "It's just a cover that let Nathaniel evade authorities. It's past time to let him go."

"Neil or Nathaniel or whoever," Nicky said. "He's ours, and we're not letting him go. You want us to vote on it or something? Bet you it'll be unanimous."

"Coach Wymack, talk some sense into your team," Browning said.

"Neil," Wymack said, and Nathaniel lifted his stare to look over Andrew at Wymack. Nathaniel had seen that look on his

[274]

face only once before, when Wymack tried putting him back together after Christmas. It was the look of a man made ancient by his players' tragedies; it was the look of a man who'd have their backs no matter what it cost him. Nathaniel felt wretched for causing that expression again but infinitely comforted by Wymack's unhesitating support. "Talk to me. What do you want?"

Nathaniel swallowed hard against an unexpected lump in his throat. His words came out so jagged they all had to go quiet to understand him. "I want—I know I shouldn't stay, but I can't—I don't want to lose this. I don't want to lose any of you. I don't want to be Nathaniel anymore. I want to be Neil for as long as I can."

"Good," Wymack said. "I'd have a hell of a time fitting 'Wesninski' on a jersey."

Browning rubbed at his temples. "I would like a word with you."

"About?"

"Your willingness to put your players in considerable danger, for one."

"Giving up on Neil now goes against everything we are," Wymack said. "I'm game to argue with you about it for as long as it takes, but not if it means using up Neil's allotted time. That's not fair to any of them."

Andrew tugged Nathaniel's hoodie and said in German, "Get rid of them before I kill them."

"They're waiting for answers," Nathaniel said. "They were never able to charge my father while he was alive. They're hoping I know enough to start decimating his circle in his absence. I'm going to give them the truth, or as much of it as I can without telling them my father was acting on someone's orders. Do you want to be there for it? It's the story I should have given you months ago."

"I have to go," Andrew said. "I don't trust them to give you back."

[275]

Andrew let go of him and got to his feet. Nathaniel got up without his help and looked past Andrew to Wymack. "I'm sorry," he said in English. "I should have told you, but I couldn't."

"Don't worry about that right now," Wymack said. "Twenty minutes isn't near long enough for this conversation. We can talk about it on the ride back to campus, right?"

"Yes," Nathaniel said. "I promise. I just have to talk to them first."

"Then go," Dan said. When Nathaniel looked back at her, she stressed, "But come back to us as soon as they're done with you, okay? We'll figure this out as a team."

"As a family." Nicky attempted a smile. It was weak, but it was encouraging.

This had to be a cruel dream. Their forgiveness threatened to burn Nathaniel up from the inside-out, as healing as it was damning. He didn't deserve their friendship or their trust. He'd never be able to repay them for rallying behind him like this. He could try the rest of his life, however long it was going to be now that Stuart was in the picture and Nathan was out, and he'd always fall short.

"Thank you," he said.

Allison waved his thanks off with an airiness that didn't match her tense expression. "No, thank you. You just closed three outstanding bets and made me five hundred bucks," she said when Nathaniel glanced at her. "I'd rather find out exactly why and when you two hooked up than think about this awfulness any longer, so let's talk about that on the ride back instead."

Aaron's gaze bounced from Allison to Nathaniel to Andrew. He was waiting for them to shoot her down, Nathaniel thought, and his expression went slack when neither one of them did. Nicky opened his mouth, then closed it again without a word and stared at Nathaniel. Kevin, surprisingly, didn't react at all.

Nathaniel didn't have the energy to confirm or deny

[276]

anything right now, so he just looked at Andrew and asked, "Ready?"

"Waiting on you," Andrew reminded him.

"I didn't invite him," Browning said.

"Trust me," Wymack said. "You'll fare a lot better if you take them both."

Browning flicked a calculating look between them and gave in with an impatient, "We're leaving now."

Wymack moved out of the way to let them pass, but as Nathaniel reached the door, he said, "We'll wait for you, all right? As long as it takes, Neil."

Nathaniel nodded and stepped out onto the balcony. He and Andrew went down the stairs behind Browning and got into the backseat of the SUV. Browning sat ahead of them and slammed the door. Nathaniel watched until the hotel disappeared out the window, then looked to Andrew and asked in German, "Can I really be Neil again?"

"I told Neil to stay," Andrew said. "Leave Nathaniel buried in Baltimore with his father."

Nathaniel looked out the window again and wondered if that was possible. He knew in a sense he could never really leave Nathaniel behind. Even if Stuart could talk the Moriyamas down, they'd all know Nathan's child was alive and kicking. Nathaniel would always be a security risk to them. But the thought was thrilling and chilling in turns, and Nathaniel turned his hand over to consider his palm. He traced Andrew's key into his skin with a bandaged finger.

"Neil Abram Josten," Neil murmured, and it felt like waking up from a bad dream.

-

Neil knew talking to the FBI wasn't going to be easy, but he hadn't expected it to be this strenuous. He spent the rest of Saturday and all of Sunday cooped up with them in their offices. The only time Andrew and Neil left each other's line of sight was when someone came by to check Neil's wounds, and the

[277]

two of them were never left alone together. The agents brought in food so he wouldn't have to leave the building, escorted him to and from the restroom, and set up cots so he and Andrew could sleep on-site under surveillance.

In exchange for their questionable hospitality, Neil told them everything. They started with Lola's phone call and went through the shootout, where Neil put as many names to faces as he could. Almost as important as who died was who'd survived. Neither Romero nor Jackson had been at the house. From there they bounced to Neil's childhood and all the terrible things that entailed.

After they ransacked his memory for everything about his father's people and known heists, they moved on to Neil's whereabouts for the seven years between Baltimore and Millport. Neil took them step by step through every alias and residence, but he refused to give up his mother's contacts. He plead ignorance based on his age at the time, and after asking him the question twenty different ways the agents eventually gave up. Neil told them where his father's people had caught up with them, the places where Nathan himself had shown up on their heels, and stopped with his mother's death.

They had to acknowledge the Hatfords at one point, but it made for a cagey conversation. The FBI couldn't admit to whatever deals they'd struck and Neil couldn't prove anything. Instead they focused on what Neil knew of Stuart from his youth. Neil didn't have much to offer, but what little he did have became a turning point in how some of the agents viewed him. Until that conversation they looked at him and saw only Nathan's son. Finding out he'd chosen a life on the run over a sedentary life with another crime family earned him points with more than one fed.

Twice on Sunday they brought up the Witness Protection Program again, but Neil refused both times. He was giving them everything they needed to build a case and he was willing to testify if they could get any of Nathan's people on the stands.

[278]

Until then he wanted to stay as he was. If they enrolled him against his will he'd simply slip his leash and go back to Palmetto State. Andrew said the Foxes would never let Neil disappear quietly. They'd raise a fuss and get the press neck-deep in it until someone turned him up. The agents called them selfish and reckless, but Neil and Andrew held their ground.

Neil didn't know they'd won the argument until Browning slapped a couple applications on the table in front of him. The first was an official name change request, the second and third were for a passport and driver's license, and the last was for a reissued social security card due to the first. A picture Neil only dimly recognized was held to the second with a paperclip; it was a mug shot Wymack had taken of him last summer for his school file. In it he still had brown hair and eyes, and his face was free of Riko's tattoo. Despite the picture, the application was half-filled out already and indicated his natural eye color as blue. Neil guessed the picture would shrink to where no one would really notice the discrepancy.

He was so distracted by the picture it took him a moment to understand the significance of what he'd been handed. Across the top of every page was the name Neil Josten. All Neil had to do was sign the dotted lines.

"Consider this a contract with us," Browning said, sounding as peeved as always. He waited for Neil to look up at him before continuing. "Once you sign this, we start the process to instate 'Neil Josten' as a valid and functioning member of society. That means no more running and no more fake IDs. You are going to be Neil from now until death. You are not allowed to change your mind. You so much as order a latte under a pseudonym and we are going to have a serious problem."

"Pen," Neil said, holding out his hand. When Browning didn't move fast enough, he said, "I get it. Just give me a pen so I can sign it."

Browning tossed it onto the table. Andrew caught it before it could roll off the edge and passed it over. Neil scribbled his name along every dotted line and handed the stack back. Browning passed them off to someone else and considered the file-strewn table.

"We're done here," Browning said. "If we think of anything else, we'll let you know."

"I'm sure you will." Neil got to his feet and stretched out the day's kinks. The conference room they'd taken over was windowless, but the clock on the wall said it was half past nine. They'd been in here for almost thirteen hours. The day had felt long as it dragged by, but knowing how many hours he'd lost pushed him one step past exhausted to drained. He carefully scrubbed the heels of his hands into his eyes and choked down a yawn.

"Stetson will give you a lift," Browning said when Neil dropped his hands to his sides.

Stetson was a humorless man they'd seen occasionally throughout the day. Neil didn't mind him half as much as he did Browning because Stetson hadn't said a single word to them. The end of the interrogation wasn't reason enough to break that silence, it seemed. He collected them with a glance and brought them to his car. Neil sat in the backseat with Andrew and toyed with the bandages on his face. Andrew popped the back of his head when he realized what Neil was doing and ignored Neil's scowl.

Stetson walked them upstairs to the hotel room, but the Foxes had spread out in their absence. Having to stay a night meant they'd needed to acquire enough beds for everyone. This room with its two queen beds now housed only Abby and Wymack. Wymack looked from Neil to Andrew, then turned his attention on Stetson.

"Giving me a ride to the bus?" he asked. He waited for a nod, then motioned for Andrew and Neil to make themselves at home. "I'll be right back. Figure out if we're staying or going."

He closed the door behind himself. Neil listened through the wood for the faint sound of footsteps on stairs, then locked the door and pulled the chain. Abby sat in the middle of one of the beds, and she held out both hands to Neil when he turned away from the door.

"Let me take a look at you."

Neil couldn't crawl across the bed to her or shove himself across with his hands, so he toed out of his shoes and stepped up onto the bed instead. He took a couple unsteady steps over to her and sat before he could fall. The mattress shifted as Andrew took up post behind him. Neil put down his bag of medicine where Abby could get to the antibiotics if necessary, but she had the Foxes' unusually well-stocked first aid kit on her night stand. She leaned over to get it, put it down at her side, and reached for the bandages on his face.

She worked in silence. She didn't need to say anything when her expression said enough. When she was finished she started unwrapping the bandages from Neil's right arm. Andrew shifted closer at that, as he still hadn't gotten a look at Neil's uncovered arms, but Neil kept his eyes on Abby. Grief and outrage warred for dominance on Abby's face, but she held her tongue until she made it to Neil's hand.

She swallowed hard. "Oh my god, Neil."

Neil finally risked a look down at his arm. His skin was striped with parallel lines that were black from bloody scabs but not quite deep enough to need stitches. Lola had filled the gaps between them with shallow burns, perfect circles leading from his elbow to an inch shy of his wrist. He'd torn his wrists open on the handcuffs in a way that couldn't yet scab; the skin was carved out in a shallow line along the scars Riko had given him a few months ago. Dark bruises made a thick band around his wrist and stretched up onto his thumb. His knuckles were burnt so badly Neil had to flex his fingers and make sure they worked.

For a half-second he was back in that car with Lola's knife on his skin and nowhere to go but six feet under. Neil didn't know what sound he made but Andrew's fingers were a sudden and unforgiving weight on the back of his neck. Andrew pushed

[281]

him forward and held him down. Neil tried to breathe but his chest was as tight as a rubber band ready to snap.

"It's over," Abby said as she gently combed her fingers through his hair. "It's over. You're going to be okay. We've got you."

Neil breathed, in-out-in-out, too shallow to reach his lungs, too fast to do him any good. He flexed his fingers again, then clenched them, knowing he was splitting the scabs open, knowing he was pulling at burned flesh trying so hard to heal, but needing to know he still had a grip. He needed to know that his father and Riko had both lost, that he could walk away from this and step back onto the court as Neil Josten. For a moment that single-mindedness was enough to startle a bit of clarity into him, and Neil was desperately grateful he didn't have the breath to laugh. He knew how panicked it would sound.

"Stop it," Andrew said, like it was really that simple.

It wasn't, but Neil's tangled mix of anger and exasperation was enough to put a hiccup in his gasping. That catch disrupted the frantic pace enough that Neil managed a real breath. He sucked in a second one as deep as he could, then a third as slowly as he could stomach it. His insides were still quaking by the time he got a sixth, but he was off that ledge and safe in their hands and Neil didn't care if he felt two seconds from getting violently ill. He went limp and let Andrew pull him back upright. Looking at him was safer than facing the damage again, so Neil studied Andrew's profile and let Abby work.

She was halfway done with his left arm when Wymack returned. Andrew had to get up to let him in, but he came right back. Wymack stood between the beds to survey the mess. His expression was unreadable, but his half-lidded eyes were dark, and Neil knew how to read the anger in every inch of an older man's frame. Neil made another fist, a silent promise that his hands were still in working order. It did nothing to take the tension from Wymack's shoulders.

"Are we spending the night here?" Wymack asked.

[282]

"I hate Baltimore," Neil said. "Can we go?"

Wymack nodded and looked to Abby. "How much longer do you need?"

"Ten minutes, maybe," Abby said. "We'll be done by the time everyone's checked out and on the bus."

"I'll round them up," Wymack said. "They won't bother you until we're back on campus."

"I promised them answers," Neil said.

"The bus isn't set up for a conversation like this. Even two to a row they'd be too spaced out to hear you easy. The locker room has a better setup. Nap back to the stadium and deal with them in familiar territory."

"My room key's on the dresser," Abby said to Wymack.

Wymack plucked it up, grabbed his paperwork, and left to get the Foxes. Abby finished cleaning and rewrapping Neil's arms, and Neil and Andrew waited while she repacked her bag. Neil swallowed some painkillers dry before handing her his medicine for the ride back. The team hadn't come to Baltimore with much, just what they'd needed for the game in New York, but Neil checked every drawer to make sure nothing was left behind.

The bus was waiting for them downstairs, door open and overhead lights on. Matt was putting the last gear bag in the storage compartment as they approached.

"I dropped my gear in New York," Neil said.

"Andrew found it while he was looking for you," Abby said. "Your bag was four gates down by the time the police broke things up. Everything's a bit worse for the wear, but at least it's all accounted for."

Matt slammed the doors closed, tugged the handles to make sure the locks caught, and gave Neil a once-over. "Hey," he said. "Coach made us promise to leave you alone, but are you okay?"

"No," Neil said, "but I think I will be."

He stepped up into the bus and found the Foxes sitting one to a row. They usually left space between the upperclassmen and

[283]

Andrew's group, but tonight Nicky, Aaron, and Kevin had settled in directly behind their older teammates. Neil would have taken the cushion behind Kevin, except Andrew headed for his usual seat in the far back. Neil followed him back and sat in front of Andrew, leaving a two-seat gap between him and the rest of the Foxes.

Getting comfortable was almost impossible thanks to the injuries on his face. He had to sleep on his back, but the seat wasn't long enough for him to completely stretch out. His thoughts kept him up most of the night, but he managed to doze off occasionally. Those stolen snatches of rest did almost more harm than good, but something was better than nothing.

Neil knew they were getting close when Wymack parked the bus outside a gas station. It took three Foxes to carry back enough coffees for everyone, and they didn't bother to pass the cups out. A couple minutes later the Foxhole Court rolled into view outside Neil's window. The sight of it was a much-needed jolt of adrenaline. Neil trailed bandaged knuckles along the cold window.

"Neil Josten," he mouthed. "Number ten, starting striker, Foxhole Court."

Even if the Moriyamas rejected Stuart's truce and came after him, the process had begun. Neil Josten was in the system to become a real person. He wouldn't die a lie.

Wymack killed the engine, and Neil painstakingly sat up. The Foxes filed off the bus and divvied up their gear. Neil looked for his bag and found it slung over Matt's shoulder. He tried to take a tray of coffee instead, but Dan sent his wrapped hands a pointed look and ignored his silent offer.

They trailed inside and settled down in the lounge. Dan, Renee, and Allison handed out drinks. Wymack had filled a plastic bag with snack foods, everything from powdered doughnuts to chips, and he upended it on the table for everyone to dig through. Nicky pulled a protein bar from the mix and passed it to Neil. Neil tried pulling the foil wrapper open and hissed through clenched teeth at the burn in his knuckles. Andrew took the bar from him, ripped it open in one easy swipe, and dumped it in Neil's waiting hands.

Kevin leaned forward to look past Andrew at Neil. He spoke in low but urgent French and said, "We need to talk about this."

"We're going to," Neil said.

"This," Kevin said, with emphasis, and touched his tattoo.

"Not now," Neil said. "Later."

"Neil."

"I said no."

Andrew couldn't understand them, but he understood the edge in Neil's voice. He put a hand on Kevin's shoulder and shoved him back. Kevin opened his mouth to argue but caught himself. He pressed a careful hand to his mottled throat and looked away. Wymack was the last to sit down, and suddenly Neil was the center of attention again.

He looked around the room at them and said uncertainly, "I don't know where to start."

"The beginning?" Dan suggested.

They were less interested in his father than they were in Neil himself, and they didn't yet need or want the level of details he'd given the FBI. Kevin had shared some of the truth on the drive from New York to Maryland, but Neil didn't know what all he'd told them. Chances were Neil was repeating a detail or two, but no one stopped him.

He told them who his parents were both officially and in reality. He admitted that he'd played little league Exy for a couple years under a different name and in a different position. He told them about his mother's abrupt decision to run away, the terrible eight years on the run, and the confrontation that ended with his mother's death. He told them how he ended up in Millport and why he tried out for the Exy team there.

He told them why he'd risked everything to come here, what it'd meant when he found out who the Moriyamas were, and how many times he'd thought about running away before he cut things too close. He swore he hadn't known until the fall banquet who his father really was to the Moriyamas and that even now he only dimly understood the intricate hierarchy between the Moriyama branches and the Wesninski circle. He knew less how his uncle was supposed to fit in there.

He told them how he'd intended to end the year, how he'd hoped to at least make it through championships and a rematch with Riko but how he'd realized months ago he wasn't going to be back the following year. It was the answer they probably deserved the most, because that fatalistic decision had colored every other interaction with them and fueled his determination to not let them get too close to him.

They listened to it all without interruption and sat in silence for a long time afterward. The eventual questions were inevitable, and Neil answered everything they asked him. They seemed startled at first by the honesty, no matter the story that had come before it, and were emboldened by his unhesitating responses. Renee said nothing until everyone else's curiosity had been temporarily assuaged, then somehow made a dire what-if sound almost kind.

"You said your uncle is negotiating a truce with Kengo. What if he can't?"

Neil didn't waste their time softening his response. "They will get rid of me."

"You're not serious," Matt said, alarmed.

"I am a loose end," Neil said, "dangerous enough on a good day and unforgivable when Kengo is dying. The Moriyamas can't afford leaks in their empire when they're about to shift that much power around."

"When will you know?" Dan asked.

"Uncle Stuart said he would get in touch with me when he was done sorting things out."

"Don't worry," Nicky said, with a failed attempt at cheer. "Andrew will protect you."

Kevin flicked him a horrified look. "These are the Moriyamas, Nicky. This is not Riko and the master; this is not Neil's father. Andrew can't—"

"I know," Nicky cut in, irritated. "Just shut up."

They fell to uncomfortable silence. Wymack looked between them, then said, "One more thing: if the press hasn't caught on yet, it's inevitable that they will. Browning told me the steps they were taking to hide your name, but if anyone followed them from the hospital to the hotel they'll put it together. It doesn't matter that the bus wasn't on-site; if they saw any of us changing rooms they'll follow us to you.

"You looking like this," he motioned up at his own face, "will be all the answer they need. The FBI can ask them to take your safety into consideration before they start running articles, but since you revoked their protection I don't know how much weight their word carries. Figure out as soon as you can how far you'll let them push and where you want us to draw the line."

"It's generally best to give them the answers they want," Allison said. "If you satisfy their curiosity they won't have to resort to more forceful methods. Besides, the press serves the fickle mind of public interest. They can't focus on you for long. Something else will distract them."

"General public, maybe," Dan said, "but Exy fans'll remember long after everyone else has moved on. They're going to drag the other teams into this and let them say whatever they like about you. It's going to be our freshman year all over again, but worse."

"Unless we find something they want more than a piece of me," Neil said.

"Like what?" Matt asked. "It's kind of a hard story to top."

Neil leaned forward and slanted a look at Kevin. He answered in French, "They won't care half as much about my father when they find out who yours is. You'll always be bigger news than I am to them."

Kevin's mouth thinned to a disapproving line. "It's not

time."

"Make it the time. I need your help, and you should have told him years ago," Neil accused him. When Kevin didn't answer, Neil interpreted it as the reluctant agreement he wanted. He straightened and went back to English. "We're going to split their attention between us. Kevin's going to out his father."

"Wait, you know who he is?" Nicky asked Kevin, startled.

"I found out," Kevin said, an edge in his words. "My mother wrote the master when she found out she was pregnant. I took the letter from his house and hid it at the stadium a few years ago."

"And I took it from Evermore," Neil said. He shrugged at the startled look Kevin flicked him. "Jean showed me where it was. I stole it so you'd do something about it."

"So who is it?" Dan asked.

"I'll contact him before I tell anyone else," Kevin said. "He deserves a forewarning."

Renee looked to Neil and said, "What do you need from us, Neil?"

It didn't take much thought. "Everything I needed, you already gave me. You let me stay."

Renee's smile was slow and sweet. Dan got up and crossed the room to give Neil a careful hug. She didn't hold him like Abby once had, like she thought he might fall apart without her support. There was a muted ferocity in the fingers that bit into his arms and he could feel the tension in her body where she leaned against him. This wasn't comfort; it was something protective and defiant. She was staking claim over him as one of her team. Somehow it was enough to ease the last of the day's stresses out of him. That much-needed peace only made Neil realize how exhausted he still was, and he barely managed to swallow a yawn.

Dan let go and took a step back when Neil finally relaxed. "Come on. It's been a long day and I'm ready to see it over with. Let's sleep this off and figure out in the morning where to go from here. Maybe we'll all get breakfast or something. All right?"

"All right," Neil agreed, and the Foxes got to their feet.

Abby handed him his medicine. "Let me check on you again tomorrow, but be careful washing, okay? Wrap your arms if you can. If you get soap in those burns it's going to hurt."

Neil nodded, looked to Wymack one last time, and followed his teammates out. Their cars were still in the parking lot where they'd left them a couple days ago. Andrew popped the locks on his car and Nicky opened the passenger door for Neil. Neil climbed in and didn't bother struggling with the buckle. As soon as his limbs were out of the way, Nicky slammed the door and got in back. The upperclassmen piled into Matt's truck and Matt pulled out after Andrew.

It was the middle of the night, but there was usually still something going on around campus. Today the grounds were dead, and it took Neil a moment to remember it was spring break. Understanding was quickly followed by a flicker of guilt; the others had had plans to fly out on Sunday morning. They'd missed their flights to stay in Baltimore with him. He asked Dan about it when they met up again at Fox Tower, but she waved it off as unimportant.

No one talked about it, but somehow they all ended up in Neil and Matt's room. Matt and Aaron shoved the couch out of the way, and the girls showed up a minute later with blankets. The living room wasn't meant to sleep nine bodies but somehow they made a workable nest out of it. Foxes came and went as they grabbed pillows and changed into pajamas. For a moment, though, Neil and Matt were alone. Matt gave Neil's shoulder a careful squeeze.

"Things could have gone much worse," Matt said, subdued. "I'm glad they didn't. You want anything, you need anything, you let us know. Okay?"

"Okay," Neil said.

"I mean it," Matt stressed.

[289]

"I know," Neil said. "I'm done lying to you, Matt. I promise."

Matt sighed, but he sounded more tired than skeptical. "Wish it didn't take all of this to get that, but I guess I understand. A lot of things about you make sense now, actually. With one notable exception," Matt added dryly, "but I'm going to let Allison handle that conversation. She'll kill me if I steal her thunder."

"Great," Neil said. Matt grinned at his unenthusiastic tone. Neil thought maybe he was better off not knowing, but he asked, "Does that mean you bet against it?"

"I bet for you and against him," Matt said, and shrugged at Neil's surprised look. "I'm your roommate. You never talked about girls, even back when Seth and I would go on and on about them. I noticed, but I figured you'd say something if you wanted us to know. Just so you know, it makes no difference to me either way," Matt said, "except I would have seriously judged your taste a couple days ago."

Neil assumed Andrew's territorial streak in Baltimore had a lot to do with Matt's change of heart. "Did he really choke Kevin?"

"Took three of us to pull him off," Matt said.

Neil didn't know what to say to that. Matt gave him a minute, then clapped his shoulder and went to get changed. Neil thought about getting undressed, decided it would take far too much effort, and sat down on his blankets to wait on the rest of the Foxes. He ended up in the dead center of the room, with Andrew on one side of him and Matt on the other. His thoughts should have kept him up all night, but with his friends this close Neil couldn't worry about anything. Neil studied Andrew's face until he couldn't keep his eyes open anymore.

He dreamed of facing his father on an Exy court, and in his dream the Foxes won.

CHAPTER FIFTEEN

Monday breakfast plans got pushed back to brunch on account of how late they'd all been up. The dining halls were closed for spring break, but there was a diner ten minutes down the road that served breakfast food all day. The Foxes dispersed to get ready, carrying blankets and pillows with them out of the room. Kevin was the only one who stayed behind. Neil knew why, but he was still too tired for this conversation. He struggled to his feet and trailed Matt to the kitchen with his bag of medicine. They'd be eating in an hour, but apparently that was too long to wait for coffee. Matt rinsed the pot in the sink and started filling it.

Neil lifted a cup down from the cabinet and shook his medicine out of the bag. There he stopped, because he could only imagine how much it'd hurt his fingers to unscrew that child-safety cap. He looked around for something to make it easier and saw Kevin waiting in the doorway.

Kevin glanced from Neil to Matt and spoke in French. "When Riko finds out what your father did to your face, he will retaliate."

By now Matt was used to them jabbering away in foreign languages around him. He gave no sign he heard them or cared what they were saying but pulled coffee beans and filters down from the cabinet. Neil warred with himself, heart tripping and skipping with unjustified nerves. He studied Matt's profile until Matt cut the grinder off, then looked past him to Kevin.

"Can he do anything about it, though?" Neil asked in English.

Matt froze with the filter halfway to the coffee maker. In the doorway, Kevin tensed up in incomprehension or disapproval.

[291]

Neil felt Matt's eyes on him but didn't return the look. Just last night he'd said he was done lying to Matt. He couldn't expect Matt to believe him if he talked behind Matt's back today. The upperclassmen knew the whole story now, anyway, so there was no reason to hide this inevitable complication.

"By now Kengo knows my father's dead and I'm alive. Worse, he knows the FBI has already talked to me. He has to make a decision on me one way or the other. Will Riko risk making the first move?"

Kevin flicked a cool look at Matt but obediently brought the conversation back to English. "They touched what they never should have. By erasing your tattoo they've swept him aside as insignificant. Riko won't tolerate that." Kevin lifted his left hand as a prime example of Riko's violent inferiority complex. "If he thinks he can sneak past his father to get you, he will."

"Let him try," Neil said. "He knows where he can find me."

"Your false bravado helps no one."

"Neither does your cowardice," Neil pointed out. "I was only afraid of Riko because he knew who I was. What can he hold against me now that everyone knows the truth?" Neil gave Kevin a moment to digest that then said, "Andrew says the Ravens have to let this feud play out this spring, so Riko can't even come after the rest of you yet. They might kick and fuss a bit but you're safe from them for now."

"You believe him?" Matt asked.

Neil shrugged. "Tetsuji calmed their crazy fans down by saying the Ravens would handle us on the court. He has to deliver, so yeah, I believe Andrew. But hey, since Riko's hands are tied," Neil said, glancing back at Kevin, "now's a perfect time to take that off your face."

It took Kevin a moment to catch on, and he jerked like he'd been struck. "Don't even joke like that."

"I'm not joking. Allison said she'd spot me the cash to take mine off. Maybe she'll do the same for you now that I don't need her help."

"No question," Matt said. "She loves a good scandal."

"Stop," Kevin said. "Shut up."

"You're supposed to be done being second-best," Neil said. "Prove it."

Kevin made a cutting gesture at him and stormed out. He didn't bother closing the door behind him, and Neil understood when Andrew wandered in a second later. Andrew brought a roll of duct tape and some garbage bags with him and went past the kitchenette to sit on Neil's blankets. Neil closed the bedroom door and went to join him in the living room. Andrew waited until he was seated before lifting the bottom edge of Neil's hoodie. He raised it an inch or two, then checked another spot, and finally poked his hand up under the edge.

"I don't have a shirt on under this," Neil said.

Andrew accepted that in silence and settled down to wait. Neil held a bandaged hand out for the tape and bags, but Andrew gazed into space and ignored him. Matt finished up in the kitchen and went past them. When the bathroom door was closed behind him and the shower cut on, Andrew motioned to Neil's hoodie. Neil tried not to wince as he popped the buttons undone. He got the shirt as far as his elbows before he had to take a breather and rest his aching hands. Andrew gave him only a second before peeling the sleeves off his arms one at a time.

Andrew pulled a garbage bag over each arm, tore the excess edges off, and taped the jagged ends to Neil's biceps. He tugged at both bags to check for any give and added another layer of tape to be sure. When Neil's arms were good, Andrew started on his face. He picked up one of the plastic ends he'd torn off, folded it over and over in on itself, and taped it over one of Neil's cheeks like a shiny black bandage. Neil was pretty sure Andrew put more tape than plastic on Neil's face, but Neil wasn't going to complain. Andrew finished his other cheek and inspected his handiwork. Neil guessed he was satisfied with the end result because Andrew tossed the scissors and roll of tape

[293]

off to one side.

Andrew tugged the blanket out from under them and draped it over Neil's shoulders like a cape. Neil tried pulling the ends together over his chest but couldn't get a good grip with bags over his fingers. Andrew watched him try twice, then pushed his hands aside and did it for him. Then there was nothing to do but wait until Matt was done. Matt went from the bathroom to the bedroom without slowing and dressed in record time. Instead of detouring back to the bathroom sink to fix his hair into its usual gelled spikes, he carried a comb into the living room and looked between them. Neil glanced his way, but Andrew didn't acknowledge their audience.

"I'm going to see if Dan needs help rescheduling her flight," Matt said. "Come next door when you're ready."

"Okay," Neil said.

Andrew stood and followed Matt to the door. Neil assumed he was leaving to shower in his own room so got up and headed for the bathroom. He let the blanket drop when he heard the door close, but the subsequent click of the lock was definitely from the inside. Neil glanced back, curious, but Andrew was standing out of sight.

Neil reached for the bathroom light. The bag around his hand stuck to the damp tiles on the wall. Neil looked at the shower and wondered if he could just skip it. The bags would protect his injuries and bandages, but they'd also make this entire process a hundred times more complicated. He hadn't showered since Friday night, though, so he didn't have a lot of choice in the matter.

Andrew's bare feet were silent against the carpet, but Neil saw a blur of colors on the fogged-up mirror and turned. Andrew studied his chest with a bored look, but the fingers he pressed to Neil's scars were a heavy and lingering weight. Neil waited to see if he had anything to say, but Andrew hadn't spoken to anyone since they checked out of the hotel in Baltimore. Neil doubted the others had noticed, since Andrew rarely talked to even Kevin or Nicky now that he was sober, but Neil wasn't used to the silent treatment.

"Hey," Neil said, just to make Andrew look up at him.

Neil leaned in to kiss him, needing to know if Andrew would lean away or push him back. Instead Andrew opened his mouth to Neil without hesitation and slid his hand up Neil's chest to his throat. Kissing hurt his injured cheeks but Neil fought to ignore that twinging pain. It'd only been a couple days since those kisses on the bus but right now it felt like forever.

Neil remembered too well what it was like to say goodbye. He remembered what it was like saying hello again. A hint of Friday's panic and outrage flickered in his chest, hot enough to burn the air from his lungs. He didn't know what this thing between them was anymore. He didn't know what he wanted or needed it to be. He just knew he had to hold on for as long as he could.

"You are a mess," Andrew said against Neil's lips.

"What else is new?"

Andrew pulled back and guided Neil out of his way. He turned the shower on and held his hand under the stream to check the temperature. Neil stepped on the hems of his pants to get them started in coming off, but Andrew did most of the work stripping him. It was awkward being naked in front of someone else, his scars and bruises on full display, but the uncomfortable curl in Neil's gut was eased somewhat by the detached way Andrew handled him. Neil stepped into the shower, tensing in preparation for pain, and was relieved when the wraps on his face and arms held. He ducked his head and let the water beat against his skull. It gave him an excuse to close his eyes and find his mental footing.

A hand in his hair jarred him from his thoughts and he cracked his eyes open to see Andrew standing in front of him. Andrew hadn't bothered to get undressed aside from stripping his bands and shoes off. Water plastered his black shirt to him, and small streams raced down his temples and over his cheeks to

[295]

drip off his chin. Neil reached for his face, remembered the bags just in time, and frowned a bit in annoyance. Andrew pushed his hand aside and yanked the shower curtain closed.

Andrew got Neil's hair washed efficiently, if not gently, but by the time he moved on to Neil's body there was more kissing than cleaning. Andrew made the mistake of turning his face away at one point, so Neil chased water down the side of Andrew's neck. Andrew's fingers clenched convulsively on Neil's sides as a shudder wracked Andrew's frame.

Andrew tried to recover with a ground-out, "Your neck fetish is not attractive."

"You like it," Neil said, unapologetic. "I like that you like it."

He bit down to prove his point and Andrew turned his head into it with a sharp hiss. Neil smiled where Andrew couldn't see it. Maybe Andrew felt the twist of his lips against oversensitive skin, because he tangled his fingers in Neil's hair and pulled his head away. Andrew put a hand flat against Neil's abdomen and pushed, backing Neil up until he was out of the spray and pressed flat against slick, chilly tile.

Andrew bit the question into the corner of Neil's jaw. "Yes or no?"

"It's always yes with you," Neil said.

"Except when it's no," Andrew said.

Neil put a plastic-wrapped finger to Andrew's chin, guiding his head up for another kiss. "If you have to keep asking because—I'll answer it as many times as you ask. But this is always going to be yes."

"Don't 'always' me."

"Don't ask for the truth if you're just going to dilute it."

Andrew clapped his hand over Neil's mouth and kept it there until going to his knees meant he couldn't reach anymore. Andrew ghosted a kiss across Neil's hip before swallowing him whole. Neil caught at Andrew's hair, but his injuries and the plastic bags made it difficult for him to get a good grip. He scrabbled at the wall instead, but it was too slick to offer much leverage. Andrew pinned him against the wall with a hand on his hip, which helped, but Neil still felt like he was falling. He did fall afterward, albeit in a controlled slide down the wall, gasping for breath and dizzy with burnt-out need.

"Do you want—" he started, voice ragged.

Andrew kissed him to shut him up. Neil grimaced a little at the taste on Andrew's tongue but was happy to burn it away. Andrew braced himself with a forearm against the wall, keeping a few comfortable inches between their bodies. Neil let him have that gap but crossed his aching arms behind Andrew's head to keep him close. Neil didn't notice the absence of Andrew's other hand until Andrew's breath caught against his lips. It confused him for a second, to the point that he was almost stupid enough to pull back and look down.

It'd been weeks since kissing Andrew became a regular thing, but every night ended the same: with Andrew getting Neil off and then sending Neil on his way. He wouldn't even unzip his pants when Neil was still around. Neil didn't know if this break in routine was grudging trust or determination to not let Neil out of sight again. Neil didn't care right now so long as Andrew stayed. Neil hummed something into Andrew's mouth that could have been approval, could have been encouragement, and got a faint growl in response.

Andrew wasn't amused by Neil's support, but he wasn't annoyed enough to pull away, either. Neil held tight until Andrew finally went still. Andrew took a couple seconds to catch his breath, then pushed at the wall until Neil obediently dropped his arms and let him go. Andrew rinsed his hand in the spray before getting to his feet and helping hoist Neil up.

Neil stepped out of the tub, getting water everywhere, and wound his towel around his waist. Andrew leaned out of the shower to get the door for him, and he pushed it closed when Neil was gone. Neil lingered long enough to hear the slap of Andrew's soaked clothes against the floor, then went into the

[297]

bedroom to air dry. He'd only bought one towel when he moved on-campus last summer, but Matt had some spares for laundry day and Dan's occasional sleepover. Neil pulled a clean one off Matt's closet shelf and hung it on the bathroom doorknob for Andrew.

He was still wet when Andrew turned up, and he shrugged at the look Andrew favored him. Andrew scrubbed him dry, careful around his injuries and too-vigorous everywhere else, and peeled the dripping bags from Neil's arms and face. Andrew ran a considering finger along the bandages on Neil's left arm before helping Neil into the loosest clothes he owned. It was cool enough out to wear long sleeves, but it wouldn't be for much longer. These wounds were going to scar where everyone could see them. Scarred was better than dead, so Neil figured he'd get over the stares eventually.

Neil loaned Andrew clothes so he wouldn't have to go back to his room in a towel but didn't stick around while Andrew dressed. He headed to the kitchen instead to grab his medicine and fill three mugs with coffee. Andrew wandered in as Neil was turning the pot off and claimed one of the mugs. Neil took the other two and his pills but hesitated at the suite door.

"I don't have my keys," he said. He'd put them in his travel duffel before the trip to New York, but Neil hadn't touched his gear since. He knew Matt had carried his bag into the stadium for him, but no one had bothered unpacking after his story last night. Neil couldn't believe he'd forgotten to check his things. He didn't know whether to chalk it up to his exhaustion or the trauma of coming clean. Maybe he could blame it on Renee and Dan, whose gestures at the end of that painful conversation had made him feel too safe to worry about anything else.

Andrew turned away without comment and fetched Matt's keys from his desk drawer. Only after he'd made it back to Neil's side did Neil remember Matt dropping them there last night after changing. Neil envied Andrew's perfect recall for only a moment; Andrew had already said most of the memories from his childhood were unpleasant. Neil didn't have many good memories, either, but at least he knew he'd forgotten some of the earliest injustices and tragedies. He couldn't imagine what it'd be like hanging on to every blow and loud word.

He considered asking Andrew if he had any good memories at all, but then he'd have to ask what someone so joyless actually considered to be "good". Instead he said, "Our game is over now, isn't it?"

"It's still my turn," Andrew pointed out.

"But after that?" Neil asked. "I have no secrets left to trade."

"Come up with something else."

"What would you take?"

"What would you give me?"

"Don't ask questions you already know the answer to," Neil said. Andrew slanted a bored look at him, unimpressed with having his own words tossed back in his face. Neil leaned a shoulder against the door before Andrew could open it and said, "I think I should get a few bonus turns, though, considering you got all your answers from me for free."

"You volunteered those," Andrew said.

"Circumstances kind of forced my hand."

Andrew gazed back at him in silence. Neil refused to take the hint or move, content to play the waiting game. It took a couple minutes, but finally Andrew held up a finger and said, "One free question."

"One?" Neil echoed. "The fewer you give me, the more you'll hate what I ask."

"I hate everything about you anyway," Andrew said. "I won't notice."

Neil moved away from the door. "I'll let you know when I come up with something."

Andrew got the door and locked it behind them. Neil lifted his little finger from his mug and let Andrew hook the key ring over it. Neil went next door, but Andrew continued down the

[299]

hall to his own room. Neil didn't have a free hand to knock, so he gave the door a light kick. It took three tries before anyone inside heard him or realized that sound was someone asking to be let in. When Matt swung the door open Neil held one of the mugs out.

"You forgot this."

"Oh, thanks." Matt took it and stepped aside to let him in.

Dan and Renee were already showered and dressed. The empty couch cushion between them had no doubt been Matt's, but Dan motioned for Neil to take it. Matt perched on the arm of the couch to Dan's left and draped his arm over her shoulder. She twined her fingers through his and studied Neil's bandages. Neil let her look her fill and waited to see if she'd come up with any new questions overnight.

All she came up with, though, was, "How are you feeling?"

"I don't know," Neil said. He thought he should be a little worried that he hadn't heard from Stuart, but he couldn't dredge up any concern. The Foxes had faced his secrets and only tightened their grip on him. How could he fear anything with them all at his back? What could he regret when he still felt Andrew's kisses on his mouth? "Right now I'm fine, I think."

The muffled sound of a hairdryer said Allison was done with her shower and on to the slow process of primping for her day. They waited for her in comfortable silence. Neil's coffee was long-gone and the mug cold by the time Allison turned up. It didn't matter that it was spring break or that they were just going out to eat eggs; Allison was dressed to the nines as usual and she left a trail of perfume from the bathroom to the den. She came around the couch to look down at Neil, hands on her hips and heel clicking idly against the floor.

"Is it out?" she asked.

"I haven't watched the news yet," Neil said.

She looked over her shoulder like she was considering turning the TV on, but Dan got to her feet and said, "I'm starving. Let's go."

[300]

They collected Andrew's lot from next door. Neil didn't miss the looks the upperclassmen sent him when they saw what Andrew was wearing, but he was more interested in the cousins' reactions. There was a tense set to Nicky's shoulders and a noticeable space between him and Andrew. Neil guessed Nicky's mouth had gotten away with him and he'd said something about Andrew showering in Neil's room. That lack of brain-to-mouth filter would be the death of him one of these days. Aaron was standing even further back with his arms folded tight across his chest and his eyes on Neil. Neil expected to see censure or disgust in his expression, considering how much grief Aaron gave Nicky for his sexuality, but Aaron's stare was heavy and unreadable.

Matt offered to pile everyone into his truck then retracted it immediately when he remembered Neil couldn't climb into the bed. Neil sat passenger in Andrew's car instead, silently relegating Kevin to the backseat with Nicky and Aaron, and watched the empty campus roll by out his window. Nicky was quiet for most of the ride, but he bounced back before they reached the parking lot. Luckily he was smart enough to stay off personal topics and instead rambled about his personal record for pancake-eating.

Brunch was a boisterous event. The Foxes were rallying the only way they knew how: by pushing on like the weekend hadn't happened. They were there for Neil if he needed anything from them, but they weren't going to pry anymore and they wouldn't linger over near-misses and ugliness. The only awkward moment was when the waitress, trying to make small talk, asked Neil about his bandages.

"Skateboarding," Matt said the same time Dan said, "Fell into a tank of piranhas."

Allison waved a hand in bored dismissal when the waitress sent a nonplussed look between the two and said, rather conspiratorially, "Bad breakup."

"Rough weekend," the waitress deduced, and moved on.

[301]

Dan picked up right where they'd left off: figuring out how to rearrange their spring break plans. Rescheduling their flights out was doable, if a bit costly, but Dan wasn't interested in heading back north anymore. She didn't say she didn't want to let Neil out of sight, but she alluded to it so tactlessly Neil knew what she meant. She didn't think there was anything worth doing around campus this week, what with everything closed down for break, and fished for ideas from the others.

"Did you have any plans to do anything?" Matt finally thought to ask Neil. "Besides the obvious, I mean."

Neil wasn't sure if Matt meant Exy or Andrew. He didn't try to guess but said, "I was going to take a road trip." Judging by the looks on their faces, it was the last thing they'd expected from him. Neil shrugged uncomfortably and said, "Mom and I traveled to survive. I've never gone anywhere just because I could. I wanted to know what it was like."

"You've never taken a vacation?" Dan asked, then caught herself with a wince and a, "Scratch that. Forget I said that."

"Where did you want to go?" Renee asked.

"I don't know," Neil admitted. "I haven't looked around yet."

Allison tapped manicured fingernails against her lips thoughtfully, then beckoned to Matt. "Resort?"

"Doesn't seem like his kind of thing," Matt said, "and it's too early for the beach. Cabin?"

Allison looked poised to argue but thought better of it. "Blue Ridge?"

"Haven't been yet," Matt said, "but I've heard they're awesome."

"Neil?" Allison asked.

"What?" Neil asked, lost.

"Yes or no?" Allison said, like she couldn't believe he wasn't following along. "We're going to the mountains for the week."

"We," Kevin echoed. When Matt looped his finger to

[302]

indicate everyone, Kevin made a cutting gesture in dismissal. "No. Regardless of what happened this weekend, we are still in the middle of spring championships. We need—"

Kevin cut off abruptly and looked down. Neil couldn't see what he was looking at, but he could guess. One of Andrew's hands was out of sight beneath the table and his knife was missing from beside his plate. Andrew's chin was cradled in his other hand as he gazed across the room at nothing in particular. Kevin stared hard at the top of Andrew's head like he was considering calling Andrew's bluff. In the end he scowled and let it drop. Neil didn't know what convinced him: the dark bruises still lining his throat or the desperate gestures Nicky was making on Neil's other side.

"Anyway," Allison said pointedly.

"Kind of last minute for booking, isn't it?" Dan asked.

"It's March," Allison said, like that explained everything. She pulled her glittering phone out of her purse and pointed it at Neil. It was a last chance to turn her offer down, Neil guessed, because a second later she nodded and pressed a couple buttons. "I'll have Sarah find us something. Sarah?" she said into her phone before Neil could ask. "I need something in the Blue Ridge that will sleep nine. Preferably with five bedrooms or more. Yes, tonight through Sunday morning is best. Yes, I'll wait."

She hung up and set her phone aside.

"Sarah?" Nicky asked.

"My parents' travel agent," Allison said. Nicky gave her an odd look, and Allison looked almost offended. "You don't think I book my own travel, do you? Who has time for that?"

"Everyone else in the real world," Dan said dryly.

"Surprised your father let you keep her when he wrote you out," Nicky said. It was a rude reminder that Allison had lost most of her inheritance by abandoning her parents' dreams for her. Even Nicky knew how bad that sounded, judging by his flinch. "Uh, that came out wrong. I just meant—"

[303]

"I know what you meant," Allison said, a little frostily. "He doesn't know."

"I'm sorry." Nicky sent a pleading look at Neil to save him from his thoughtlessness.

Neil didn't have to intervene, because Allison followed Nicky's frantic glance to Neil. "You do like the mountains, don't you?"

"I cut through them once," Neil said. "We didn't stay. Is this really okay?"

"Is it okay, he says," Dan said, "like we didn't all just invite ourselves to his vacation."

"Give us a number?" Renee asked Allison.

Allison waved it off. "Don't worry about it."

The waitress and two servers turned up with their plates then, and the conversation temporarily derailed as everyone helped sort the orders out. Halfway through brunch Allison got a confirmation call for a five-bedroom cabin in the Smokies. They could get their keys from the main office anytime before eight, and it was just over two hours from campus by car. Allison checked the clock on her phone as she relayed the details to her teammates and nodded in satisfaction. It wasn't even one; they had plenty of time to pack and get on the road.

When they started trying to lock down a departure time, Neil had to say, "I have to see Abby before we go."

"Oh," Dan said, "then no rush, take your time. We'll pack while she fixes you up."

Having a plan and a destination meant no one was interested in lingering over their food. They wolfed down what was left of their breakfasts and flagged the waitress down for their check. Neil didn't know when Dan had swiped the team's purchasing card from Wymack but she charged their meal and tip to it. Neil's phone was with his bag at the stadium still, so Nicky called Abby on the way across the parking lot.

"Hey," Nicky said. "When do you want to see Neil? We've decided we're all gonna bail out of town for the week. Soon as

[304]

you green-light Neil we can go. Yeah, okay, see you in a bit."

He hung up and clambered into the backseat. When they were on the road he leaned forward between the front seats to say, "She's gonna meet you at the stadium so she can get to all her stuff. She says Coach is already there trying to rebook his tickets. Hopefully he signs everyone we need before the news scares them off."

"Can I take the car?" Neil asked Andrew.

Andrew didn't answer, but he drove to the dormitory instead of the stadium. Neil climbed out when the others did and started around the hood. As he turned he saw Kevin get into the passenger seat. Andrew glanced back when he realized Kevin wasn't with him but didn't slow and didn't ask.

As soon as Kevin was settled Neil got them on the road again. Abby's and Wymack's cars were parked side-by-side at the curb at the Foxhole Court. Neil punched in the newest security code and led the way down the hall. As they neared the locker room he looked back at Kevin and said, "Let me talk to him first. He won't be in the mood to talk to anyone when you're through with him."

Kevin kept his eyes on the floor and said nothing.

Abby was sitting in the lounge waiting for them. She started to get up, but Kevin detoured to her and bought Neil time to make for Wymack's office. Wymack's door was open just wide enough for Neil to see his desk. Wymack was surrounded by his usual paper chaos and had his phone to his ear. He didn't bother to move itineraries off his keyboard before trying to type one-handed. He looked up at movement in the doorway and motioned for Neil to come in.

Neil closed the door behind him and took one of the chairs opposite Wymack to wait. It only took a couple minutes more for Wymack to get his flight fixed. Neil heard "Columbus" and knew Wymack was looking at the striker Neil had chosen. Finally Wymack hung up and set his phone back on its stand. A couple taps of his keys locked his monitor and Wymack sat back

[305]

to give Neil his full attention.

Neil stared back at him, suddenly lost. He was fluent in two languages, nearly there in a third, and could string together some useful survival phrases in a half-dozen more. But with the whole truth bared between them Neil didn't have the right words to say.

"You should have thrown my file away," Neil said at last. "You should have walked away when I threw your contract back in your face. But you took a chance on me and you brought me here. You saved my life. Three times," Neil said, "you've saved my life. I can't just say 'thank you' for that."

"You don't have to," Wymack said. "I brought you here, but you saved yourself. You're the one who decided to stay. You're the one who stopped being afraid long enough to realize you could get a grip here and a foothold there. You found your own way.

"If anything," Wymack continued when Neil tried to protest, "I should be thanking you. You told us last night you intended to end the year dead or in federal custody. You could have shut everyone and everything out and worried about yourself this year. Instead you agreed to help Dan fix this team. You're saving the two I thought we couldn't reach, and you're a living example for Kevin to follow. He never used to watch you," Wymack said, "but he's had eyes on you since December trying to figure out how you stand your ground."

"He can't be taught," Neil said.

"So you think," Wymack said. "From where I'm sitting, you're making real progress."

It could have been wishful thinking, except Wymack had a way of seeing through all of them. Neil believed him because he wanted to believe Kevin could be gotten to. He needed to see the day Kevin took that number off his face and bested Riko at his own game. He needed Kevin to believe he could usurp Riko's throne and survive. Until Kevin believed that, he'd never fully believe in the Foxes' ability to reach finals.

"Neil," Wymack said after a minute, "it's all over the news.

We tried staying in our rooms and out of sight while you were with the FBI, but they waited us out. They have pictures of the bus and all of us loading up to leave. It didn't take them long to put the pieces together. My phone's been ringing all morning between the press, the board, and Chuck. School board's going to want to talk to you before you return to classes."

Neil had known this would happen, but for a moment he thought his breakfast would come back up. "Okay."

"You want me to play the 'no comment' game with the press?"

"If you can. I'll—" Neil faltered, but thought about Allison's advice and Kevin's reluctant promise to help him tackle the storm, "—talk to them next week. You can tell them that."

"Tuesday?" Wymack suggested. "Tuesday or Wednesday would give you Monday to deal with all the on-campus reactions. I'll schedule a time and see what I can do to distract them in the meantime. Maybe I'll let them know you've accepted vice-captaincy for next year."

"I'm not qualified to be that," Neil said. He gestured to the recruits' files that were spread across Wymack's desk. "All of them have more experience than I do, and they're not going to want to follow a gangster's son."

"Andrew didn't want to follow you, either," Wymack said. "Look how that turned out. You'll figure something out one way or another."

Neil looked down at his hands. He'd counted his life and losses on his fingers just a few weeks back. Now it was up in the air, resting solely on Stuart's ability to sway the Moriyamas to his side. Wymack was asking Neil to commit to a future neither of them was sure he would actually have. Practicality said to wait until they knew for sure. After a moment, though, Neil curled one hand into a fist and focused on the path he wanted.

"I'll do my best," he said.

"Good," Wymack said. "Now get going. Dan called to tell me you're all going out of town. Get away from all of this for a bit, get some fresh air in you, and come back ready to make the impossible happen."

"Yes, Coach," Neil said.

Kevin stood up when Neil returned to the lounge. Neil saw the tension in Kevin's shoulders and the hard line of Kevin's mouth and knew Kevin was going to put this off until they returned. Kevin glanced at him, then past him at Wymack's open door, and opened his mouth on an excuse Neil didn't want to hear.

"Don't do this to him," Neil said.

Kevin hesitated, and Neil knew he'd won. Abby looked between them, lost. Neil didn't wait for her to figure it out but went next door to her office. Abby joined him a moment later, still confused. Neil didn't explain but listened for the muffled sound of Wymack's door closing. Only then could he relax and turn his attention back on Abby.

Facing his injuries today wasn't any easier. Neil quickly averted his eyes from the mess on his arms as Abby unwound his bandages. Abby cupped Neil's face in one hand before getting to work. Afterward she packed a travel kit for him to take to the mountains and kissed his forehead farewell. Neil eased off the bed and went out to the car to wait.

Twenty minutes later Kevin showed up looking hollow-eyed and defeated. He started to open the passenger door, then got in back. Neil said nothing to him but turned the key in the ignition. It was a short ride back to Fox Tower, and Kevin didn't get out when Neil parked. Neil waited only a minute before getting the hint and starting for the door. Two steps from the car he turned back and opened his door again. Kevin had his elbow on the windowsill and his face in his hand. Neil rethought what he was going to say.

"I'll tell them so you don't have to."

Kevin gestured with his free hand: "Get out" or "I don't care" but not "Don't you dare." He didn't say anything; Neil didn't think he could. Neil closed the door and left him to his

[308]

misery.

Neil collected Nicky and the twins from their room and took them all next door to Dan's room. A pile of backpacks and travel suitcases in the middle of the living room said they were all ready to go. Matt and Allison were sitting on the couch while Renee unplugged electronics around the room. Renee went and got Dan from the bedroom when Neil asked her to. Dan sank into the open spot between Matt and Allison and grabbed a mug off the coffee table. Neil waited until everyone was settled before looking across the room at Dan.

"Coach is Kevin's father."

Dan spat her coffee halfway across the table and choked on what little didn't make it out of her mouth. Matt stared slack-jawed at Neil for an endless second before he realized Dan was coughing, and then he gave her an enthusiastic thump on the back. Dan tried to say something, but it was an unintelligible hoarse wheeze. Allison and Renee stared at Neil like he'd grown a second head, and Aaron looked to Andrew like Andrew should have warned them of this at some point. If Andrew noticed the attention, he didn't return it; he had eyes only for Neil.

"No way!" Nicky burst out. "No way! Are you serious? You can't be serious. When the hell did that happen?"

"She taught Coach Exy," Neil reminded him.

"And what, he didn't notice that he knocked her up?" Aaron asked.

"She told him Kevin wasn't his," Neil said. "She knew Coach wanted to have an NCAA team one day. She thought he'd abandon his dreams to help her raise Kevin. She didn't want that, but she didn't want to give up what she was doing and move to the States, either. So she lied. The only person she told was Coach Moriyama."

Dan finally got her voice back. "How long has Kevin known?"

"Only a couple years," Neil reminded her.

"A couple years," Dan echoed, voice dangerous, "and he

[309]

didn't say anything?"

"He was trying to protect him," Neil said. "If Coach knew Kevin was his son, he'd have tried to take him from Edgar Allan."

Nicky grimaced. "They'd have never let Kevin go."

"He should have said something when he ran away," Dan insisted. "He's been down here a year and a half now. He had no right to keep something like this from Coach for so long. Jesus, he didn't—" Dan's voice cracked a bit, more grief than outrage, and Neil assumed she was imagining Wymack's reaction to being blindsided by the truth. "That's not right. That's not fair."

"No," Neil agreed quietly, "but at least Coach knows now."

"Damn," Matt said. "How'd he take it?"

"I wasn't there for the conversation," Neil said, "but I don't think it went well."

Dan made an awful noise and got up from the couch. Matt reached for her only to get his hand smacked away. Dan bolted for the bedroom and slammed the door behind her. Matt looked flabbergasted by that violent rejection, but Renee took over Dan's empty spot and slipped her arm through his. Despite that silent show of support, Renee was looking at Allison. The look they exchanged was tired.

"She's never going to forgive him for this," Allison said.

"When Coach comes to terms with it, she will too," Renee said.

Allison said nothing; her skeptical look said enough. Neil silently agreed with Allison. He'd spent enough time with the upperclassmen to know how much Dan admired Wymack. He was the only father figure she'd ever had and was everything she aspired to be in life. Dan had forgiven a lot of injustices over her years with the Foxes, but most of those insults had been directed at her and her friends. Forgiving someone for hurting Wymack might be more than she could handle.

"Keep an eye on her?" Neil asked.

"Of course," Renee said.

Neil went next door to pack. It didn't take long, but he didn't return to them when he was done. Instead he sat on the couch and waited for his teammates to pull themselves together again. Matt showed up fifteen minutes later, but it was another twenty after that before Nicky came looking for them. Matt slung Neil's duffel over one shoulder and his own over the other and let Neil get the lock. Kevin had come inside at some point, and he looked utterly exhausted where he stood at Andrew's side. Dan was obviously still mad as hell where she stood apart from everyone else. She didn't even look at Matt at his approach but stomped off toward the stairwell.

The Foxes headed downstairs in a scattered line and tossed their bags into the bed of Matt's truck. Andrew was the only one to keep his, and Matt didn't try taking it from him. Matt had a net cover tucked away under the passenger seat that took only a minute to snap into place. With their bags secured, the Foxes split up between Matt's truck and Andrew's car and got on the road.

Andrew detoured to the ABC store on the way to the interstate. Nicky went inside alone, was gone for fifteen minutes, and came back with an obscene amount of bottles. Without their bags in the trunk there was plenty of room for the haul. Andrew unzipped and upended his bag. It was full of sweaters, an odd choice for the mountains until Neil realized they were using the shirts just as packing for the bottles. Neil hoped Andrew had packed more practical attire in with Nicky's or Kevin's things.

They were back on the road a couple minutes later. It was a bit over two hours from campus to the mountains, but it felt like a short ride to athletes who were used to traveling for games. Neil thought they'd catch up to Matt's truck at some point, but the upperclassmen made it to the site first. Matt messaged Neil with directions from the main office to their cabin and a confirmation that he had all their keys.

Ten minutes later Andrew pulled into the dirt drive outside their home away from home. The massive cabin looked rustic on

[311]

the outside and refined on the inside, with smooth log walls and polished wooden floors. The main room had heavy rugs strewn everywhere and decorative bones and art on the wall. The kitchen was stocked with all-new appliances, and an oversized magnet on the fridge advertised what time buffet meals were served at the office. The back room had both a Foosball table and a billiards table. There was also a TV mounted on the wall.

One bedroom was downstairs. The other four bedrooms were upstairs, one at each corner. Two bedrooms already had bags in them, which meant Andrew's group was splitting up between floors. Nicky immediately voted for Neil and Andrew to have the private bedroom downstairs, and neither Aaron nor Kevin contested it. Neil almost said something because the downstairs bedroom only had a king bed in it, but since Andrew didn't argue he kept his own mouth shut.

All four upstairs bedrooms had doors to a balcony that surrounded the entire building. Two back doors downstairs led onto a deck that wound around two sides of the building, overlooking the mountainside and a seemingly endless stretch of trees. Rocking chairs lined the porch, and little lanterns were set at intervals on the railing. A hot tub was installed in the corner of the L-shaped deck, and that was where they found the upperclassmen. They'd already changed into swimsuits and were sitting inside the tub as it filled.

"Isn't this awesome?" Matt asked. "I want to move here."

"There's so much... nature," Nicky said. "I'd live here if I could stay indoors."

Allison rolled her eyes and slouched lower against the tub wall. "The only thing missing is a daiquiri."

"Funny you should mention that," Nicky said, and all four upperclassmen turned to stare at them. Nicky feigned shock, then hurt, and put a hand to his chest dramatically. "Seriously, you guys? It's like you don't know us."

"We try not to," Allison said.

At the same time, Matt asked, "What did you bring?"

"Ha." Nicky made a face at Allison. "What didn't we bring, you mean?"

"I got us the cabin," Allison said. "You make the drinks. There's a blender in the kitchen."

"Two, actually," Renee said. "I saw a backup one in the cabinet over the fridge."

Nicky took a quick vote on who wanted what and recruited Aaron and Kevin to help him bring the bags inside. Neil and Andrew went into the kitchen to investigate. The freezer had a built-in ice machine and the bucket was full, so Andrew slid it onto the counter and scrounged up the second blender. Neil stood out of the way while the others unloaded their liquor haul and watched with vague interest as Andrew and Nicky each set to work with the blenders. Kevin and Aaron sat at the table and cracked open a bottle of vodka.

"You doing Renee's?" Nicky asked as he poured the first drink. "It's against my religion to make virgin daiquiris."

Andrew didn't answer, but Neil knew he'd take care of it. Nicky recruited Kevin to carry drinks out as they were finished. Kevin and Aaron were fine drinking shots, but Nicky blended something colorful for himself when everyone else was taken care of. He followed Aaron and Kevin out to the deck, likely assuming Neil and Andrew wouldn't be far behind them.

Andrew stayed to clean the blenders out, then took two rocks glasses from the cabinet. He filled both to the brim with scotch and held one out to Neil. Neil looked from it to Andrew.

"I don't drink," Neil reminded him.

"You don't drink because you are afraid of losing control," Andrew said. "What do you have to hide now?"

That easy accusation brought Neil up short. He looked at the drink again. Andrew moved it closer, and Neil took the glass. Andrew lifted his a little in either challenge or invitation, and they knocked their drinks back together. The whisky burned its way down Neil's throat. Neil thought about too many nights on the road and too many bruises. He thought about Wymack

[313]

putting him back together in his apartment this past December and letting Neil keep his secrets. He wavered between extremes, unsure if the heat pooling in his gut was nausea or relief.

Andrew pulled a pack of cigarettes out of his back pocket and traded Neil for his empty glass. Neil shook the pack, felt the distinctive weight of a lighter shifting, and went out back. He stood halfway down the porch from the tub so the others wouldn't have to smell the cigarette smoke and lit up. He turned the cigarette between his hands, dimly aware of the others' laughing conversation, more aware of the taste in his mouth. He ran his tongue along his teeth, wondering what to think.

In the end the cigarette was enough to tip the scales. Andrew smelled of cigarette smoke and whisky the night he gave Neil a key to his house and told him to stay. Neil was always going to carry his past with him, but he didn't have to be weighed down by it. With enough time he could smooth the wretched edges out and replace his triggers with better memories.

Andrew came up alongside him and set the bottle of scotch at his feet. Neil slid his cigarettes across the wooden railing toward him. In exchange Andrew set a refilled glass halfway between them. Neil watched sunlight flash off the rocking surface and flicked ash to the dirt fifteen feet below. He held the cigarette out of the way when he picked up the glass, and he downed the whisky in one slow go. It was just as harsh as the first shot had been, but it didn't taste like death this time.

"Oh my god," Nicky said, too loud. "Was that alcohol? Did you just give Neil alcohol, and did he really just drink it? Did I miss the memo that Neil was suddenly going to start drinking with us?"

Despite Nicky's stunned approval, Andrew didn't serve Neil a third shot. They finished their cigarettes away from the others, then drifted closer so Neil could join the conversation.

The office opened its doors for dinner at eight, so they walked a half-mile down a dirt road to the main building. There

[314]

was more than enough food to satisfy the pack of hungry athletes and the property owners were on hand to greet each arriving group of guests. Their black eyes and bruises and Neil's extensive bandages drew more than a few curious looks, but the staff were polite enough to keep their mouths shut.

Dan hauled Kevin to a stop halfway back to the cabin. Neil heard Matt utter a low warning not to strike Kevin where it'd leave a mark, but it was a toss-up as to whether or not Dan heard him. Matt built a fire in the main fireplace when they made it back to the cabin, and the Foxes curled up on the couches and rocking chairs to watch the flames dance. Allison told stories of other resorts she'd visited, with an obligatory disclaimer that every place paled in comparison to her family's properties. She and Matt started a debate as to how the Foxes should celebrate when they won first place in championships. Neil didn't know if it was all in good fun or if they were making serious plans; he'd have assumed the former if not for how easily Allison had secured them this cabin.

As his teammates argued cruises versus Hawaii or Vegas, he thought of the money stashed in his safe at the dorm. Neil was done running and his father was never getting that money back. He couldn't think of anything better to do with it than repay his teammates' friendship. He didn't say anything, unsure what they'd think of a vacation bought with blood money, but listened carefully for the winning dream vacation. Their plans got more elaborate the more they drank until Neil was sure none of them would remember this debate in the morning.

Neil got up for another glass of water when the conversation slid toward more normal topics. When he cut the sink off and turned around he found Aaron waiting for him in the middle of the kitchen. Aaron jerked his chin in a silent order to follow and stepped out the back door onto the balcony. Neil set his drink aside and followed. He closed the door as quietly as he could and went to lean against the railing. Aaron made no move to close the gap between him.

[315]

"Nicky's kind of stupid," Aaron said. "He made the mistake of saying something to Andrew instead of waiting until he could get you alone. Andrew almost cut him open when he didn't take the hint fast enough." He glanced over his shoulder at the back door, maybe making sure the kitchen was still empty, before turning back on Neil. "That leaves you with me, since Andrew didn't see fit to warn me off you."

"When's the last time Andrew saw fit to talk to you at all?" Neil asked.

"Last Wednesday," Aaron reminded him.

It wasn't the answer Neil expected. He'd laid the groundwork for Aaron and Andrew's therapy and it'd been weeks since Aaron first muscled his way into one of Andrew's sessions, but this was the first hint that they were actually doing something real with that time. Aaron's awful attitude that first Wednesday was the only reaction they'd ever gotten from the brothers. Neil had assumed the two were still getting nowhere fast. Triumph was a quiet, smoldering heat in his stomach quickly snuffed out by Aaron's next words.

"So now you're going to talk to me," Aaron said, "and I'm going to give you exactly one chance to tell me the truth. Are you really fucking my brother?" He waited a beat, but when Neil just gazed back in silence, asked, "Do you take your cues from dead men?"

"What?" Neil asked.

"Just wondering how you went from your whole I-don't-date high horse to Andrew's bed," Aaron said. "Either you were lying to us to hide the fact you're a flamer, or you saw Drake rape Andrew and realized he's easy prey."

Neil punched him—a terrible mistake in retrospect, as he ended up half-crumpled over his screaming hand. Aaron took a couple bored steps out of Neil's reach and calmly checked the corner of his mouth with his thumb. He spat to one side and crouched to get a look at Neil's face. Despite his cruel words, his expression was calm and searching. Neil had the distinct feeling

[316]

he'd been had, but that didn't soothe his outrage any.

"Fuck you," Neil said in a voice like gravel. "Walk away while you still can."

"Nicky guesses it's nothing more than hate sex," Aaron said like Neil hadn't even spoken. "I'm hedging my bets on it being something else. We'll know soon enough, right?"

"Stay out of it."

"I won't," Aaron said. "You wanted me to fight for her. Do you think he'll fight for you?"

"No," Neil said.

Aaron shrugged, got to his feet, and went inside without another word. Neil waited until the fire in his hand became a dull roar, then eased upright and checked his bandages. There was enough light filtering through the glass back door for him to see clean gauze. Neil couldn't believe something could hurt so much and not leave a mark.

He sucked in a slow breath to throttle his lingering anger and headed indoors. His cup was where he'd left it, and Aaron was back in his chair when Neil stepped into the living room. Aaron didn't look Neil's way again that night, and Neil was happy to pretend Aaron didn't exist.

Kevin and Dan showed up not much later. Neil didn't see any fresh bruises on either of them but they looked like they'd gone through an emotional wringer. Nicky got up without being asked and collected a few bottles from the kitchen. By the time he returned Kevin had found a seat on the outskirts and Dan was practically sitting in Matt's lap. Dan and Kevin were more interested in getting tanked than contributing to the conversation, so their teammates filled in the silence as best they could.

By the time the Foxes split up for bed, most of them were unsteady on their feet. Luckily Renee was sober enough to help shepherd the shakiest ones up the stairs. Neil almost followed before remembering his room was downstairs. As if Allison could read his mind, she leaned dangerously far over the railing

[317]

and pointed at him.

"This cabin isn't soundproof. Don't keep me up. That goes for you two, too," she said, and turned her accusing finger on Dan and Matt. Dan tried for an innocent look but was too drunk to pull it off. Allison shook her finger for emphasis. "No fucking where I can hear it. It isn't fair to those of us who aren't getting any."

"Maybe if you ask Kevin very nicely," Nicky started.

Kevin's scathing look was almost louder than Allison's revolted noise. Neil shook his head and started for the bedroom. Andrew wasn't far behind him, and together they got Neil changed out for bed. Neil eyed the bed with some consternation. The only person he'd ever shared a bed with was his mother. She crammed them onto the same narrow mattress so she'd always know where he was; it was the only way she could get any sleep at night. Hesitation did neither of them any favors, though, so Neil picked a side and tugged the blankets back as carefully as he could.

Despite his reservations, there was something painfully familiar about the weight of another body in his bed. Less familiar was the way it felt being pushed deeper into the mattress, Andrew's hands on his shoulders and tongue in his mouth, but that was something Neil could definitely get used to.

He wouldn't let himself dwell on Aaron's ugly words, but it was harder to let go of Nicky's assumption that this was nothing more than an anger-fueled attraction. Nicky was more right than Neil wanted him to be, but Neil had no reason to resent that. He'd known going into this what Andrew thought of him— Andrew's apathy was precisely why Neil had decided to accept Andrew's advances.

But it wasn't that easy anymore, and Neil didn't know why or when it changed. He knew less what he was supposed to do about it. He'd have to warn Andrew at some point, but now wasn't the time. He buried his unease and confusion deep and worked bandaged fingers into Andrew's hair. He didn't care how

[318]

much it hurt so long as he could pull Andrew closer, and he let Andrew take him apart until he couldn't think anymore.

CHAPTER FOURTEEN

The Foxes spent most of the next day outdoors, hiking up and down the nearby trails and signing up for some afternoon horseback riding. Getting onto the horse set every cut and burn on Neil's arms screaming in pain, but Neil was too stubborn to sit it out. He had time to catch his breath once he was up in the saddle and he gritted his teeth against the throbbing pain. By the time they finished the two-hour trek he'd almost forgotten about his injuries. Dismounting was an unhappy reminder, and when they got back to the cabin he dug his bandages and antibiotics out of his bag. Andrew collected Renee when he saw what Neil was doing.

"I can do it," Neil said when Renee sat cross-legged on the bed in front of him.

"I know you can," Renee said. "but perhaps it's easier if someone helps you."

He could have argued further, but there was no winning with Renee, so he submitted to her ministrations. She didn't bat an eye at the ugly injuries she uncovered or waste his time with apologies and questions. She simply bent her head to the task and cleaned every cut and burn as thoroughly and carefully as possible.

Afterward she asked, "Are you going to let them air?"

"I should," Neil said, "but I don't want these on display."

"I will ask them not to say anything," Renee said, correctly guessing Neil's concern. When Neil didn't argue, she slid off the bed and left the room. Allison was right about sound in the cabin; Neil heard every word Renee said to the Foxes with two rooms between them.

Neil would have stalled, but Andrew grew tired of waiting

[320]

on him. He motioned for Neil to follow and left in search of
Kevin. Neil swallowed a sigh and went after him. He braced for
his teammates' reactions when he stepped into the kitchen with
all his injuries bared. Nicky flinched and looked away, whereas
Aaron surveyed the damage with keen interest. Dan opened her
mouth but caught herself in the nick of time. Matt went from
shock to anger in a nanosecond, and Allison averted her gaze as
quickly as she could. Renee watched her friends with a smile on
her lips and a calm stare, ready to intervene if one of them broke
their word.

Kevin was the first and only to do so, and his reaction was
predictable. "Can you play?"

"Yes," Neil said, before anyone could tear into Kevin. "It's
going to hurt, and if the Bearcats get too rough next week I'll
have some problems, but I still have my grip." He made a fist at
Kevin as proof and carefully did not wince at the tearing feeling
along his knuckles. "I'll just be extra careful."

"Absolutely not," Dan said. "You're not playing. You think
Coach will let you on the court when you look like that? I'll sub
in for you, Neil. Renee can help Allison out one more time,
right?" She looked to Renee long enough to see Renee's nod.
"Trust us to hold the line. You focus on healing so we can use
you in semifinals."

Neil's first instinct was to argue and to call unfair, to say he
hadn't survived his father and Lola's abuse just to sit out, to
protest that they needed all the help he could get. Then he
looked down at his arms and took a realistic assessment of his
chances. It was disappointing to know she was right, but
somehow it was still okay.

"I trust you," he said. "Thank you."

"Oh, wow," Nicky said. "Who's humanizing who in that
relationship, anyway?"

Andrew casually reached for the wooden block of knives.
Renee moved it out of his reach without batting an eye and
smiled at the look Andrew gave her for interfering. Nicky took

advantage of Andrew's distraction by hiding out of sight behind Kevin's taller body. Neil didn't miss the look Aaron sent Andrew, and a new flush of anger had him clenching his hand again. The ache in his knuckles warned him to relax, but then Aaron turned a shrewd look on Neil that made Neil want to knock him out. The pain would be worth it.

"Speaking of," Allison said, "I'm still waiting for an explanation, Neil. When are we going to talk about this?" She waggled her fingers at Neil and Andrew.

"Apparently never," Nicky said, a little sullenly.

"Don't be ridiculous," Allison said.

Neil dragged his stare away from Aaron with great effort. "Not anytime soon," he said, and when Allison looked affronted, explained, "I spent all weekend telling people every secret I've ever kept and I'll have to do it all over again as soon as we get back to campus. I think I've given up enough this week, don't you?"

Allison opened her mouth like she was going to argue but said nothing. After an eternity she looked to Dan and Renee. Dan gave a small jerk of her chin; Renee only smiled. Allison grimaced at them both before turning back on Neil.

"Fine. Be stingy—for now. We'll get the details out of you eventually."

They had time to kill before the office opened for dinner, so they headed to the back room. Kevin made a beeline for the TV and changed stations until he found a sports network. Dan and Allison claimed the Foosball table, so the others split into teams for pool. Neil had no idea what he was doing, but Renee and Nicky walked him through it. He failed miserably, but Andrew and Renee could hold their own against Matt and the cousins.

Neil bandaged his arms before the walk to dinner. Dan and Matt disappeared afterward, and Nicky and Aaron piled into the hot tub with Renee and Allison. Kevin settled down by the fireplace with a history book, so Andrew and Neil ended up in the kitchen. Andrew poured drinks and let Neil deliver them to their teammates. Andrew had a shot for him when he was done making the last trip. Andrew offered silent toast and they drank together. Andrew's kiss was hotter than the whisky and more than enough to take the bite off his tongue.

When Dan and Matt returned the team migrated to the den with more drinks. They spent another late night talking about anything in the world except Exy. The fresh air and alcohol had Neil nodding off earlier than he meant to, but he wasn't the only one ready for an early night. Renee and Aaron headed upstairs right when Neil gave up staying awake. Andrew stayed behind to keep an eye on Kevin, so Neil went alone to the bedroom and made himself comfortable on his side of the bed. He woke up when Andrew came in, but drifted off again as soon as Andrew settled down.

Fingernails tapping on the door woke them both up some indeterminable time later. Neil reached for a gun and hit Andrew's arm instead. Andrew glanced back at him before rolling off the bed. The cabin was practically pitch black this late at night, but it was a straight shot from Andrew's side of the bed to the door. Neil couldn't see who was standing outside, but Renee's calm voice was unmistakable.

"I'm sorry," she said. "I need to borrow your car. I will bring it back before we check out."

"Light," Andrew said.

Neil reached blindly for the lamp on the bedside table. He found it on the fifth try and shielded his eyes against the sudden harsh glow. Andrew squinted at it in displeasure before heading for his bag. Renee stood fully dressed in the doorway, looking wide awake and grim.

"Renee?" Neil asked, because it was obvious Andrew wasn't going to make her explain.

Renee's words were a cold shock to his system: "Kengo is dead."

Neil stared blankly at her, but it didn't take long to figure the rest out. "Jean?"

[323]

"Riko hurt him," Renee said. "I am going to get him."

"They won't let you into Evermore," Neil said.

Renee's smile didn't reach her eyes. "Yes, they will."

Andrew pressed the keys into her waiting palm. Renee nodded gratitude and turned away. Andrew followed her out, presumably to lock the front door behind her. Neil heard the engine hum to life outside, and headlights splashed a sharp beam through the bedroom window as she pulled out of the gravel drive. Andrew came back alone and closed the door on his way to the bed. Neil waited until he was under the sheets before killing the lights again. He listened to Andrew's breathing smooth out, but he didn't get anymore sleep that night. He couldn't stop thinking about Riko and Jean, and Tetsuji and Evermore, and what Kengo's death meant for the truce with his uncle.

Explaining Renee's absence the next day somehow fell to Neil. Kevin took the news as well as Neil thought he might and locked himself in the upstairs bedroom to have a panic attack. The morning started with Irish coffee for everyone. The afternoon was a little better until they realized Renee had turned her phone off. The Foxes trusted her judgment, but their vacation wasn't the same without her.

Renee returned mid-morning on Sunday since they needed both cars to make it back to South Carolina. Neil was on the back porch with Andrew, watching a cigarette burn to nothing, when he heard tires on gravel. Nicky was dozing in one of the rocking chairs, a mug of coffee forgotten in a loosely-cradled hand. Neil got him up and inside. The others had heard the car and were heading to the den. By the time Renee walked through the door they were all waiting for her.

"Oh," she said. "Good morning."

"How is he?" Kevin asked.

"He's not well," Renee said, "but Abby is doing what she can for him."

"You didn't seriously kidnap Jean," Dan said.

"I didn't have to." Renee shrugged out of her coat and draped it neatly over the back of a chair. "Edgar Allan's president lives on campus, so I stopped by his house and asked him to intervene."

"You didn't really," Allison said, staring at her.

"I put him on the phone with Stephanie," Renee said, meaning her foster mother. "She made it clear he had two choices: he could settle this quietly between us or she'd get all her industry friends to run with news of Evermore's violent hazing. He chose the one that would hurt his school the least, or at least he tried. Coach Moriyama couldn't produce Jean when Mr. Andritch asked him to, so we made an unannounced trip to the stadium. Did you know not even the president has access to the court? I don't think he knew his codes were out of date. He had to get the new ones from security. Either way, the Ravens weren't expecting us."

"That sounds like an understatement," Matt said dryly.

"The master would have covered his tracks," Kevin said. "If he knew Andritch was looking for Jean for some reason, he would have found a way to hide him from view."

"Coach Moriyama wasn't there. He was in New York," Renee said. Kevin stared at her, blank-faced in disbelief. Renee shook her head and said, "He was invited to the funeral. Riko wasn't."

Kevin's flinch was full body. "No."

Riko was his father's son in name only; he had been estranged from his father and brother his entire life. Despite that cold shoulder, Riko always believed he could win his father's attention and approval through his successes on the court. Kengo's death was a disastrous blow to Riko's dreams, and Kevin had warned Neil Riko's reaction would be ugly. That Ichirou had reached out to his uncle but skipped his brother entirely was acid on an open wound. With no one there to stay Riko's hand or distract him from his furious grief, Jean hadn't stood a chance.

[325]

"Mr. Andritch let me take Jean away when he saw the shape he was in," Renee said. "I left him my number and promised to keep in touch while the school investigates. Abby has also promised to keep them updated on his recovery. Unfortunately—or not—Jean is unwilling to name names or press charges. He is not happy to be in South Carolina. He has already tried leaving twice."

"To go where?" Nicky asked. "Not back to Evermore. Is he crazy?"

"It's self-preservation," Neil said. "If Riko and Tetsuji think he's pointing fingers behind their backs, they'll kill him. Even this could be considered defiance since he's not where he's supposed to be."

"How bad is it?" Matt asked. "Kevin got out of his school contract when he got injured."

"They had no choice. I couldn't play," Kevin said. "If Jean will heal, they can still claim him as theirs and there is nothing we can do about it."

"But the president's involved, right?" Nicky said. "So the school board's going to get in on it soon enough, and they're going to do whatever it takes to hide this. It'll kill their precious reputation if this gets out."

"If Jean won't implicate anyone and my mother agrees to keep quiet, they might be willing to let him transfer to another school," Renee said. "That is the best-case scenario, anyway."

"Jean won't agree," Kevin said quietly.

"Perhaps you can talk him into it," Renee said. "I would appreciate the help."

"He isn't safe with us," Kevin said. "I won't give him false hope."

"Some hope is better than none at all," Renee said. "It is the same deal we offered you, and you are still here."

"I stayed because of Andrew," Kevin said.

"And I'm not taking in any more refugees," Andrew said.

"I know," Renee said. "Jean is my problem, not yours. The

[326]

consequences and fallout are mine to deal with, I promise."

"He doesn't have family he could stay with?" Dan asked.

"His parents sold him to the Moriyamas to repay a debt," Kevin said. "The Ravens are all he has."

Neil shook his head. "Kevin will talk to him when we get back."

"I didn't say that," Kevin said.

"But you're going to," Neil said. "You already walked away from him once knowing what Riko would do to him in your absence. Don't do it again. If you don't protect him now, his death is on you."

"Damn, Neil," Nicky said. "A little harsh?"

Neil ignored him. "Renee already did the hard part. She got him out of there. You just have to put your foot down and keep him here. You outrank him in Riko's imaginary hierarchy. He'll listen to you."

"Yeah," Matt said. "Weren't you two friends once?"

Kevin opened his mouth, closed it again, and looked away. "That was a long time ago."

"Kevin," Renee said. "Please."

Kevin said nothing for so long Neil thought he was going to refuse. Finally Kevin said, "I'll do what I can, but I won't promise anything."

"Thank you," Renee said, and glanced at Neil to include him in that.

Kevin jerked his hand in cutting dismissal and turned away. "I'm going to pack."

Neil watched him stomp upstairs, only dimly aware of Dan and Allison peppering Renee with more questions. When Kevin was out of sight and his footsteps stopped in his bedroom, Neil headed after him. He took the stairs as quietly as he could, but the cabin wasn't designed with sneakiness in mind, and he knew Kevin heard him coming. The bedroom door was wide open, but Neil pushed it closed behind him. Kevin was sitting on his bed, one knee tucked to his chest, as he stared dully into the distance.

[327]

Neil sat cross-legged on the end of the bed and waited.

It didn't take long. Kevin propped his chin on his knee and said, "How do you do it?" Kevin flicked his fingers as if frustrated by his own vagueness and said, "After everything that's happened this year, after Riko and your father and the FBI and knowing Lord Ichirou has found out about you, why aren't you afraid?"

"I am," Neil said. "But I'm more afraid of letting go than I am of holding on."

"I don't understand."

"You do, or you wouldn't have trusted Andrew and Coach in the first place. Problem is you put yourself in their hands and refused to commit any further than that. You think Riko will hurt you for your defiance, so you're afraid to step too far out of line. But this middle ground won't save you forever.

"Kevin," Neil said, and waited for Kevin to finally look at him. "Figure out what you want more than anything, what it would kill you to lose. That's what's at stake if you let Riko win. Calculate the cost of your fear. If it's too much, you need to fight. Wouldn't you rather die trying than never try at all?"

"It's death either way," Kevin pointed out.

"Die free or die a failure," Neil said. "The choice is yours, but pick your side before you see Jean again. If he thinks you're bluffing you'll never win him over."

Kevin said nothing, so Neil slid off the bed and left him there. The others were talking about breakfast as he headed back downstairs. Renee had stopped by a drive-through on her way up but the others had been putting off breakfast until they had to turn in their keys at the main office. All that was left to do was pack, so they split up to their rooms and dug their bags from their closets.

They packed the cars and walked to the office building for the last time. Renee drank tea while the others chowed down on eggs and bacon. No one said a word about Jean where someone might overhear them, though it was questionable anyone else in

[328]

the breakfast hall knew who they were and could put it all together. They returned their keys on the way out and split up between the cars. Andrew pulled out of the drive first, and they started back to campus.

They made a shortstop by Abby's house so Kevin could see Jean. Abby had left the front door unlocked as usual, so the team let themselves in without knocking. Dan called out a greeting on her way inside so Abby would know she had guests, and Abby answered from further down the hall.

They found Abby and Wymack seated at the kitchen table. Dishes on the counter and crumpled napkins on the table said they'd just finished lunch. Abby cleared away the mess and took Kevin down the hall to wherever Jean was resting. Neil looked to Wymack, searching for the lingering trauma of Kevin's confession. Wymack's calm mask was fool-proof. That didn't stop Dan from staring like she could see through him.

"Consensus?" Wymack asked when they heard a door shut.

"He can hide with us until he's better," Dan said. "What he does after that is up to him."

Wymack nodded. "Neil, the board knows you were coming back today."

"They want to talk," Neil said, not really a question.

"They told me to call them as soon as you returned," Wymack said. "Have you returned?"

It was tempting to take that subtle offer and hide a bit longer, but Neil was out of time. Spring break was over. Classes started up again tomorrow and his classmates would have heard the news a week ago. In a day or two Neil would have to face the press and confirm everything they'd already figured out. Inexplicably Neil wondered how Coach Hernandez reacted to the news. He wondered if reporters had called him looking for insight. His former teammates no doubt had plenty to say. Small towns grew up on gossip.

"Yeah," Neil said. "I'm back."

Wymack stepped out to make the call.

[329]

Abby came back alone and looked around at the team. "Jean can't handle this many guests."

"We were just dropping Renee and Kevin off," Matt said.

Abby settled back into her chair and looked around at the Foxes. "Renee said the cabin was lovely."

They fell over themselves to describe the cabin's highlights to her. Aaron had little to contribute, but he at least looked like he was paying attention to the conversation. They'd only just started telling her about the horseback riding when Wymack came back. He stopped in the doorway instead of heading for his chair. Neil took the hint and headed for him. Andrew stayed behind like Neil knew he would; Kevin needed Andrew more than Neil did today.

Charles Whittier, the president of Palmetto State University, lived in an oversized house near the front gates to campus. Wymack and Neil followed the stone sidewalk around the building to the door, and Neil hung back while Wymack rang the bell. Wymack had called ahead, so Whittier answered almost immediately.

"Chuck," Wymack said in lieu of hello.

"Coach," Whittier said, but he was looking past Wymack at Neil. "Come in."

They passed a living room that could fit Wymack's entire apartment and a conference room bigger than Neil's dorm suite. Whittier's office was in the back of the house near the kitchen. He gestured for them to take their seats and closed the door behind them. His desk was cleared off of everything except a computer and phone, but a tray on a nearby filing cabinet held glasses of iced tea. He passed two to Wymack, who handed one off to Neil, and took his own to his chair. Neil held on to his drink like it'd give him the courage he needed for this.

Whittier was still looking at him like Neil would explode in another minute, but at length he said, "Let's begin."

He tapped his mouse button, and a second later his phone rang. An automated voice welcomed them to the conferencing

[330]

system. After Whittier keyed his access code in the voice stated, "There are twenty callers connected including you," and a series of loud beeps followed as everyone was linked in.

"This is Whittier," Whittier said. "I have Coach David Wymack and—Neil Josten," he said after a brief hesitation and a glance at Wymack, "here with me. Who do we have signed on already?"

They went down the list, offering names and titles. Neil felt like the entire administration department had shown up for this call; the people checking in ranged from Student Affairs to Alumni Relations to all eleven members of the Board of Trustees. Once everyone was introduced and accounted for, Whittier got them started.

What followed was one of the longest hours of Neil's life. It was quickly obvious this wasn't the first call they'd had since Neil's truth came out; they were picking this conversation up from the last time they'd spoken and they referenced Wymack's last arguments. Neil was given time to present his case, and Wymack staunchly vouched for him when the Board peppered him with questions and demands.

When they were done with him they switched to fighting amongst themselves. They debated the risks of keeping Neil around but were equally interested in the publicity: how would they look for releasing him at the end of the year versus how they would look for standing with him. Neil wanted to remind them he was still listening in on the call. Instead he counted to ten and drank his tea. Wymack wasn't any happier about their callous calculations, and he tolerated it for only a few more minutes.

"Look," he broke in, ignoring Whittier's gesture to stay out of it. "Look," he said again, louder, when the others kept talking over him. Wymack gave them a couple seconds then started talking loudly anyway. "Since day one you've questioned every single decision I've made. Time and time again I've proven that I always know what's best for this team—both for the players and

[331]

for the school's interests. Haven't I?

"This should be an easier call than signing off on Andrew was," Wymack pushed on without waiting for their agreement. "With Andrew I asked you to have faith and patience because I knew it'd take time before you saw your endorsement pay off. This time the results are already in. You've reaped the benefits of Neil's presence since August.

"Neil is a critical member of my team," Wymack said, stabbing his finger against the desk for emphasis. "You can ask any person on my line-up and they will all agree: we would not be where we are today if he wasn't here with us. And where we are today is on the cusp of finals. We are four games—four!—from being NCAA champions. We are on the verge of being the first team in the nation to best the Edgar Allan Ravens. We have a line-up that will graduate to pros and Court. We are reshaping the way everyone thinks about Palmetto State's Exy program. Taking Neil off the team won't save face and it sure as hell isn't the smart decision. It will backfire so hard you'll never want to see a reporter again."

They were quiet for a minute, then started arguing amongst themselves again. Finally they put it to vote, and they voted in favor of Neil.

"Thank you," Wymack said, in a tone that clearly said he was more annoyed by their pigheadedness than grateful for their support. "Now that that's finally settled, there's something else I need to say so long as I have you all with me. You should hear this from me before you see it on the news."

"What now?" one of the Trustees asked.

"It's recently come to my attention that I have a son," Wymack said. He kept his tone and expression even, but he looked tense in his chair. "I'm scheduling a paternity test now that we're back on campus only because I want the paperwork on file."

"Congratulations," someone said, more obligatory than anything else.

[332]

Wymack opened his mouth, closed it, and tried again. "It's Kevin Day."

The silence that followed was profound. At last someone managed, "It's what?"

"He told me last week. He was—inspired," Wymack said after a brief search for words, "by Neil's situation to come clean with me. I'm telling you now because he plans on making it public this week. We're going to use it to help combat the negative press surrounding Neil. I'd like to state for the record that this discovery will have no impact on my coaching."

"Noted," a woman said, sounding uncertain, right before another argument broke out. This one was shorter, mostly centered on how the school was going to publicly react to the news. Finally everything was squared away and the conference drew to a close. As each person hung up the line beeped to indicate people dropping out. Whittier waited until he heard all nineteen before releasing the conference.

"That was unexpected," Whittier said, with a long look at Wymack. Neil thought he was looking for a sign that Wymack had been sitting on this secret for years instead of a week.

Wymack had no problems interpreting that stare, but instead of declaring his innocence Wymack simply said, "I am his coach first."

Whittier shook his head. "Speaking president to coach, that's exactly what I want to hear and I expect you to keep your word. Speaking Chuck to David, I'm sorry. That couldn't have been an easy discovery."

"Thank you," Wymack said after a moment.

Whittier got to his feet and walked them to the door. Wymack gave Neil a ride back to the dorm. Neil spent it staring out the window and wondering if he should say anything. In the end he decided to trust Abby and Dobson to keep an eye on Wymack. He settled for a hollow "Thanks" when Wymack dropped him off at the back curb, and he didn't look back before heading inside.

[333]

Monday meant classes, though Neil would have happily stayed in bed at the dorm. His injuries drew more lingering stares than he could stomach and a couple classmates were bold enough to press him for gossip. There was no point lying about it, but no one said Neil had to tell the truth either. He warded off all of their questions with an insistent, "I don't want to talk about it," that got louder every time someone ignored that warning.

When the bell sounded at the end of his last class, the relief Neil felt was almost crippling. He all but bolted from the classroom and followed the crush of rowdy students out of the building and down the stairs. He made it ten steps away from the building before someone stopped in his path. Neil was used to dodging bodies on campus, so he neatly sidestepped and kept going. The man spoke on Neil's way by.

"You will stop."

Neil didn't really think he was being addressed, but looking back was instinctive. He regretted it immediately and rocked to a startled stop. The man who'd spoken was Japanese, older than the oblivious students that flowed past them but dressed casually so as not to stand out. He considered Neil like Neil was the bane of his existence and gestured, not an invitation but an order.

"We are leaving."

Neil almost asked where they were going but thought better of it at the last second. He followed the stranger to the library parking lot. A car idled at the curb and Neil got in the backseat when someone inside opened the door for him. His escort slammed the door behind him and got in the passenger seat.

No one said a word. Neil stared out the window, keeping track of where they were going in case he needed to find his way back, but he didn't have long to wonder. They took him to the construction site on the far side of campus. Neil saw parked cars and idle equipment but no workers. Enough of the new dorm's exterior was up now that they were likely busy inside, but Neil would have preferred some witnesses.

[334]

There was only one other car parked out back. The driver pulled up alongside it and killed the engine, but no one moved. Neil got the hint after a minute of tense silence and got out. The door opposite him was unlocked. He opened it but hesitated halfway into the car when he saw who was waiting for him.

At first glance, Ichirou Moriyama didn't look like much. His black silk suit spoke of excessive wealth, but his youthful features undermined that pretentiousness. He only had a couple years on Neil to start with and genetics made him look even younger. He was just another hopeful businessman, maybe, another rich kid CEO living life in the vertical fast lane. Neil was fooled for all of one second: the moment it took him to meet Ichirou's eyes across the backseat.

This man was not like Neil's father, with his temper and thugs and ugly reputation. He was not like Riko, with his selfish cruelty and childish tantrums. This was a man who could hold both of them in check with a glance, a man who'd been raised to rule. He was the Moriyamas' power in living, breathing form, and with his father's death he sat alone and untouchable on its throne.

Neil considered turning around and walking away but suspected that was a good way to get shot in the back. He didn't know why he was here, since not even Riko had ever met his brother face-to-face, but he knew one misstep meant his uncle's hopeful truce was void. Neil pawed desperately at his memory, searching for any advice on how to handle this encounter. Neil couldn't face Ichirou as Neil Josten; he had to face Ichirou as a Wesninski would. That meant every word had to be the truth and this had to be the biggest lie Neil had ever told.

He bit down on his doubts and the first flicker of panic and said, very carefully, "May I come in?"

Ichirou flicked two fingers in silent command, and Neil climbed into the car. He closed the door behind himself, firmly but not loudly, and fixed his stare on Ichirou's shoulder.

"Do you know who I am?" Ichirou asked.

[335]

"Yes," Neil said, and faltered for a half-second as he grasped at a proper title. "Sir" didn't have the necessary respect, but Kevin had referred to Kengo more than once as "lord". It was an outdated and clumsy term but it was all Neil had right now. "You are Lord Moriyama."

"Yes," Ichirou said, with a measured calm Neil didn't trust for a second. "You are aware my father is dead? I have not yet heard your condolences."

"Offering them seems presumptuous," Neil said. "It assumes you value my words, but I am just a no-one."

"You are not no one," Ichirou said. "That is why I am here. You understand."

It wasn't a question, but Neil lowered his head and said, "My father is dead at my uncle's hands and the FBI is investigating what is left of his ring. I am a loose end that must be dealt with one way or another."

"I could stop it," Ichirou said, and Neil believed him. It didn't matter that the FBI already had boxes full of Neil's stories and names. If Ichirou wanted the story killed and rumors quieted, he could do it with a couple phone calls and enough money. "Instead I am here. I like to know the value of things before I throw them away so I know how to compensate for their loss."

"I have no value now," Neil said, "but if given the time and chance to do so I would repay your family for the inconveniences I've caused. The average professional Exy player makes three million dollars a year. I don't need that kind of money for myself. Let me donate it to your family instead. I can route it through whichever holdings and charities you've inherited."

"An unsubtle attempt to buy your safety."

"My lord," Neil said, "I am attempting to right a wrong and fulfill a broken promise. I was supposed to belong to your uncle. I should have been raised at Evermore to be a Raven and play for Court. My potential revenue has always belonged to you. I

[336]

returned to Exy as soon as my mother died because I know my purpose."

"And yet you did not return to my uncle," Ichirou said.

It felt like a test where failure meant death. Neil knew what the safe answer probably was, but a dangerous thought burned his tongue. His father had served Kengo, but to hold so much territory and power Kengo would have had to trust him. Nathan would have had the right to bring threats and potential complications to Kengo's attention. Neil didn't have that authority, but he had to try.

"I know you have no reason to trust my word," Neil said, very carefully, "and I know I have not earned your ear or consideration. But I am a Wesninski. My family is your family. Please believe me when I say I would never risk the safety of your empire. Playing for Edgar Allan would betray everything my family is supposed to stand for."

He hesitated as if afraid of continuing and crossing a fragile line. Ichirou waited for him to make up his mind. Neil wished he could read something, anything, on Ichirou's face, but his expression was serene and his tone hadn't changed since this awful conversation started. Neil didn't know if he was fooling Ichirou, and he didn't know if it would make a difference even if he could.

Neil finally took a steadying breath and said, "Your brother is going to destroy everything of yours unless someone collars him."

It was enough to earn a thin smile from Ichirou. It was all Neil could do to not flinch when Ichirou said, "That is very bold."

"Yes," Neil said, "but it is the truth."

Ichirou said nothing for so long Neil wondered if he was supposed to get out of the car and walk away. Finally Ichirou gestured for him to continue.

"Riko has spent his entire life aiming to be the best player on the court," Neil said. "When he feels his superiority is

[337]

threatened he lashes out without concern for collateral damage. This past year alone is proof of his increasing instability.

"Kevin Day was your uncle's second largest investment, but Riko destroyed him over injured pride. At the start of his sophomore year Kevin had a seven-digit net worth between his professional contract, his spot on the national team, and his endorsements. He could have earned your family fifteen, twenty million a year after graduation. Now Kevin is starting over from scratch.

"Riko killed one of my teammates in August and admitted to it in a public location," Neil said. "In November he interfered with the Oakland justice system and left a money trail from California to South Carolina all for the sake of hurting another teammate, and in December he bought out a psychiatrist at Easthaven in Columbia to continue that torture. Over Christmas break he gave me back my natural looks so my father's people could find and kill me. He laid the groundwork for the confrontation in Maryland that ended with my father's death and this entire federal investigation.

"Last week he reacted to your father's death by beating one of his teammates within an inch of his life. He is lucky it was Jean Moreau; Jean knows who your family is and would never speak out against Riko. But Jean is in our custody now while he heals and Edgar Allan University has launched a quiet investigation into the Ravens. They will find out about the hazing and abuse your uncle condones and someone will have to answer for it. What happens if they stumble across evidence of Riko's manipulations during their search?

"I am not saying your brother is out of line," Neil lied, "but he is not being careful. He is escalating because he feels threatened, but there are too many people watching us now. They will catch him soon enough, and I am afraid of what will fall back on you. I won't ally myself with such a risk, so I cannot play for your uncle at Edgar Allan. I'm sorry."

Another endless silence followed. A day or week or year

[338]

passed before Ichirou said, "Look me in the eye and listen very carefully." Neil dragged his stare up to Ichirou's face. Ichirou's smile was long gone and his coal eyes seemed to bore right through Neil. "Where I come from, a man's word is only as good as his name and his name earns weight from the blood he has spilled for my family. You are untested and untrue. You are not worth the air you breathe. I would balance the red in my ledger with your death and consider it a fair repayment.

"However," Ichirou said, "you are your father's son, and your father was someone to me. He is the reason I came down here myself when I could have sent anyone to speak to you. Do you know what I will do to you if I think you are wasting my time? Do you know what I will do to anyone you have ever met or spoken to? I will kill everyone who has ever stood by you and I will make each death last a lifetime."

It didn't sound like a threat; it sounded like a promise.

"What can I do to convince you I'm telling the truth?" Neil said.

"Nothing," Ichirou said, and said a few words in Japanese to the two men seated up front.

The front passenger pulled a cell phone out of his pocket. Neil couldn't understand a word the man said, but he understood that angry tone just fine. For a wild moment he thought the man was arranging messy deaths for all of the Foxes. He clenched his teeth against a spike of panic and stared at the empty cushion between him and Ichirou. The passenger went back and forth for several minutes, then hung up and put his phone away. His tone was deferential when he said something to Ichirou.

Whatever the news was, Ichirou's expression didn't change. Ichirou tapped his thumb idly on his ankle as he thought. Neil didn't know how long they sat there in silence, ten minutes or ten lifetimes, but he was sure he'd die before Ichirou finally made up his mind.

"Perhaps your life has a price tag after all," Ichirou said. "Eighty percent of your earnings for the entirety of your career

[339]

will be sufficient. I expect similar tithes from Day and Moreau; it is only reasonable considering my family funded their training. Someone will be in touch with you to make arrangements. If you fail to make the cut after graduation, the deal is forfeit and you will be executed. Do you understand?"

Disbelief knocked the air from his lungs; relief was so intense Neil thought for a moment he'd be violently ill. Somehow he kept his tone even when he said, "I understand. I'll talk to Kevin and Jean immediately. We will not fail you."

Ichirou slanted a hooded look at him. "Then for now you are dismissed."

It was so abrupt Neil almost forgot to say, "Thank you."

He tried to get out of the car without looking like he was making a mad dash for it and wasn't entirely sure he succeeded. He closed the door behind him and both drivers cut the engines on. Neil stood stock still as the cars pulled away and watched numbly as they rolled out of sight. Knowing they were gone did nothing to make him feel safer and Neil sank to his knees on the asphalt. He dug his fingers into the taut denim over his knees and fought to get his racing heart under control.

When he thought he could stand without falling down he followed Perimeter Road back around campus to the building where Kevin had his history class. The clock on Neil's phone said there were fifteen minutes left of the period, so Neil propped himself against the wall outside the door and waited. Kevin was one of the last out and he drew up short when he saw Neil.

"I'm taking you to Abby's," Neil said in French. "We have to talk to Jean."

"Not right now," Kevin said.

"Yes now." Neil put an arm out when Kevin looked ready to walk away. "Ichirou just came to see us."

Kevin choked on his first denial. His second attempt was hoarse with disbelief. "Don't joke about such things." Neil stared back at Kevin in silence until Kevin flinched and took a half-

[340]

step back. "No. He won't even meet Riko. He wouldn't come here."

"Come on," Neil said.

He messaged Andrew on their way to Fox Tower, so Andrew was waiting for them on the trunk of his car. He had a small package in one hand and a cigarette in the other. The latter he tossed aside at their approach, and he got the locks undone as he slid to his feet. It was a short drive from the dorm to Abby's place. Neil knocked even though her door was unlocked, and Abby answered a few seconds later. She frowned at the sight of them on her doorstep but moved aside to let them in.

"Don't you have class right now?"

"No," Neil said. "Where's Jean?"

"He was asleep the last time I checked in on him."

"It's important," Neil said. "I'll wake him up."

Abby studied Kevin's bleak expression a moment before stepping aside. Neil took Kevin and Andrew down the hall, leaving Abby staring after them, and gave the bedroom door a cursory knock on his way in. Jean startled awake at the noise and started to sit up. Moving was a mistake, judging by the sound he made as he sank back to the mattress. Neil took advantage of his distraction and surveyed Riko's handiwork on his way to the bedside. Jean's face was pretty much a swollen bruise. Both eyes were blackened courtesy of a broken nose and stitches had patched his chin and cheek back together. Chunks of hair had been ripped from his skull, leaving bald and scabbing patches throughout. Neil forced back an unexpected rush of anger and sat on the edge of the mattress.

"Hello, Jean," Neil said.

"Go away," Jean said, voice raw with loathing. "I have nothing to say to you."

"But you'll listen," Neil said, "because I just told Ichirou where you are."

It was enough to get Jean's undivided attention. Kevin sat down on Jean's other side, white-faced all over again at the

[341]

sound of Ichirou's name. Neil looked back to make sure Andrew was listening, then told them about Ichirou's visit: why he'd come, how he'd chosen to spare their lives, and what it would cost them to repay his favor. Kevin and Jean listened to all of it without saying a word.

"It's not a pardon and it's not really freedom, but it's protection." Neil looked from one shell-shocked face to the other. "We're assets for the main family now. The King's lost all his men and there's nothing he can do about it without crossing his brother. We're safe—for good."

Jean made a terrible sound and buried his face in his hands. Kevin opened his mouth, closed it again, and flicked a haunted look down at Jean. Neil waited, but neither man seemed able to react beyond that. Finally he slid off the bed and left them to each other's questionable comfort. Andrew preceded him out of the room, but Neil snagged his sleeve as he tugged the door closed behind them. Andrew obediently turned to face him.

"How does it feel to sell yourself out?" Andrew asked.

"Worth every penny," Neil said. "Let him have however much he wants. I don't need the money. All I need is what he gave me: a promise that I have a future. I have permission—no, orders—to live my life how I want to. I'm going to graduate from Palmetto State in four more years and play Exy until they force me to retire. Maybe I'll even die of old age."

"You sound more like them every day," Andrew said.

Neil guessed he meant their more optimistic teammates. "You're going to have to come up with something of your own to hold onto. I'm safe, Kevin doesn't need your protection anymore, Nicky's going back to Erik eventually, and Aaron's got Katelyn. What are you going to live for if you're not playing sheepdog for us?"

"Aaron doesn't have Katelyn."

"Denial doesn't suit you. We talked about this."

"You talked," Andrew said. "I didn't listen."

"Choose us," Neil said. It was enough to shut Andrew up—

maybe only for a second, but Neil would take any opening he could get. "Kevin's going to retake his spot on Court before he graduates. He thinks I can make the cut with enough practice and time. Come with us. Let's all play in the Olympics together one day. We'd be unstoppable."

"That's your obsession, not mine."

"Borrow it until you have something of your own." Neil held tighter to Andrew's sleeve when Andrew started to pull free. "Isn't any of this fun? Having a place, having a team, a different city every week and cigarettes and drinks in-between? I don't want this to end."

Andrew yanked loose. "Everything ends."

He pushed his package against Neil's chest and headed down the hall. Andrew had already slit the tape from the ends, so Neil pried the flap open without much trouble or pain. He shook the box over a waiting palm, but nothing fell out. He had to dig the contents out with his fingers and he considered the wadded cloth with some consternation. He didn't understand until he shifted his grip and let the ends unravel. He was holding a set of arm bands identical to Andrew's. They were long enough to hide the bandages and fresh scarring on Neil's forearms.

He looked up at Abby's approach. She glanced from him to the closed bedroom door to the gift Neil was holding. "Everything all right?"

Neil thought about it, but not for long. "Never been better."

CHAPTER FIFTEEN

The Foxes reacted to Neil's news with almost unanimous jubilation. Even Aaron perked up enough to offer congratulations. Kevin couldn't recover that quickly from having his world upended, though, and was distracted the entire afternoon. He missed shots he should have made with his eyes closed and spent his breaks sitting alone in the stands. Wymack said nothing to him about his poor performance and quieted Dan the one time she tried to say something.

Dan managed to get everyone downtown for a celebratory dinner. They couldn't talk about Ichirou's deal in public, but they could and did yammer about everything else that came to mind. No one missed Neil's new bands, but after a couple good-natured taunts they kept their word to stay out of Neil and Andrew's not-relationship.

Neil spent most of the meal watching Kevin and Andrew. Kevin said nothing to anyone but stared at his plate as he played with his food. Andrew sat forward in his seat between the two strikers, fingers laced and propped against his face to hide his mouth. He watched everyone with a hooded gaze and had nothing to add. When someone made the mistake of trying to include him he stared them down until they moved on. Neil saw the tired look Matt and Dan exchanged, the disappointment evident in the frowns tugging at their lips. They'd made real progress in the mountains, or so they thought, but Andrew had closed up again without warning. Neil wanted to say Andrew was conserving all his energy for Kevin's quiet meltdown, but he wasn't sure how to say it without drawing Andrew's ire.

Finally they headed back to the dorm. Neil followed Nicky into the cousins' room. Kevin made a beeline for the bathroom but left the door open behind him. Neil looked from his white-knuckled grip on the sink edge to Kevin's reflection. He didn't know what put that intense look on Kevin's face unless Kevin was staring at the number on his cheek. Kevin had been second-best and second-class all his life. Now he had the freedom to reach for the rank he'd always deserved and always been too afraid to want. Neil didn't blame Kevin for his fear, but he needed to see Kevin overcome it.

When Kevin gave no sign he was moving any time soon, Neil had to give up. Andrew was sitting on his desk, so Neil perched beside him. Nicky and Aaron claimed the beanbag chairs and loaded a game on the TV. They powered through three levels before Kevin reappeared.

Kevin looked from Neil to Andrew and said, "Take me to the court."

It was obvious he didn't care which one of them complied, but Neil looked to Andrew. Andrew had the window open so he could blow cigarette smoke through the screen. He was only halfway through the stick but he didn't hesitate to stub it out on the windowsill. He set the butt aside for later and slid off the desk. When he was halfway across the room Neil got up and invited himself along. Kevin didn't seem to notice and Andrew acknowledged his presence with a brief glance. Nicky sent them off with a cheery farewell and went back to mowing down monsters.

They left Kevin in the locker room and continued down to the court. Neil stood near the wall to study the polished floor and gleaming fox paws. Andrew sat on the home bench and said nothing. Kevin didn't make them wait long but showed up with a bucket of balls in one hand and his racquet in the other. Neil watched him stride across the empty court to the first-fourth line. Kevin set the bucket down, tightened his gloves, and began firing on the empty goal.

Andrew tolerated the spectacle only until the bucket was empty, then got up with a bored, "He really is pathetic."

[345]

"Aren't we all?" Neil asked without taking his eyes off Kevin.

Kevin surveyed the mess around him and rocked his racquet to-and-fro. He used the butt of his racquet to bring a few stray balls closer, then handed his racquet off from his right hand to his left one. Neil expected him to shake his right hand out before starting a second around. Instead Kevin reached right-handed for the nearest ball.

Neil banged his hands on the court wall in warning. The reverberations sent heat curling through every healing cut and burn on his arms and he ground out a pained, "Andrew."

Kevin ignored the thump and slipped the ball into the net of his racquet. He gave his racquet an experimental twirl, then fired at the goal. Neil thought he was aiming for the same spot he'd been pummeling for the last five minutes, but the ball landed a half-foot off. Kevin flicked his racquet in obvious irritation and scooped up another ball. He took another shot, but it still landed wide of the target. Kevin systematically went through the rest of the balls within easy reach. He made his mark on the fifth try, then landed the next four balls in the exact same spot.

Neil looked over his shoulder. Andrew had turned back to watch at his name, and the look on his face was indecipherable. The twitch at the corner of his mouth might have been scorn, but Neil wasn't convinced. Finally Andrew turned sharply on his heel and left. Neil looked back to the court as Kevin rounded up balls. He clenched his teeth, braced himself for the pain, and pounded on the wall again.

Kevin pointed his stick at Neil in a clear order to knock it off. Neil ignored the way his hand was pulsing hot and cold in turns and waved his left hand at Kevin. Kevin made a dismissive gesture and went back to work. Neil resisted the urge to go on-court and choke Kevin for his recklessness, but it was a near thing. Instead he watched as Kevin slowly picked up speed, going from stationary goals to running shots. Kevin dashed for the balls as they rebounded and tried to fire them back as fast as possible. He drew two crosses on the goal, the cardinal directions first followed by the four corners, and hit the center of the goal with every ball after that.

Neil felt cold all over watching him, but he didn't know if it was fear that Kevin was going to injure himself again or awe. He'd always known Kevin was the best, but he'd almost forgotten what Kevin used to be like at his peak.

A flash of orange in his peripheral vision was enough at last to distract him from Kevin, and Neil stared as Andrew set his helmet on the home bench. Andrew had to notice the attention, but he focused on tightening his gloves. He wasn't going to volunteer an explanation, so Neil asked, "You're going to play with him?"

"Someone needs to keep an eye on that idiot," Andrew said.

He yanked the last strap into place, strapped his helmet on, and headed for the door. He didn't bother to knock a warning before throwing open the court door, but Kevin was facing the door and stumbled to a stop at the sight of him. He shot a quick look Neil's way. His face guard and the distance between them made it impossible to see his expression, but Neil could guess there was something accusing in it. He shook his head and gave an exaggerated shrug, trying to convey his innocence. Andrew slammed the door behind him and headed for goal.

Kevin shepherded balls back toward the first-fourth line. Andrew made an expansive gesture at whatever Kevin said to him and slung his racquet carelessly against his shoulder. He refused to budge even when Kevin signaled readiness. Kevin stood with his racquet back for a few seconds longer, then gave up and fired a shot. Andrew didn't so much as twitch, and the ball shot right past his helmet. The goal lit up red. Kevin took another shot, and another, then grew impatient and aimed for Andrew himself. It cracked off Andrew's helmet, and Andrew finally shifted into a ready position.

The next time Kevin fired at goal, Andrew shot it straight back at him. Kevin caught it but had to retreat to hold onto it. As

[347]

soon as he had his footing he aimed at the goal. Andrew popped that one right at Kevin's knees, and Kevin sidestepped out of the way just in time. They went back and forth for a while before Kevin scored again. Kevin scored twice more in quick succession, but Andrew deflected the shot after that with an impossible twist of his racquet. It escalated from there in speed.

This wasn't a practice anymore; it was a fight. Andrew was trying to cut Kevin off at the pass, and Kevin was daring Andrew to keep up somehow. Exy had been a raw point between them since they'd met. It was the critical part of their friendship Andrew refused to acknowledge and Kevin couldn't fix, a dream Andrew wouldn't believe in and Kevin couldn't give up on. This was a shootout years in the making, and Neil could barely breathe as he watched them struggle. Neil could see their tempers starting to flare in the little things, a jerk of Kevin's racquet here and there and the increasing viciousness of Andrew's deflections.

It was inevitable that Kevin would win. Even left-handed, Kevin put too much of himself into his practices to lose to Andrew here. Andrew had all the raw talent to be a champion but none of the finesse; he couldn't beat Kevin with sheer force alone. When Kevin landed five shots in a row, he dropped his racquet and stomped toward the goal. Andrew put his racquet to his shoulder and watched him come.

Neil expected Kevin to start yelling. Instead Kevin caught the grill of Andrew's helmet and slammed him back against the goal wall. Neil flinched and started for the door, knowing he'd be too late to stop Andrew from gutting Kevin but needing to try. Halfway there he stopped, because Andrew hadn't moved. His fist was at his side in an aborted punch and he hadn't even thrown Kevin off of him. He simply stood there and listened to whatever Kevin was snarling in his face. At length Kevin let go and turned away. Andrew shoved him in the back with the butt of his racquet hard enough Kevin stumbled and stepped up to the goal line again.

[348]

A few seconds later they were back at it as if nothing had ever happened, and they kept going until Kevin finally had to sit down. Neil collected balls from the court while they showered and wisely didn't say anything to either of them. The ride back to Fox Tower was silent and Kevin went straight to bed. Andrew collected his cigarette butt from the window, lit up, and stared out at the dark campus. Neil watched him a few minutes before going back to his own room.

Kevin was his usual self the next day, domineering and caustic as always. He was back to his right hand as well and said nothing about last night's practice. Neil thought maybe he'd strained his hand by pushing so hard against Andrew, but he was back to his left hand as soon as he was alone at the court that night. Andrew followed him on again without hesitation and the two battled it out like they'd already forgotten yesterday's results. Neil was relegated to the sidelines still, but tonight he didn't mind as much. He saw his future in every shot fired and deflected, every point stolen and thwarted, and he could barely breathe through his excitement.

-

Wednesday afternoon the press came by for interviews and footage. Neil remembered Allison's advice to be honest and attempted to answer as much as he could stomach. He avoided some of the more awful questions by reminding them there was still an ongoing investigation into his father's businesses. He didn't expect them to back down, but they got the hint after a couple tries and moved on to other things. Unsurprisingly they asked about the extent of his injuries. Neil confirmed he'd be out of Friday's game but would be back on the court for semifinals. His unflagging confidence in the Foxes' ability to proceed earned him a grin here and a nod there and established that, Nathaniel or Neil or whoever, the Foxes' mouthy rookie was the same person he'd always been. When they were done with him they went down the rest of the Fox line, even cornering Abby and Wymack. Finally they left and let the Foxes focus on their

[349]

scrimmage.

On Thursday Neil found Andrew outside his classroom door. Andrew set off without a word, knowing Neil would follow. Neil was content to tag along until he realized they were going to the library. Nicky said last fall Andrew avoided the library at all costs. Neil had only seen Andrew in it once, when Andrew collected him for practice this past January. He might have asked what they were doing, but Andrew spoke first. He was only four steps up the staircase to the second floor when he rounded on Neil.

"Take these or I'll use them," he said, holding out his hands.

Neil stared at his empty palms, mystified, then reached under the hems of Andrew's long sleeves and caught the edges of Andrew's bands. He knew there were sheathes in Andrew's bands and had handled them before, but the weight still caught him off-guard. He tucked the bands and their hidden weapons into his backpack. Andrew watched until Neil's bag was zipped closed and slung over his shoulder again before turning away.

There was only one reason Andrew would give up his knives in here, but Neil couldn't believe it. He didn't have long to wonder. The right wall was lined with computers, and alongside the computer stations were oversized tables for studying. Halfway toward the back Katelyn sat with three unfamiliar students. The boy at her right was gesturing expansively at his open textbook as he spoke. Katelyn twirled a pen through her hair as she listened. Andrew was only two tables away before she noticed him, and she jumped so hard she dropped her pen. Andrew flicked her a cool look and kept going. Neil paused to make sure she understood that summons.

Her classmates sent her odd looks, startled to silence by her violent reaction. Katelyn turned in her chair to watch Andrew leave, then sent a nervous look Neil's way. Neil only shook his head and motioned after Andrew.

Katelyn got to her feet. "I'll be right back."

Andrew must have checked the library layout before

coming, because he cut through rows of aging reference volumes to a section so obscure there were no browsing students. Neil noticed the isolation immediately and was glad Andrew had turned over his knives. Andrew turned at the end of the row, sized up the empty corner just a couple steps away, and waited for Neil and Katelyn to catch up.

Katelyn made the mistake of stopping too close to him. She barely had time to cry out before Andrew caught her shoulder and threw her at the wall. Neil winced at the sound she made as she slammed into it. She stumbled but didn't fall and turned to stare wide-eyed at him.

"Please," she said. "Please, I—"

"Shut up," Andrew said. He snapped his arm out like a barricade, and the slap of his hand against the wall near her head made her cower. "Don't speak. The sight of you is intolerable as it is. The sound of your voice tips the scales out of your favor."

Neil took a careful step toward them, trying to convey silent support and backup, but Katelyn was too afraid of Andrew to look at Neil. Andrew leaned forward to get in her face and jabbed a finger into her temple.

"You are a tumor," he said. "I should have cut you out and thrown you away when you were still benign. Now it's too late, so here we are. Don't you dare fucking speak," Andrew said, voice savage, when Katelyn opened her mouth. Katelyn clamped her lips together and finally darted a terrified look at Neil. Andrew seized her chin and forced her attention back to him. "Do not ignore me. Your life hinges on how well you can listen. Can you listen?"

She nodded frantically, but Andrew didn't let go. "The conditions for your survival are simple: do not ever mistake this for acceptance and do not ever, ever speak to me. You are part of his life but you will never be part of mine. If you forget that I will remind you, and you will not survive the lesson. Do you understand?"

Andrew waited for her to nod again before letting go. He

[351]

considered his hand a moment, then wiped his fingers off on his jeans like he could erase the feel of her skin. He gave Katelyn a long look, then pushed off the wall and stepped back out of her space. "I hope you two are miserable together."

With that, he turned and strode off. Neil turned after him, but Katelyn gave a quiet sob behind him. He hesitated and looked back at her. She clamped both hands over her mouth to stifle the noise, but Neil could see her shoulders shaking. Neil wasn't good at comforting people and wasn't overly fond of Katelyn to begin with, but he felt obligated to make a rough attempt seeing how this confrontation was partly his fault.

"You won," Neil said. She just stared at him with tear-bright eyes. "Aaron's not in class now, if you want to call him."

He turned and left her there with her shock and fear. Andrew hadn't slowed to see if Neil was following. Neil jogged after him and caught up at the stairs. Andrew strode out the front door into a sunny afternoon. Neil let him get to the railing overlooking the campus pond before catching hold of Andrew's elbow. Andrew wrenched out of his grip but stopped moving.

Neil stood where he could see Andrew's face. "What changed your mind?"

Andrew ignored him. Neil propped his back against the railing and looked past Andrew at the library. He turned the overdue encounter over in his head and imagined how Aaron would react when Katelyn called him crying. It had the potential to make practice uncomfortable, but Neil doubted Aaron would hold onto his irritation for long. Aaron knew firsthand how callous Andrew's methods were and he finally had what he wanted. If the ends justified the means for him, he'd comfort Katelyn appropriately but never hold those threats against his brother.

"That reminds me, is now a bad time to take my bonus turn?" Neil interpreted Andrew's silence how he wanted and said, "Who said 'please' that made you hate the word so much?"

Andrew gazed at him in silence for a minute. "I did."

[352]

Neil didn't know what answer he'd been expecting but this wasn't it. He felt it like a pop to his chest, sharp and startling. He opened his mouth to say something, anything, but what could he possibly say to something like that?

Andrew tolerated his blank stare for only a couple seconds before waving this all off as inconsequential and uninteresting. "He said he would stop if I said it."

"You believed him," Neil guessed.

"I was seven," Andrew said. "I believed him."

"Seven," Neil echoed stupidly.

Andrew hadn't moved in with the Spears until he was twelve. Before Drake turned Andrew's life into a living hell Andrew had gone through twelve other houses, and Andrew had told Neil just the other week that none of them had been good. Neil hadn't asked how bad they'd been; he'd assumed Drake was the worst by far.

Neil regretted asking, but it was too late to take it back. "You—" Neil said, but words failed him. He looked for the lie in Andrew's calm stare and came up empty. Andrew had nearly killed four men for assaulting Nicky and would have broken Allison's neck for hitting Aaron, but when it came to crimes against his own person Andrew couldn't care less. He held his life in less regard than he did anything else. Neil hated that with a ferocity that was nauseating.

"After everything they did to you, how can you stand me?" Neil asked. He was unwilling to put the details into words with so many people around. He doubted anyone was paying attention to them, but he wasn't going to risk it. He gestured between them, knowing Andrew would understand. "How is this okay?"

"It isn't a 'this'," Andrew said.

"That's not what I'm asking. You know it isn't. Andrew, wait," he insisted, because Andrew was turning away like he couldn't hear Neil anymore. Neil reached for him, unwilling to let him leave without a real answer.

[353]

"No," Andrew said, and Neil's hand froze a breath from Andrew's arm. Andrew went still as well, and they stood for a minute in awful silence. Finally Andrew looked back at him, but for a moment Neil didn't know who he was looking at. In the space of one breath Andrew's expression went so dark and distant Neil almost retreated. Then Andrew was back, as calm and uncaring as always, and he caught Neil's wrist to push his hand to his side. He dug his fingers in before letting go, not quite hard enough to hurt, and said, "That's why."

Neil stopped when Andrew told him to. It wasn't much, but it was more than enough. Neil managed a nod, too numb to speak, and watched Andrew walk away from him.

-

Kevin took the court right-handed Friday night. Neil started to say something about it, but the quelling look Kevin sent him killed his questions. Dan mistook Neil's expression for worry and paused in the court doorway to reassure him.

"We've got this," she promised.

"I know," Neil said, and Dan's grin went ear-to-ear.

Dan headed to the half-court line as the Foxes' second striker, and the rest of the Foxes filed on behind her as their names were called. Renee and Nicky were left on the sidelines with Neil as the night's subs. Renee would be in and out for the backliners, since the Bearcats would run defense into the ground, and Andrew would hold the goal the entire game.

The Binghamton Bearcats strode onto the court with palpable arrogance. Neil didn't blame their overconfidence, considering the Foxes' sorry state tonight, but he didn't have to forgive it either. The stadium roared excited as the last ten seconds counted down. The Bearcats took first serve and the game got violent inside the first minute. It took Neil all of ten minutes to realize the Bearcats were trying to eliminate another player. The Foxes were a skeleton crew as-is. Down another body they had no chances.

Wymack's vicious swearing at his side said he understood

why yellow cards were popping up all over the place. Abby grimly unpacked her first aid kit and waited for the first injury. Nicky paced irritated lines and yelled colorful insults at the Bearcats through the walls. Renee attempted to quiet him when he got too loud but said nothing otherwise. Neil attempted to leech off Renee's calm but he could feel his blood starting to boil as he watched Allison take another spill. Behind that growing outrage was the chill of inevitability. The Foxes could only tolerate this type of play for so long. They'd been pushed aside and stomped on most their lives; the court was the last place they would put up with this kind of insult. Seth would have thrown a punch eight minutes ago. The others would snap before long.

Except the minutes raced by, two Bearcats were evicted with red cards, and the Foxes kept their cool. They let hits land and racquets fall and gave ground when pushed. Matt didn't even fight back when his striker mark took a swing at him. He dropped his arms to his sides and let the punches land until the referees tore them apart. Dan scored on the foul shot and hugged Matt on her way back to half-court. Neil watched the short exchange and finally relaxed. The Foxes had chosen victory over pride tonight.

It was a necessary sacrifice, but it took an emotional and physical toll on all of them. They spent most of halftime fuming, too angry at their opponents to appreciate how well they were doing. Wymack toned down his halftime recap, not wanting to set anyone's fraying tempers off with his usual gruff approach. If anyone heard him, they gave no sign of it.

Wymack looked around when he was done and asked, "Anyone else have something to say?"

Dan rapped the butt of her racquet against the floor. "We're halfway there. Let's wipe the floor with these assholes and then get wasted. Tell me someone has alcohol back at the dorm. ABC will be closed by the time the game is over and I'm down to half a case of beer."

Nicky grimaced at the expectant look she sent him. "Not

[355]

enough to make up for this. We went through most of it Monday."

"Something's better than nothing, I guess," Matt said, a little dejectedly.

"Katelyn has some," Aaron said without looking up from where he was tightening his net. "Between her and the Vixens we might get a decent haul."

Surprise wiped the disappointment off his teammates' faces; the Foxes flicked quick looks between Aaron and Andrew as they waited for a reaction. Andrew was as usual standing alone on the far side of the room. He didn't say anything, and his bored expression didn't so much as twitch at the sound of Katelyn's name.

Aaron finally looked up, but he looked to Dan, not Andrew. "Unless you don't want it?"

Dan sent a cautious look at Andrew. "Uh, yeah. Sure. If they've got some to share, the more the merrier. Right?"

The last was directed at Andrew, a careful prod expecting a violent reaction. Andrew stared into space and continued to ignore all of them.

Aaron nodded as if this wasn't at all a strange turn of events and set his racquet aside. "I'll get a headcount when we're back down there. We can borrow the basement study room again."

"Uh," Matt said.

"Don't," Neil said, cutting him off before he could ask the obvious.

Nicky was harder to shush, and he gave Aaron an unsubtle nudge. Aaron brushed him off with a bored flick of his fingers. Nicky sent a wide-eyed look at Andrew that Andrew didn't return. Luckily a warning chime went off before Nicky's mouth got him in trouble.

Wymack ushered his Foxes to their feet. "Up and out. We've got a team to send home crying. You can gossip on your own time."

Second half was just as rough as first had been, but halftime had restored the Foxes' spirits. Sending Aaron and Nicky on together to start the half was the best decision Wymack made all night. Aaron played with an energy and focus Neil had never seen from him, and Nicky's excitement gave him a much-needed edge. Andrew held his ground behind them and watched their blind spots. Their flawless teamwork let offense pace themselves for a hard last-quarter push. When Matt and Renee stepped onto the court with twenty-five minutes to go, Dan and Kevin went all-out.

The final bell heralded a seven-five Fox win. Neil and the subs were on the court as soon as the referees opened the door. The Foxes spared only a couple seconds to celebrate; they'd had enough of the Bearcats to last them two lifetimes and would rather enjoy their success with drinks in their hands. They went through handshakes as fast as they could go.

Aaron was one of the first off the court. He shoved his racquet at Nicky and dropped his helmet and gloves on his way to the cheerleaders. Katelyn tossed her pom-poms aside at his approach and jumped into his waiting arms to kiss him. The Vixens bounced around them, cheering and waving to the crowd.

"Holy shit," Nicky said, looking from them to Andrew's unimpressed countenance. "Holy shit, am I dreaming?"

It was Kevin's turn to deal with the press, but he sent Neil a significant look on his way over to them. Neil had nothing to add since he'd been sidelined all night, but he stepped closer in case Kevin needed to redirect anything his way. Kevin gave his best press-ready smile to the camera before motioning Andrew over. Andrew took up post alongside Neil but didn't look at the reporters. The interview started off predictably with comments on the game and the impossible points Kevin had scored.

Neil half-tuned it out until Kevin was asked about semifinals. The Bearcats were going home as the lowest-scoring team of this elimination round. In two weeks the Foxes would be taking on two of the Big Three.

"I'm looking forward to playing USC again," Kevin said. "I

haven't spoken to Jeremy or Coach Rhemann since I transferred but their team is always amazing. Their season was nearly flawless this year. There's a lot we can learn from them."

"Still their biggest fan," the interviewer joked. "You're up against Edgar Allan again, too, in the biggest rematch of the year. Thoughts?"

"I don't want to talk about the Ravens anymore," Kevin said. "Ever since my mother died it's been Ravens this and Ravens that. I am not a Raven anymore. I never will be again. To be honest, I never should have been one in the first place. I should have gone to Coach Wymack the day I found out he was my father and asked to start my freshman year at Palmetto State."

"The day—" She floundered, then said, "Did you say Coach Wymack is your father?"

"Yes, I did. I found out when I was in high school," Kevin said, "but I didn't tell him because I thought I wanted to stay at Edgar Allan. Back then I thought the only way to be a champion was to be a Raven. I bought into their lies that they would make me the best player on the court. I shouldn't have believed it; I've been wearing this number long enough to know that wasn't what they wanted for me.

"Everyone knows the Ravens are all about being the best. Best pair, best line-up, best team. They drill it into you day after day, make you believe it, make you forget that in the end 'best' means 'one'. They let you forget until other people buy into it, be it fans swaying too far the wrong way or the ERC calling them out on their schemes. Then they don't want to play that game anymore, and they skip straight to the elimination round. Did you know I've never been skiing? I'd like to try it one day, though."

It was too much all at once for her to catch the significance of that last remark, but it would only take a couple moments. Neil understood right away, and the adrenaline that flooded his veins made him sway a little on his feet. He shot Andrew a quick

[358]

look. Andrew didn't return it, but he was definitely paying attention. The stare he had trained on the back of Kevin's head was intense.

Kevin didn't wait for her to put two and two together. "Tell the Ravens to be ready for us, would you? We're already ready for them."

Kevin turned and walked away. The interviewer stared after him for an endless moment, then spun back toward the camera and started rambling away about everything Kevin had just said. Neil and Andrew didn't stick around for the recap or bewildered speculating but followed close behind Kevin.

Kevin didn't slow or look around on his way to the locker room, and he pushed right past his celebrating teammates in the foyer. He dropped his helmet and gloves on his way across the changing room and caught hold of the edge of the sink. He swayed a bit like his legs wanted to give out from under him and his hands were trembling so violently Neil could see it from the doorway. Instead of falling he leaned forward and pressed his forehead to the mirror.

"We're all going to die," Kevin said at last.

"No, we're not," Neil said.

Kevin thought about that for a minute, then straightened. After staring at his reflection for an age he lifted his hand and covered his tattoo on the glass. The result sent an odd tremor along Kevin's shoulders. Neil didn't know if it was approval or fear. All that mattered was that Kevin nodded and turned back to them. He looked at Neil first, then Andrew.

"We have a lot of work to do."

"Tomorrow," Andrew said, and ignored the way Neil looked at him.

Kevin accepted that promise with a nod, and he and Andrew headed for the showers. Neil was clean, so he went back to the foyer to meet the rest of his teammates. They quieted down a bit at his arrival.

Dan gestured past Neil toward the changing room. "What

[359]

happened?"

Neil counted it off on his fingers. "Kevin told them Coach is his father, said he's never going back to Edgar Allan, and called the Ravens out as two-faced assholes. Oh," he said, looking up from his hand, "and he said his injury wasn't an accident. Not in so many words, but it won't take them long to figure out what he meant."

Dan gaped. "He what?"

"Great," Wymack said. "He's turning into another you. That's just what I needed."

"At least you can legally take out life insurance on one of them," Nicky said.

"Out," Wymack said. "Everyone out. Get washed up before your stench kills me."

Neil waited with Wymack and Abby in the lounge while the Foxes showered and dressed. Wymack turned the TV on and watched the post-game recap mesh with snips of Kevin's interview. One sportscaster called it sour grapes and sensationalism; another referred back to how easily Edgar Allan let Kevin go and how long both Kevin and Riko stayed out of sight after that so-called accident. The third was more neutral but brought up Kathy Ferdinand's show in August. Kevin had gone cagey and quiet as soon as Riko showed up, and perhaps they finally had an explanation for Neil's unexpected antagonism and staunch defense of Kevin.

Wymack turned the TV off as his Foxes started filing in. When they were all seated he swept them with a brief look. "Going to make this quick. You've got a well-deserved party to get to. We'll go over the nitty-gritty and ugly details Monday morning as usual. This wasn't the cleanest game you've played but it was by far the most mature. You did what you had to do and you came out on top.

"Also: welcome to the semifinals. It's you, USC, and Edgar Allan. You're toe-to-toe with what's left of the Big Three. No, don't make that face," Wymack said, because Dan blanched a little at that reminder. "Don't be afraid. Be rowdy. Be proud. No one thought you could get this far—no one except the people seated in this room. You've earned this. You've earned this," he stressed, with another look around. "Now get out and get trashed."

"Carefully," Abby said. "Off the road, out of sight, out of trouble. Okay?"

"Yes, Mom," Nicky quipped.

"We won't leave the dorm," Dan promised.

Traffic made the trip back to Fox Tower endless. The dead silence in Andrew's car didn't help. Aaron looked content where he was leaning against the window and Nicky was practically vibrating with excitement, but no one spoke.

Getting out of the car again was almost a relief, and Neil helped his teammates lug what was left of their alcohol down to one of the basement rooms. By the time Matt and Nicky got the tables cleared out of the way the Vixens were starting to show up. Andrew acknowledged their arrival by taking a handle of vodka and leaving again.

"Ahem," Nicky said at his elbow. Neil attempted a neutral look that fooled Nicky not at all. "You realize we're going to be out of the room for a couple hours, right? Get lost."

"I'm fine here," Neil said.

"Goodbye," Dan said, showing up out of nowhere on Neil's other side. "First rule of college dating: never waste an empty dorm room."

Neil wanted to tell her they weren't dating and Andrew could take or leave his presence at any given point. He wanted to stay and celebrate his teammates' brilliant success. He wanted to watch the way Aaron became a completely different person with Katelyn at his side. But half of the Vixen squad was already here, taking up the room with bright laughter and thick perfume, and noise in the hall said more were on the way. Neil had nothing against the cheerleaders, but if he could choose between playing nice with half-strangers for hours or bothering Andrew

[361]

in private, the latter was the obvious choice.

"You were amazing tonight," Neil said, because they deserved at least that much before he disappeared on them. "All of you."

"None of that," Dan said breezily, but her grin said she appreciated his compliment all the same. "We'll talk about the game Monday, remember? Tonight is for drinking and general craziness. Now get out of here and get some."

"Speaking of getting some," Nicky said in German. He wheeled on Aaron and flailed at him. "How is he suddenly okay with this? What the hell did you do?"

"I returned the favor," Aaron said with a cool look in Neil's direction. "Neil used Katelyn against me, so I used Neil against Andrew. Depending on how you look at it, Neil's as much a violation of our deal as Katelyn was. Andrew could break our deal and let me go or break things off with Neil."

Neil was fluent in German, but Aaron's words were a jumbled mess he couldn't make sense of. Aaron had warned Neil he was ready to fight for Katelyn, but if Neil was the ammunition he'd used Aaron should have lost. This had to be a misunderstanding or Aaron's skewed take on Andrew's intentions.

Nicky found his tongue first. "Wait, he chose Neil over you? That sounds a little serious for a fling, don't you—" Nicky glanced at Neil's blank face and faltered. "News to you too, huh?"

Aaron ignored Nicky and tossed a key to Neil. "You're trading rooms with me tomorrow. I'm allowed to bring Katelyn by the dorm now but I'm not putting her in the same room as Andrew if I can help it. He might've agreed to stand down but I still trust him as far as I can throw him."

"I'll pack in the morning," Neil said.

Aaron turned back to Katelyn. Nicky was still looking at Neil like he was the world's biggest mystery. Neil slipped out before Nicky said anything else and took the stairs up. Andrew's door was locked, but Aaron's key let Neil in. He found Andrew half-buried in a beanbag chair with the open bottle of vodka in his hands. The TV was off, but Andrew studied the screen like he could see something on its dark surface. He didn't ask how Neil got inside. Maybe he and Aaron had already talked about the upcoming switch.

Neil locked the door behind him and crossed the room to Andrew's side. Andrew let him take the vodka away without argument or resistance. Neil screwed its cap on tight and set it where neither of them could knock it over. Andrew was ready when Neil turned back to him, and he caught Neil's collar to pull him down. Neil planted one hand against the rough carpet to keep himself leveraged off Andrew's body. The other he buried in the beanbag near Andrew's head. Andrew dragged a hand down Neil's arm from his shoulder to his wrist.

"Last I checked you hated me," Neil said against Andrew's mouth.

"Everything about you," Andrew said.

Neil pushed himself up a bit. "I'm not as stupid as you think I am."

"And I'm not as smart as I thought I was," Andrew said. "I know better than to do this again. Perhaps it's the self-destructive streak in me?"

If it wasn't for that "again" Neil would think this had to do with Wednesday's terrible conversation. Neil ticked through all the possible explanations as fast as he could, from Roland's advances to Andrew's complicated family issues to the Foxes and Drake. Pressure on his wrist finally turned his thoughts where they needed to go. Neil had once asked Andrew if it would kill him to let something in. He should've known better than to say such a thing after seeing Andrew's scars. Andrew had nearly killed himself trying to hang onto Cass Spear, but he'd still lost her in the end.

"I am not a pipe dream," Neil said. "I'm not going anywhere."

[363]

"I didn't ask you."

"Ask me," Neil insisted, "or stick around long enough to figure it out for yourself."

"I'll get bored of you eventually."

"You sure?" Neil asked. "Rumor has it I'm pretty interesting."

"Don't believe everything you hear."

Neil ignored that dismissal because Andrew was already pulling him down again. They kissed until Neil felt dizzy, until he wasn't sure he could hold himself up anymore, and then Andrew pulled Neil's hand off the beanbag chair. He held it up away from them for an eternity, then slowly pressed it flat against his chest and let go. Andrew tensed up underneath Neil's hand but relaxed before Neil could pull away.

Neil wasn't fooled. Andrew had made it very clear the first time he kissed Neil how important an actual "yes" was. This casual surrender wasn't genuine consent. Andrew was doing this because of what they'd said on Wednesday, but Neil wasn't sure which one of them Andrew was trying to convince. It'd only been three months since Proust's abuse and four months since Drake's attack. Neil didn't know when Andrew would be okay with this but he knew it wasn't today. Neil left his hand on Andrew but refused to move it from that spot.

"I won't be like them," Neil said. "I won't let you let me be."

"One hundred and one," Andrew said, "going on one hundred and two."

"You're a terrible liar," Neil said, and Andrew kissed him into silence.

CHAPTER SIXTEEN

Saturday morning Wymack stopped by Fox Tower with a guest. Andrew's bedroom door was open as Neil and Aaron traded rooms, so Wymack settled for rapping on the doorframe. Neil glanced up at the first sign of movement in the doorway but forgot what he was going to say when he saw the woman standing at Wymack's side.

Theodora Muldani was a former Raven backliner who now played for the Houston Sirens and the US Court. Her thick black hair was pulled back in intricate braids, and pastel make-up looked shockingly bright against her dark skin. Her stony expression was the same look she favored cameras with when she caught them watching her. A short dress did nothing to hide long, thick legs and chiseled arms. She looked like she could hold her own against Matt in a fight. Neil bet she was absolute hell on the court, an unmoving tank unimpressed by strikers stupid enough to oppose her.

"Kevin," Neil said.

Kevin was planted in front of the TV, laptop open in his lap, as he watched the repercussions of last night's incendiary remarks. None of them expected much to come of it. The Ravens denied everything, of course, but it was a toss-up as to what they honestly believed. The team was used to a violent hierarchy and harsh punishments, but willfully handicapping one of their own—handicapping Kevin Day of all people—might seem farfetched to even them. None of the Ravens had been there when Riko broke Kevin's hand. Jean was the only witness, and he was also the only one the press couldn't yet find for comments.

"Kevin," Neil said again, but Thea wasn't waiting any

longer.

She came around Wymack and strode across the room toward Kevin. Kevin was too engrossed to care who was coming up on him, so Thea grabbed his laptop and threw it off to one side. Kevin started and looked up, mouth open on an angry retort he abandoned the second he recognized his guest. Thea grabbed his left wrist and hauled his arm around where she could see the scars on the back of his hand. Kevin let her move him, too stunned to fight back. Thea surveyed the white lines across his fair skin and flicked a hooded look at Neil.

"Get out."

Neil didn't know what caught Andrew's attention, the clatter of Kevin's laptop across the carpet or an unfamiliar woman's voice, but he materialized in the doorway a second later. He looked from Thea to Kevin and back again and didn't intervene. Neil shouldn't have been surprised; Renee only knew about Thea and Kevin's relationship because Andrew knew about it. Andrew knew Thea wasn't a real threat to anyone here.

Thea was less accepting and swiveled her stare to Andrew. "You get out, too."

Andrew stared back at her like she hadn't even spoken.

"Thea," Kevin finally said, and scrambled to his feet. "What are you doing here?"

Thea cut a hard look from Kevin to the TV, but all she said was, "They'll leave or I will. I won't talk to you in mixed company."

"We are mixed company regardless," Kevin said. "I am not a Raven anymore."

He didn't say "Neither are you". Even though Thea graduated from Edgar Allan almost three years ago she still wore her Raven jersey number on a pendant around her throat. It made Neil wonder how Ravens fared after they'd left the Nest's hive mind. Maybe it took years for them to recover. Maybe they never did. Maybe they broke and carried pieces of Evermore with them the rest of their lives.

[366]

The look on Thea's face said she was not at all impressed by Kevin's logic. "I will count to three. One."

"Stop it," Kevin said. "Just talk to me."

"Now you want to talk," Thea said, a tad derisively. "Two."

"I always wanted to talk, but it was complicated."

"'Complicated'," Thea echoed. The air quotes she threw him were angry and mocking. "'Complicated' is having to find out from a press conference that you broke your hand and left the line-up. 'Complicated' is finding out the hard way you disconnected your old number and having to hear from Jean that you didn't want anything to do with any of us effective immediately. Don't you dare use 'complicated' on me. I deserve better than that. Three."

She turned to go, but Kevin caught her wrist. "Jean," Kevin said, like that somehow answered all of her accusations. The twitch of Thea's mouth was as much anger as it was incomprehension. Kevin shook his head and insisted, "If you're going to believe me, you need to see Jean first."

"What's left of him, anyway," Wymack said. He ignored the piercing look Thea sent him and looked past her at Kevin. "I came so I could get her into the dorm, but she picked up a rental car at the airport. Catch a ride to Abby's with her so I can figure out what the hell is going on around here."

Thea hesitated a moment longer, then tugged out of Kevin's grip and gestured for him to follow. Wymack stepped aside so they could leave and watched them disappear down the hall. Neil knew they were out of sight when Wymack turned back toward the room. Wymack surveyed the mess Neil and Aaron had made of the place, their stuff in quasi-organized stacks all around the living room, and arched a brow at Andrew.

"I called Nicky before coming over to make sure you were here," Wymack said. "When he told me what Neil and Aaron were doing I thought he was fucking with me."

It wasn't a question, so Andrew only stared back at him in calm silence. Wymack pushed on after only a moment. "Dorm

[367]

room applications are due in a few weeks. With nine men and six women on the line it's easiest for us to get five rooms of three. I'd prepared a speech to talk you into it, but I guess I wasted my time. I assume Nicky's the next-best person to take away from you?"

"You assume he'll survive until summer," Andrew said.

"You break him, you owe me a new defenseman," Wymack said.

"You have one at Abby's house."

Wymack shook his head. "Jean won't stay next year. I already suggested it, but he and Kevin know they can never play together again. There's too much between them, good and bad and ugly, for them to ever make things right. We'll figure out what to do with him eventually."

Neil considered that, then looked past Wymack at the door. "You don't think Kevin will tell Thea the whole truth, do you?"

"Unlikely," Wymack said. "We've got a lot of eyes on us now and most of them aren't friendly. I don't think he'll put her at risk like that."

Wymack waited a minute to see if Neil had anything else, then started to turn away. He only took one step before he turned back on them. "Oh, that reminds me." He dug something out of his pocket. Maybe he knew Andrew wouldn't spare the effort to catch it because he tossed it to the ground at Andrew's feet. Keys jangled as they hit the carpet, and Neil stared in disbelief. He couldn't be right, except last summer Wymack had given Neil three new keys, too: a set for all of the important doors at the Foxhole Court. Neil's suspicions were confirmed when Wymack said, "Kevin said to give you those."

He left without waiting for a response. Andrew considered the keys a minute longer before finally scooping them up and pocketing them. Neil knew better than to comment, but his heart was pounding as he turned back to his desk. He imagined a world wherein Andrew actually gave a damn about the game. He thought about four more years with the Foxes and a professional contract after that. He thought about fighting for a spot on the US Court and facing the best the world had to offer, Kevin at his side and Andrew at his back.

Daydreaming was almost too distracting, but eventually Neil got everything settled into his new room. It was still hours more before Kevin returned, and by then Neil was dozing on a textbook at his desk. The sound of the door opening woke him, and Neil sat up to study Kevin's relaxed expression. Neil assumed that meant he'd convinced Thea of Riko's role in Kevin's "accident".

Kevin didn't come far into the room but looked from Neil to where Andrew was half-buried in a beanbag chair. "Let's go."

Neil looked to Andrew, but he needn't have worried. Andrew got up without argument or comment, and they followed Kevin to the Foxhole Court.

-

The Trojans' and Foxes' stadiums were the same size, but USC's darker red-and-gold theme made the Trojan Court appear significantly smaller. Somehow that illusion did nothing to make the Foxes feel better about standing in the inner ring. They'd made sure to get here a half-hour before the doors opened, needing time to mentally steel themselves for the upcoming game. For now they were alone. In ninety minutes they'd take on the number-two team in the nation.

"Yeah," Matt said at last, the first one to speak since security let them in. "No problem."

Not even Kevin had something to say to that, but that might have been because Kevin was too busy soaking in the joy of being back on Trojan territory. His contented expression was at complete odds with the nerves and dread evident on his teammates' faces. Neil wanted to tell him to tone it down, but he couldn't remember the last time he'd seen Kevin in a good mood.

The doors opened, letting the crowd in as an unending wave. Wymack ushered his Foxes back to the locker room. One of USC's staff stopped by not much later to give them a rundown on the night's outlook. The game was completely sold out, there were six news stations in attendance, and twelve recruiters from summer major leagues and pros would be watching. She had to know none of those representatives would be looking at the Foxes but she listed their cities and teams anyway.

"We don't have USC's line-up," Wymack said. "Any idea when we'll get that?"

"I'll see if I can get a copy," she promised. "Do you need anything else?"

"That's about it," Wymack said, so she left. As soon as the door closed behind her Wymack looked to Dan. "You and Kevin start thinking about what you're going to say in pre-game."

Dan rubbed hard at her arms, struggling to hold herself together and give her team a captain's unwavering confidence. "Does 'We're excited to be here' and 'We're going to do our best' cover pretty much everything?"

"How about 'We're gonna own these losers'?" Nicky suggested.

"And that's why you're not allowed to talk to the press," Matt said dryly.

The locker room was built to accommodate much larger teams, so it was easy for the Foxes to spread out. They found breathing space wherever they could, needing a couple minutes to get their heads on straight before tonight's match. Neil didn't know how much it helped, but when the reporters showed up they were all out of time. Kevin and Dan offered polite praise for USC and promised an interesting match. Wymack saw the press out as soon as possible and sent his Foxes to get changed.

They reentered the inner court with thirty minutes until serve. The stands were packed all the way to the rafters, and the noise the fans made was a physical weight crushing Neil's skin against his bones. If the Foxes' arrival wasn't enough to set the fans into a frenzy, the sight of the Trojans' captain making his way toward the small team did the trick.

Jeremy Knox was dressed to go in everything but his gloves

[370]

and helmet. He'd taken the Trojans' helm his junior year and did well enough to keep the position this year. Neil thought he'd come to size them up as the most unpredictable and unworthy contenders to ever set foot in his stadium, but Jeremy's serious expression dissolved to a toothy grin as soon as he spotted Kevin. Kevin slipped past Allison and Renee to meet him.

Jeremy had to pass Wymack to get to the Foxes, so he gave Wymack's hand a firm shake. "Coach Wymack, welcome to SoCal. We're excited to host you tonight. Kevin, you crazy fool," he said, less formally, and clapped Kevin's shoulder in cheery greeting. "You never cease to amaze. You've got a thing for controversial teams, I think, but I like this one much better than the last one."

"They're mediocre at best but they're easier to get along with," Kevin said.

"Same old Kevin, as unforgiving and obnoxious as always," Jeremy said, but his tone was fond. "Some things never change, hm? Some things do." His grin faded and he treated Kevin to a searching look. "Speaking of your last team, you, uh, you created quite a stir with that thing you said two weeks ago. About your hand, I mean, and it maybe not being an accident."

Two weeks later people were still talking about it, if a bit quieter than they had in the immediate aftermath. Kevin hadn't had anything else to say on the matter, and the Ravens maintained their innocence and outrage at the allegations. It was a stalemate that satisfied no one, but it was all anyone was going to get.

Kevin said nothing for a minute, as if debating how much he trusted Jeremy with, then only said, "I have a backliner for you. Do you have room on next year's line-up?"

It wasn't the answer Jeremy was expecting. Kevin walked Jeremy out of earshot of the Foxes before explaining. Jeremy's smile was long-gone by the time Kevin finished his pitch. Jeremy gestured expansively—between them, past Kevin at the court, and up over his head at the stands. Neil's first thought was

[371]

he was refusing whatever truths Kevin was giving him. Then Kevin gave one of his rare real smiles, and Jeremy gave his shoulder a hard squeeze.

Jeremy held a folded piece of paper up. Instead of taking it Kevin walked him back to the Foxes. Jeremy turned it over to Wymack, who unfolded it and skimmed the printed list.

"Our line-up," Jeremy explained. "It's late to be getting it to you, I know, but we were trying to avoid as much of a backlash as possible."

"Backlash?" Dan asked.

Wymack handed her the sheet and watched her face go white. When she looked up at him again Wymack shook his head and turned on Jeremy. "Your pity's a little misplaced. Tell Coach Rhemann we don't want handouts."

"This isn't pity," Jeremy said. "We're doing this for us, not you. Your success this year has us rethinking everything about how we play. Are we second because we're talented or because we have twenty-eight people on our line-up? Are we good enough as individuals to stand against you? We have to know."

Kevin snatched the paper from Dan's hands and looked at it. Matt leaned over his shoulder to see and said, "You're joking. You're joking. You're not?" he asked with an incredulous look at Jeremy. Allison yanked hard on his sleeve, wanting an explanation, so Matt said, "There are only nine names on it."

"Two goalies, three backliners, two dealers, two strikers," Jeremy said. "You've made it this far with those numbers. It's time to see how we'd fare in that situation. I'm excited," he said, with another toothy smile. "None of us have ever played a full game before. Hell, most of us don't even play full halves anymore. We don't have to because the numbers are always in our favor."

"And you called me a crazy fool," Kevin said. "You'll lose tonight if you play like this."

"Maybe," Jeremy agreed, unconcerned. "Maybe not. Should be fun either way, right? I don't remember the last time I was this psyched for a game. Look at this." He held his hands out to them and laughed. "Bring it, Foxes, and we'll bring it too."

He left them staring after him, his head high and his smile honest. Neil thought he finally understood how the USC Trojans had won the Day Spirit Award eight consecutive years. That trophy was intended for the best sports in the game and required a unanimous vote from the ERC. The Trojans had never gotten a red card and never been caught on camera saying something rude about an opponent. Neil had assumed it was an act the same way people assumed Wymack's recruiting standards were a complicated publicity stunt.

"I take back what I said about earthquakes," Nicky said weakly. "I have a new favorite team."

"That was always the crucial difference between USC and Edgar Allan," Kevin said, handing the roster over to Dan again. "That's why more Trojans make Court than Ravens do. Both teams are obsessed with being the best, but only the Trojans would risk their standings to improve. They'll play tonight with everything they've got and they'll be better for it. Next year is going to be interesting."

"Interesting" was too tame a word for the look in Kevin's eyes. The smile that finally slipped free and curved his lips was hungry.

Wymack nodded and turned on his team. "USC just gave us an open door to finals. Don't be fooled and don't waste it. They'll still put up a hell of a fight and they're going to take first half away from us. You have to control the point gap so you can make a comeback in second. Understand?"

"Are we really going to beat USC?" Dan asked, staring at Matt.

"And go on to beat Edgar Allan in a few weeks? Hell yeah we are."

"I might be sick."

"Puke later," Wymack said. "Right now take these lazy mongrels on some laps."

[373]

They warmed up nice and slow, though how Dan kept the pace so conservative when the Foxes' hearts were pounding a mile a minute Neil didn't know. Neil stared at the court as he ran, hoping to hell and back this wasn't a cruel dream. Every lap helped drive it home until Neil thought anticipation would kill him. The Trojans entered the inner ring on the Foxes' fourth lap; Neil saw the first flash of red and gold as he passed their benches but didn't see the entire line-up until the Foxes came around again. The Trojans' mascot passed them running the other direction and the stands' cheers followed.

They stretched in the locker room and changed out into court gear. Neil assumed Dan hadn't puked because she kissed Matt before bringing her team to the court for drills. Only nine Trojans would be playing tonight but all twenty-eight came on for passing and shots. Eventually referees shooed everyone off the court save the captains. Neil swigged water at the bench as the announcer finally explained USC's challenge. The response from the crowd was deafening and outraged: the fans were not as pleased by the trick as the Trojans themselves were.

"Hear that?" Wymack said. "Their own school knows they're dead. Let's line it up and win this thing."

It was easier said than done. The first forty-five minutes were a fierce struggle as the nation's second-best and the tiny southern team went head-to-head. No matter how hard the Foxes fought, USC stayed several steps ahead of them. Frustration and helplessness put a sick heat in Neil's veins, pushing him harder and faster against the Trojan defense line, but nothing he did seemed to make a difference. They were the little kids playing in the big kids' park and it was painfully obvious they were out of their league.

Allison and Dan fell back time and time again, more interested in helping guard Renee and clear the ball than passing forward for goals. Despite their collective best efforts, the Trojans bagged seven goals against the Foxes' four. The defense line hit half-time break so exhausted they could barely breathe.

[374]

Neil couldn't remember the last time Matt looked so worn out.

"Fuck," Matt said weakly. "What just happened?"

"I'm sorry," Renee said.

"No, no," Nicky was quick to say. "That's on us, not you. They're just so good."

"They're brilliant," Wymack said, "but they're doomed. They don't know how to pace themselves for a full game. Don't know if you could see it out there, but they were starting to slow down by the thirty-minute mark. Second half is going to kill them."

"I hope so," Dan said, with a grim look at Kevin and Neil. "It's a bigger point gap than we wanted. Can you close it?"

"We are not the problem here," Kevin said, gesturing between Neil and himself. Nicky was too tired to bristle at that accusation, but Aaron sent Kevin a sour look and Matt scowled. Kevin didn't care who he offended and kept his eyes on Dan. "If you'll actually get the ball to us, we can do something with it."

Matt looked at Andrew. "One of these days you have to let me hit him."

Andrew gazed back at him in unimpressed silence.

A bell summoned them back to the inner court, and the teams were called on for second half. Neil knew it was coming, but it was still jarring to see the same faces staring back at him. The only new players to the court were the goalkeepers, Andrew in for the Foxes and Laila Dermott for the Trojans. Behind that bolt of surprise was a sudden thrill, because the Trojans looked tired.

They'd had fifteen minutes to catch their breaths, so the half started on even footing. It didn't stay there long. The Foxes operated best on their second wind. No matter how hard they fought in first half, their subconscious instinct was to reserve their strength for the last push. Now there was no reason to hold back, and each successive minute tapped deeper into their desperation and grit.

At twenty-five minutes, the Foxes finally closed the gap.

[375]

Laila was a nightmare in goal, but Kevin and Neil had an advantage few teams who faced the Trojans had: they had a nightmare in their own goal who they had to practice against daily. They'd spent all year trying to outsmart the best goalkeeper in the south. They didn't have that much time to figure Laila out, but they didn't need it. Laila's defense was quickly falling apart in front of her and she couldn't hold her goal alone. Kevin and Neil combined Fox and Raven footwork to break past the stumbling backliners and slammed goals home one after the other.

USC could have taken control of the game in a heartbeat if only they'd rethink their strategy. If they pulled their three subs from the sidelined players the Foxes' night was over. But the Trojans had made up their mind and they weren't backing down. Instead of interfering, the rest of the line-up stood shoulder-to-shoulder at the wall and watched their teammates' slow collapse. Their four coaches stood behind them, taking notes and talking amongst themselves. Neil could hear the crowd losing its mind through the court walls, but the Trojans seemed oblivious to that chorus of betrayal.

The final bell sounded on a thirteen-nine win, Foxes' favor. Neil stumbled to a stop and pried his helmet off, needing to see the scoreboard without his visor in the way. No matter how many times he blinked the score remained the same.

"Is it over?" Neil's backliner mark gasped out. "Oh, thank god."

Neil looked over at Alvarez and was floored to see her smiling. She thrust a gloved hand his way even as her legs wobbled and gave out. Neil caught her somehow and helped haul her back to her feet. She propped herself against him and scrabbled ineffectually at the straps on her helmet. It took her a few tries before she realized her fingers were too numb to manage it. She gave up and tapped her helmet against his instead.

"Is this what dying feels like?" she asked, and called over

[376]

her shoulder, "Babe, I think I'm dying. Do I still have legs? I can't look down. I don't think I have legs. I don't think I'll ever walk again."

"Uh-huh," Laila said, trotting over to them. "You'd better figure something out, because you're definitely too heavy for me to carry off this court."

"Rude."

Alvarez groped blindly for Laila's shoulder until Laila hooked an arm around her waist and pulled her off Neil. Alvarez was still smiling, that half-crazy too-wide look that reminded Neil a little of Lola and a little of Nicky. Neil tried to remember if she'd been hit in the head at any point tonight but the Foxes had kept the violence within excusable limits. It seemed only fair considering what good sports the Trojans were.

"That was fantastic," Alvarez said. "I want to do it again. Next year, maybe, when my legs grow back."

"Stop being such a baby," Laila said.

"Ignore her," Alvarez said to Neil. "She's just sour because she lost nine goals in forty-five minutes. Don't know why, not like it's a new personal record or—ohhh, it is. Ouch, that's gotta sting a bit. So much for being first-draft."

"Bitch," Laila said without any heat.

"That's what you get for calling me fat," Alvarez said. She looked back at Neil and gestured past him. "Oops, looks like the party started without you. Go, go, go!"

Neil looked over his shoulder to see the Foxes celebrating on the half-court line. He started to turn toward them, then looked back at Alvarez and Laila. "Your team is terrifying," he said, inspired by Alvarez's enthusiasm to be honest. "We'll be cheering for you next week."

Alvarez flashed a thumbs-up, so Neil jogged to meet his team. He heard Alvarez ask how anyone could still run after "the world's longest game", but he figured it was directed at Laila and didn't slow to hear the answer. Dan saw Neil coming and broke free of the Foxes to bolt for him. She popped nearly every

[377]

vertebrae in Neil's spine with how hard she hugged him and she couldn't seem to let go again. A second later they were swamped by the rest of the team; the Foxes had obediently shifted their raucous party over to Neil and Dan.

It took great effort to calm down enough for the post-game handshake. The entire Trojan line-up came onto the court for it, but the nine who'd played tonight could barely form a line. The Foxes went to them instead. Jeremy had an exhausted smile and nothing but compliments for them. Alvarez's partner in crime who'd spent most of the night shadowing Kevin sat down when he saw them coming but held his hand up ready for them. As soon as Neil made it past the last of the Trojans he followed his teammates off the court. The stands were a third empty already, though Neil didn't know when the students had started storming out.

Neil didn't care how many hearts they broke that night. They'd beaten USC. When the Trojans lost to the Ravens next week they'd be eliminated from championships. The Foxes were going to finals, and that was the only thing that mattered.

-

Since the Foxes had Friday night off and Andrew and Aaron's cold war was over, Andrew's lot was free to return to Columbia for the first time in months. They got a late start down there, though, as Neil and Kevin wanted to watch the USC-Edgar Allan match. The Trojans went all-out against the Ravens, but their best wasn't good enough. They lost, albeit by the smallest margin they'd ever managed.

Jeremy took the loss well in his post-game interview and expressed no regrets for how things had turned out. He sidestepped every opportunity to call the Ravens out on their ugly playing style but perked up when attention was drawn to how close they'd been to a win.

"We almost had it, right?" Jeremy said. "I don't think anyone was expecting us to get that close. It feels really different out there without Kevin and Jean on the line."

"Worst time of year for someone to be injured," the reporter agreed. Tetsuji had announced earlier in the week that Jean was off the court with a bad sprain. "Rumor has it Jean won't make it back in time for finals."

"Yeah, I spoke to Jean earlier this week. He's definitely done for the year, but he'll be back in the fall. He just won't be back in black." Jeremy flashed his toothy grin and didn't wait to be asked to explain. "Yesterday he faxed us over the last of the paperwork we needed to make this thing official, so I'm allowed to tell you: he's transferring to USC for his senior year."

"Let me make sure I heard you correctly," the reporter said. "Jean Moreau is leaving Edgar Allan for USC?"

"We ordered his gear this morning," Jeremy said. "We'll have to get him some sun this summer, though! He's a little pale to pull off red and gold right now." He laughed like this news wasn't going to cause an uproar with Edgar Allan's rabid fans. "Unfortunately his number was taken already, but Jean said we can reassign him to whatever's open. I'll let him tell you what his new one is going to be."

"Can you tell us why he's transferring?"

"I can't get into all the details because it's not my place to tell his personal business, but I can say we're excited to have him. I think we have a lot to learn from each other. Next year is going to be amazing. I think you're going to see a lot of changes across the board. We've all got to take another look at what we bring to the court."

Nicky reached for the remote and cut the TV off. "I've got a theory that Renee and Jeremy are long-lost siblings. What do you think would happen if they ever joined forces?"

"They'd get murdered," Aaron said, getting up from the other beanbag chair. "War's profitable; no one wants their world-peace nonsense."

Nicky made a face at him. "Thanks for that cheery dose of reality."

The five of them went down to the car together, and Neil

rode in back between Aaron and Nicky. Andrew took them by
Sweetie's first for some ice cream. Nicky and Aaron were
distracted talking about their room assignments next year and
didn't seem to notice that Andrew bypassed the salad bar and its
bowl of crackers. It wasn't until the end of the meal when Aaron
was paying that either of them clued in. Aaron picked up every
single napkin on the table looking for cracker dust and frowned
across the table at Andrew.

"How many?"

Andrew hadn't said a word to any of them all evening, but
he finally dragged his stare away from the far wall and looked at
his brother. "Zero."

"Zero," Aaron echoed, like it was an unfamiliar number.
"What do you mean, zero?"

"We're not getting any?" Nicky asked, stupefied.

Andrew ignored him, uninterested in repeating himself.
Nicky and Aaron exchanged a long look, confusion on one face
and disbelief on the other. Andrew didn't stick around for them
to figure it out but slid off the bench and started for the door.
Neil followed with Kevin right behind him, and the cousins
caught up to them at the car. The ride from Sweetie's to Eden's
Twilight was silent, and Andrew dropped them off at the curb as
usual. Kevin collected a parking tab for him while the bouncers
gave Nicky and Aaron enthusiastic welcome-backs. They went
inside to find a table as Andrew pulled away.

There weren't tables open yet, but there was enough room
for a body at the bar. Nicky stole the stool and waved when he
caught Roland's eye. Roland came by as soon as he'd caught up
with his current orders.

"Long time no see," Roland said, and added a pointed,
"Again. You guys have got to stop dropping out of contact."

"It's been a crazy year," Nicky said.

"So I heard," Roland said, and looked past Nicky at Neil.
"How're you holding up?"

"I'm fine," Neil said.

Roland looked ready to say something else, but after a glance between Nicky and Aaron he shook his head. He got to work mixing their drinks instead, and Nicky regaled him with stories about their spring break. The club was too loud for Neil to hear Andrew's approach, but suddenly Andrew was pressed into his side by the crowd. Roland looked from Andrew to Neil and back again, brow furrowed a bit in badly-concealed concern. Neil realized then he was looking for a sign they were all right after what he'd let slip back in January.

Nicky knew when he was being ignored, and he had no problem interpreting Roland's searching stare. He interrupted his own story to demand, "Don't you dare tell me you knew about them before I did! Oh my god," he said at Roland's startled, guilty look. "Oh my god, you did. How the hell? We just figured it out a couple weeks ago. How long have you known Andrew was gay?"

"Are they a 'them' now?" Roland asked instead of answering. His smile was back, wide and pleased, and he stopped filling their tray to pour them shots. Ever the optimist, he set one out for Neil, too. Nicky passed the glasses out and Neil accepted his after a slight hesitation. Roland plucked his own shot up and tipped it in a toast. "I'll drink to that. It's about damned time."

"It's not something to be proud of," Aaron said.

"Hater," Nicky said, and half-turned to make sure Neil wasn't pawning his drink off on Andrew. They knocked their drinks back as one and Roland collected empty glasses. Nicky pointed at Roland as he went back to mixing drinks. "I noticed you avoided my questions, by the way. You're not sneaky. And what do you mean 'about damned time'?"

"You can pry that story out of Andrew," Roland said.

"Getting answers out of these two is like trying to get a stone to bleed," Nicky said. "It's impossible and I'm about to get my fingers broken for trying. How'd you know? Is your gaydar more advanced than mine is or—" Nicky's jaw dropped as he

[381]

clued in. "Wait. No way. No way! Did you two—?"

"Don't," Aaron cut in. "Just don't. I don't want to hear it. I don't want to think about it. I want to drink and pretend I don't know any of you."

"I thought we were friends," Nicky said to Roland. "How could you keep this from me?"

"I'm a bartender," Roland said. "I don't spill drinks or other people's secrets. With that one ill-timed exception," he corrected himself with a small grimace at an impassive Andrew. "Sorry about that, by the way. Didn't mean to jump the gun."

"Roland, we are fighting effective immediately," Nicky said with a huff. "Maybe you can win my friendship back with enough drinks tonight. Come on, Aaron, let's see if a table opened up."

Kevin went with them, likely to get away from the turn this conversation had taken. Andrew took the stool so no one could get between him and his drinks, and Neil stood as close to his back as he could. Roland split a shaker's contents between two tall glasses, poured a couple straight sodas for Neil, and was finished. He rinsed the shaker out in a waist-high sink and slid their impossibly full tray closer to Andrew.

"So about those padded cuffs," Roland said, and laughed at the look Andrew gave him.

As soon as Roland ducked away to check on the rest of his customers Andrew set about rearranging their drinks into an indeterminable new order. Nicky still wasn't back by the time Andrew finished, so Andrew started on the closest drink. Standing there watching him, Neil thought he wouldn't mind waiting for a seat all night. His clock was still ticking down, but his numbered days followed a different schedule now. Neil had all the time in the world, and that left a heat in his gut stronger than any whisky could.

CHAPTER SEVENTEEN

Because USC lost both semifinal games back-to-back, the ERC canceled the third semifinals match. There was no point in pitting the Foxes and Ravens against each other when they had both already qualified for finals. Instead the two schools were given a week off to rest, recharge, and fend off a story-hungry press.

The Foxes sounded confident whenever they had a microphone in or camera their faces, and it wasn't always an act. Their all-consuming hatred of Riko helped smooth out the jittery edges of their nerves. The Ravens had little to say about the Foxes, but that was probably because they were dealing with fallout from Jean's abrupt transfer. Jean was the most sought-after athlete in NCAA news these days, but he refused to announce his current whereabouts or speak to the press. His silence did the Ravens no favors so soon after Kevin's bold interview, and the speculations and rumors were starting to get a little wild.

On Monday afternoon Wymack told his team the final game would be hosted at Castle Evermore. It wasn't welcome news, but it wasn't a surprise, either. Because it doubled as the national team's court, Edgar Allan's stadium was half-again as large as Palmetto State's. They needed every seat they could get. Wymack still didn't think it'd be big enough for a showdown like this, but there definitely wasn't room in South Carolina to accommodate a championship finals crowd.

On the tail-end of that announcement, Wymack passed around a clipboard. Edgar Allan was going to reserve a "friends and family" section right behind the Away bench. They were given eighteen seats to divvy up between the nine of them, and

[383]

Wymack needed a list of names so he could get those seats reserved as soon as possible and start working on travel arrangements from the airport to Edgar Allan.

Eighteen didn't sound like very many, but the Foxes couldn't fill them. No one in Andrew's group needed any, and Allison passed the clipboard on without hesitation. Renee needed one for her foster mother and donated the second to Matt so his father could bring his current mistress. Dan went last so she knew how many spare seats she could steal. Several of her stage sisters had moved on from their old club to quieter jobs, but the few who were still there were unlikely to get approved for a Friday night off.

That night Nicky and Aaron showed up to evening practice uninvited. Neil expected Kevin to send them packing with a "too-little, too-late" speech, but he put them to work immediately. On Wednesday the upperclassmen tagged along too. A week and a half wasn't enough time to make anyone an expert on Raven drills and scrimmages, but Kevin tried his best. His caustic attitude and rude dismissal of his teammates' abilities earned him no favors during the day, but at night the Foxes submitted with a silent and grim determination. Matt was the first one to realize Kevin played left-handed at night, since he was the one getting in Kevin's face to block him. Having a secret weapon against the Ravens buoyed their spirits.

Bringing all the Foxes along made it harder for Neil to get Andrew alone afterward, since it was more obvious that they weren't heading straight for bed. Living in the same room made it only marginally easier to catch Andrew alone between classes. The Foxes had such long practices that most of their classes were crammed into the same time blocks. It would have been completely impossible if not for Nicky's interference. Nicky spent a lot of his free time hanging out with the rest of the Foxes in their rooms, and he dragged Kevin with him whenever he could. It forced Andrew to choose between Neil and his controlling nature. Sometimes Neil won; other days Andrew's

[384]

spite had him hunting the wayward pair down as soon as he realized what was going on.

The following week was significantly harder to get through, in part because it was the last week of classes. Friday night the Foxes would face the Ravens in NCAA Exy finals; Monday they'd start academic finals. Three of Neil's teachers made classes optional, allowing their students to come in for reviews and practice tests or opt for self-study elsewhere. Neil tried going to his first class but left halfway through. He intended to find an empty seat at the library, but somehow he ended up at the Foxhole Court instead.

Wymack didn't look surprised to see him, but he made Neil swear he wouldn't fail any classes before he'd loan Neil games to watch. The next morning Neil didn't even try to go to class. Between matches Neil ran laps and suicide drills. He ran the stadium steps early in the day so his legs could recover before afternoon practice. He pushed himself to go faster, faster, faster and knew it wouldn't help.

The Ravens were lightning on the court; they rarely carried the ball for more than a few steps because they'd perfected the art of impossible passes. They'd destroyed the Foxes with their tricks last October. Kevin had spent months teaching Neil how to play like that, but that meant nothing now. It didn't matter if Neil and Kevin could score if their defense couldn't hold the line and control that point gap. Every match Neil watched drove that further home until he thought he'd be sick.

Aaron and Andrew canceled their Wednesday session with Dobson to come to practice on time, but Kevin skipped Thursday night's practice. He had no real explanation aside from, "I need to take care of something," and he left Neil in charge. Telling the others what to do was every bit as awful as Neil expected it would be, but Neil didn't have time to hesitate. They had a game to win and Neil was the only other person who knew all of the Ravens' drills. He walked his teammates through them, knowing they couldn't master them in such a short time

[385]

but needing them to know what they were up against on Friday. They asked a lot of questions but didn't push back, and afterward Dan murmured, "Nicely done, captain," at his ear.

They didn't leave the court until after one, but by the time they made it back to the dorm Neil's nerves overrode his exhaustion. He stood at his desk while the others changed for bed, staring at his textbooks without really seeing them. He flipped halfheartedly through one of his notebooks, then pushed everything aside. He wanted to go for a run, but he also knew his body needed to rest after today's long practices. He'd settle for pacing, but he didn't want the others to know he was getting anxious. It felt like doubt could undo everything they'd been working toward.

Nicky came back into the living room. "Hey. You good?"

"I'm fine," Neil said. "Just thinking."

Nicky said nothing, but it was a minute before he turned away. Neil had the living room light on, so Nicky closed the bedroom door. Neil stood quiet and still until the bedroom descended to silence, then sat down at his desk and stared at the wall. He stayed there so long with his twisting thoughts he couldn't believe the sky wasn't lightening with sunrise. At last Neil's thoughts slowed to a drained crawl and he got up to sleep. He only made it a few feet from his desk before the suite door opened and let Kevin in.

Kevin reeked so strongly of alcohol Neil could smell him halfway across the room, but Neil forgot the stench the second he saw the bandage on Kevin's face. It was too much to hope for and too impossible to believe in, but Neil froze in his tracks and stared. Kevin pushed the door closed and stumbled backward into it. He almost fell, braced himself in the nick of time, and stared blearily at Neil. That was about all Kevin could manage, it seemed, so Neil went to him. Kevin made a limp gesture near his side. Neil worked a corner of the tape up and pulled the gauze off Kevin's face.

It felt a bit like falling and a bit like flying; Neil's stomach

[386]

bottomed out a second before adrenaline flooded his veins. Kevin had worn a "2" since his first days in the Moriyamas' cruel care. Riko and Kevin used markers for years, writing over their numbers any time they threatened to fade. As soon as they were old enough they'd switched to a more permanent ink. Now that number was gone, covered up by the jet-black image of a chess piece. Neil's knowledge of chess was hazy at best, but he knew for sure that wasn't a king.

"You did it," Neil said, too stunned to manage anything else.

"Let Riko be King," Kevin said, with the exaggerated enunciation of the thoroughly sloshed. "Most coveted, most protected. He'll sacrifice every piece he has to protect his throne. Whatever. Me?" Kevin gestured again, meaning to indicate himself but too drunk to get his hand higher than his waist. "I'm going to be the deadliest piece on the board."

"Queen," Andrew said somewhere behind Neil. Neil hadn't heard him get out of bed, but of course the bang of the door would have woken him. A sober Andrew was as light a sleeper as Neil was, maybe moreso because Andrew was used to unfriendly people sneaking into his room. Neil looked back at him, but Andrew was studying Kevin. Andrew crossed the room to stand at Neil's side and caught Kevin's chin in his hand. He turned Kevin's head to inspect the new ink. "He is going to be furious."

"Fuck him," Kevin said, sliding a little further down the door. "Fuck all of them. Waste of time to be angry. They should be afraid."

"Hell hath no fury," Andrew said.

Kevin gestured feebly to Neil, so Neil pressed the bandage back into place over swollen, reddened skin. Neil dropped his hand back to his side and clenched his fingers into a fist to hide the excited tremor. He doubted either Kevin or Andrew noticed; they were too busy staring each other down. At length Andrew smiled, slow and cold. It was the first time he'd smiled since

[387]

coming off his drugs, and Neil couldn't help but stare.

"Now it's getting fun," Andrew said.

"Finally," Kevin said, equal parts exhaustion and exasperation.

It took both of them to get Kevin to the bedroom. Neil didn't know how Kevin was going to make it up the ladder to his loft, but somehow he managed. He was asleep almost as soon as his head hit the pillow. Neil felt completely recharged as he stared up at Kevin's bunk. He was unsteady on his feet, too buzzed to stand still. The darkness should have hidden the jittery wreck he'd become, but Andrew wasn't fooled. He jabbed Neil's shoulder on his way back out of the room. Neil tore his gaze away from Kevin's unconscious form and followed.

Andrew pushed him up against the wall with heavy hands and hard kisses. "Junkie."

"I've been waiting for that since June," Neil said. "You've been waiting longer."

Andrew didn't bother denying it. It was nearly dawn by the time they finally went to bed, but Neil could make up the hours on the bus ride north. He burrowed under his blankets and dreamed of Evermore coming down on his head.

-

By an hour to serve, every parking lot on Edgar Allan's campus was packed. The stadium grounds were swarming with black-clad fans. Staccato bursts of camera flashes and hefty bodies in suits marked the arrival of big-name celebrities. Everywhere Neil looked he saw cops, and an entire section was cordoned off for news vans.

Neil looked over at his teammates. Nicky drummed his fingers on his hips as he took it all in. Aaron stood shoulder-to-shoulder with Katelyn, knuckles white with how tight he was holding her hand. Andrew looked unimpressed by the madhouse they'd stepped into, but his calm gaze tracked the crowd for threats. Renee was fiddling with her cross necklace, gaze distant as she prayed. Dan and Matt stood arm-in-arm behind her, twin pillars of strength ready for a fight. The rapid tap-tap-tap of Allison's heel against the asphalt gave her unease away but she wore a contemptuous look.

At Neil's side, Kevin was untouchable. Kevin had shown off his new tattoo as soon as they'd gotten on the bus. The team's celebration made it hard for Neil to sleep, but he couldn't begrudge them their excitement. Wymack hadn't reacted with more than a quick, tight smile, which meant he'd known about it before any of them did. Neil thought of the tribal flame tattoos on Wymack's arms and wondered if Wymack recruited his own artist for the job. It would at least explain how Kevin got back into the dorm last night when he could barely walk.

Neil didn't know what the last straw was to break Kevin's chain, but apparently last night's spectacle wasn't born of drunken grandeur. Kevin had committed; there was no going back. He faced Castle Evermore now like it was just another worthless stop on his way to glory. Neil didn't know if that determination was genuine or pure force of will, just as he didn't know how much of that disdain was a front for the press to pick up on. Neil had a feeling Kevin's defiance was at least nine-tenths truth, and that was enough to keep Neil's nerves at bay.

Two women collected the Vixen squad. Four security guards escorted the Foxes from the bus to the stadium while another six stood guard along the short route. It was a little excessive, perhaps, but Edgar Allan's board wasn't taking any chances. Cameras flashed as the Foxes went by, and it was only a matter of time before someone realized Kevin's ink had changed. An incredulous shout got all attention on Kevin's face, and suddenly ten guards seemed entirely insufficient. There was a chorus of boos on all sides as the news swept through the crowd, but breaking through that vicious disapproval were a few scattered shouts of "Queen!" Kevin endured all of it with a haughty expression locked in place.

It was Neil's first time in Evermore's Away locker room. Kevin had warned them about it on the ride up, but words

[389]

couldn't keep Neil from feeling like he'd stepped into a tomb. It was twice as large as the Foxes' locker room but it seemed a hundred times smaller. The walls were bare of any decoration and everything was pitch black from the floor to the ceiling. It took an immediate toll on the Foxes and they spread out as quickly as they could, slinging orange bags into every corner of the room to try and break up the crushing illusion.

"Edgar Allan extends its welcome to tonight's opponents," one of the guards said when the team stopped moving. "The stadium has sold out, as have the towers. State and school officials are in North, the Court is in South, and the ERC is in West. We are hosting twelve representatives from the major leagues and six from professional teams. You will not approach any of them unless you are invited to do so by a member of my staff."

He waited a beat to make sure they understood. "You have free use of the inner ring for the next half-hour, at which point the Ravens will arrive on the Home side and you will be restricted to your half of the stadium. Do you have any questions?"

Nicky raised his hand. "Yeah. Who's in the eastern tower?"

"East is reserved for Moriyama guests and business clients," Kevin said.

The guard nodded confirmation, looked around for any other questions, and left.

"Well," Dan said when the door closed behind him, "this is what we've been waiting for."

"Let's do it," Matt said.

They left their gear and went into the inner ring. Outside it'd seemed like no one was on the Foxes' side, but the stands were broken up by small clumps of students and fans in every shade of orange. The Foxes waved at every friendly face they could see, earning ragged cheers and enthusiastic fist-pumping. The Raven fans were fast to retaliate, leaping to their feet and roaring boos at the tops of their lungs.

Halfway up each section was a fan dressed in red and black stripes, and one after the other they thrust a hand into the air. The closest one was still too far for Neil to clearly see what she was holding, but he thought it looked like a bike bell. It made no sense until five seconds later, when the entire section, floor to rafters, jumped as one. As they landed the next section jumped, and the thundering wave circled the stadium. It was a deafening cacophony and more unsettling than Neil wanted it to be. The striped fans put their arms up again as the wave made it back to them and signaled a second go-around.

"Jesus Christ," Nicky said, barely audible even though he was standing right behind Neil. "I don't think I can—Erik!"

Nicky darted around Neil and bolted for the stands. The first row was empty, with a security guard standing to either end, but a man had just shown up to present his ticket. How Erik Klose heard Nicky over the noise from the stands, Neil didn't know, but he turned away from the guard immediately and leaned over the security railing to give Nicky a fierce hug. Nicky clung to him like it'd been years since they last stood in the same room, oblivious to or completely unconcerned with the looks he was attracting.

The rest of the Foxes' guests showed up only a couple seconds later, since Wymack had arranged van transportation from the airport for them. Wymack dismissed his team, knowing how badly they needed friendly faces right now. Allison hadn't brought anyone, but she followed the upperclassmen to the stands. Aaron headed for the Vixens to talk to Katelyn. Neil stayed behind with Andrew and Kevin and simply watched.

Four of Dan's sisters had made it. They wore white sundresses they'd altered so three spelled out FOX. The fourth sported a fox paw that was already starting to lose a toe pad. They practically crushed Dan, smothering her with a group hug before fawning over her. They were just as quick to hug Allison, and the familiarity in their easy smiles said they'd met her at least once before.

[391]

Stephanie Walker had the next seat, and she held on to Renee forever. Matt's parents had the seats next to her. His mother's braid was dyed orange and she'd come in equally bright overalls. Matt had talked about his mother often enough that Neil knew how much Matt adored her. Somehow he was still surprised at how blatantly that love was returned. There was a fierce pride in Randy Boyd's grin that reminded Neil of Dan, and she toyed with the spikes he'd gelled his hair into. Matt's father was a little more reserved but smiled as he clapped Matt's shoulder in greeting. The woman he'd brought as his guest looked barely older than Matt was, and neither she nor Matt acknowledged each other.

Betsy Dobson was the last to walk in. Andrew hadn't saved a ticket for her, so Neil assumed Wymack and Abby had invited her. Andrew didn't seem at all surprised to see her but went to her as soon as she was settled. She smiled at his approach and gestured around her. Neil couldn't hear her over the crowd but assumed she was making her usual redundant observations. Neil looked away before she caught his eye and turned his attention back on the crowd.

"You two could at least say hello," Wymack said, somewhat aggrieved.

"There's no point," Kevin said. "All they are is a distraction."

"It's called a support network. Look it up."

"Thea is watching from South tonight," Kevin said, looking to the elevated VIP box. It was too far away and too high up for Neil to make out any faces, but there was a small crowd gathered at the windowed walls already. Knowing the Court was here to watch them play sent a chill through Neil's veins. Kevin dragged his stare back to Wymack's face and said, "and my father comes to all of my games. That is enough."

On Wymack's other side, Abby's gaze softened. Wymack's jaw worked for a moment before he could say in an even tone, "Your mother would be proud of you."

"Not just of me," Kevin said in a rare bout of humanity.

It was getting too personal, or maybe that sharp spike of discomfort in Neil's chest was a fit of loneliness and loss. Neil left them to each other and went to join his teammates. Erik's handshake was firm and his smile wide. Neil mixed the sisters up almost immediately after their cheery introductions. Stephanie's patient smile was as unnerving as Renee's peaceful demeanor had once been, and Neil was sure Randy popped a couple vital organs with how hard she hugged him. Matt's father skipped a simple "hello" to offer Neil his services as a plastic surgeon, if Neil wanted someone to clean up his face a bit.

"Dad," Matt said, horrified. "The fuck?"

"Neil Josten," a security guard said, "a Stuart Hatford is here to see you."

Neil followed the guard halfway down the inner ring. A wall separated the inner ring from the stands, and Stuart waited on the other side of it with his arms folded along the top. He dismissed the guard with a simple nod and turned a considering look on his long-lost nephew.

"I'd have thought you'd be back in England by now," Neil said.

"I've been going back and forth," Stuart said. "I would have come for you sooner, but he told us not to interfere until he made a decision." Neil didn't have to ask who Stuart meant by "he". Stuart waited for Neil's nod before continuing. "Your father's death left a void that's not easy to fill. Little boss is cleaning house and cutting losses everywhere he can, taking out people from California to South Carolina. Cops, doctors, moles— doesn't matter. If there's even a chance they're a liability to his new rule they're gone. Interesting stuff, the reshaping of an empire. Bloody, too."

"There were people in South Carolina?" Neil asked. As soon as he said it his heart skipped a beat. "Wait, doctors? Medical doctors or shrinks? Do you have names?"

"I stay out of the specifics unless they pertain to me," Stuart said. "Someone in particular you're looking for?"

"A psychiatrist in Columbia, Proust. Worked at Easthaven, let himself be bought out and used by the wrong brother. I told—the little boss," Neil said after a moment's hesitation, "about him."

"I'll look into it," Stuart said. He sent a casual look around and said, "You know they're still watching you, right? They're waiting for you to slip up, waiting to see if someone's stupid enough to take a bite. Bait and a mole in one. Be smart, would you? You bought into this, which means I can't protect you if things go sideways again."

"I'll be careful," Neil said. "Thank you."

"Chin up," Stuart said, straightening. "Eyes forward. Little boss is here tonight. Don't make him regret investing in you."

Neil wasn't stupid enough to look at the eastern tower. He just nodded and watched Stuart disappear into the crowd. He jogged back to Wymack and decided it best not to tell Kevin who was in attendance tonight. Wymack gave his team another minute to socialize, then herded them into the locker room. They changed out as quickly as they could, moods restored by their guests' enthusiasm, and ran laps in the inner ring until the Ravens showed up.

Neil thought the crowd was loud before, but the welcome they gave their home team had his ears ringing. The Foxes pulled back to the locker room to stretch and save their eardrums. They took their time putting the rest of the gear on and met up again in the main room. Wymack gave them a minute to breathe before sending them to the inner ring once more. Tonight's referees were split up between Home and Away and were waiting by the court doors to let the teams on. The Ravens were an endless stream of black as they entered from the far side, and Neil tried not to stare. Warm-ups had never felt so short; one minute Neil was taking his place and the next they were being recalled for pregame introductions.

Palmetto State's traveling band Orange Notes had found

their spots at some point, and they blared the fight song with unabashed pride as soon as the announcer finished reading off the Foxes' roster. The announcer waited for the last note to fade out before moving on to the Ravens' line-up. Edgar Allan's fight song sounded as malicious as always, and the drums continued in a heavy beat long after the rest of the band went quiet. The crowd stomped along until the whole stadium seemed to be a writhing, angry mass. Neil didn't know if it was the reverberations of their madness or his chaotic pulse that was choking him.

Dan met Riko on the court for a coin toss and won the Foxes first serve. The crowd was still carrying on like they intended to go all night. Wymack had a few minutes before starting line-ups were needed on the court, so he pulled his small team close enough that they could hear him.

"I suck at this pep talk thing, but Abby threatened me with gruesome death if I didn't make some sort of effort tonight. This is what I've come up with after an hour of hard brainstorming. I haven't rehearsed it yet, so you'll have to pretend it's something polished and encouraging. Deal?"

He looked around at them, catching and holding each player's eyes for a moment. "I want you to close your eyes and think about why you're here tonight. Don't tell me 'revenge' because you've already gotten it just by being here tonight.

"This isn't about Riko anymore," Wymack said. "This isn't about the Ravens. This is about you. This is about everything it took you to get to this point, everything it cost you, and everyone who laughed when you dared to dream of something big and bright. You're here tonight because you refused to give up and refused to give in. You're here where they all said you'd never be, and no one can say you haven't earned the right to play this game.

"All eyes are on you. It's time to show them what you're made of. There's no room for doubt, no room for second guesses, no room for error. This is your night. This is your game. This is your moment. Seize it with everything you've got. Pull out all the stops and lay it all on the line. Fight because you don't know how to die quietly. Win because you don't know how to lose. This king's ruled long enough—it's time to tear his castle down."

A warning bell sounded overhead. Wymack clapped his hands at them and said, "Let's go!"

"Foxes!" they roared in response, and the starting line-up headed for the door.

The Ravens took the court first and settled into their places. Riko was the first one called out, so Neil assumed he'd play this game like he had last: showing up on the court for the first and fourth quarters of the game. Kevin was the first called out for the Foxes, but Neil was close behind him. They headed for the strikers' starting spots on the half-court line. Neil kept his eyes on Riko, knowing Riko had to have heard about Kevin's tattoo by now. He was right; Neil was still twenty feet away when he saw the icy anger on Riko's face.

Riko didn't speak until Kevin and Neil had gone still, and then he let out a slew of vicious Japanese. Kevin ignored him until Riko said something else, then slid a cool look Riko's way and answered. Neil didn't know what he said, but Riko twisted his gloved hands around his stick like he was imagining breaking Kevin's neck. Pissing Riko off right before such an important match was as stupid as it was exhilarating. Neil could no longer hear the crowd through the blood rushing in his ears.

He looked up at the clock as the last Fox went still and watched until they passed the ten-second mark. He glanced past the other striker to the dealer and his first mark, counting down in his head. At two he saw the goalkeeper, and he imagined the goal blossoming red with a Fox point. At one the buzzer sounded, and Dan fired off the first serve of the night.

It'd been almost seven months since the Foxes and Ravens last faced each other on the court, and it didn't take the Ravens long to realize they were facing an entirely different team. Last fall the Foxes wrote the game off as a sure loss before they even stepped on the court. They'd played the Ravens because they had to but they looked past it to the hope of spring championships. Tonight, buoyed by determination and half-drunk on desperation, the Foxes had the strongest start they'd had all year.

The Foxes were fierce, but the Ravens were angry. Neil could feel it like poison on the court, a bad vibe that set every survival instinct hissing. The laughingstock of the NCAA should not have made it this far or cost them this much. They'd lost Jean, suffered a thorough internal investigation, and put up with Riko's violent grief in the wake of his father's death. Their fans' attack on Palmetto State and Kevin's veiled accusations had brought a lot of bad press down on them. There were rumors Edgar Allan wanted to close the Nest and reintegrate the team with the rest of campus for their own psychological safety. Now Kevin showed up on their court with a sneer and a new tattoo, and the Foxes rushed them like they had no doubts they'd win.

The Foxes weren't the same team, but neither were the Ravens. They hadn't taken the Foxes seriously last fall. Now they had to, and they didn't pull any punches.

The game didn't start off violent, but it took no time at all to get there. Bodies slammed against court walls and the floor; sticks cracked together and barely missed glancing off jerseys and helmets. The clatter and skid of racquets sliding against the ground, forcefully knocked out of gloved hands, echoed in Neil's ears as he pushed himself faster. The Foxes' defense and dealers fought tooth and nail to protect their goal and clear the ball, but good intentions and grit couldn't hold out long. The backliners simply weren't fast enough to compete. Renee gave it everything she had behind them, but Riko and Engle popped balls past her in rapid succession. Every time the goal lit up red for the Ravens Neil flinched.

They were an exhausted, anxious mess by the time they were dismissed for halftime break. Nicky barely made it to the locker room before he started dry-heaving. Abby eased him off to one side and started foisting drinks off on him. Renee stood

[397]

white-lipped and tense in the center of the room. They were sitting seven-and-three, and the Ravens would be out with a fresh line-up when the bell sounded. There wasn't a sure comeback like they'd had against the Trojans. The only way to go was down.

Renee opened her mouth but couldn't speak. Neil assumed from the guilt in her eyes that she was trying to apologize. He'd never seen her look so disappointed, but they'd never had so much riding on a single game. Renee closed her mouth, cleared her throat, and tried again. What came out wasn't "Sorry", but a quiet, "Are you sure?"

Neil didn't understand, but Andrew said, "Yes."

"Okay," Renee said. "Excuse me."

She walked out of the room, and a door closed behind her as she disappeared into the women's changing room. Dan looked ready to go after her, but Wymack shook his head and motioned for her to keep stretching.

"Leave her alone," Wymack said, subdued. "She didn't want to play goal tonight after how USC's game went. We talked her into it." He said "we" but he glanced at Andrew at that. "Andrew said he could control the score if she showed him how they played."

"You should have let her step down," Aaron said. "She'd've been more use as a fourth backliner. It's not a good gap."

"Whose fault is that?" Kevin asked.

Aaron and Matt bristled but stayed quiet. Nicky managed a shaky breath and said, "How are we supposed to stop them if they won't carry the ball?"

"You have to drive them back," Kevin insisted. "Keep them past the fourth-court line so they can't take those quick shots. Force them to shoot further out and Andrew will have a better chance of deflecting them."

"Great plan," Aaron said with heavy sarcasm, "except they're almost as fast as your mini-me is. Can't push them if we can't keep up with them."

"Find a way," Kevin insisted, and that was that.

The fifteen minute break was over far too soon. Renee rejoined them as they headed back down to the court. Dan gave her a quick hug but said nothing, knowing not even encouragement and comfort would be appropriate right now. Cameras were waiting by the court door for the Foxes' starting line-up, so Neil followed Kevin over. Kevin stood calm and quiet until a referee opened the door for them. Before he stepped on Kevin tapped the butt of his racquet against the floor and passed his stick to his other hand. He strode to half-court head high and left-handed, and the crowd went wild.

Neil wasn't the only one who'd forgotten what Kevin was like at his peak. The Ravens had written Kevin off when he broke his hand then learned his right-handed style when they realized they'd be facing him again. Even if they'd known this was coming they wouldn't be ready, because Kevin was no longer afraid of showing Riko up. He exploited his former teammates' weaknesses every chance he got and, without Jean around to overhear, used French to call warnings across the court to Neil. Kevin scored just three minutes into second half, and five minutes later he did it again.

The Ravens rallied like Kevin and Neil knew they would, and the game became a vicious fight. Again and again they knocked Matt and Aaron aside to fire on goal; again and again Andrew blocked their shots. Andrew rarely called out to the defense, maybe understanding they were halfway to running on fumes, maybe too focused on the Raven strikers to be distracted with his own backliners. Neil had never seen him play like this, so intense and fast and determined, but Andrew had promises to keep and a goal to defend.

With seventeen minutes down, the score was eight-six, and the Ravens finally lost their tempers. Reacher reacted to Kevin's third goal by punching him. He didn't stop with one blow but kept whaling on him. The referees opened the doors, but the teams were faster to converge on the fight. The only ones who

[399]

didn't join the fray were the goalkeepers, who each stood at the lines marking their boundaries and watched. It took all six referees to break up the fight. Reacher was thrown off the court with a red card, and Kevin and Matt were handed yellows.

Kevin scored on the foul shot, and that did nothing to improve the mood. Instead of going after Kevin again, the Ravens turned their sights on the backliners and Andrew. Matt and Aaron were stumbling more than usual as their marks tripped them up at every turn. Irritation made Matt and Aaron push back a little harder and Neil knew it wouldn't be long before one of them snapped. For now Allison was the voice to their rage, yelling ugly threats and insults at every Raven on the court.

The next time Jenkins got around Aaron she fired the ball to rebound short of the goal. It was obvious Andrew would get to it first, but Williams went after it anyway. When Andrew cleared the ball, Williams should have veered off-course and wheeled back to regroup. Instead Williams crashed full-speed into Andrew and crushed him up against the wall. The goal went red as the embedded sensors mistook his weight as a point. The crowd outside was startled to temporary silence; fouling a goalkeeper was one of the worst offenses in the game. By the time they recovered their wits enough to roar, Andrew had already pushed Williams off him. He took a stumbling step away from the wall and rocked to a stop. Goalkeepers' armor was meant to protect them from high-speed balls, not racquets and bodies. Andrew had gotten the breath knocked out of him.

Neil closed the space between them like it was nothing. He didn't remember dropping his racquet but suddenly he had both hands free. He planted them against Williams' shoulder blades and shoved as hard as he could to throw him off his feet. Jenkins made a wild grab at her teammate but couldn't stop his fall, and Williams hit his knees hard. Matt hauled Neil back before he could go after him again.

"Easy!" Matt said, because the livid referees were already

[400]

halfway to them. "You can't get carded, all right? We can't replace you. I'm the backliner," he insisted when Neil opened his mouth. "It's my job to defend the goal, okay?"

Neil wasn't carded for his unsportsmanlike shove, but one of the referees gave him a blistering warning. Neil stared back in baleful silence. Matt pushed Neil behind him before Neil got carded for attitude and apologized in his stead. Neil turned away to check on Andrew. Andrew returned Neil's intent look with a bored stare, then looked past Neil at the hubbub surrounding Williams. The Ravens were getting another red card, but it didn't feel like a victory. Tetsuji was taking advantage of the card to sub out his players.

The only Raven making a second appearance on the court tonight was Riko. The other two filing on were brand new, another striker to balance Riko out and an offensive dealer Neil remembered from last October's game. The Ravens intended to tear the Foxes' defense wide open, and by this point it wouldn't take a lot of work. They were almost halfway through the second half. Even though the Foxes were built for the long haul they were quickly running out of steam. It cost them too much to go up against a team like this.

"They're not fast enough," Andrew said.

He had to mean their defense line, so Neil said, "I know."

"Are you tired?" Andrew asked.

It wasn't concern, Neil knew, but that didn't make it a less confusing question. He hadn't gotten the ball often enough tonight to be tired, but he couldn't say that with Matt standing two feet away from him. "Not yet."

"Then I'm taking my turn. Matt," Andrew said, and Matt turned toward them immediately. Andrew lifted a finger from his racquet to point at Neil. "We're subbing Dan for Neil and Neil for you."

Matt stared. "We're what?"

"You're limping," Andrew returned. Neil hadn't even noticed, too focused on the ball and the Ravens. He shot a startled look down at Matt's feet like he could somehow see the source of Matt's pain. "You're no use to me right now. Get Abby to put a brace on that. Neil can hold them in the meantime."

They'd said all night that speed was the fatal weakness on their defense line. Neil was the fastest player in Class I Exy, but how Andrew thought this was a feasible solution Neil didn't know. Neil wanted to point out every reason this was a bad idea, but he didn't have the right to turn Andrew down.

"I started this game as a backliner, remember?" Neil said to Matt. "The Ravens put me up against Riko when I stayed with them in December. I know how he moves."

"Two weeks of practice don't make you ready to face the best striker in the game."

"Kevin's the best striker," Neil corrected him, "and I don't have to be the best backliner to counter Riko. I just have to be faster than he is. We both know I am. Trust me. I can keep him away from Andrew while you rest."

"Coach will never go for it," Matt said.

"Tell him he has to," Andrew said, like it was that simple.

Maybe it was Andrew's conviction that swayed Matt. Andrew had never given half a damn about this game before and only honestly tried in scattered bursts. That he cared enough to argue now was unexpected and unprecedented. There were still doubts and arguments in Matt's troubled expression, but Matt turned away without another word. As he headed for the door Neil finally saw the limp in his step. Matt no longer needed to put up an invincible front, so he stopped trying to hide how much he was hurting.

Matt stopped in the doorway to argue with Wymack and Abby. Maybe invoking Andrew's name did the trick, or maybe Wymack was desperate enough to try anything at this point. Either way Dan stepped onto the court a couple seconds later. Allison started toward her, assuming she was being traded. Dan called for her to hold her place and took up a striker's starting spot for a foul goal.

[402]

"You're crazy," Neil said to Andrew in an undertone.

"This is news to no one," Andrew said.

Neil shook his head and shifted to his new spot at Riko's side. Riko looked from him to Dan to Andrew and back again. It took him only a second to put it all together, and Riko's smile was cold.

Maybe he had a right to feel smug. It didn't matter that Neil had started this game as a backliner. He'd been away from the court for half his life and had spent the last two years honing his skills as a striker. Riko had seen for himself over Christmas break how out of practice and miserable Neil was at defense.

What Riko forgot was that Neil hadn't stepped onto the Raven court until after Tetsuji beat him unconscious. Neil's health had gotten steadily worse from there thanks to Riko's constant abuse. Tonight Neil was in perfect form, and he was mad as hell at the Ravens for hurting his Foxes.

Andrew slammed the ball up-court, and the fight to the last bell began. Neil dogged Riko every step of the way, using his stick and body to ruin Riko's shots and force him away from Andrew. They fought each other back and forth across the court, ducking and darting, sidestepping and lunging, nearly tripping each other up at every turn. Riko used every trick he had to get around Neil, but he couldn't outrun Neil for long.

Minutes stretched by without a clear shot on goal. Riko snarled something hateful at Neil as Andrew batted away his latest shot. Neil laughed at him, knowing it'd only infuriate him further. Riko's impatience and rage were fuel, lending Neil speed and making him forget the growing burn in his thighs and calves.

Something in his shoulder popped and went a little numb as he and Riko hit the ground for the nth time. Since it didn't hurt, Neil didn't stop to worry about it. He was up and after the ball before Riko was, and he passed it up to Allison. Allison gave it to Kevin, Kevin to Dan, Dan to Kevin, and Kevin scored. Just like that they were tied eight-eight.

[403]

No one scored for ten more minutes, and not for lack of trying. Finally Berger got around Aaron for a quick shot on goal. Andrew wasn't quite fast enough, and he smashed his racquet against the wall as the goal went red. Andrew's irritation was as inspiring as Riko's was, but Neil couldn't hold defense alone and Aaron had gone as far as he could. The next time the Ravens fouled the Foxes and the Foxes gained possession, Wymack sent Nicky and Matt on.

Neil expected to be pulled, but Nicky traded places with an exhausted Allison and Matt took over for Aaron. The grin Matt shot Neil was at once encouraging and apologetic. Neil flashed a tight smile back at him, and they pushed forward as one. With three backliners on the court the defense line finally had a chance to regroup, and by the last five minutes of the game they'd shut the Raven offense out. Riko and Berger were taking their shots from further out because they had no other choice, and Andrew slammed every attempt away. On the other side of the court Kevin scored on a rebound, tying them up once again.

They were going to a shootout, Neil realized, and the thought of facing down the Ravens' goalkeeper when he was this worn out was a terrifying prospect. Neil had used up all his energy, burned through all his fumes, and kept moving now out of some mindless sense of self-preservation. His legs and lungs were burning, and the numbness in his shoulder had been replaced by heat. His wrists and arms were sore, and he hurt from hitting Riko and the ground so often. His elbows ached from the constant stick checks, he couldn't feel his feet anymore, and there was a chance Riko had broken a toe or two the last time he stomped on Neil's foot.

Neil didn't know they'd reached the last minute of the game until the buzzer blared overhead. His body knew what that sound meant and finally gave out on him. He fell to his knees and barely managed to catch himself with his hands. His stomach twisted inside him, but he didn't have the strength to throw up. Oxygen-starved muscles felt like they were disintegrating but it hurt too much to breathe. Neil's mouth worked on short gasps that did nothing for him.

The buzzer went off again, and Neil's heart stopped.

The ringing in his ears wasn't all him. His teammates were screaming, wordless war cries of disbelief and victory. Neil's fingers shook so badly it was almost impossible to get the straps of his helmet undone, but finally he managed to throw his helmet off to one side. He blinked sweat out of his eyes and looked up at the scoreboard.

Ten-nine, Foxes' favor—Kevin had scored in the last two seconds of the game.

Neil wished he could smile, but it took all his strength just to look at Riko. The Raven captain and Exy King was staring at the scoreboard like he expected it to change. The Foxes were running for each other, still screaming their fool heads off, but the Ravens stood still as stone. It was the first loss in Edgar Allan's history, and they'd fallen to the unlikeliest of opponents.

Neil sucked in a deep breath that ripped him open on its way down. "I'd ask you how it feels, but I guess you've always known what it's like to be second, you worthless piece of shit."

Riko finally dragged his gaze away from the board. He stared at Neil, blank-faced and stunned, and then revulsion twisted his expression into something terrible. His racquet went up over his head but it took Neil a moment to realize Riko really intended to take a swing at him. Dan screamed his name from halfway across the court, but there was nothing Neil could do except watch Riko's racquet start down. He barely had the strength to breathe. Dodging was out of the question.

Riko's racquet got close enough that Neil heard wind whistling through the strings, and then a second racquet came out of nowhere, big and bright and orange. Andrew put everything he had left behind his swing and caught Riko across his forearm. Bones gave a sickening crunch as they shattered. Riko's racquet clattered harmlessly off to one side, and then Riko was the only one screaming. He stumbled a few steps away

[405]

from them before falling to his knees and holding his arm to his gut. Andrew put his racquet down in front of Neil like a shield and watched Riko's breakdown with a bored stare.

Neil lost sight of Riko when the Foxes swarmed him. Gloved fingers patted his head and shoulders, looking for any sign that he'd been hurt. Neil tuned out their frantic demands, more interested in listening to Riko's endless, agonized screaming. Then Dan caught his face in her hands and gave him a shake.

"Neil," she said, so desperate and afraid Neil had to look at her.

"Hey," Neil said, hoarse with exhaustion and heady triumph. "We won."

Dan threw her arms around him and buried a choked laugh against his padded shoulder. "Yeah, Neil. We won!"

EPILOGUE

There should have been a ceremony as Edgar Allan passed the championship trophy to their successors. Instead the celebration was postponed until the morning. In its place were cops and EMTs, statements and interviews. Neil didn't know why he'd expected anything else when the Foxes were involved.

Riko was rushed out in an ambulance, but the Ravens and Foxes were kept at the stadium until half past two in the morning. The crowd left only when the police forced them to go, and they were deathly silent on their way out of Evermore's gates. The Foxes' guests and Vixens argued for the right to stay but lost. As they left they promised to meet the Foxes at their hotel.

The Foxes were quiet when they were finally allowed to shower and change. The long hours since the last bell had temporarily worn away their well-deserved excitement. They were sore all over and drained to the point that moving was a terrible chore. Neil leaned against the shower wall because he knew better than to sit down. He fell asleep without meaning to but woke up again when the water ran cold. He yawned as he dressed and went in search of his teammates.

A security guard was waiting outside the changing room door to intercept him. "Neil Josten, they have a few last questions for you."

Neil turned soundlessly after him and followed him back to the inner ring. The stadium was completely empty and the police were long gone. Neil was too tired to ask what was going on so plodded along behind the guard in silence. A third of the way down was a gate the security guards used for moving between the inner ring and the stands. The guard unlocked it and

[407]

motioned Neil through. Spilled soda made Neil's shoes stick to the ground, and the entire place reeked of greasy food and beer.

Past the next stairwell was one of the tunnel entrances that let fans into the stadium from the outer ring. Neil had been in the Foxes' outer ring only once, since the Foxes' locked entrance let him bypass the food stands and paraphernalia shops. The Ravens' outer ring looked much the same as the Foxes' did except for the dated championship banners that hung from the rafters. Once a source of pride, they would now serve as a visible reminder of tonight's failure.

EAST was written above an elevator in bold red letters, and Neil forgot about the banners. The guard had to swipe his badge and key in a six-digit code to get access. There were only two buttons inside, "Floor" and "Tower". Neil closed his eyes for the ride to the top.

The guard stayed behind when Neil stepped out, so Neil went on alone. A short hall opened up into a spacious room Neil recognized. Nine years ago he'd been here with Riko and Kevin while his father carved a man into a hundred pieces.

Stuart Hatford and a man Neil didn't recognize stood in the far corners. Tetsuji and Riko sat on one of the couches, Tetsuji straight-backed and stone-faced, Riko shuttered and hollow. Neil saw the white plaster of a cast poking out of the sling the doctors put Riko's arm in. Neil could have stared at it forever, but Ichirou was standing by the windows overlooking the court and Neil knew better than to ignore him. Neil stood halfway between the brothers and fixed his eyes on Ichirou's collar.

It was so quiet Neil heard someone's watch ticking. Neil counted a minute, then two, and still no one said a word. At last Ichirou drew a gloved hand from his pocket and gestured. The stranger brought him a handgun. Neil waited, silent and breathless, for Ichirou to turn that gun on him. He could ask for a second chance, but there was no point in trying. His words wouldn't change what happened tonight, and not even Neil could lie well enough to convince Ichirou he was sorry.

[408]

Ichirou started forward, but he didn't go to Neil. He stood before his uncle and spoke in quiet Japanese. Tetsuji listened to it all in silence, expression unchanging. When Ichirou went quiet, Tetsuji bowed low over his knees. He didn't sit up again, even when Ichirou turned his heavy stare on Riko. Riko finally stirred enough to look up, and the brothers faced each other for the first time. Ichirou crouched in front of him, wordless and slow.

"Ichirou," Riko said, so choked with emotion Neil almost couldn't understand him. He could have been cursing Ichirou's name for waiting so long to come into his life. He could have been begging for justice or revenge. Riko opened his mouth to say something else but closed it again when Ichirou cradled Riko's cheek in his free hand.

It wasn't comfort, but Neil didn't figure that out until it was too late. Ichirou put the gun to Riko's temple and pulled the trigger without hesitation. The gunshot was so unexpected, so loud, that Neil jumped. Riko's body jerked under the force of impact. Blood splattered across Tetsuji's back and the leather couch they shared. Ichirou withdrew his hands and let Riko fall.

As Ichirou straightened the stranger stepped forward. Ichirou passed the gun back, and the stranger knelt to press it into Riko's lifeless hand. Neil watched him curl Riko's fingers around the grip. In a distant corner of his mind Neil knew what was going on, but right now Neil was too shocked to make full sense of it.

Ichirou stopped in front of Neil. "You have cost the Ravens their coach and their captain. Are you satisfied?"

It made no sense at first, because Tetsuji was still alive. When Neil caught on he stopped breathing. Tetsuji Moriyama was stepping down—not necessarily because Neil had asked for it, but because Ichirou had been here firsthand to see what the Ravens had become under Tetsuji's guidance. Stuart had said Ichirou was cutting his losses. The Ravens' reckless violence and fraying sanity made them a glaring liability. Ichirou wanted

[409]

nothing to do with Edgar Allan's tarnished reputation.

Neil was suddenly wide awake. "Your people are safe, as are mine. Yes, I'm satisfied."

Ichirou's smile was cold and fleeting. "Let them call you by whatever name they like. You will always be a Wesninski at heart." Ichirou gestured to Neil like he was shooing away an insignificant fly. "You are dismissed."

The security guard took Neil back to the locker room and left him at the door. Neil went inside alone and found all of the Foxes waiting for him. Neil looked from one tired face to the next, soaking them in, reveling in everything they'd accomplished tonight and imagining how they'd react when they heard the news tomorrow.

"What's so funny?" Nicky asked when he spotted Neil in the doorway.

Neil hadn't realized he was smiling. "Life?"

His good mood seemed to inject a little life back into the room. Dan sat up a bit straighter, and Matt managed a grin. Kevin pressed his fingers hard against his new tattoo. Aaron and Nicky exchanged triumphant looks, and Allison reached out to squeeze Renee's hand. Wymack's nod was approving; Abby's smile was proud.

"Let's blow this joint," Wymack said. "We've got a party to get to. Anyone who's not on the bus in two minutes gets to stay here overnight."

In no world would Wymack ever really leave his team behind, but the Foxes hustled out of there like they believed him. Neil waited off to one side while the others filed out, knowing Andrew would be the last to leave. Wymack knew better than to stick around and followed his Foxes down the hall.

Andrew brought Neil's duffel to him. Neil took it but dropped it off to one side. Andrew studied it for a moment, then shrugged out of his own bag and put a hand to the wall near Neil's head.

"Your close calls are getting old," Andrew said. "I thought

[410]

you knew how to run."

Neil affected confusion. "I thought you told me to stop running."

"Survival tip: no one likes a smart mouth."

"Except you," Neil reminded him.

A year ago Neil had been a scared nobody, hating himself for signing the Foxes' contract and counting down days until he moved in with Wymack. Tonight he was the starting striker for the first-ranked team in the NCAA. In two years he'd be captain, and in four he'd graduate from Palmetto State. Neil would find a professional team first and then fight tooth and nail to make the cut for Court. Neil could already imagine the weight of an Olympics medal around his neck. He didn't even care what color it was so long as it was his.

Better than that bright future was what he already had: a court that would always be home, a family who'd never give up on him, and Andrew, who for once hadn't wasted their time denying that this thing between them might actually mean something to both of them. Neil hadn't even noticed the silence at first, too distracted by his dizzying thoughts. Now he couldn't help but smile and pull Andrew in.

This was everything he wanted, everything he needed, and Neil was never letting go.

Acknowledgements

My undying gratitude to some of my favorite people in the word: KM, Amy, Z, Jamie C, and Miika. You've done the impossible by cleaning up this wreck of a series. Thank you to my sisters, who put together this cover for me when I'd just about given up on it.

All my love to you: to the person holding this book, who took a chance on Neil and the Foxes and Exy. This story would be nothing without you. Thank you for believing in something crazy with me.